THE GUINEA
STAMP

MORE WILDSIDE CLASSICS

Please see www.wildsidepress.com for a complete list!

THE GUINEA STAMP

STAMP

A Tale of Modern Glasgow

ANNIE S. SWAN

WILDSIDE PRESS

THE GUINEA STAMP

This edition published 2005 by Wildside Press, LLC.
www.wildsidepress.com

CHAPTER I.

FATHERLESS.

It was an artist's studio, a poor, shabby little place, with a latticed window facing the north. There was nothing in the furnishing or arrangement of the room to suggest successful work, or even artistic taste. A few tarnished gold frames leaned against the gaudily-papered wall, and the only picture stood on the dilapidated easel in the middle of the floor, a small canvas of a woman's head, a gentle Madonna face, with large supplicating eyes, and a sensitive, sad mouth, which seemed to mourn over the desolation of the place. The palette and a few worn brushes were scattered on the floor, where the artist had laid them down for ever. There was one living creature in the room, a young girl, not more than sixteen, sitting on a stool by the open window, looking out listlessly on the stretch of dreary fenland, shrouded in the cold and heavy mist. It was a day on which the scenery of the fen country looked desolate, cheerless, and chill. These green meadows and flat stretches have need of the sunshine to warm them always. Sitting there in the soft grey light, Gladys Graham looked more of a woman than a child, though her gown did not reach her ankles, and her hair hung in a thick golden plait down her back. Her face was very careworn and very sad, her eyes red and dim with long weeping. There was not on the face of the earth a more desolate creature than the gentle, slender girl, the orphan of a day. At an age when life should be a joyous and lovely thing to the maiden child, Gladys Graham found herself face to face with its grimmest reality, certain of only one thing, that somewhere and somehow she must earn her bread. She was thinking of it at that moment, with her white brows perplexedly knitted, her mouth made stern by doubt and apprehension and despair; conning in her mind her few meagre accomplishments, asking herself how much they were likely to bring in the world's great mart. She could read and write and add a simple sum, finger the keys of the piano and the violin strings with a musicianly touch, draw a little, and dream a great deal. That was the sum total of her acquirements, and she knew very well that the value of such things was *nil*. What, then, must become of her? The question had become a problem, and she was very far away yet from its solution.

The house was a plain and primitive cottage in the narrow street of a little Lincolnshire village — a village which was a relic of the old days, before the drainage system was introduced, transforming the fens into a fertile garden, which seems to bloom and blossom summer and winter through. Its old houses reminded one of a Dutch picture, which the quaint bridges across the waterways served to enhance. There are many such in the fen country, dear to the artist's soul.

John Graham was not alone in his love for the wide reaches, level as the sea, across which every village spire could be seen for many a mile. Not very far away, in clear weather, the great tower of Boston, not ungraceful, stood out in awe-inspiring grandeur against the sky, and was pointed out with pride and pleasure by all who loved the fens and rejoiced in the revived prosperity of their ancient capital. For ten years John Graham had been painting pictures of these level and monotonous plains, and of the bits to be found at every village corner, but somehow, whether people had tired of them, or hesitated to give their money for an unknown artist's work, the fortune he had dreamed of never came. The most of the pictures found their way to the second-hand dealers, and were there sold often for the merest trifle. He had somehow missed his mark, — had proved himself a failure, — and the world has not much patience or sympathy with failures. A great calamity, such as a colossal bankruptcy, which proves the bankrupt to be more rogue than fool, arouses in it a touch of admiration, and even a curious kind of respect; but with the man out at elbows, who has striven vainly against fearful odds, though he may have kept his integrity throughout, it will have nothing to do; he will not be forgiven for having failed.

And now, when he lay dead, the victim of an ague contracted in his endeavour to catch a winter effect in a marshy hollow, there was nobody to mourn him but his motherless child. It was very pitiful, and surely in the wide world there must have been found some compassionate heart who would have taken the child by the hand and ministered unto her for Christ's sake. If any such there were, Gladys had never heard of them, and did not believe they lived. She was very old in knowledge of the world, that bitterest of all knowledge, which poverty had taught. She had even known what it was, that gentle child, to be hungry and have nothing to eat — a misery enhanced by the proud, sensitive spirit which was the only heritage John Graham had left the daughter for whom, most cheerfully, he would have laid down his life. The village people had been kind after their homely way; but they, working hard all day with their hands, and eating at eventide the substantial bread of their honest toil, were possessed of a great contempt for the worn and haggard man who tramped their meadow-ways with his sketch-books under his arm, his daughter always with him, preserving still the look and manners of the gently born, though they wore the shabbiest of shabby garments, and could scarcely pay for the simple food they ate. It was a great mystery to them, and they regarded the spectacle with the impatience of those who did not understand.

It was the month of November, and very early that grey day the chilly darkness fell. When she could no longer see across the narrow street, Gladys let her head fall on her hands, and so sat very still. She had eaten nothing for many hours, and though feeling faint and weak, it did not occur to her to seek something to strengthen her. She had something more important than such trifling matters to engross her thoughts. She was so sitting, hopeless, melancholy, half dazed, when she heard the voice of an arrival down-stairs, and the unaccustomed tones of a man's voice mingling with the shriller notes of Miss Peck, their little landlady. It was not the curate's voice, with which Gladys had grown quite familiar during her father's illness. He had been very kind; and in his desperation, when his end approached, Graham had implored him to look after Gladys. It was a curious charge to lay upon a young man's shoulders, but Clement Courtney had accepted it cheerfully, and had even written to his widowed mother, who lived alone in a Dorsetshire village, asking her advice about the girl. Gladys was disturbed in her solitude by Miss Peck, who came to the door in rather an excited and officious manner. She was a little, wiry spinster, past middle life, eccentric, but kind-hearted. She had bestowed a great deal of gratuitous and genuine kindness on her lodgers, though knowing very well that she would not likely get any return but gratitude for it; but times were hard with her likewise, and she could not help thinking regretfully at times of the money, only her due, which she would not likely touch now that the poor artist was gone. She had a little lamp in her hand, and she held it up so that the light fell full on the child's pale face.

'Miss Gladys, my dear, it is a gentleman for you. He says he is your uncle,' she said, and her thin voice quite trembled with her great excitement.

'My uncle?' repeated Gladys wistfully. 'Oh yes; it will be Uncle Abel from Scotland. Mr. Courtney said he had written to him.'

She rose from her stool and turned to follow Miss Peck down-stairs.

'In the sitting-room, my dear, he waits for you,' said Miss Peck, and a look of extreme pity softened her pinched features into tenderness. 'I hope — I hope, my dear, he will be good to you.' She did not add what she thought, that the chances were against it; and, still holding the lamp aloft, she guided Gladys down-stairs. There was no hesitation, but neither was there elation or pleasant anticipation in the girl's manner as she entered the room. She had ceased to expect anything good or bright to come to her any more, and perhaps it was as well just then that her outlook in life was so gloomy; it lessened the certainty of disappointment. A little lamp also burned on the round table in the middle of the narrow sitting-room, and the fire feebly blinked behind Miss Peck's carefully-polished bars, as if impressed by the subdued atmosphere without and within. Close by the table stood a very little man, enveloped in a long loosely-fitting overcoat, his hat in one hand and a large damp umbrella in the other. He had an abnormally large head, and a soft, flabby, uninteresting face, which, however, was redeemed from vacancy by the gleam and glitter of his remarkably keen and piercing black eyes. His hair was grey, and a straggling beard, grey also, adorned his heavy chin. Gladys was conscious of a strong sense of repulsion as she looked at him, but she tried not to show it, and feebly smiled as she extended her hand.

'Are you Uncle Abel, papa's brother?' she asked — a perfectly unnecessary question, of course, but it fell from her involuntarily, the contrast was so great; almost she could have called him an impostor on the spot.

'Yes,' said Uncle Abel in a harsh undertone; 'and you, I suppose, are my niece?'

'Yes. Can I take your overcoat or your umbrella?' asked Gladys; 'and would you like some tea? I can ask Miss Peck to get it. I have not had any myself — now I come to think of it.'

'I'll take off my coat. Yes, you can take it away, but don't order tea yet. We had better talk first — talking always makes one hungry; then we can have tea, and we won't require any supper. These are the economics poor people have to study. I guess you are no stranger to them?'

Gladys again faintly smiled. She was not in the least surprised. Poverty had long been her companion, she expected nothing but to have it for her companion still. She took her uncle's hat and overcoat, hung them in the little hall, and returned to the room, closing the door.

'Perhaps you are cold, uncle?' she said, and, grasping the poker, was about to stir up the fire, when he hastily took it from her, with an expression of positive pain on his face.

'Don't; it is quite warm. We can't afford to be extravagant; and I daresay,' he added, with a backward jerk of his thumb towards the door, 'like the rest of her tribe, she'll know how to charge. Sit down there, and let us talk.'

Gladys sat down, feeling a trifle hurt and abashed. They had always been very poor, she and her father, but they had never obtruded it on their own notice, but had tried cheerfully always to accept what they had with a thankful heart. But Love dwelt with them always, and she can make divine her humblest fare.

Mr. Abel Graham fumbled in the inner pocket of his very shabby coat, and at last brought out a square envelope, from which he took the curate's letter.

'I have come,' he said quite slowly, 'in answer to this. I suppose you knew it had been written?'

'If it is Mr. Courtney's letter, yes,' answered Gladys, unconsciously adopting her uncle's businesslike tone and manner. 'Of course he told me he had written.'

'And you expected me to come, of course?'

'I don't think I thought about it much,' Gladys answered, with frankness. 'It is very good of you to come so soon.'

'I came because it was my duty. Not many people do their duty in this world, but though I'm a very poor man, I won't shirk it — no, I won't shirk it.' He rubbed his hands together slowly, and nodded across the hearth to his niece. Instead of being pleased, as she ought to have been, with this announcement, she gave a quick little shiver. 'My brother John — your father, I mean — and I have not met for a good number of years, not since we had the misfortune to disagree about a trifle,' continued the old man, keeping his eyes fixed on the girl's face till she found herself made nervous by them. 'Time has proved that I was right, quite right; but my brother John was always, if you will excuse me saying it, rather pigheaded, and' —

'Don't let us speak about him if you do not feel kindly to him!' cried the girl, her great eyes flashing, her slender frame trembling with indignation. 'I will not listen, I will go away and leave you, Uncle Abel, if you speak harshly of papa.'

'So' — Abel Graham slapped his knee as he uttered this meditative monosyllable, and continued to regard his niece with keener scrutiny, if that were possible, than before. 'It is John's temper — a very firebrand. My dear, you are very young, and you should not be above taking advice. Let me advise you to control that fiery passion. Temper doesn't pay — it is one of the things which nothing can ever make pay in this world. Well, will you be so kind as to give me a little insight into the state of your affairs? A poor enough state they appear to be in, if this parson writes truly — only parsons are accustomed to draw the long bow, for the purpose of ferreting money out of people's pockets. Well, my dear, have you nothing to tell me?'

Gladys continued to look at him with dislike and distrust she made no attempt to disguise. If only he would not call her 'my dear.' She resented the familiarity. He had no right to presume on such a short acquaintance.

'I have nothing to tell you, I think,' she said very coldly, 'except that papa is dead, and I have to earn my own living.'

CHAPTER II.

WHAT TO DO WITH HER.

'Your own living? I am glad to hear you put it so sensibly. I must say I hardly expected it,' said the old man, with engaging frankness. 'Well, but tell me first what your name is. I don't know what to call you.'

'Gladys,' she answered; and her uncle received the information in evident disapproval.

'Gladys! Now, what on earth is the meaning of such a name? Your father and mother ought to be ashamed of themselves! Why can't people name their children so that people won't stare when they hear it? Jane, Susan, Margaret, Christina, — I'm sure there are hundreds of decent names they might have given you. I think a law should be passed that no child shall be named until he is old enough to choose for himself. Mine is bad enough, — they might as well have christened me Cain when they were at it, — but Gladys, it beats all!'

'I have another name, Uncle Abel. I was baptized Gladys Mary.'

'Ah, that's better. Well, I'll call you Mary; it's not so heathenish. And tell me what you have thought of doing for yourself?'

'I have thought of it a great deal, but I have not been able to come to any decision,' answered Gladys. 'Both papa and Mr. Courtney thought I had better wait until you came.'

'Your father expected me to come, then?'

'Yes, to the last he hoped you would. He had something to say to you, he said. And the last morning, when his mind began to wander, he talked of you a great deal.'

These details Gladys gave in a dry, even voice, which betrayed a keen effort. She spoke almost as if she had set herself a task.

'I came as soon as I could. The parson wrote urgently, but I know how parsons draw the long bow, so I didn't hurry. Business must be attended to, whatever happens. You don't know what it was your father wished to say? He never asked you to write it, or anything?'

'No, but in his wandering he talked of money a great deal, and he seemed to think,' she added, with a slight hesitation, 'that you had taken some from him. Of course it was only his fancy. Sick people often think such things.'

'He could not possibly in his senses have thought so, for I never had any money, or he either. We could not rob each other when there was nothing to rob,' said the old man, but he avoided slightly his niece's clear gaze. 'Well, Mary, I am willing to do what I can for you, as you are my brother's only child, so you had better prepare to return to Scotland with me.'

Gladys tried to veil her shrinking from the prospect, but her sweet face grew even graver as she listened.

'I am a very poor man,' he repeated, with an emphasis which left no doubt that he wished it to be impressed firmly on her mind, — 'very poor; but I trust I know my duty. I don't suppose, now, that you have been taught to work with your hands — in the house, I mean — the woman's kingdom?'

This sentimental phrase fell rather oddly from the old man's lips. He looked the very last man to entertain any high and chivalrous ideal of womanhood. Gladys could not forbear a smile as she answered, —

'I am afraid I am rather ignorant, Uncle Abel. I have never had occasion to do it.'

'Never had occasion; hear her!' repeated the old man, quite as if addressing an audience. 'She has never had any occasion. She has been born and cradled in the lap of luxury, and I was a born fool to ask the question.'

The desolate child felt the keenness of the sarcasm, and her eyes filled with hot tears. 'You don't understand, Uncle Abel, you never can understand, and there is no use trying to make you,' she said curiously. 'I think I had better call Miss Peck to get tea for us.'

'Not yet; we must settle everything, then we needn't talk any more. I am your only relation in the world, and as I have been summoned, perhaps unnecessarily, on this occasion, I must, and will, do my duty. I have not taken the long and expensive journey from Scotland for nothing, remember that. So sit down, Mary, and tell me exactly how matters stand. How much money have you?'

The colour mounted high to the girl's white brow, and her proud mouth quivered. Never had she so felt the degradation of her poverty! Now it seemed more than she could bear. But she looked straight into her uncle's unlovely countenance, and made answer, with a calmness which surprised herself, —

'There is no money, none at all — not even enough to pay all that must be paid.'

Abel Graham almost gasped.

'All that must be paid! And, in Heaven's name, how much is that? Try to be practical and clear-headed, and remember I am a poor man, though willing to do my duty.'

'Mr. Courtney and I talked of it this morning, when we arranged that the funeral should be tomorrow,' Gladys answered in a calm, straight, even voice, 'and we thought that there might be five pounds to pay when all was over. Papa has some pictures at the dealers' — two in Boston, and three, I think, in London. Perhaps there might be enough from these to pay.'

'You have the addresses of these dealers, I hope?' said the old man, with undisguised eagerness.

'Yes, I have the addresses.'

'Well, I shall apply to them, and put on the screw, if possible. Will you tell me, if you please, how long you have lived in this place?'

'Oh, not long, — in this village, I mean, — only since summer. We have been all over the fens, I think; but we have liked this place most of all.'

'Heathens, wandering Jews, vagabonds on the face of the earth,' said the old man to himself. 'So you have arranged that it will be tomorrow — you and the parson? I hope he understands that he can get nothing for his pains?'

'I don't know what you are talking about,' said Gladys, and her mouth grew very stern — her whole face during the last hour seemed to have taken on the stamp and seal of age.

'And what hour have you arranged it for?'

'Eleven, I think — yes, eleven,' answered Gladys, and gave a quick, sobbing breath, which the old man elected not to notice.

'Eleven?' He said it over slowly, and took a penny time-table from his pocket, and studied it thoughtfully. 'We can get away from Boston at one. It's the worst kind of place this to get at, and I don't know why on earth your father should have chosen it' — 'to die in,' he had almost added; but he restrained these words. 'We can't get to Glasgow before midnight, I think. I hope you won't object to travelling in the night-time? I must do it. I can't be away any longer from business; it must be attended to. I hope you can be ready?'

'I don't mind it at all,' answered Gladys in a still, quiet voice. Her heart cried out against her unhappy destiny; but one so desolate, so helpless and forlorn, may not choose. 'Yes, I shall be ready.'

'Well, see that you are. Punctuality is a virtue — one not commonly found, I am told, in your sex. You will remember, then, Mary, that I am a very poor man, struggling to get the necessaries of life. You have no false and extravagant ideas of life, I hope? Your father, surely, has taught you that it is a desperate struggle, in which men trample each other remorselessly under foot. Heaven knows he has had experience of it, so far as I can hear and see.'

'He never told me anything, Uncle Abel. We were happy always, he and I together, because we loved each other. But I know that life is always hard, and that the good suffer most,' said Gladys simply.

A strange and unwonted thrill touched the selfish heart of the old man at these words, as they fell gravely from the young lips, formed in their perfect sweetness for the happy curves of joy and hope.

'Well, well, if these are your views, you are less likely to be disappointed,' he said, in gruff haste. 'Well, to go on. I am a poor man, and I have a poor little home; I hope, when you come to share it, you will be a help, and not altogether a burden on it?'

'I shall try. I can learn to work. I must learn now,' Gladys answered, with exemplary meekness.

'There is an old woman who comes to do my little turn of a morning. There is no reason why now I should not dispense with her services. She is dear at the money, anyhow. I have often grudged it.'

'I wonder to hear that you are so poor,' said Gladys, looking straight into his face with her young, fearless eyes. 'Papa told me once that you were quite rich, and that you had a splendid business.'

Abel Graham looked distinctly annoyed at this unexpected statement regarding his worldly affairs.

'Your father, Mary, was as ignorant of the practical affairs of life as an unborn babe. He never showed his ignorance more than when he told you that fabrication — a pure fabrication of his fancy. I have a little trade in the oil and tallow line. No, not a shop, only a little warehouse in a back street in Glasgow. When you see it you will wonder how it has ever kept body and soul together. A splendid business! Ha! ha! That is good!'

'And do you live near it, Uncle Abel?'

'I live at it — in it, in fact; my house is in the warehouse. It's not a very genteel locality, nor a fine house, it is good enough for me; but I warn you not to expect anything great, and I can't alter my way of life for you.'

'I hope I should never expect it,' answered Gladys quietly. 'And you live there quite alone?'

'Not quite. There is Walter Hepburn.'

'Who is Walter Hepburn?' asked Gladys, and the Scotch name fell most musically from her lips for the first time, the name which was one day to be the dearest to her on earth.

'He's the office boy — an imp of the devil he is; but he is sharp and clever as a needle; and then he is cheap.'

'Are cheap things always good, Uncle Abel?' Gladys asked. 'I have heard papa say that cheap things are so often nasty, and he has spoken to me more than once of the sin of cheapness. Even genius must be bought and sold cheaply. Oh, he felt it all so bitterly.'

'Mary Graham, your foolish father was his own worst enemy, and I doubt he will prove yours too, if that is all he has taught you. You had better get tea at once.'

Thus rebuked, Gladys retired to the kitchen, and, to the no small concern of the little landlady, she sat down on the low window-seat, folded her hands on the table, and began helplessly to weep.

'My dear, my dear, don't cry! He hasn't been good to you, I know he hasn't. But never mind; better times will soon dawn for you, and he will not stay. I hope he will go away this very night,' she said very sympathetically.

'No, he will stay till tomorrow, then I must go with him. He has offered me a home, and I must go. There is nothing else I can do just now,' said Gladys. 'I can't believe, Miss Peck, that he is papa's brother. It is impossible.'

'Dear Miss Gladys, there is often the greatest difference in families. I have seen it myself,' said Miss Peck meditatively. 'But now you must have something to eat, and I suppose he must be hungry too' —

'If you would get tea, please, we should be much obliged; and oh, Miss Peck, do you think you could give him a bed?'

'There is nothing but the little attic, but I daresay it will do him very well. He doesn't look as if he were accustomed to anything much better,' said Miss Peck, with frank candour. So it was arranged, and Gladys, drying her eyes, offered to help the little woman as best she could.

Abel Graham looked keenly and critically at his niece when she returned to the room and laid the cloth for tea. His eye was not trained to the admiration or appreciation of beauty, but he was struck by a singular grace in her every movement, by a certain still and winning loveliness of feature and expression. It was not the beauty sought for or beloved by the vulgar eye, to which it would seem but a colourless and lifeless thing; but a pure soul, to which all things seemed lovely and of good report, looked out from her grave eyes, and gave an expression of gentle sweetness to her lips. With such a fair and delicate creature, what should he do? The question suggested itself to him naturally, as a picture of his home rose up before his vision. When he thought of its meagre comfort, its ugly environment, he confessed that in it she would be quite out of place. The house in which he had found her, though only a hired shelter, was neat and comfortable and homelike. He felt irritated, perplexed; and this irritation and perplexity made him quite silent during the meal. They ate, indeed, without exchanging a single word, though the old man enjoyed the fragrant tea, the sweet, home-made bread, and firm, wholesome butter, and ate of it without stint. He was not, indeed, accustomed to such dainty fare. Gladys attended quietly to his wants, and he did not notice that she scarcely broke bread. When the meal was over, he wiped his mouth with the back of his hand, and rose from the table.

'Now, if you don't mind,' he said almost cheerfully, the good food having soothed his troubled mind, 'I would like to take a last look at my brother. I hope they have not screwed down the coffin?'

Gladys gave a violent start. The word was hideous; how hideous, she had never realised till it fell from her uncle's lips. But she controlled herself; nothing was to be gained by exhibitions of feeling in his presence.

'No, they will come, I think, tomorrow, quite early. I did not wish it done sooner,' she answered quietly. 'If you come now, I can show you the door.' She took the lamp from the table, and, with a gesture of dignity, motioned him to follow her. At the door of the little room where the artist had suffered and died she gave him the lamp, and herself disappeared into the studio. Not to sit down and helplessly weep. That must be over now; there were things to be thought of, things to do, on the threshold of her new life, and she was ready for action. She found the matches, struck a light, and began at once to gather together the few things she must now sacredly cherish as mementoes of her father. First she took up with tender hand the little canvas from the easel, looked at it a moment, and then touched the face with her lips. It was her mother's face, which she remembered not, but had been taught to love by her father, who cherished its memory with a most passionate devotion. She wrapped it in an old silk handkerchief, and then began a trifle dreamily to gather together the old brushes with which John Graham had done so much good, if unappreciated, work. Meanwhile the old man was alone in the chamber of death. He had no nerves, no fine sensibilities, and little natural affection to make the moment trying to him. He entered the room in a perfectly matter-of-fact manner, set the lamp on the washstand, and approached the bed. As he stood there, looking on the face, calm, restful, beautiful in its last sleep, a wave of memory, unbidden and unwelcome, swept over his selfish and hardened heart. The years rolled back, and he saw two boys kneeling together in childish love at their mother's knee, lisping their evening prayer, unconscious of the bitter years to come. Almost the white, still outline of the dead face seemed to reproach him; he could have anticipated the sudden lifting of the folded eyelids. He shivered slightly, took an impatient step back to the table for the lamp, and made haste from the room.

CHAPTER III

THE NEW HOME.

Next day at noon that strangely-assorted pair, the sordid old man and the gentle child, set out in a peasant's waggon, which he had hired for a few pence, to ride across the meadows to Boston. The morning was very fair. In the night the mist had flown, and now the sun shone out warm and cheerful, giving the necessary brightness to the scene. It lay tenderly on the quaint fen village, and the little gilt vane on the church steeple glittered proudly, almost as if it were real gold.

Gladys sat with her back to the old horse, quite silent, never allowing her eyes for a moment to wander from that picture until distance made it dim. She had no tears, though she was leaving behind all that love had hallowed. She wondered vaguely once or twice whether it would be her last farewell, or whether, in other and happier years, she might come again to kneel by that nameless grave. Abel Graham paid small attention to her. He tried to engage in a conversation with the peasant who sat on the front of the waggon, holding the reins loosely in his sunburnt hands; but that individual was stolid, and when he did vouchsafe a remark, Abel did not understand him, not being familiar with fen vernacular. They reached Boston in ample time for the train, even leaving half an hour to spare. This half hour the old man improved by hunting up the dealer in whose hands were two of his brother's pictures, leaving Gladys at the station to watch their meagre luggage. He drove a much better bargain than the artist himself could have done, and returned to the station inwardly elated, with four pounds in his pocket; but he carefully concealed from his niece the success of his transaction — not that it would have greatly concerned her, she was too listless to take interest in anything. At one o'clock the dreary railway journey began, and after many stoppages and changes, late at night Gladys was informed that their destination was reached. She stepped from the carriage in a half dazed manner, and perceived that they were in a large, brilliantly-lighted, but deserted, city station. All her worldly goods were in one large, shabby portmanteau, which the old man weighed, first in one hand and then in the other.

'I think we can manage it between us. It isn't far, and if I leave it, it will cost tuppence, besides taking Wat Hepburn from his work tomorrow to fetch it.'

'Can't we have a cab?' asked Gladys innocently.

'No, we can't; you ought to know, if you don't, that a cab is double fare after midnight,' said the old man severely. Just look in the carriage to make sure nothing is left.'

Gladys did so, then the melancholy pair trudged off out from the station into the quiet streets. Happily the night was fine, though cold, with a clear, star-begemmed sky, and a winter moon on the wane above the roofs and spires. A great city it seemed to Gladys, with miles and miles of streets; tall, heavy houses set in monotonous rows, but no green thing — nothing to remind her of heaven but the stars. She had the soul of the poet-artist, therefore her destiny was doubly hard. But the time came when she recognised its uses, and thanked God for it all, even for its moments of despair, its bitterest tears, because through it alone she touched the great suffering heart of humanity which beats in the dark places of the earth. In the streets after midnight there is always life — the life which dare not show itself by day, because it stalks in the image of sin. Gladys was surprised, as they slowly wended their way along a wide and handsome thoroughfare, past the closed windows of great shops, to meet many ladies finely dressed, some of them beautiful, with a strange, wild beauty, which half fascinated, half terrified her.

'Who are these ladies, Uncle Abel?' she asked at length. 'Why are so many people in the streets so late? I thought everybody would be in bed but us.'

'They are the night-birds, child. Don't ask any more questions, but shut your eyes and hold fast by me. We'll be home in no time,' said the old man harshly, because his conscience smote him for what he was doing.

Gladys again became silent, but she could not shut her eyes. Soon they turned into another street, in which were even more people, though evidently of a different order. The women were less showily dressed, and many of them had their heads bare, and wore little shawls about their shoulders. As they walked, the crowd became greater, and the din increased. Some children Gladys also saw, poorly clad and with hungry faces, running barefoot on the stony street. But she kept silence still, though growing every moment more frightened and more sad.

'Surely this is a terrible place, Uncle Abel,' she said at last. 'I have never seen anything like it in my life.'

'It isn't savoury, I admit; but I warned you. This is Argyle Street on a Saturday night; other nights it is quieter, of course. Oh, he won't harm you.' A lumbering carter in a wild state of intoxication had pushed himself against the frightened girl, and looked down into her face with an idiotic leer.

Gladys gave a faint scream, and clung to her uncle's arm; but the next moment the man was taken in charge by the policeman, and went to swell the number of the drunkards at Monday's court.

'Here we are. This is Craig's Wynd, or The Wynd, as they say. We have only to go through here, and then we are in Colquhoun Street, where I live. It isn't far.'

In the Wynd it was, of course, rather quieter, but in the dark doorways strange figures were huddled, and sometimes the feeble wail of a child, or a smothered oath, reminded one that more was hidden behind the scenes. Gladys was now in a state of extreme mental excitement. She had never been in a town larger than Boston, and there only on bright days with her father. It seemed to her that this resembled the place of which the Bible speaks, where there is weeping and wailing and gnashing of teeth. To the child, country born and gently reared, whom no unclean or wicked thing had ever touched, it was a revelation which took away from her childhood for ever. She never forgot it. When years had passed, and these dark days seemed almost like a shadow, that one memory remained vivid and most painful, like a troubled dream.

'Now, here we are. We must let ourselves in. Wat Hepburn will be away long ago. He goes home on Saturday night,' said the old man, groping in his pocket for a key. It was some minutes before he found it, and Gladys had time to look about her, which she did with fearful, wondering eyes. It was a very narrow street, with tall houses on each side, which seemed almost to touch the sky. Gladys wondered, not knowing that they were all ware-houses, how people lived and breathed in such places. She did not know yet that this place, in comparison with others not many streets removed, was paradise. It was quiet — quite deserted; but through the Wynd came the faint echo of the tide of life still rolling on through the early hours of the Sabbath day.

'Here now. Perhaps you had better stay here till I bring a light,' said the old man at length.

'Oh no, I can't; I am terrified. I will come in, cried Gladys, in affright.

'Very well. But there's a stair; you must stand there a moment. I know where the matches are.'

Gladys stood still, holding in to the wall in silent terror. The atmosphere of the place depressed her — it smelt close and heavy, of some disagreeable oily odour. She felt glad to turn her face to the door, where the cool night air — a trifle fresher — could touch her face. Her uncle's footsteps grew fainter and fainter, then became louder again as he began to return. Presently the gleam of a candle appeared at the farther end of a long passage, and he came back to the door, which he carefully closed and locked.

Then Gladys saw that a straight, steep stair led to the upper floor, but the place Abel Graham called his home was on the ground floor, at the far end of a long wide passage, on either side of which bales of goods were piled. He led the way, and soon Gladys found herself in a large, low-ceiled room, quite cheerless, and poorly furnished like a kitchen, though a bed stood in one corner. The fireplace was very old and quaint, having a little grate set quite unattached into the open space, leaving room enough for a stool on either side. It was, however, choked with dead ashes, and presented a melancholy spectacle.

'Now,' said the old man, as he set the portmanteau down, 'here we are. One o'clock in the morning — Sunday morning, too. Are you hungry?'

'No,' said Gladys, 'not very.'

'Or cold, no? That's impossible, we've walked so fast. Just take off your things, and I'll see if there's anything in the press. There should be a bit of bread and a morsel of cheese, if that rascal hasn't gobbled them up.'

Gladys sat down, and her eyes wandered over all the great wide room into its shadowy corners, and it was as if the frost of winter settled on her young heart. The old man hung up his coat and hat behind the door, and, opening the press, brought therefrom the half of a stale loaf, a plate on which reposed a microscopic portion of highly-coloured butter, and a scrap of cheese wrapped in paper. These he laid on the bare table, where the dust lay white.

'Eat a mouthful, child, and then we'll get to bed,' he said. 'You'll need to sleep here in my bed tonight, and I'll go to the back room, where there's an old sofa. On Monday I'll get some things, and you can have that room for yourself. Tired, eh?'

Uncle Abel's spirits rose to find himself at home, and the child's sank lower at the prospect stretching out before her.

'No — that is, not very. It seems very long since morning.'

'Ay, it's been a longish day. Never mind; tomorrow's Sunday, and we needn't get up before ten or eleven.'

'Don't you go to church, Uncle Abel?'

'Sometimes in the afternoon, or at night. Oh, there are plenty of churches; they grow as thick as mushrooms, and do about as much good. Won't you eat?'

The fare was not inviting; nevertheless, Gladys did her best to swallow a few morsels, because she really felt faint and weak. It did not occur to the miser that he might kindle a cheerful spark of fire to give her a welcome, and to make her a cup of tea. He was not less cold and hungry himself, it may be believed, but he had long inured himself to such privation, and bore it with an outward semblance of content.

When they had eaten, he busied himself getting an old rug and a pillow from the chest standing across one of the windows, and carried them into the other room, then he bade Gladys get quickly to bed, and not burn the candle too long. He went in the dark himself, and when Gladys heard his footsteps growing fainter in the long passage a great terror took possession of her, the place was so strange, so cold, so unknown. For some time she was even afraid to move, but at last she rose and crossed the floor to the windows, to see whether from them anything friendly or familiar could be seen. But they looked into the street, and had thick iron bars across them, exactly like the windows of a gaol. It was the last straw added to the burden of the unhappy child. Her imagination did not lack in vividness, and a thousand unknown terrors rose up before her terrified eyes. If only from the window she might have looked up to the eyes of the pitying stars, she had been less desolate, less forlorn. A sharp sense of physical cold was the first thing to arouse her, and she took the candle and approached the bed. Now, though they had ever been poor, the artist and his child had kept their surroundings clean and whole-some. In her personal tastes Gladys was as fastidious as the highest lady in the land. She turned down the covering, and when she saw the hue of the linen her lip curled, and she hastily covered it up from sight. In the end, she laid herself down without undressing above the bed, spreading a clean handkerchief for her head to rest upon; and so, worn-out, she slept at last an untroubled and dreamless sleep, in which she forgot for many hours her forlorn and friendless state.

CHAPTER IV.

A RAY OF LIGHT.

Sunday was a dreary day. It rained again, and the fog was so thick that it seemed dim twilight all day long in Gladys's new home. Her uncle did not go out at all, but dozed in the chimney-corner between the intervals of preparing the meagre meals. On Sunday Abel Graham attended to his own housekeeping, and took care to keep a shilling off Mrs. Macintyre's pittance for the same. Gladys, though unaccustomed to perform household duties except of the slightest kind, was glad to occupy herself with them to make the time pass. The old man from his corner watched with much approval the slender figure moving actively about the kitchen, the busy hands making order out of chaos, and adding the grace of her sweet young presence to that dreary place. On the morrow, he told himself, he should dismiss the expensive Mrs. Macintyre. Yes, he had made a good investment, and then the girl would always be there, a living creature, to whom he might talk when so disposed.

'It isn't at all a bad sort of place, my dear,' he said quite cheerfully. 'At the back, in the yard, there's a tree and a strip of grass. In spring, if you like, you might put in a pennyworth of seeds, and have a flower.'

This was a tremendous concession. Gladys felt grateful for the kindly thought which prompted it.

'One tree, growing all by itself. Poor thing, how lonely it must be!'

The old man looked at her curiously.

'That's an odd way to look at it. Who ever heard of a tree being lonely? You have a great many queer fancies, but they won't flourish here. Glasgow is given up to business; it has no time for foolish fancies.'

Gladys gravely nodded.

'Papa told me so. Is it very far to Ayrshire, Uncle Abel?'

The old man gave a quick start.

'To Ayrshire! What makes you ask the question? What has put such a thing into your head?'

'Papa spoke of it so often, of that beautiful village where you and he were born. He was so sorry I could not pronounce it right, Mauchline.'

As that sweet voice, with its pretty English accent, uttered the familiar name, again a strange thrill visited the old man's withered heart.

'No, you don't say it right. But I wonder that he spoke of it so much; we were poor enough there, herd boys in the fields. We couldn't well have a humbler origin, eh?'

'But it was a beautiful life — papa said so — among the fields and trees, listening to the birds — the same songs Burns used to hear. I seem to know every step of the way, all the fields in Mossgiel, and every tree in the woods of Ballochmyle. Just before he died, he tried to sing, — oh, it was so painful to hear his dear, trembling voice, — and it was "The Bonnie Lass o' Ballochmyle." If it is not very far, will you take me one day, when you have time, Uncle Abel, to see Mauchline and Mossgiel and Ballochmyle?'

She looked at him fearlessly as she made her request, and her courage pleased him.

'We'll see. Perhaps at the Fair, when fares are cheap. But it will only be to please you; I never want to see the place again.'

'Oh, is not that very strange, Uncle Abel, that papa and you should think of it so differently? He loved it all so much, and he always said, when we were rich, we should come, he and I together, to Scotland.'

'He was glad enough to turn his back on it, anyhow. If he had stayed in Glasgow, and attended to business, he might have been a rich man,' said he incautiously.

'*You* are not rich, though you have done so,' said Gladys quickly, looking at him with her young, fearless eyes. 'I think papa was better off than you, because he could always be in the country, and not here.'

The undisguised contempt on the girl's face as she took in her surroundings rather nettled the old man, and he gave her a snappish answer, then picked himself up, and went off to his warehouse.

Next day Gladys had to rise quite early — before six — and with her own hands light the fire, under the old man's superintendence, thus receiving her first lesson in the economy of firelighting. She was very patient, and learned her lesson very well. While she was brushing in the hearth she heard another foot on the passage, and was further astonished by the tones of a woman's voice giving utterance to surprise.

'Mercy on us! wha's he gotten noo?'

The words, uttered in the broadest Scotch, and further graced by the unlovely Glasgow accent, fell on the girl's ears like the sound of a foreign tongue. She paused, broom in hand, and looked in rather a bewildered manner at the short stout figure standing in the doorway, with bare red arms akimbo, and the broadest grin on her coarse but not unkindly face.

'I beg your pardon, what is it?' Gladys asked kindly, and the surprise deepened on the Scotchwoman's face.

'Ye'll be his niece, mebbe — his brither's lass, are ye, eh? And hae ye come to bide? If ye hiv, Almichty help ye!'

Gladys shook her head, not understanding yet a single word. At this awkward juncture the old man came hurrying along the passage, and Mrs. Macintyre turned to him with a little curtsey.

'I'm speakin' to the young leddy, but she seemin'ly doesna understand. I see my work's dune; mebbe I'm no' to come back?'

'No; my niece can do the little that is necessary, so you needn't come back, Mrs. Macintyre, and I'm much obliged to you,' said the old man, who was polite always, in every circumstance, out of policy.

'Ye're awn me wan an' nine, fork it oot,' she answered brusquely, and held out her brawny hand, into which Abel Graham reluctantly, as usual, put the desired coins.

'Yer brither's dochter, genty born?' said Mrs. Macintyre, with a jerk of her thumb. 'Gie her her meat; mind, a young wame's aye toom. Puir thing, puir thing!'

Abel Graham hastened her out, but she only remained in the street until she saw his visage at one of the upper windows, then she darted back to the kitchen, and laid hold of the astonished Gladys by the shoulder. 'If ye ever want a bite — an' as sure as daith ye will often — come ye to me, my lamb, the second pend i' the Wynd, third close, an' twa stairs up, an' never heed him, auld skin o' a meeser that he is!'

She went as quickly as she came, leaving Gladys dimly conscious of her meaning, but feeling intuitively that the words were kindly and even tenderly spoken, so they were not forgotten.

When the water had boiled, the old man came down to supervise the making of the porridge — a mystery into which Gladys had not been yet initiated. Three portions were served on plates, a very little tea put in a tiny brown teapot, and breakfast was ready. Then Abel went into the passage and shouted to his young assistant to come down.

Gladys was conscious of a strong sense of curiosity as she awaited the coming of the 'imp,' which was his master's favourite name for him, and when he entered she felt at first keenly disappointed. He was only a very ordinary-looking street boy, she thought, rather undersized, but still too big for his clothes, which were stretched on him tightly, his short trousers showing the tops of his patched boots, which were several sizes too large for him, and gave him a very ungraceful appearance. He had not even a collar, only an old tartan scarf knotted round his neck, and from the shrunk sleeves of the old jacket his hands, red and bony, appeared abnormally large. But when she looked at his face, at the eyes which looked out from the tangle of his hair, she forgot all the rest, and her heart warmed to him before he had uttered a word.

'This is Walter Hepburn — my niece, Mary Graham; and you may as well be friendly, because I can't have any quarrelling here,' was the old man's introduction; then, without a word of thanksgiving, he fell to eating his porridge, after having carefully divided the sky-blue milk into three equal portions.

The two young persons gravely nodded to each other, and also began to eat. Gladys, feeling intuitively that a kindred soul was near her, felt a wild desire to laugh, her lips even trembled so that she could scarcely restrain them, and Walter Hepburn answered by a twinkle in his eye, which was the first bright thing Gladys had seen in Glasgow. But though she felt kindly towards him, and glad that he was there, she did not by any means admire him, and she even thought that if she knew him better she would tell him of his objectionable points. For one thing, he had no manners; he sat rather far back from the table, and leaned forward till his head was almost on a level with his plate. Then he made a loud noise in his eating, which disturbed Gladys very much — certainly she was too fastidious and delicate in her taste for her present lot in life. When that strange and silent meal was over, the old man retired to the warehouse and left the children alone. But that did not disconcert them, as might have been expected. From the first moment they felt at home with each other. Walter was the first to speak. He leaned up against the chimneypiece, and meditatively watched the girl as she began deftly to clear the table.

'I say, miss,' he said then, 'do you think you'll like to be here?'

The English was pretty tolerable, though the accent was very Scotch.

'No. How could I?' was the frank reply of Gladys. 'But I have nowhere else, and I should be thankful for it.'

'Um.'

Walter thrust his hands into his diminutive pockets, and eyed her with a kind of meditative gravity.

'Are you always thankful when you should be?' he inquired.

'I am afraid not,' Gladys answered, with a little shake of her head. 'You live here all the week, don't you, till Saturday night, when you go home?'

'Yes; and I'm always thankful, if you like, when Monday comes.'

Gladys looked at him in wonder.

'You are glad when Monday comes, to come back here? How strange! — and the other place is home. Have you a father and mother?'

'Yes, worse luck.'

Again Gladys looked at him, this time with strong disapproval.

'I don't understand you. It is very dreadful, I think, that you should talk like that.'

'Is it? Perhaps if you were me, and had it to do, you'd understand it. I wish I was an orphan. When a man's an orphan he may get on, but he never can if he has relations like mine.'

'Are they — are they wicked?' asked Gladys hesitatingly.

The lad answered by a short, bitter laugh.

'Well, perhaps not exactly. They only drink and quarrel, and drink again, whenever they have a copper. Saturday and Sunday are their head days, because Saturday's the pay. But I'm better off than Liz, because she has to be there always.'

'Is Liz your sister?'

'Yes. She isn't a bad sort, if she had a chance, but she never will have a chance there; an' perhaps by the time I'm able to take care of her it will be too late.'

Gladys did not understand him, but forbore to ask any more questions. She had got something fresh to ponder over, another of the many mysteries of life.

'I say, he's a queer old buffer, the boss, isn't he?' asked Walter, his eye twinkling again as he jerked his thumb towards the door. 'They say he's awful rich, but he's a miserable old wretch. I'd rather be myself than him any day.'

'I should think so,' answered Gladys, looking into the fine open face of the lad with a smile, which made him redden a little.

'I say, you might tell me why you think I'm so much better off than him. I sometimes think myself that I'm the most miserable wretch in the world.'

'Oh no, you're not; you are quite young, and you are a man — at least, you will be soon. If I were you I should never think that, nor be afraid of anything. It isn't very nice to be a girl like me; with you it is so different.'

'Well, perhaps I ought to be thankful that I'm not a woman. I never thought of that. Women have the worst of it mostly, now I think of it. I'm sorry for you.'

'Thank you.'

Gladys looked at him gratefully, and both these young desolate hearts, awaking to the possibilities and the sorrows of life, felt the chord of sympathy responding each to the other.

'He gives me five shillings a week here and my meat. They take it all at home, and I want so awful to go to the night school. Do you know, it takes me all my time to read words of three or four letters?'

'Oh, how dreadful! I can read; I'll teach you,' she cried at once. 'Perhaps it would do till you can go to school.'

'Could you? Would you?'

The boy's whole face shone, his eyes glowed with the light of awakened hope. He felt his own power, believed that he could achieve something if the first great stumbling-block were removed. Something of his gladness communicated itself to Gladys — showed itself in the heightened, delicate colour in her cheek, in the lustre of her eyes. So these two desolate creatures made their first compact, binding about them in the very hour of their meeting the links of the chain which, in the years to come, love would make a chain of gold.

CHAPTER V.

LIZ.

Abel Graham's business was really that of a wholesale drysalter in a very small way. His customers were chiefly found among the small shopkeepers who abounded in the neighbourhood, and as he gave credit for a satisfactory time, he was much patronised. To give credit to a certain amount was the miser's policy. When he once got the unhappy debtors in his toils it was hopeless to extricate themselves, and so they continued paying, as they were able, high prices and exorbitant interest, which left them no chance of making any profit in their own humble sphere. He had also lent a great deal of money, his income from that source alone being more than sufficient to keep himself and his niece in modest comfort, had he so willed. But the lust of gold possessed him. It was nothing short of physical pain for him to part with it, and he had no intention of changing his way of life for her. He was known in the district under the elegant *sobriquet* of Skinny Graham; and when Gladys heard it for the first time, she laughed silently to herself, thinking of its fitness. The simple-hearted child quickly accommodated herself to her surroundings, accepting her meagre lot with a serenity a more experienced mind might have envied. She even managed to make a little atmosphere of brightness about her, which at once communicated itself to the two who shared it with her. They viewed this exquisite change, it may be believed, from an entirely different standpoint. The old man liked the comfort and the cleanliness which the girl's busy hands made in their humble home; the boy looked on with deep eyes, wonderingly, catching glimpses of her white soul, and knowing that it was far above and beyond the sordid air it breathed. She went out a great deal, wandering alone and fearlessly in the streets — always in the streets, because as yet she did not know that even in that great city, where the roar and the din of life are never still, and the air but seldom clear from the smoke of its bustle, are to be found quiet resting-places, where the green things of God grow in hope and beauty, giving their message of perpetual promise to the heart open to receive it. Gladys would have welcomed that message gladly, ear and heart having been early taught to wait and listen for it, but as yet she believed Glasgow to be but a city of streets, of dull and dreadful stones, against which the tide of life beat remorselessly for ever. And such life! For very pity the child's heart grew heavy within her often as she looked upon the stream of humanity in these poor streets, on the degraded, hopeless faces, the dull eyes, the languid bearing of those who appeared to have lost interest in, and respect for, themselves. She believed it wholly sad. Standing on the outside, she knew nothing of the homely joys, the gleams of mirth, the draughts of happiness possible to the very poor. She thought their laughter, when it fell sometimes upon her ears, more dreadful than their tears. So she slipped silently about among them, quite unnoticed, looking on with large sad eyes, and almost as an angel might. Sometimes looking to the heavens, which even walls and roofs of stone could not shut out, she wondered how God, who loved all with such a tender love, could bear to have it so. It vexed her soul with doubts, and made her so unhappy that even in her dreams she wept. Of these things she did not speak to those about her yet, though very soon it became a habit with her and Walter to discuss the gravest problems of existence.

The old man offered no objections to the lessons, only stipulating that no unnecessary candles should be consumed. He allowed but one to lighten the gloom of the large kitchen; and every evening after tea the same picture might have been seen — the old man dozing in the chimney-corner, and the two young creatures at the little table with books and slates, the unsteady light of the solitary candle flickering on their earnest faces. Teacher and taught! Very often in the full after years they looked back upon it, and talked of it with smiles which were not far off from tears. It is not too much to say that the companionship of Walter was the only thing which saved Gladys from despair; but for the bright kinship of his presence she must have sunk under the burden of a life so hard, a life for which she was so unfitted; but they comforted each other, and kept warm and true in their young hearts faith in humankind and in the mercy of Heaven.

As the days went by, Walter dreaded yet more the coming of Saturday, and Sunday to be spent in his own house in Bridgeton, but as yet he had not spoken of his great sorrow to Gladys, only she was quick to notice how, as the week went by and Saturday came, the shadow deepened on his face. She felt for him keenly, but her perception was so delicate, so quick, she knew it was a sorrow with which she must not intermeddle. There were very many things in life, Gladys was learning day by day, more to be dreaded than death, which is so often, indeed, the gentlest friend.

One Monday morning Walter appeared quite downcast, so unusual with him that Gladys could not forbear asking what troubled him.

'It's Liz,' he said, relieved to be asked, though diffident in volunteering information. 'She's ill, — very badly, too, — and she is not looked after. I wish I knew what to do.'

Gladys was sympathetic at once.

'What is it? — the matter, I mean. Have they had a doctor?'

'Yes; it's inflammation of the lungs. She's so much in the streets at night, I think, when it's wet; that's where she's got it.'

'I am very sorry. Perhaps I could do something for her. My father was often ill; he was not strong, and sometimes caught dreadful chills painting outside. I always knew what to do for him. I'll go, if you like.'

The lad's face flushed all over. He was divided between his anxiety for his sister, whom he really loved, and his reluctance for Gladys to see his home. But the first prevailed.

'If it wouldn't be an awful trouble to you,' he said; and Gladys smiled as she gave her head a quick shake.

'No trouble; I shall be so glad. Tell me where to find the place, and I'll go after dinner, before it is dark. Uncle Abel says I must not go out after dark, you know.'

'It's a long way from here, and you'll have to take two cars.'

'I know the Bridgeton car; but may I not walk?'

'No; please take these pennies. When you are going to see my sister, I should pay. Yes, take them; I want you to.'

Gladys took the coppers, and put them in her pocket. She knew very well they would reduce the hoard he was gathering for the purchase of a coveted book, but she felt that in accepting them she was conferring a rare pleasure on him. And it was so. Never was subject prouder of a gift accepted by a sovereign than Walter Hepburn of the fact that that day Gladys should ride in comfort through the wet streets at his expense. It was another memory for the after years.

In the afternoon, accordingly, Gladys dressed and went out. Her uncle had provided her with a warm winter cloak, which enveloped her from head to foot. It was not new. Had Gladys known where it came from, and who had worn it before her, she might not have enjoyed so much solid satisfaction in wearing it, but though she had been told that it was an unredeemed pledge she would not have known what it meant.

It was a dry afternoon, though cloudy and cold. It was so near Christmas that the shops were gay with Christmas goods; but in those who have no money to spend in such luxuries, the Christmas display can only awaken a dull feeling of envy and discontent. By dint of much asking, after leaving the car, Gladys found the street where the Hepburns lived. It was not so squalid as the immediate neighbourhood of her own home, but it was inexpressibly dreary — one of these narrow long streets, with high 'lands' on either side, entered by common stairs, and divided into very small houses. Outwardly it looked even respectable, and was largely occupied by the poorer labouring class, who often divided their abodes by letting them out to lodgers. It was one of the streets, indeed, where the overcrowding had attracted the serious consideration of the authorities.

A bitter wind, laden with the promise of snow, swept through it from end to end, and caught Gladys in the teeth as she entered it. It was not a very cheerful welcome, and Gladys looked with compassion upon the children playing on the pavement and about the doorways, but scantily clad, though their blue fingers and pinched faces did not seem to damp their merriment. The child-heart, full of glee and ready for laughter, always will assert itself, even in the most unfavourable circumstances. Round the door which Gladys desired to enter, a little band of boys and girls were engaged playing the interesting game of 'Here's the Robbers passing by,' and Gladys stood still, watching them with a kind of quiet, tender interest, trying to understand the words, to which they gave many strange meanings. They grew shy of the scrutiny by and by, and the spell was broken by an oath which fell glibly from the lips of a small boy, showing that it was no stranger to them. Gladys looked inexpressibly shocked, and hastened into the stair, which was very dirty, and odorous of many evil smells. The steps seemed endless, but she was glad as she mounted to find the light growing broader, until at last she reached the topmost landing, where the big skylight revealed a long row of doors, each giving entrance to a separate dwelling. The girl looked confusedly at them for a moment, and then, recalling sundry directions Walter had given, proceeded to knock at the middle one. It was opened at once by a young woman wearing a rusty old black frock and a large checked apron, a little shawl pinned about her head quite tightly, and making her face look very small and pinched. It was a very pale face, — quite ghastly, in fact, — the very lips white, and her eyes surrounded by large black circles, which made Gladys think she must be very ill.

'Well, miss?' she said coolly and curtly, holding the door open only about three inches.

'Does Mrs. Hepburn live here?' asked Gladys, thinking she had made a mistake.

'Yes, but she's no' at hame. Come back the morn. Eh, Liz, will yer mither be oot the morn?'

'Ay; ask her what she wants,' a somewhat husky voice announced from the interior, followed by a fit of coughing quite distressing to hear.

'Oh, is that Walter's sister, who is ill?' said Gladys eagerly. 'Please, may I come in? Ask her. Tell her that I have come from

Colquhoun Street to see her. I am Gladys Graham.'

The young woman disappeared into the interior; a whispered consultation followed, and a general hurrying movement of things being put straight, then Gladys was bidden come in.

She stepped into the little narrow dark passage, closed the door, and entered the kitchen where the two girls were. It was quite a comfortable place, clean and warm, though the air was close, and not wholesome. It had a few articles of kitchen furniture, and two beds, one in each corner, which rather crowded the space. On one of the beds, half lying, half sitting, was Liz, Walter's sister, with a blanket pinned round her shoulders, and a copy of the *Family Reader* in her hand, open at a thrilling picture of a young lady with an impossible figure being rescued from a runaway horse by a youth of extraordinary proportions.

Gladys entered the kitchen rather hesitatingly, — the young woman with the sullen grey face disconcerted her — but when she looked at Liz she smiled quite brightly, and came forward with a quick, ready step.

'How are you? I am so sorry you are ill. Walter thought I might come to see you. I hope you will soon be better.'

Liz allowed her hand to be shaken, and fixed her very bright blue eyes keenly on the girl's sweet face. Gladys felt that she was being scrutinised, that the measure of her sincerity was gauged by that look, but she did not evade it. With Liz, Gladys was much surprised. She was so different from the picture she had drawn, so different from Walter; there was not the shadow of a resemblance between them. Many would have called Liz Hepburn beautiful. She was certainly handsome after her kind, having straight, clear-cut features, a well-formed if rather coarse mouth, brilliant blue eyes, and a mass of reddish-brown hair, which set off the extreme fairness of her skin. Gladys felt fascinated as she looked, though she felt also that there was something fierce, and even wild, in the depths of these eyes. Evidently they found satisfaction in their survey of the stranger's face, for she laid down the paper, and gave her head a series of little nods.

'Gie her a chair, Teen, and shove the teapot on to the hob,' she said, offering to her guest such hospitality as was in her power.

CHAPTER VI.

PICTURES OF LIFE.

Gladys sat down, and suddenly became conscious of what she was carrying, a little flower-pot, in which bloomed a handful of Roman hyacinths, their delicate and lovely blossoms nestling among the tender green of their own leaves, and a bit of hardy fern. It was her only treasure, which she had bought for a few pence in the market one morning, and she had nothing else to bring to Liz.

'Will you take this? Is it not very pretty? I love it so much, but I have brought it for you. My father liked a flower when he was ill.'

Liz gave another enigmatical nod, and a faint, slow, melancholy smile gathered about the lips of Teen as she sat down to her work again, after having stirred the fire and pushed the dirty brown teapot on to the coals. In this teapot a black decoction brewed all day, and was partaken of at intervals by the two; sometimes they ate a morsel of bread to it, but other sustenance they had none. Little wonder the face of Teen was as cadaverous as the grave.

Then followed an awkward silence, during which Liz played with the frayed edge of the blanket, and Teen stitched away for dear life at a coarse garment, which appeared to be a canvas jacket. A whole pile of the same lay on the unoccupied bed, and Gladys vaguely wondered whether the same fingers must reduce the number, but she did not presume to ask. She did not feel drawn to the melancholy seamstress, whose thin lips had a hard, cold curve.

'Were you reading when I came in? I'm afraid I have stopped you,' said Gladys at length.

'Ay, I was readin' to Teen "Lord Bellew's Bride; or the Curse of Mountford Abbey." Splendid, isn't it, Teen?' said Liz quite brightly. 'We buy'd atween us every week. I'll len' ye'd, if ye like. It comes oot on Wednesday. Wat could bring'd on the Monday.'

'Thank you very much,' said Gladys. 'I haven't much time; I have a great deal to do in the house.'

'Hae ye? Ay, Wat telt me; an', michty! ye dinna look as if ye could dae onything. The auld sinner, I'd pooshin him!'

Liz looked quite capable of putting her threat into execution, and Gladys shrank a little away from the fierceness of her eyes.

'Ye are ower genty. His kind need somebody that'll fecht. If he was my uncle, and had as muckle money as they say he has, I'd walk oot in silk and velvet in spite o' his face. I'd hing them a' up, an' then he'd need to pay.'

Gladys only vaguely understood, but gathered that she was censuring the old man with the utmost severity.

'Oh, I don't think he is as rich as people say, and he is very kind to me,' said she quickly. 'If he had not taken me when my father died, I don't know what would have become of me.'

'Imphm! The tea's bilin', Teen. Look in my goon pocket for a penny, an' rin doon for twa cookies.'

The little seamstress obediently rose, pushed back the teapot, and disappeared.

'If I wis you,' said Liz the moment they were alone, and leaning forward to get a better look at Gladys, 'I wadna bide. Ye wad be faur better workin' for yersel'. If ye like, I'll speak for ye whaur I work, at Forsyth's Paper Mill in the Gorbals. I ken Maister George wad dae onything I ask him.'

She flung back her tawny locks with a gesture of pride, and the rich colour deepened in her cheek.

'Oh, you are very kind, but I don't think I could work in a mill. I don't know anything about it, and I am quite happy with my uncle — as happy as I can be anywhere, away from papa.'

Liz regarded her with a look, in which contempt and a vague wonder were oddly mingled.

'Weel, if you are pleased, it's nae business o' mine, of course. But I think ye are a fule. Ye wad hae yer liberty, onyway, and I could show ye a lot o' fun. There's the dancin'-schule on Saturday nichts. It's grand; an' we're to hae a ball on Hogmanay. I'm gettin' a new frock, white book muslin, trimmed wi' green leaves an' a green sash. Teen's gaun to mak' it. That's what for I'll no' gang to service, as my mither's aye wantin'. No me, to be ordered aboot like a beast! I'll hae my liberty, an' maybe some day I'll hae servants o' my ain. Naebody kens. Lord Bellew's bride in the story was only the gatekeeper's dochter, an' that's her on the horse, look, after she was my Lady Bellew. Here's Teen.'

Breathless and panting, the little seamstress returned with the cookies, and made a little spread on the bare table. Gladys was not hungry, but she accepted the proffered hospitality frankly as it was given, though the tea tasted like a decoction of bitter aloes. She was horrified to behold the little seamstress swallowing it in great mouthfuls without sugar or cream. Gladys had sometimes been hungry, but she knew nothing of that painful physical sinking, the result of exhausting work and continued insufficiency of food, which the poisonous brew for the time being overcame. Over the tea the trio waxed quite talkative, and 'Lord Bellew's Bride' was discussed to its minutest detail. Gladys wondered at the familiarity of the two girls with dukes and duchesses, and other persons of high degree, of whom they spoke familiarly, as if they were next-door neighbours. Although she was very young, and knew nothing of their life, she gathered that its monotony was very irksome to them, and that they were compelled to seek something, if only in the pages of an unwholesome and unreal story, to lift them out of it. It was evident that Liz, at least, chafed intolerably under her present lot, and that her head was full of dreams and imaginings regarding the splendours so vividly described in the story. All this time Gladys also wondered more than once what had become of the parents, of whom there was no sign visible, and at last she ventured to put the question —

'Is your mother not at home today?'

This question sent the little seamstress off into a fit of silent laughter, which brought a dull touch of colour into her cheeks, and very much improved her appearance. Liz also gave a little short laugh, which had no mirth in it.

'No, she's no' at hame; she's payin' a visit at Duke Street.' And the little grave nod with which Gladys received this information further intensified the amusement of the two.

'Ye dinna see through it,' said Liz, 'so I'll gie ye'd flat. My faither and mither are in the gaol for fechtin'. They were nailed on Saturday nicht.'

'Oh!'

Gladys looked genuinely distressed, and perhaps for the first time Liz thought of another side such degradation might have. She had often been angry, had felt it keenly in her own passionate way, but it was always a selfish anger, which had not in it a single touch of compassion for the miserable pair who had so far forgotten their duty to each other and to God.

'Gey bad, ye think, I see,' said Liz soberly. 'We're used to it, and dinna fash oor thoombs. She'll be hame the nicht; but he's gotten thirty days, an' we'll hae a wee peace or he comes oot.'

Gladys looked at the indifferent face of Liz with a vague wonder in her own. That straight, direct glance, which had such sorrow in it, disconcerted Liz considerably, and she again turned to the pages of 'Lord Bellew.'

'Don't you get rather tired of that work?' asked Gladys, looking with extreme compassion on the little seamstress, who was again hard at work.

'Tired! Oh ay. We maun tire an' begin again,' she answered dully. 'It's sair on the fingers.'

She paused a moment to stretch out one of her scraggy hands, which was worn and thin at the fingertips, and pricked with the sharp points of many needles.

'It's dreadful; the stuff looks so hard. What do you make?'

'Men's canvas jackets, number five, thirteenpence the dizen,' quoted the little seamstress mechanically, 'an' find yer ain threed.'

'What does that mean?' asked Gladys.

'I get a penny each for them, an' a penny ower.'

'For making these great things?'

'Oh, I dinna mak' them a'. The seams are run up wi' the machine afore I get them. I pit in the sleeves, the neckbands, an' mak' the buttonholes. There's mair wark at them than ye wad think.'

'Is the money not very little?'

'Maybe; but I'm gled to get it. I'm no' able for the mill, an' I canna sterve. It keeps body an' soul thegither — eh, Liz?'

'Nae mair,' said Liz abstractedly, again absorbed in her paper. 'But maybe oor shot 'll come.'

Gladys rose to her feet, suddenly conscious that she had made a very long visit. Her heart was heavier than when she came. More and more was the terrible realism of city life borne in upon her troubled soul.

'I'm afraid I must go away,' she said very quietly. 'I am very much obliged to you for being so kind to me. May I come again?'

'Oh, if ye like,' said Liz carelessly. 'But ye'll no' see Teen. She lives doon the street. My mither canna bide her, an' winna let her nose within the door, so we haud a jubilee when she's nailed.'

'Oh, please don't speak like that of your mother!'

Liz looked quite thunderstruck.

'What for no'? I've never gotten onything frae her a' my days but ill. I'll tell ye what — if I had ta'en her advice, I'd hae gane to the bad lang syne. Although she is my mither, I canna say black's white, so ye needna stare; an' if ye are no' pleased ye needna come back, I didna spier ye to come, onyway.'

'Oh no; pray forgive me if I have made a mistake. I am so sorry for it all, only I cannot understand it.'

'Be thankfu' if ye dinna, then,' replied Liz curtly. 'I'm no' very ceevil to ye. I am much obleeged to ye for comin', for the flooers, an' mair than a', for teachin' Wat to read.'

Her face became quite soft in its outline; the harshness died out of her bright eyes, leaving them lovely beyond expression. Gladys felt drawn to her once more, and, leaning forward, without a moment's hesitation she kissed her on the brow. It was a very simple act, no effort to the child who had learned from her English mother to give outward expression to her feelings; but its effect on Liz was very strange. Her face grew quite red, her eyes brimmed with tears, and she threw the blanket over her head to smother the sob which broke from her lips. Then Gladys bade good-bye to the little seamstress, and slipped away down the weary stair and into the grimy street, where already the lamps were lit. Her mind was full of many new and strange thoughts as she took her way home, and it was with an effort she recovered herself sufficiently to attend to her simple duties for the evening. But when the old man and the boy came down from the ware-house, supper was ready as usual, and there was nothing re-marked, except that Gladys was perhaps quieter than usual.

'Yes, I have been, and I saw your sister, Walter,' she said at last, when they had opportunity to talk alone. 'She is much better, she says, and hopes to get out soon.'

'Did you see anybody else?'

'Yes, a friend whom she called Teen; I do not know her other name,' answered Gladys.

'Teen Balfour — I ken her. An' what do you think of Liz?'

He put the question with a furtive anxiety of look and tone not lost on Gladys.

'I like her. At first I thought her manner strange, but she has a feeling heart too. And she is very beautiful.'

'You think so too?' said the lad, with a strange bitterness; 'then it must be true.'

'Why should it not? It is pleasant to be beautiful, I think,' said Gladys, with a little smile.

'For ladies, for you, perhaps it is, but not for Liz,' said Walter. 'It would be better for her if she looked like Teen.'

Gladys did not ask why.

'I am very sorry for her too. It is so dreadful her life, sewing all day at these coarse garments. I have many mercies, more than I thought. And for so little money! It is dreadful — a great sin; do you not think so?'

'Oh yes, it's a sin; but it's the way o' the world,' answered Walter indifferently. 'Very likely, if I were a man and had a big shop, I'd do just the same — screw as much as possible out of folk for little pay. That's gospel.'

Gladys laid her hand on his arm, and her eyes shone upon him. 'It will not be your gospel, Walter, that I know. Some day you will be a rich man, perhaps, and then you will show the world what a rich man can do. Isn't there a verse in the Bible which says, "Blessed is he that considereth the poor"? You will consider the poor then, Walter, and I will help you. We shall be able to do it all the better because we have been so poor ourselves.'

It was a new evangel for that proud, restless, bitter young heart, upon which the burden of life already pressed so heavily. Gladys did not know till long after, that these words, spoken out of the fulness of her sympathy, made a man of him from that very day, and awakened in him the highest aspirations which can touch a human soul.

CHAPTER VII.

LIZ SPEAKS HER MIND.

'Wat,' said Liz Hepburn to her brother next time he came home, 'wat kind o' a lassie is thon?'

It was a question difficult for Walter to answer, and, Scotch-like, he solved it by putting another.

'What do you think of her?'

'I dinna ken; she's no' like ither folk.'

'But you liked her, Liz?' said Walter, with quite evident anxiety.

'Oh ay; but she's queer. How does she get on wi' Skinny?'

'Well enough. I believe he likes her, Liz, if he would let on.'

Liz made a grimace.

'I daursay, if he can like onything. I telt her my mind on the business plain, an' offered to get her into our mill.'

'Oh, Liz, you might have had more sense! Her work in a mill!' cried Walter, with more energy than elegance.

'An' what for no'?' queried Liz sharply. 'I suppose she's the same flesh and bluid as me.'

'Shut up, you twa,' said a querulous, peevish voice from the ingle-neuk, where the mother, dull-eyed, depressed, and untidy, sat with her elbows on her knees. She was in a poor state of health, and had not recovered from the last week's outburst. It was Saturday night, but there was no pay forthcoming from the head of the house, who was still in Duke Street Prison. Walter looked at his mother fixedly for a moment, and the shadow deepened on his face. She was certainly an unlovely object in her dirty, unkempt gown, her hair half hanging on her neck, her heavy face looking as if it had not seen soap and water for long, her dull eyes unlit by any gleam of intelligence. Of late, since they had grown more dissipated in their habits, Walter had fallen on the plan of keeping back his wages till the beginning of the week — the only way in which to ensure them food. Seldom, indeed, was anything left after Saturday and Sunday's carousal.

'Is there anything the matter the day, mother?' he asked quite kindly and gently, being moved by a sudden feeling of compassion for her.

'No, naething; but I'm clean dune. Wad ye no' bring in a drap, Wat?' she said coaxingly, and her eye momentarily brightened with anticipation.

'It won't do you any good, mother, ye ken that,' he said,

striving still to speak gently, though repulsion now mingled with his pity. 'A good dinner or supper would do ye more good. I'll bring in a bit steak, if ye'll cook it.'

'I've nae stammick for meat,' she said, relapsing into her dull state. 'I'm no' lang for this world, an' my wee drap's the only comfort I hae. Ye'll maybe wish ye hadna been as ill to me by an' by.'

'I'm comin' alang some nicht, Wat,' said Liz, who invariably treated such remarks with the most profound contempt, ignoring them entirely. 'D'ye think Skinny'll let me in?'

'I daresay,' answered Walter abruptly, and, sitting down on the window-box, he looked through the blindless window upon the masses of roofs and the twinkling lights of the great city. His heart was heavy, his soul sick within him. His home — so poor a home for him, and for all who called it by that sweet name — had never appeared a more miserable and homeless place. It was not the smallness nor the poverty of its furnishing which concerned him, but the human beings it sheltered, who lay a burden upon his heart. Liz was out of bed, crouching over the fire, with an old red shawl wrapped round her — a striking-looking figure in spite of her general *deshabille*, a girl at whom all men and many women would look twice. He wished she were less striking, that her appearance had matched the only destiny she could look for — grey, meagre, commonplace, hopeless as a dull November day.

'Your pecker's no' up, Wat?' she said, looking at him rather keenly. 'What are ye sae doon i' the mooth for?'

Walter made no reply. Truth to tell, he would have found it difficult to give expression to his thoughts.

'He's aye doon i' the mooth when he comes here, Liz,' said the mother, with a passing touch of spirit. 'We're ower puir folk for my lord noo that he's gettin' among the gentry.'

'The gentry of Argyle Street an' the Sautmarket, mother?' asked Walter dryly. 'They'll no' do much for ye.'

'Is Skinny no' gaun to raise yer screw, Wat?' asked Liz. 'It's high time he was thinkin' on't.'

'I'll ask him one o' these days, but he might as well keep the money as me. This is a bottomless pit,' he said, with bitterness. 'It could swallow a pound as quick as five shillings, an' never be kent.'

'Ye're richt, Wat; but I wad advise ye to stick in to Skinny. He has siller, they say, an' maybe ye'll finger it some day.'

One night not long after, Liz presented herself at the house in Colquhoun Street, to return the visit of Gladys. As it happened, Walter was not in, having heard of a night school where the fees were so small as to be within the range of his means. Gladys looked genuinely pleased to see her visitor, though she hardly recognised in the fashionably-dressed young lady the melancholy-looking girl she had seen lying on the kitchen bed in the house of the Hepburns.

'Daur I come in? Would he no' be mad?' asked Liz, when they shook hands at the outer door.

'Do you mean my uncle?' asked Gladys. 'He will be quite pleased to see you. Come in; it is so cold here.'

'For you, ay; but I'm as warm's a pie, see, wi' my new fur cape — four an' elevenpence three-farthings at the Polytechnic. Isn't it a beauty, an' dirt cheap?'

Thus talking glibly about what was more interesting to her than anything else in the world, Liz followed Gladys into the kitchen, where the old man sat, as usual, in his arm-chair by the fireside, looking very old and wizened and frail in the flickering glow of fire and candle light.

'This is Walter's sister, Uncle Abel,' Gladys said, with that unconscious dignity which singled her out at once, and gave her a touch of individuality which Liz felt, though she did not in the least understand it.

The old man gave a little grunt, and bade her sit down; but, though not talkative, he keenly observed the two, and saw that they were cast in a different mould. Liz looked well, flushed with her walk, the dark warm fur setting off the brilliance of her complexion, her clothes fitting her with a certain flaunting style, her manner free from the least touch of embarrassment or restraint. Liz Hepburn feared nothing under the sun.

'And are you quite better, Liz?' asked Gladys gently, with a look of real interest and sympathy in her face.

'Oh ay, I'm fine. Wat's no' in?' she said, glancing inquiringly round the place.

'No; he has heard of a teacher who takes evening pupils for book-keeping and these things, and has gone to make arrangements with him.'

Never had the nicety of her speech and her sweet, refined accent been more marked by Abel Graham. He looked at her as she stood by the table, a slender, pale figure, with a strange touch of both child and maiden about her, and he felt glad that she was not like Liz. Not that he thought ill of Liz, or did not see her beauty, such as it was, only he felt that the maiden whom circumstances had cast into his care and keeping was of a higher type than the red-cheeked, bright-eyed damsel whom so many admired.

'An' when hae ye been oot, micht I ask?' inquired Liz calmly. 'Ye're a jimpy-looking thing.'

'Not since Sunday.'

'Sunday! Mercy me! an' this is Friday. She'll sune be in her grave, Mr. Graham. Folk maun hae fresh air. What way d'ye no' set her oot every day?'

'She is welcome to go if she likes, miss. I don't keep her in,' answered the old man tartly.

'Maybe no', but likely she has that muckle adae she canna get,' replied Liz fearlessly. 'It's a fine nicht — suppose ye tak' a walk wi' me? The shops is no' shut yet.'

'Shall I go, uncle?' asked Gladys.

'If ye want, certainly; but come in in time of night. Don't be later than nine.'

'Very well,' answered Gladys, and retired into her own room to make ready for her walk.

Then Liz, turning round squarely on her seat, fixed the old man fearlessly with her eyes, and gave him a piece of her mind.

'I saw ye lookin' at her a meenit ago, Maister Graham, an' maybe ye was thinkin' the same as me, that she's no' lang for this world. Is't no' a sin an' a shame for a cratur like that to work in a place like this? but it's waur, if it be true, as folk say, that there's nae need for it.'

So astonished was Abel Graham by this plain speaking on the part of a girl he had never seen in his life, that he could only stare.

'It's true,' added Liz significantly; 'she's yin o' the kind they mak' angels o', and that's no' my kind nor yours. If I were you, I'd see aboot it, or it'll be the waur for ye, maybe, after.'

Happily, just then Gladys returned for her boots, and in her mild excitement over having a companion to walk with, she did not observe the very curious look on her uncle's face. But Liz did, and gave an inward chuckle.

'How's your father and mother?' he asked, making the commonplace question a cover for the start he had got.

'Oh, they're as well as they can expect to be,' Liz replied. 'He cam' oot on Monday. I spiered if they had gi'en him a return ticket available for a week.'

The hard little laugh which accompanied these apparently heartless words did not in the least deceive Gladys, and, looking up from the lacing of her boots, she flashed a glance of quick sympathy upon the girl's face, which expressed more than any words.

'They're surely very ill-kinded,' was Abel Graham's comment, in rather a surprised tone. Liz had given him more information about her people in five minutes than Walter had done in the two years he had been with him. The difference between the two was, that while sharing the bitterness of their home sorrows, the one found a certain relief in telling the worst, the other shut it in his heart, a grief to be brooded over, till all life seemed tinged and poisoned by its degradation.

'Oh, it's drink,' she said carelessly, — 'the same auld story. Everything sooms awa' in whisky; they'll soom awa' theirsel's some day wi'd, that's wan comfort. I'm sure that's wan thing Wat an' me's no' likely to meddle wi'. We've seen ower muckle o' the misery o' drink. It'll never be my ruin, onyway. Are ye ready, Gladys?'

'In a minute, just my hat and gloves,' Gladys answered, and again retired.

'I say, sir, d'ye no' think ye should raise Wat's wages? I had twa things to say to ye the nicht, an' I've said them. Ye needna fash to flyte; I'm no' feared. If ye are a rich man, as they say, ye're waur than oor auld yin, for he haunds oot the siller as lang as it lasts.'

'You are a very impudent young woman,' said Abel Graham, 'and not a fit companion for my niece. I can't let her go out with you.'

'Oh, she's gaun the nicht, whether you let her or no',' was the calm answer. 'And as to being impident, some folk ca's the truth impidence, because they're no' accustomed to it. But aboot Wat, ye ken as weel as me, ye micht seek east an' west through Glesca an' no' get sic anither. He's ower honest. You raise his wages, or he'll quit, if I should seek a place for him mysel'.'

The calm self-assertion of Liz, which had something almost queenly in it, compelled the respect of the old man, and he even smiled a little across the table to the chair where she sat quite at her ease, delivering herself of these remarkably plain statements. In his inmost soul he even enjoyed them, and felt a trifle sorry when Gladys appeared, ready to go. Liz sprang up at once, and favoured the old miser with a gracious nod by way of farewell.

'Guid-nicht to ye, then, an' mind what I've said. I was in deid earnest, an' I'm richt, as ye'll maybe live to prove. An' mind that there's ower wee a pickle angels in Glesca for the ither kind, and we'd better tak' care o' what we hae.'

CHAPTER VIII.

EDGED TOOLS.

'Noo, whaur wad ye like to gang?' inquired Liz, as they shut the outer door behind them.

'Anywhere; it is pleasant to be out, only the air is not *very* good here. Do you think it is?'

'Maybe no'. We'll look at the shops first, onyhoo, an' then we'll gang an' meet Teen Ba'four. D'ye mind Teen?'

'Oh yes. Is she quite well? She looked so ill that day I saw her. I could not forget her face.'

'Oh, she's well enough, I think. I never asks. Oor kind gangs on till they drap, an' then they maistly dee,' said Liz cheerfully. 'But Teen will hing on a while yet — she's tough. I dinna see her very often. My mither disna like her. She brings me the *Reader* on Fridays. Eh, wummin, "Lord Bellew's Bride" is finished. Everything was cleared up at the end, an' the young man Lord Bellew was jealous o' turns oot to be only her brither. The last chapter tells aboot the christenin' o' the heir, an' she wears a white brocade goon, trimmed wi' real pearls an' ostrich feathers. Fancy you an' me in a frock like that! Wad it no' mak' a' the difference?'

'I don't know, I'm sure. I never thought of it,' answered Gladys, quietly amused.

'Hae ye no'? I often think o'd. If I lived in a big hoose, rode in a carriage, an' wore a silk dress every day, I wad be happy, an' guid too, maybe. It's easy to be guid when ye are rich.'

'The Bible doesn't say so. Don't you remember how it explains that it is so hard for a rich man to enter the kingdom of heaven?'

Liz looked round in a somewhat scared manner into her companion's face.

'D'ye read the Bible?' she asked bluntly. 'I never dae, so I canna mind that. I never thocht onybody read it — or believed it, I mean — except ministers that are paid for it.'

'Oh, that is quite a mistake,' said Gladys warmly. 'A great many people read it, because they love it, and because it helps them in the battle of life. I couldn't live without it. Walter and I read it every night.'

Liz drew herself a little apart doubtfully, and looked yet more scrutinisingly into the face of Gladys.

'Upon my word, ye're less fit than I thocht for this warld. What were ye born for? Ye'll never fecht yer way through,' she said, with a kind of scornful pity.

'Oh yes, I will. Perhaps if it came to the real fight, I should prove stronger than you, just because I have that help. Dear Liz, it is dreadful, if it is true, to live as you do. Are you not afraid?'

'I fear naething, except gaun into consumption, an' haein' naebody to look after me,' responded Liz. 'If it cam' to that, I'd *tak'* something to pit an end to mysel'. My mind's made up on that lang syne.'

She looked quite determined; her full red lips firmly set, and her eyes looking straight before her, calm, steadfast, undaunted, in corroboration of her boast that she feared nothing in the world.

'But, Liz, that would be very wicked,' said Gladys, in distress. 'We have never more to bear than we are able; God takes care of that always. But I am sure you are only speaking in haste. I think you have a great deal of courage — too much to do that kind of thing.'

'Dinna preach, or we'll no' 'gree,' said Liz almost rudely. 'Let's look at the hats in this window. I'll hae a new one next pay. Look at that crimson velvet wi' the black wings; it's awfu' neat, an' only six-and-nine. D'ye no' think it wad set me?'

'Very likely. You look very nice always,' answered Gladys truthfully, and the sincere compliment pleased Liz, though she did not say so.

'Well, look, it's ten meenits past aicht. We were to meet Teen in the Trongate at the quarter. We'll need to turn back.'

'And where will we go after that?' inquired Gladys. 'The shops are beginning to shut.'

'You'll see. We've a ploy on. I want to gie ye a treat. Ye dinna get mony o' them.'

She linked her arm with friendly familiarity into that of Gladys, and began to chatter on again, chiefly of dress, which was dear to her soul. Her talk was not interesting to Gladys, who was singularly free from that feminine weakness, love of fine attire. No doubt she owed this to her upbringing, having lived always alone with her father, and knowing very few of her own sex. But she listened patiently to Liz's minute account of the spring clothes she had in view, and even tried to make some suggestions on her own account.

It was with something of a relief, however, that she beheld among the crowd at last the slight figure and pale countenance of Teen.

'Guid-e'enin' to ye,' Teen said in her monotonous voice, and without a smile or brightening of her face. 'Fine dry nicht. We're late, Liz, ten minutes.'

'Oh, it doesna matter. We'll mak' a sensation,' said Liz, with a grim smile. 'A' the same, we'd better hurry up an' get oor sixpenceworth.'

'Where are we going?' asked Gladys rather doubtfully.

'Oh, ye'll see. I promised ye a treat,' answered Liz; and the trio quickened their steps until they came to a narrow entrance, illuminated, however, by a blaze of gas jets, and adorned about the doorway with sundry bills and pictures of music-hall *artistes*.

Before Gladys could utter the least protest, she was whisked in, paid for at the box, and hurried up-stairs into a brilliantly-lighted hall, the atmosphere of which, however, was reeking with the smoke and the odour of tobacco and cheap cigars. Somebody was singing in a high, shrill, unlovely voice, and when Gladys looked towards the platform behind the footlights, she was horrified at the spectacle of a large, coarse-looking woman, wearing the scantiest possible amount of clothing, her face painted and powdered, her hair adorned with gilt spangles, her arms and neck hung with sham jewellery.

'Who is she? Is it not awful?' whispered Gladys, which questions sent the undemonstrative Teen off into one of her silent fits of laughter.

But Liz looked a trifle annoyed.

'Don't ask such silly questions. That's Mademoiselle Frivol, and she's appearin' in a new character. It's an awful funny song, evidently. See how they're laughin'. Be quiet, an' let's listen.'

Gladys held her peace, and sank into the seat beside Liz, and looked about her in a kind of horrified wonder.

It was a large place, with a gallery opposite the stage. The seats in the body of the hall were not set very closely together, and the audience could move freely about. It was very full; a great many young men, well-dressed, and even gentlemanly-looking in outward appearance at least; the majority were smoking. The women present were mostly young — many of them mere girls, and there was a great deal of talking and bantering going on between them and the young men.

Those in the gallery were evidently of the poorer class, and they accompanied the chorus of the song with a vigorous stamping of feet and whistling accompaniment. When Mademoiselle Frivol had concluded her performance with a little dance which brought down the house, there was a short interval, and presently some young men sauntered up to the three girls, and bade them good-evening in an easy, familiar way, which made the colour leap to the cheek of Gladys, though she did not know why. She knew nothing about young men, and had no experience to enable her to discern the fine shades of their demeanour towards women; but that innate delicacy which is the safeguard and the unfailing monitor of every woman until she wilfully throws it away for ever, told the pure-minded girl that something was amiss, and that it was no place for her.

'Who's your chum, old girl?' asked a gorgeous youth, who wore an imitation diamond breastpin and finger-ring. 'Give us an introduction, Miss Hepburn.'

He did not remove his cigar, but looked down upon the pale face of Gladys with a kind of familiar approval which hurt her, and made her long to flee from the place.

'No; shut up, an' let her a-be,' answered Liz tartly. 'Hae ye a programme?'

'Yes, but you don't deserve it for being so shabby,' said the gorgeous youth, putting on a double eyeglass, and still honouring Gladys with his attention.

'I hope you will enjoy the performance, miss,' he added. 'Did you hear Frivol's song? It was very clever, quite the hit of the evening.'

Gladys never opened her mouth. When she afterwards looked back on that experience, she wondered how she had been able to preserve her calm, cold unconcern, which very soon convinced the youth that his advances were not welcome. Liz looked round at her, and, noting the proud, contemptuous curl of the girl's sweet lips, laughed up in his face.

'It's no go, Mr. Sinclair. Let's see that programme, an' dinna be mean.'

But the discomfited Mr. Sinclair, in no little chagrin, departed as rudely as he came.

'Ye dinna want a gentleman lover, Gladys,' whispered Liz. 'He's struck, onybody can see that, an' he's in business for himsel'. I'm sure he's masher enough for you. Wull I gie him the hint to come back?'

'I'm going home, Liz. This is no place for me, nor for any of us, I know that,' said Gladys, quite hotly for her.

'Oh no, you're no'. We must hae oor sixpenceworth. Bide or nine, onyhoo. That's just twenty meenits. Here's the acrobats; ye'll like that.'

The acrobatic performance fascinated Gladys even while it horrified and almost made her sick. She watched every contortion of the bodies with the most morbid and intense interest, though feeling it to be hideous all the time. It excited her very much, and her cheeks flushed, her eyes shone with unwonted brilliance. When it was over, she rose to her feet.

'I'm going out, Liz. This is a bad place; I know it is. I'm going home.'

Liz looked up, with annoyance, at the clock.

'It's too bad; aichteenpence awa' for naething, but I suppose we maun gang. I've to leave mysel', onyway, at nine. Ye'll bide, Teen, yersel'?'

'No' me. There's no' much the nicht, onyway,' answered Teen; and her weird black eyes wandered restlessly through the hall, as if looking in vain for an absent face. So the three quitted the place in less than half an hour after they had entered it.

One of the audience watched their movements, and left the hall immediately behind them by another door. As they moved along the busy street some one touched Liz on the shoulder, and Gladys felt her hand tremble as it lay on her arm.

'I maun say guid-nicht here, Gladys,' she said hurriedly, and her cheeks were aflame. 'I'm vexed ye didna like the play. I meant it weel. Ye'll see her hame, Teen?'

'Ay,' answered Teen, and next moment Liz was gone.

Gladys, glancing back, saw her cross the street beside a tall, broad-shouldered, handsome-looking man, though she could not see his face.

'That's her bean,' said Teen, with a nod. 'He's a swell; that's what for she has her best claes on. They're awa' for a walk noo. He was in the hall, but I didna see him.'

'Is she going to be married to him?' inquired Gladys, with interest.

'She hopes sae; but — but — I wadna like to sweer by it. He's a slippery customer, an' aye was. I ken a lassie in Dennistoun he carried on as far as Liz, but I'm no' feared for Liz. She can watch hersel'.'

A strange feeling of weariness and vague terror came over Gladys. Day by day more of life was revealed to her, and added to her great perplexity. She did not like the phase with which she had that night made acquaintance. Conversation did not flourish between them, and they were glad to part at the corner of the Lane. Gladys ran up to the house, feeling almost as if somebody pursued her, and she was out of breath when she reached the door. Walter had returned from his first evening lesson, and great had been his disappointment to find Gladys out. He was quick to note, when she entered the kitchen, certain signs of nervous excitement, which made him wonder where she had been.

'It's nearly half past nine,' said the old man crossly; 'too late for you to be in the streets. Get to bed now, and be up to work in the morning.'

'Yes, uncle,' said Gladys meekly, and retired to her own room thankfully, to lay off her bonnet and cloak.

Walter hung about by the dying fire after the old man went up to take his nightly survey of the premises, and at last Gladys came back.

'Did you have a good lesson, Walter?' she asked, with a slight smile.

'Oh, splendid. What a thing it is to learn! I feel as if I could do anything now I have begun,' he cried enthusiastically. 'Mr. Robertson was so kind. He will give me Euclid as well for the same money. He says he sees I am in earnest. Life is a fine thing after all, sometimes.'

'Yes.' Gladys looked upon his face, flushed with the fine enthusiasm of youth, with a slight feeling of envy. She felt very old and tired and sad.

'And you've been out with Liz?' he said then, seeing that for some unexplained reason she was not so interested as usual in his pursuits. 'Where did she take you?'

'To a music hall — not a nice place, Walter,' said Gladys almost shamefacedly.

His colour, the flush of quick anger, leaped in his cheek.

'A music hall! I should just say it isn't a nice place. How dared she? I see Liz needs me to talk to her plainly, and I will next time I see her,' he began hotly; but just then the old man returned, and they kept silence. But the evening's 'ploy' disturbed them both all night, though in a different way.

CHAPTER IX.

AN IMPENDING CHANGE.

It was an uneventful year. Spring succeeded the fogs and frosts of winter, sunny skies and warmer airs came again, bringing comfort to those who could buy artificial heat, so making gladness in cities, and a wonder of loveliness in country places, where Nature reigns supreme. The hardy flowers Gladys planted in the little yard grew and blossomed; the solitary tree, in spite of its loneliness, put forth its fresh green buds, and made itself a thing of beauty in the maiden's eyes. In that lonely home the tide of life flowed evenly. The old man made his bargains, cutting them perhaps a trifle less keenly than in former years. The lad, approaching young manhood, did his daily work, and drank yet deeper of the waters of knowledge, becoming day by day more conscious of his power, more full of hope and high ambition for the future. And the child Gladys, approaching womanhood also, contentedly performed her lowly tasks, and dreamed her dreams likewise, sometimes wondering vaguely how long this monotonous, grey stream would flow on, yet not wishing it disturbed, lest greater ills than she knew might beset her way.

Again winter came, and just when spring was gathering up her skirts to spread them benignly over the earth, a great change came, a very great change indeed.

It was a March day — cold, bitter, blustering east winds tearing through the streets, catching the breath with a touch of ice — when the old man, who to the observant eye had become of late decrepit and very frail-looking, came shivering down from his warehouse, and, creeping to the fire, tried to warm his chilled body, saying he felt himself very ill.

'I think you should go to bed, uncle, and Walter will go for the doctor,' said Gladys, in concern. 'Shall I call him now?'

'No; I'll go to bed, and you can give me some toddy. There's my keys; you'll get the bottle on the top shelf of the press in the office. I won't send for the doctor yet. You can't get them out when once they get a foot in, and their fees are scandalous. No, I'll have no doctors here.'

Gladys knew very well that it was useless to dispute his decision, and, taking his keys, ran lightly up-stairs to the warehouse.

'I am afraid Uncle Abel is quite ill, Walter,' she said, as she unlocked the cupboard. 'He shivers very much, and looks so strangely. Do you not think we should have the doctor?'

'Yes; but he won't have him. I think he looks very bad. He's been bad for days, and his cough is awful, but he won't give in.'

'If he is not better tomorrow, you will just go for the doctor yourself, Walter. After he is here, uncle can't say much,' said Gladys thoughtfully. 'I will do what I can for him today. I am afraid he looks very like papa. I don't like his eyes.'

She took the bottle down, and retired again, with a nod and a smile — the only inspiration known to the soul of Walter. It was not of the old man he thought as he busied himself among the goods, but of the fair girl who had come to him in his desolation as a revelation of everything lovely and of good report.

The hot fumes of the toddy sent the old man off into a heavy sleep, during which he got a respite from his racking cough. It was late afternoon when he awoke, and Gladys was sitting by the fire in the fading light, idle, for a wonder, though her work lay on her lap. It was too dark for her to see, and she feared to move lest she should awaken the sleeper. He was awake, however, some time before she was aware, and he lay looking at her intently, his face betokening thought of the most serious kind. She was startled at length by his utterance of her name.

'Yes, uncle, you have had a fine sleep, so many hours. See, it is almost dark, and Walter will be down presently,' she said brightly. 'Are you ready for tea now?'

She came to his bed-side, and looked down upon him as tenderly as if he had been the dearest being to her on earth.

'You are a good girl, a good girl,' he said quickly, — 'the best girl in the whole world.'

Her face flushed with pleasure at this rare praise.

'I am very glad, uncle, if you think so,' she said gently. 'And now, what can the best girl in the world do to keep up her reputation? Is the pain gone?'

'Almost; it is not so bad, anyhow. Do you think I'm dying, Gladys?'

She gave a quick start, and her cheek blanched slightly at this sudden question.

'Oh no. Why do you ask such a thing, uncle? You have only got a very bad cold — a chill caught in that cold place up there. I wonder you have escaped so long.'

'Ay, it is rather cold. I've been often chilled to the bone, and I've seen Walter's fingers blue with cold,' he said. 'You'll run up soon and tell him to haul all the soap-boxes out of the fireplace, and build up a big fire to be ready for the morning, lighted the first thing.'

'Very well, uncle; but I don't think I'll let you up-stairs tomorrow.'

'It's for Walter, not for me. If I'm better, I've something else to do tomorrow.'

'Well, we'll see,' said Gladys briskly. 'Now I must set on the kettle. Wouldn't you like something for tea?'

'No, nothing. I've no hunger,' he answered, and his eyes followed her as she crossed the floor and busied herself with her accustomed skill about the fireplace.

'You're an industrious creature. Nothing comes amiss to you,' he said musingly. 'It's a poor life for a young woman like you. I wonder you've stood it so long?'

'It has been a very good life on the whole, uncle,' Gladys replied cheerfully. 'I have had a great many blessings; I never go out but I feel how many. And I have always tried to be contented.'

'Have you never been very angry with me,' he asked unexpectedly.

'No, never; but' —

'But what?'

'Sorry for you often.'

'Why?'

'Because you did not take all the good of life you might.'

'How could I? A poor man can't revel in the good things of life,' he said, with a slight touch of irritation.

'No, quite true; but some poor people seem to make more out of small things. That was what I meant,' said Gladys meekly. 'But we must not talk anything disagreeable, uncle; it is not good for you.'

'But I want to talk. I say, were you disappointed because I never took you into Ayrshire in the summer?'

'Yes, uncle, a little, but it soon passed. When summer comes again, you will take me, I am sure.'

'You will go, anyhow, whether I do or not,' he said pointedly. 'Will you tell me, child, what you think of Walter?'

'Of Walter, uncle?' Gladys paused, with her hand on the cupboard door, and looked back at him with a slightly puzzled air.

'Yes. Do you think him a clever chap?'

'I do. I think he can do anything, Uncle Abel,' she replied warmly. 'Yes, Walter is very clever.'

'And good?'

'And good. You and I know that there are few like him,' was her immediate reply.

'And you like him?'

'Of course I do; it would be very strange if I did not,' she replied, without embarrassment.

'Do you think he would be capable of filling a much higher post than he has at present?'

'Of course I do; and if you will not be angry, I will say that I have often thought that you do not pay him enough of money.'

'There's nothing like going through the hards in youth. It won't do him any harm,' said the old man. 'He won't suffer by it, I promise you that.'

'Perhaps not; but when he has educated himself, — which won't be long now, Uncle Abel, he is getting on so fast, — he will not stay here. We could not expect it.'

'Why not, if there's money in it?'

'*Is* there money in it?'

A shrewd little smile wreathed her lips, and her whole manner indicated that her sense of humour was touched.

'There's money in most things if they are attended to,' he said, with his usual evasiveness; 'and a young, strong man can work up a small thing into a paying concern if he watches his opportunity.'

'Money is not everything,' Gladys replied, as she began to spread the cloth, 'but it can do a great deal.'

'Ay, you are right, my girl; this is a poor world to live in without it. Suppose you were a rich woman, what would you do with your money?'

'Help people who have none; it is the only use money is for.'

'Now you speak out of ignorance,' said the old man severely. 'Don't you know that there's a kind of people — Walter's parents, for instance — whom it is not only useless, but criminal, to help with money? Just think of the poor lad's case. He has only had a small wage, certainly; but if it had been three times bigger it would have been the same thing.'

Gladys knit her brows perplexedly.

'It is hard, uncle, certainly. The plan would be, to help them in a different way.'

'But how? There are plenty rich and silly women in Glasgow who are systematically fleeced by the undeserving poor — people who have no earthly business to be poor, who have hands and heads which can give them a competence, only they are moral idiots. No woman should be allowed full use of large sums of money. She is so soft-hearted, she can't say no, and she's imposed on half the time.'

'You are very hard on women, Uncle Abel,' said Gladys, still amused with his enthusiasm. She had no fear of him. Although there was not much in common between them, there was a kind of quiet understanding, and they had many discussions of the kind. 'I would rather be poor always, Uncle Abel, if I were not allowed to spend as I wished. I should just have to learn to be prudent and careful by experience.'

'Ay, by experience, which would land you in the poorhouse.

Have you no desire for the things other women like — fine clothes, trinkets, and such-like?'

'I don't know, uncle, because I have never had any,' said Gladys, with a little laugh. 'I daresay I should like them very well.'

The old man gave a grunt, and turned on his pillow, as if tired of talk.

Gladys busied herself with the evening meal, and when it was ready called Walter down. It was a pretty sight to see her waiting on the old man, attending to his comforts, and coaxing him to eat. In the evening she ran out to get some medicine for him, and when he was left with Walter, busy at his books at the table, he sat up suddenly, as if he had something interesting and important to say.

'How are you getting on with your learning, Wat? You are pretty constant at it. If there's anything in application, you should succeed.'

'It's pretty tough work, though, when a fellow's getting older.'

'Older,' repeated the old man, with a quiet chuckle. 'How old are you?'

'Nineteen.'

'Nineteen, are you? Well, you look it. You've vastly improved of late. I suppose you think yourself rather an ill-used sort of person — ill used by me, I mean?'

'I don't think you pay me enough, if you mean that,' said Walter, with a little laugh; 'but I'm going to ask a rise.'

'Why have you stayed here so long, if that is your mind? Nobody was compelling you.'

'No; but I've got used to the place, and I like it,' returned Walter frankly; but he bent his eyes on his books, as if there was something more behind his words which he did not care should be revealed.

'I see — it's each man for himself in this world, and deil tak' the hindmost, as they say; but I don't think you'll be hindmost. Suppose, now, you were to find yourself the boss of this concern, what would you do?'

'Carry it on as best I could, sir,' answered Walter, in surprise.

'Ay, but how? I suppose you think you'd reorganise it all?' said the old man rather sarcastically.

'Well, I would,' admitted Walter frankly.

'In what way? Just tell me how you'd do it?'

'Well, I'd be off, somehow or other, with all these old debts, sir, and then I'd begin a new business on different principles. I couldn't stand so much carrying over of old scores to new accounts, if I were on my own hook. You never know where you are, and it's cruel to the poor wretches who are always owing; they can't have any independence. Its a poor way of doing business.'

'Oh, indeed! You are not afraid to speak your mind, my young bantam. And pray, where did you pick up all these high and mighty notions?'

'They may be high and mighty, sir, but they're common-sense,' responded Walter, without perturbation. 'You know yourself how you've been worried to death almost, and what a watching these slippery customers need. It is not worth the trouble.'

'Is it not? Pray, how do you know that?' inquired the old man, his eyes glittering as he asked the question. 'I don't know, of course, but you always say you are a poor man,' replied Walter, as he put down the figures of a sum on his slate.

'But you don't believe it, eh? Perhaps that's why you've stuck to me like a leech so long,' he said, with his most disagreeable smile; but Walter never answered. They had been together now for some years, and there was a curious sort of understanding — a liking, even — between them; and of late Walter had taken several opportunities of speaking his mind with a candour which really pleased his strange old master, though he always appeared to be in a state of indignation.

'The only thing I am anxious about is the girl,' he muttered, more to himself than to the lad. 'But she'll find friends — more of them, perhaps, than she'll want, poor thing, poor thing!'

These words gave Walter something of a shock, and he looked round in quick wonderment. But the return of Gladys just then prevented him asking the question trembling on his lips.

CHAPTER X.

IN AYRSHIRE.

The old man passed a quiet night, and was so much better in the morning that he insisted on getting up.

'What kind of a morning is it?' was the first question he put to Gladys when she entered the kitchen soon after six o'clock.

'A lovely morning, uncle, so balmy and soft. You can't think what a difference from yesterday, and there's a bird singing a spring song in my tree.'

Often yet she said such things. The grey monotony of her life had not quite destroyed the poetic vein, nor the love of all things beautiful.

'Warm, is it? Have you been out?'

'Not yet; but I opened my window and put my head out, and the air was quite mild. A spring morning, Uncle Abel, the first we have had this year.'

'Any sun?'

'Not yet, but he will be up by and by. How have you slept?'

'Pretty well. I am better this morning — quite well, in fact, and directly you have the fire on I'll get up.'

'Don't be rash, uncle, I really think you ought to stay in bed today.'

'No; I have something to do. How soon can you be ready — finished with your work, I mean? Have you anything you can leave ready for Wat's dinner?'

'Why, Uncle Abel?' asked Gladys, in surprise.

'Because I want you to go somewhere with me.'

'You are not going out of this house one foot today,' she answered quickly. 'It would be very dangerous.'

The old man smiled, slightly amused, but not displeased, by the decision with which she spoke. 'We'll see, if it keeps fine, and the sun comes out. I'm going today, whatever the consequences, and you with me. It's been put off too long.'

Gladys asked no more questions, but made haste to build up the fire and get him a cup of tea before he rose.

'Put on your warm clothes, and make ready for a journey in the train, Gladys,' he said after breakfast.

She looked at him doubtfully, almost wondering if his mind did not wander a little.

'Uncle Abel, what are you thinking of? You never go journeys in trains. It will not be safe for you to go today, with such a cold,' she exclaimed.

'I am going, my dear, as I said, and so are you, whatever the consequences, so get ready as fast as you like, so that we may have the best of the day.'

'Is it a far journey?'

'You'll see when you get there,' he replied rather shortly; and Gladys, still wondering much, made haste with her work, and began to dress for this unexpected outing. But she felt uneasy, and, stealing a moment, ran up to Walter, who was busy in the warehouse, and revelling in the unaccustomed luxury of a blazing fire.

'How nice it is, and what a difference a fire can make, to be sure,' she said quickly. 'I say, Walter, such a thing! Uncle Abel is going a journey, — a railway journey, actually, — and I am going with him. Has he said anything to you? Have you any idea what it means?'

'Not I. He's a queer old chap. Not off his head, I hope?'

'Oh no, and he says he is quite well. I don't know what to think. Perhaps I shall understand it when I come back. You will find your dinner in the oven, Walter; and be sure to keep up a good fire all day down-stairs, in case uncle should come back very cold and tired. I am afraid he will, but it is no use saying anything.'

Walter leaned his elbows on the soap-boxes, and looked into the girl's face with a curious soberness.

'Something's going to happen, I feel it — something I don't like. I'm oppressed with an awful queer feeling. I hope they're not worse than usual at home.'

'Oh no, you are letting your imagination run away with you,' she said brightly. 'I hope you will have such a busy day you won't have time to think of such things;' and, bidding him good-morning, she ran down again to her uncle.

Then, for the first time since that memorable and dreary journey from the fen country, these two, the old man and the maiden, went forth together. Both thought of that journey, though it was not spoken of. She could not fail to see that there was a certain excitement in the old man; it betrayed itself in his restless movements and in the gleam of his piercing eye. Gladys no longer feared the glance of his eye nor the sound of his voice. A quiet confidence had established itself between them, and she really loved him. It was impossible for her to dwell beside a human being, not absolutely repulsive, without pouring some of the riches of her affection upon him. As for him, Gladys herself had not the remotest idea how he regarded her, did not dream that she had awakened in his withered heart a slow and all-absorbing affection, the strength of which surprised himself. He bade her stand back while he went to the booking-office for the tickets, and they were in the train before she repeated her question regarding their destination.

'I think it would only be fair, Uncle Abel, if you told me now where we are going,' she said playfully.

For answer, he held out the ticket to her, and in amazement she read 'Mauchline' on it. The colour flushed all over her face, and she looked at him with eager, questioning eyes.

'Oh, Uncle Abel, what does it mean? Why are you going there today? I cannot understand it.'

'I have my reasons, Gladys. You will know them, perhaps, sooner than you think.'

'Is it a long journey, uncle? I am so afraid for you. Let me shut the window up quite. And are we really, really going into Ayrshire at last?'

She was full of excitement as a child. She sat close to the window, and when the train had left the city behind, looked out with eagerest interest on the wintry landscape.

'Oh, Uncle Abel, it is so beautiful to see it, the wide country, and the sky above it so clear and lovely. Oh, there is room to breathe!'

'I am sure it looks wintry and bleak enough,' the old man answered, with a grunt. 'I don't see much beauty in it myself.'

'How strange! To me it is wholly beautiful. Is this Ayrshire yet? Tell me when we come to Ayrshire.'

A slow smile was on the old man's face as he looked and listened. He enjoyed her young enthusiasm, but it seemed to awaken in him some sadder thought, for once he sighed heavily, and drew himself together as if he felt cold, or some bitter memory smote him.

In little more than an hour the train drew up at the quiet country station, and Gladys was told they had reached their journey's end. It was a lovely spring morning; the sun shone out cheerfully from a mild, bright sky, the air was laden with the awakening odours of spring, and the spirit of life seemed to be everywhere.

'Now, my girl, we have a great deal to do today,' said the old man, when they had crossed the footbridge. 'What do you want most to see here?'

'Mossgiel and Ballochmyle, and the house where you lived in Mauchline.'

'We'll go to that first; it's not a great sight, I warn you — only a whitewashed, thatched cottage in a by-street. When we've seen that, we'll take a trap and drive to the other places.'

'But that will cost a great deal,' said Gladys doubtfully, recalled for the moment to the small economies it was her daily lot to practise.

'Perhaps; but we'll manage it, I daresay. It is impossible for us to walk, so there's no use saying another word. Give me your arm.'

Gladys was ready in a moment. Never since the old fen days had she felt so happy, because the green earth was beneath her feet, the trees waving above her, the song of birds in her ears instead of the roar of city streets. They did not talk as they walked, until they turned into the quaint, wide street of the old-fashioned village; then it was as if the cloak of his reserve fell from Abel Graham, and he became garrulous as a boy over these old landmarks which he had never forgotten. He led Gladys by way of Poosie Nancie's tavern, showed her its classic interior, and then, turning into a little narrow lane, pointed out the cottage where he and her father had been boys together.

It was the girl's turn to be silent. She was trying to picture the dear father a boy at his mother's knee, or running in and out that low doorway, or helping to swell the boyish din in the narrow street; and when they turned to go, her eyes were wet with tears.

'I would rather have come here today, Uncle Abel, than anywhere else in the whole wide world. But why did you wish to come? Did you take a sudden longing to see the old place?'

'No; that was not my object at all. You will know what it was some day. Now we'll go to the inn and get something to eat while they get our machine ready. See, there's the old kirk; there's a lot of famous folk buried in that kirkyard. We'd better go in, and I'll show you where I want to be laid.'

They got the key of the churchyard gates, and, stepping across the somewhat untidily kept graves, stood before an uneven mound, surrounded by a very old mossgrown headstone.

'There's a name on it, child. You can't read it, but it doesn't matter,' he said; but Gladys, bending down, brushed the tall grass from the stone, and read the name, John Bourhill Graham of Bourhill, and his spouse, Nancy Millar.

'Whose names are these, uncle — your father's and mother's?'

'Oh no; *they* were not Grahams of Bourhill,' he answered dryly. 'That's generations back.'

'But the same family?'

'I suppose so — yes. I see you would like to explore this place; but we can't, it's not the most cheerful occupation, anyhow. Come on, let us to the inn.'

The lavish manner in which her uncle spent his money that day amazed Gladys, but she made no remark. Immediately after their hot and abundant dinner at the inn, they drove to the places Burns has immortalised, and which Gladys had so long yearned to see. Ballochmyle, in lovely spring dress, so far exceeded her expectation that she had no words wherein to express her deep enjoyment.

'Do not let us hurry away, uncle,' she pleaded, as they wandered through the wooded glades, 'unless you are very tired. It is so warm and pleasant, and it cannot be very late.'

'It is not late, half past two only; but I want you to see Bourhill, where our forbears lived when we had them worth mentioning,' he said grimly. 'Did your father never speak to you about Bourhill?'

'No, never, Uncle Abel. I am quite sure I never heard the name until I read it today in the churchyard.'

'I will tell you why. He had a dream — a foolish one it proved — a dream that he might one day restore the name Graham of Bourhill again. He hoped to make a fortune by his pictures, but it was a vain delusion.'

A shadow clouded the bright face of Gladys as she listened to these words.

'This place, Bourhill, is it an estate, or what?' she asked.

'Not now. A hundred years ago it had some farms, and was a fair enough patrimony, but it's all squandered long syne.'

'How?'

'Oh, drink and gambling, and such-like. My grand-father, David Graham, kent the taste of Poosie Nancie's whisky too well to look after his ain, and it slipped through his fingers like a knotless thread.'

He had become even more garrulous, and unearthed from the storehouse of his memory a wealth of reminiscences of those old times, mingled with many bits of personal history, which Gladys listened to with breathless interest. She had never seen him so awakened, so full of life and vigour; she could only look at him in amazement. They drove leisurely through the pleasant spring sunshine over the wide, beautiful country, past fields where the wheat was green and strong, and others where sowing was progressing merrily — sights and sounds dear to Gladys, who had no part nor lot in cities.

'Oh, Uncle Abel, Ayrshire is lovely. Look at these low green hills in the distance, and the woods everywhere. I do not wonder that Burns could write poetry here. There is poetry everywhere.'

'Ay, to your eyes, because you are young and know no better. Look, away over yonder, as far as your eyes can see, is the sea. If it was a little clearer you would see the ships in Ayr Harbour; and down there lies Tarbolton; away over there, the way we have come, Kilmarnock. And do you see that little wooded hill about two miles ahead to the left? Among these trees lies Bourhill.'

'It is a long drive to it, Uncle Abel. I hope it has not tired you very much?'

'No, no; I'm all right. We'll drive up the avenue to the house and back. I want you to see it.'

'Does nobody live in it?'

'Not just now.'

Another fifteen minutes brought them to an unpretending iron gateway, which gave entrance to an avenue of fine old trees. The gate stood open, and though a woman ran out from the lodge when the trap passed, she made no demur.

The avenue was nearly half a mile in length, and ended in a sharp curve, which brought them quite suddenly before the house — a plain, square, substantial family dwelling, with a pillared doorway and long wide windows, about which crept ivy of a century's growth. It was all shut up, and the gravel sweep before the door was overgrown with moss and weeds, the grass on the lawns, which stretched away through the shrubberies, long and rank; yet there was a homely look about it too, as if a slight touch could convert it into a happy home.

'This is Bourhill, my girl; and whatever ambitions your father may have had in later years, it was once his one desire to buy it back to the Grahams. Do you like the place?'

'Yes, uncle; but it is very desolate — it makes me sad.'

'It will not be long so,' he said; and, drawing himself together with a quick shiver, he bade the driver turn the horses' heads. But before the house vanished quite from view he cast his gaze back upon it, and in his eye there was a strange, even a yearning glance. 'It will not be long so,' he repeated under his breath, — 'not long; and it will be a great atonement.'

CHAPTER XI.

DARKENING DAYS.

In the night Gladys was awakened by her uncle's voice sharply calling her name, and when she hastened to him she found him in great pain, and breathing with the utmost difficulty. Her presence of mind did not desert her. She had often seen her father in a similar state, and knew exactly what to do. In a few minutes she had a blazing fire, and the kettle on; then she ran to awaken Walter, so that he might go for the doctor. The simple remedies experience had taught the girl considerably eased the old man, and when the doctor came he found him breathing more freely. But his face was quite grave after his examination was made.

'I suppose my hour's come?' said Abel Graham in a matter-of-fact way. 'I don't think much of your fraternity, — I've never had many dealings with you, — but I suppose you can tell a man what he generally knows himself, that he'll soon be in grips with death?'

The doctor looked at him with an odd smile. He was a young man, fighting his way up against fierce competition — an honest, straightforward fellow, who knew and loved his work.

'You don't think highly of us, Mr. Graham, but I daresay we have our uses. This young lady appears to be an accomplished nurse; she has done the very best possible under the circumstances.'

He turned to Gladys, not seeking to hide his surprise at finding such a fair young creature amid such surroundings. Walter Hepburn, standing in the background, experienced a strange sensation when he saw that look. Though he knew it not, it was his first jealous pang.

'I had to nurse my father often in such attacks,' Gladys answered, with her quiet, dignified calm. 'If there is anything more I can do, pray tell me, and I will follow your instructions faithfully.'

'There is not much we can do in such a case. I never heard anything so foolhardy as to go off, as you say he did yesterday, driving through the open country for hours on a March day. I don't think a man who takes such liberties with himself can expect to escape the penalty, Mr. Graham.'

'Well, well, it doesn't matter. If my hour's come, it's come, I suppose, and that's the end of it,' he retorted irritably. 'How long will I last?'

'Years, perhaps, with care — after this attack is conquered,' replied the doctor; and the old man answered with a grim, sardonic smile.

'We'll see whether you or I am right,' he replied. 'You needn't stay any longer just now.'

Gladys took the candle, and herself showed the doctor to the outer door.

'Will he really recover, do you think?' she asked, when they were out of hearing.

'He may, but only with care. The lungs are much congested, and his reserve of strength is small. What relation is he to you, may I ask? Your grandfather?'

'No; my uncle?'

'And do you live here always?'

'Yes, this is my home,' Gladys answered, and she could scarcely forbear a smile at the expression on the young doctor's face.

'Indeed! and you are contented? You seem so,' he said, lingering at the door a moment longer than he need have done.

'Oh yes; I have a great deal to be thankful for,' she answered. 'You will come again tomorrow early, will you not?'

'Certainly. Good-morning. Take care of yourself. You do not look as if your reserve of strength were very great either.'

'Oh, I am very strong, I assure you,' Gladys answered, with a smile; and as she looked into his open, honest face, she could not help thinking what a pleasant face it was.

Then she went back to keep her vigil by the sick-bed, and to exercise her woman's prerogative to ease and minister to pain. There was so little any one could do now, however, to help Abel Graham, the issue of his case being in the hand of God. In obedience to the request of Gladys, Walter went back to bed, and she sat on by the fire, thoroughly awake, and watchful to be of the slightest use to her uncle. He did not talk much, but he appeared to watch Gladys, and to be full of thoughts concerning her.

'Do you remember that night I came, after your father died?' he asked once.

'Yes,' she answered in a low voice. 'I remember it well.'

'You felt bitter and hard against me, did you not?'

'If I did, Uncle Abel, it has long passed,' she answered. 'There is no good to be got recalling what is past.'

'Perhaps not; but, my girl, when a man comes to his dying bed it is the past he harks back on, trying to get some comfort out of it for the future he dreads, and failing always.'

'It is not your dying bed, Uncle Abel, I hope; you are not so old yet,' she said cheerfully.

'No, I'm not old in years — not sixty — but old enough to regret my youth,' he said. 'Are you still of the same mind about the spending of money, if you should ever have it to spend?'

'Yes; but it is so unlikely, Uncle Abel, that I shall ever have any money to spend. It is quite easy saying what we can do in imaginary circumstances. Reality is always different, and more difficult to deal with.'

'You are very wise for your years. How many are they?'

'Seventeen and three months.'

'Ay, well, you look your age and more. You'd pass for twenty, but no wonder; and' —

'I wish you would not talk so much, uncle; it will excite and exhaust you,' she said, in gentle remonstrance.

'I must talk, if my time is short. Suppose I'm taken, what will you do with yourself, eh?'

'The way will open up for me, I do not doubt; there must be a corner for me somewhere,' she said bravely; nevertheless, her young cheek blanched, and she shivered slightly as she glanced round the place — poor enough, perhaps, but which at least afforded her a peaceful and comfortable home. These signs were not unnoticed by the dying man, and a faint, slow, melancholy smile gathered about his haggard mouth.

'You believe, I suppose, that the Lord will provide for you?' he said grimly.

'Yes, I do.'

'Does He never fail, eh?'

'Never. He does not always provide just as we expect or desire, but provision is made all the same,' answered the girl, and her eyes shone with a steadfast light.

'It's a very comfortable doctrine, but not practicable, nor, to my thinking, honest. Do you mean to say that it is right to sit down with folded hands waiting for the Lord to provide, and living off other people at the same time?'

Gladys smiled.

'No, that is not right, but wrong, very wrong, and punishment always follows. Heaven helps those who help themselves; don't you remember that?'

'Ay, well, I don't understand your theology, I confess. But we may as well think it out. What do you suppose will become of me after I shuffle off, eh?'

'I don't know, uncle. You best know what your own hope is,' she replied.

'I have no hope, and I don't see myself how anybody can presume to have any. It's all conjecture about a future life. How does anybody know? Nobody has ever come back to tell the tale.'

'No; but we know, all the same, that there are many mansions in heaven, and that God has prepared them for His children.'

'You would not call me one of them, I guess?' said the old

man, with a touch of sarcasm, yet there was something behind — a great wistfulness, a consuming anxiety, which betrayed itself in his very eye, as he awaited her reply. It was a curious moment, a curious scene. The old, toilworn, world-weary man, who had spent his days in the most sordid pursuit of gold — gold for which he would at one time almost have sold his soul, hanging on the words of a young, untried maiden, whose purity enabled her to touch the very gates of heaven. It was a sight to make the philosopher ponder anew on the mysteries of life, and the strange anomalies human nature presents.

She turned her sweet face to him, and there was a mixture of pathos and brightness in her glance.

'Why not, uncle? I may not judge. It is God who knows the heart.'

'Ay, maybe. But what would you think yourself? You have shrewd enough eyes, though you are so quiet.'

'But I cannot know this, uncle; only if you believe that Christ died for you, you are one of God's children, though' — she added, with a slight hesitation — 'you may not have served Him very well.'

'Then you think I have not served Him, eh?' he repeated, with strange persistence.

'Perhaps you might have done more, uncle. If you get better you will do more for others, I feel sure,' she said. 'But now you must be still and keep quiet. I shall not talk another word to you, positively not a word.'

'Ay,' he said dryly, and, turning on his pillow, closed his eyes — not to sleep, oh no, brain and heart were too full of conflicting and disturbing thought.

In the dull hours of the early morning Gladys dozed a little in her chair, imagining the sick man slept. When the light grew broader she roused herself, and began to move about with swift but noiseless steps, fearing to awake him. But he did not sleep. Lying there, with his face turned to the wall, Abel Graham held counsel with himself, reviewing his life, which lay before him like a tale that is told. None knew better than he what a poor, mean, sordid, selfish life it had been, how little it had contributed to the good or the happiness of others, and these memories tortured him now with the stings of the bitterest regret. It was not known to any save himself and his Maker what agony his awakened soul passed through in the still hours of that spring day. Seeing him lie apparently in such restfulness, the two young creatures spoke to each other at their breakfast only in whispers, and when Walter went up to the warehouse, Gladys continued to perform her slight tasks as gently and noiselessly as possible; but sometimes, when she looked at the face on the pillow, with its closed eyes and pinched, wan features, she wished the doctor would come again.

About half past nine a knock came to the door, and Gladys ran out almost joyfully, expecting to see the young physician with the honest face and the pleasant eyes, but a very different-looking personage was presented to her view when she opened the door. A man in shabby workman's garb, dirty, greasy, and untidy — a man with a degraded type of countenance, a heavy, coarse mouth, and small eyes looking out suspiciously from heavy brows. She shrank away a little, and almost unconsciously began to close the door, even while she civilly inquired his business.

'Is Wat in? I want to see my son, Walter Hepburn,' he said; and when he opened his mouth Gladys felt the smell of drink, and it filled her with both mental and physical repulsion. So this was Walter's father? Poor Walter! A vast compassion, greater than any misery she had before experienced, filled the girl's gentle soul.

'Yes, he is in, up-stairs in the warehouse. Will you come in, please?' she asked; but before the invitation could be accepted, Wat came bounding down the stairs, having heard and recognised the voice, and there was no welcoming light in his eye as he gazed on his father's face.

'Well, what do you want?' he asked abruptly; and Gladys, slipping back hastily, left them alone.

And after she had returned to the kitchen she heard the hum of their voices in earnest talk for quite five minutes. Then the door was closed, and she heard Walter returning to his work. It appeared to her as if his step sounded very heavy and reluctant as it ascended the stair.

Presently her uncle roused himself up, and asked for something to eat or drink.

'Are you feeling better?' she asked, as she shook up his pillows, and did other little things to make him comfortable.

'No; there's a load lying here,' he answered, touching his chest, 'which presses down to the grave. If they can't do something to remove that, I'm a dead man. No word of that young upstart doctor yet?'

'Not yet. Shall I send for him, uncle?'

'No, no; he'll come sure enough, and fast enough — oftener than he's wanted,' he answered. 'Who was that at the door?'

'Walter's father.'

'Eh? Walter's father? What did he want? Is he smelling round too, to see if he can get anything?' he said querulously. 'When you've given me that tea, I wish you to take my keys from my coat pocket and go up to the safe. When you've opened it, you'll find an old pocket-book, tied with a red string. I want you to bring it down to me.'

'Very well.'

Gladys did exactly as she was bid, and, leaving the old man at his slender breakfast, ran up to the warehouse. To her surprise, she found Walter, usually so active and so energetic, sitting on the office stool with his arms folded, and his face wearing a look of deepest gloom. Some new trouble had come to him, that was apparent to her at once.

'Why, Walter, how troubled you look! No bad news from home, I hope?'

'Bad enough,' he answered in a kind of savage undertone. 'I knew something was going to happen. Haven't I been saying it for days?'

'But what has happened? Nothing very bad, I hope?'

'So bad that it couldn't be worse,' he said. 'Liz has run away.'

CHAPTER XII.

SETTING HIS HOUSE IN ORDER.

Gladys opened her eyes.

'Run away! How? Where? I don't understand.'

'All the better if you don't,' he answered harshly. 'She's run away, anyhow, and it's their blame. Then they come to me, after the mischief's done, thinking I can make it right. I'm not going to stir a foot in the matter. They can all go to Land's End for me.'

He spoke bitterly — more bitterly than Gladys had ever heard him speak before. She stood there, with the keys on her forefinger, the picture of perplexity and concern. She did not understand the situation, and was filled with curiosity to know where Liz had run to.

'Have they quarrelled, or what?' she asked.

'No; I don't suppose there's been any more than the usual amount of scrimmaging,' he said, with a hard smile. 'I don't blame Liz; she's only what they've made her. I'll tell you what it is,' he said, suddenly clenching his right hand, his young face set with the bitterness of his grief and shame, 'if there's no punishment for those that bring children into the world and then let them go to ruin, there's no justice in heaven, and I don't believe in it.'

Gladys shrank back, paling slightly under this torrent of passionate words. Never had she seen Walter so bitterly, so fearfully moved. He got up from his stool, and paced up and down the narrow space between the boxes in a very storm of indignation; and it seemed to Gladys that a few minutes had changed him from a boy into a man.

'Dear Walter,' she said gently, 'try to be brave. Perhaps it will not be so bad as you think.'

'It's so bad for Liz, poor thing, that it won't be any worse. She's lost, and she was the only one of them I cared for. If she'd had a chance, she'd have been a splendid woman. She has a good heart, only she never had anybody to guide her.'

Gladys could not speak. She had only the vaguest idea what he meant, but she knew that something terrible had happened to Liz. A curious reticence seemed to bind her tongue. She could not ask a single question.

'Just when a fellow was beginning to get on!' cried Walter rebelliously, 'this has to happen to throw him back. It was a fearful mistake trying to better myself. I wish I had sunk down into the mud with the rest. If I do it yet, it will be the best thing for me.'

Then Gladys intervened. Though she did not quite comprehend the nature of this new trouble which appeared so powerfully to move him, she could not listen to such words without remonstrance.

'It is not right to speak so, Walter, and I will not listen to it. Whatever others may do, though it may grieve and cut you to the heart, it cannot take away your honour or integrity, always remember that.'

'Yes, it can,' he said impetuously. 'That kind of disgrace hangs on a man all his days. He has to bear the sins of others. That is where the injustice comes in. The innocent must suffer for and with the guilty always. There is no escape.'

Gladys sighed, and her face became pale and weary-looking. Never had life appeared so hard, so full of pain and care. Looking at the face of Walter, which she had always thought so noble and so good, — the index to a soul striving, though sometimes but feebly, yet striving always after what was highest and best, — looking at his face then, and seeing it so shadowed by the bitterness of his lot, her own simple faith for the moment seemed to fail.

'You saw him, then, this morning, and I hope you admired him,' said Walter, with harsh scorn. 'Reeking with drink, speaking thick through it at ten o'clock in the morning! What chance has a fellow with a father like that? Ten to one, I go over to drink myself one of these days. Well, I might do worse. It drowns care, they say, and I know it destroys feelings, which, from my experience, seem only given for our torture.'

Gladys gave a sob, and turned aside to the safe. That sound recalled Walter to himself, and in a moment his mood changed. His eyes melted into tenderness as he looked upon the pale, slight girl, whom his words in some sad way had wounded.

'Forgive me. I don't know what I am saying; but I had no right to vex you, the only angel I know in this whole city of Glasgow.'

His extravagant speech provoked a smile on her face, and she turned her head from where she knelt before the safe, and lifted her large earnest eyes to his.

'How you talk! You must learn to control yourself a little more. It is self-control that makes a man,' she said quietly. 'I do not know how to comfort you, Walter, in this trouble, which seems so much heavier than even I think; but in the end it will be for good. Everything is, you know, to them that love God.'

She was so familiar with Scripture, and depended so entirely on it for comfort and strength, that her words carried conviction with them. They fell on the riven heart of Walter like balm, and restored a measure of peace to it. Before he could make any answer, a quick knocking, and the uplifting of the feeble voice from below, indicated that the old man was impatient of the girl's delay. She hastily lifted the pocket-book, relocked the safe door, and, with a nod to Walter, ran down-stairs.

'What kept you so long chattering up-stairs?' queried the old man, with all the peevishness of a sick person. 'You don't care a penny-piece, either of you, though I died this very moment.'

'Oh, Uncle Abel, hold your tongue; you know that is not true,' she said quickly. 'Walter is in great trouble this morning. Something has happened to his sister.'

'Ay, what is it, eh?'

'I don't know exactly, but she has left home.'

'Ay, ay, I'm not surprised; she was a bold hussy, and had no respect for anything in this world. And is Walter taking on badly?'

'Very badly. I never saw him so distressed.'

'Well, it's hard on a chap trying to do well. It's a hopeless case trying to fly out of an ill nest.'

'Uncle Abel, you must not say that. Nothing is hopeless, if only we are on the right side,' said Gladys stoutly, though inwardly her heart re-echoed sadly that dark creed.

'Well, well, you're young, and nothing seems impossible,' he said good-naturedly. 'Here, take off this string. My fingers are as feckless as a thread.'

Gladys opened the pocket-book, which was stuffed full of old papers. The old man fingered them lovingly and with careful touch, until he found the one he sought. It was a somewhat long document, written on blue, official-looking paper, and attested by several seals. He read it from beginning to end with close attention, and gave a grunt of satisfaction when he laid it down.

'Is Wat busy?' he asked then.

'He has not much heart for his work today, uncle,'

'Cry him down; I've a message for him. Or, stop, you'd better go yourself, in case anybody comes to the warehouse. Do you know St. Vincent Street?'

'Yes, uncle.'

'You don't know Fordyce & Fordyce, the lawyers' office, do you?'

'No, but I can find it.'

'Very well; go just now and ask for old Mr. Fordyce. If he isn't in, just come back.'

'And what am I to say to him?'

'Tell him to come here just as soon as ever he can. I want to see him, and there is not any time to lose.'

The girl's lip quivered. A strange feeling of approaching desolation was with her, and her outlook was of the dreariest. If it were true, as the old man evidently believed, that his hour had come, she would again be friendless and solitary on the face of the earth. Abel Graham saw these signs of grief, and a curious softness visited his heart, though he could scarce believe one so fair and sweet could really care for him.

Gladys made the utmost haste to do her errand, and to her great satisfaction was told when she reached the large and well-appointed chambers of that influential firm, that Mr. Fordyce senior would attend to her in a moment. She stood in the outer office waiting, unconscious that she was the subject of remark and speculation among the clerks at their desks, still more unconscious that one day her name would be as familiar and respected among them as that of the governor himself. After the lapse of a few minutes the office boy ushered her into the private room of Mr. Fordyce senior. He was a fine, benevolent-looking, elderly gentleman, with a rosy, happy face, silver hair and whiskers, and a keen but kindly blue eye. He appeared to be a very grand gentleman indeed in the eyes of Gladys.

'Well, my dear miss, what can I do for you, eh?' he asked, beaming at her over the gold rims of his double eyeglass in a very reassuring way.

'Please, my uncle has sent me to ask you to come and see him at once, as he is very ill.'

'And who is your uncle, my dear? It will be necessary for you to tell me that,' he said, with the slightest suggestion of a twinkle in his eye.

'My uncle, Mr. Graham, who lives in Colquhoun Street.'

'Abel Graham? Oh yes. Is he ill? And, bless me, are *you* his niece?'

Never was surprise so genuinely felt or expressed as at that moment by Mr. Fordyce.

'Yes, I am his niece; and, please, could you come as soon as possible? He is very ill. I am afraid he thinks he is dying.'

The girl's voice trembled, and a tear fell like a dew-drop from her long eyelashes. These things still more amazed the soul of Mr. Fordyce. That anybody should shed a tear for a being so sordid and unsociable as Abel Graham struck him as one of the extraordinary things he had met with in his career; and to see this fair young creature, fitted by nature for a sphere and for companionship so different, sincerely grieving for the old man's distress, seemed the most extraordinary thing of all. Mr. Fordyce rose, and, calling the boy, bade him bring a cab to the door, then he began to get into his greatcoat.

'I'll drive you back, if you have nowhere else to go. So *you* are his niece? Well, there's more sense and shrewdness in the old man than I gave him credit for.'

These remarks were, of course, quite enigmatical to Gladys; but she felt cheered and comforted by the strong, kindly presence of the genial old lawyer. As for him, he regarded her with a mixture of lively interest, real compassion, and profound surprise. Perhaps the latter predominated. He had, in the course of a long professional career, encountered many strange experiences, become familiar with many curious and tragic life stories, but, he told himself, he had never met a more interesting case than this.

'It's a romance,' he said loud out in the cab; and Gladys looked at him in mild surprise, but though she did not stand in awe of him at all, she did not presume to ask what he meant.

'Now tell me, my dear, have you been happy in this — this place?' he inquired significantly, as the cab rumbled over the rough causeway of the Wynd into Colquhoun Street.

'Yes, I have been happy. I only know now, when I think it may not be my shelter very long.'

Mr. Fordyce looked at her keenly.

'Poor girl, she knows nothing, absolutely nothing,' he said to himself. 'What a revelation it will be to her! Yes, it's a thrilling romance.'

The greeting between the well-known lawyer and his strange client was not ceremonious. It consisted of a couple of nods and a brief good-morning. Then Gladys was requested to leave them alone. Nothing loath, she ran up-stairs to Walter, whose sorrow lay heavy on her heart.

'Your niece has surprised me, Mr. Graham,' said the lawyer.

'Yes, very much indeed.'

'Why? What did you expect to see? Eh?'

'Not a refined and lovely young woman in a place like this, certainly,' he said frankly, and looking round with an expression of extreme disgust. 'Has it never occurred to you what poor preparation Miss Graham has had for the position you intend her to fill?'

'That's none of your business,' retorted the old man sharply. '*She* doesn't need any preparation, I tell you. Cottage or palace are the same to her; she'll be a queen in either.'

This strange speech made the lawyer look at the old man intently. He perceived that underneath his brusque, forbidding exterior there burned the steady light of a great love for his brother's child, and here, surely, was the greatest marvel of all.

'I did not bring you here to make remarks on my niece,' he said peevishly. 'Read that over, see, and tell me if it's all right, if there's anything to be added or taken away. There's a clause I want added about the boy, Walter Hepburn. He's been with me a long time, and though he's a very firebrand, he's faithful and honest.

He won't rue it.'

Mr. Fordyce adjusted his eyeglass and spread out the will before him. Up-stairs the two young beings, drawn close together by a common sorrow and a common need, tried to look into the future with hopeful eyes, not knowing that, in the room below, that very future was being assured for them in a way they knew not.

CHAPTER XIII.

THE LAST SUMMONS.

'You'll look after her, Mr. Fordyce, promise me that?' said the old man when they had gone over the contents of the will.

'Why, yes, I will, so far as I can,' answered the lawyer, without hesitation. 'She will not lack friends, you may rest assured. This,' he added, tapping the blue paper, 'will ensure her more friends than she may need.'

'Ay, it's from such I want you to guard her. I know how many sharks there are who would regard an unprotected girl like her as their lawful prey. She'll marry some day, I hope, and wisely. But it is in the interval she needs looking after.'

'How old is she?'

'Seventeen and a half, I think.'

'She looks her age — a remarkably calm and self-possessed young lady, I thought her today. And she has no idea of this, you say?'

'Positively none,' answered the old man, with something like a chuckle. 'Why, this very morning we spoke of what she would do when I'm away, but it doesn't seem to be worrying her much. I never saw a person, old or young, with greater powers of adapting themselves to any circumstances, — *any* circumstances, mind you, — so you needn't be exercised about her future deportment. She'll astonish you, I promise you that.'

'You really believe, then, that you won't get better?'

'I know I won't; a man knows these things in spite of himself,' was the calm reply.

The lawyer looked at him keenly, almost wonderingly. He did not know him intimately. Only within recent years had he been engaged to manage his monetary affairs, and only six months before had drawn up the will, which, it may be said, had considerably surprised him. Looking at him just then, he wondered whether there might not be depths undreamed of under the crust of the miser's soul.

'You are behaving very generously to this young-fellow Hepburn,' he said then, leaving his deeper thoughts unspoken. 'He may consider himself very fortunate. Such a windfall comes to few in a position like his.'

'Ay, ay. I daresay it depends on how you look at it,' responded the old man indifferently. 'Well, I'm tired, and there's no more to talk about. Everything is right and tight, is it? No possibility of a muddle at the end?'

'None,' answered Mr. Fordyce promptly, as he rose to his feet.

'Well, good-day to you. I have your promise to see that the girl doesn't fall into the hands of Philistines. I don't offer you any reward. You'll pay yourself for your lawful work, I know; and for the rest, well, I inquired well what I was doing, and though I'm not a Christian myself, I was not above putting myself into the hands of a Christian lawyer.'

A curious dry smile accompanied these words, but they were spoken with the utmost sincerity. They conveyed one of the highest tributes to his worth Tom Fordyce had ever received. He carefully gathered together the loose papers, and for a moment nothing was said. Then he bent his keen and kindly eye full on the old man's wan and withered face.

'Sir,' he said, 'if you are not a Christian, as you say, what is your hope for the next world?'

'I have none,' he answered calmly. 'I am no coward. If it be true, as they say, that a system of award and punishment prevails, then I'm ready to take my deserts.'

The lawyer could not reply to these sad words, because Gladys at the moment entered the kitchen.

'I have come,' she said brightly,'because I fear you are talking too much, uncle. Oh, are you going away, Mr. Fordyce? I am glad the business is all done. See, he is quite exhausted.'

She poured some stimulant into a glass and carried it to him, holding it to his lips with her own hand. The old man looked over her bent head significantly. The lawyer's eyes met his, and he gravely nodded, understanding that that mute sign asked a further promise.

Gladys accompanied him to the door, and the lawyer laid his hand on her shoulder with a fatherly touch.

'My dear, I am very sorry for you.'

'Do you, then, think him so very ill?' she asked breathlessly. 'He says he will die; but I have nursed my own father through much worse attacks.'

'He appears to have given up hope; but while life lasts we need not despair,' he said kindly. 'Good-bye. I shall come back perhaps tomorrow.'

He thought much of her all day, and when he returned to his happy home at night, told the story to his wife, and there is no doubt that the strong sympathy of these two kind hearts supported Gladys through the ordeal of that trying time.

In the evening Walter took himself off to Bridgeton, reluctant to go, yet anxious to hear further particulars regarding the flight of Liz. He arrived at the dreary house, to find his mother engaged with the weekly wash. Now, there was no reason why the washing should be done at night, seeing she had the whole day at her disposal; but it seemed to take these hours to rouse her up to sufficient energy. She was one of those unhappy creatures who have no method, no idea of planning, so that the greatest possible amount of work can be done in the shortest, and at the most fitting time. This habit of choosing unfavourable and unseasonable hours for work, which upsets the whole house, had, no doubt, in the first instance, helped to drive her husband outside for his company. She looked round from the tub, and gave her son a nod by way of greeting, but did not open her mouth. Her little kitchen was full of steam, the floor swimming in soapsuds, the whole appearance of the place suggestive of confusion and discomfort. Walter picked his way across the floor, and sat down on the window-box, his favourite seat.

'Always washing at night yet, mother?' he said discontentedly. 'Have you no time through the day?'

'No; it's meat-makin' frae mornin' till nicht. This is the only time there's a meenit's peace,' she answered stolidly.

'You'll have one less to cook for now, then,' he said gloomily. 'When did Liz go off? and have you any idea where she's gone?'

Mrs. Hepburn shook her head.

'I was oot a' Tuesday nicht, an' when I cam' in, on the back o' eleeven, she was aff, bag an' baggage. Mrs. Turnbull says she gaed doon the stair wi' her Sunday claes on, an' carryin' her tin box, a wee efter aicht. "Are ye for jauntin', Liz?" says she; but Liz never gi'ed her an answer, guid or bad, an' that's a' I ken.'

'Did she never give a hint that she was thinking of going?' Walter asked.

'No' her. Liz was aye close, as close as yersel',' said his mother rather sarcastically. 'She's aff, onyhoo.'

'Do you think she has gone away with any one — a man, I mean?' asked Walter then, and his face flushed as he asked the question.

'I couldna say, I'm sure,' answered his mother, with a stolid indifference which astonished even him. 'Ye ken as muckle as me; but as she's made her bed she maun lie on't. I've washed my hands o' her.'

'It's long since you washed your hands of us both, mother, so far as interest or guidance goes,' the lad could not refrain from saying, with bitterness. But the reproach did not strike home.

'If it's news ye want, I'll tell ye where ye'll get it,' she said sourly. 'At Teen's. Eh, she's an ill hizzie. If Liz comes to grief, it's her wyte. I canna bide thon smooth-faced, pookit cat. She'll no' show her face here in a hurry.'

'I've a good mind to look in at Teen's, and ask. Where's the old man tonight?'

'Oh, guid kens whaur he aye is. He's on hauftime the noo, an' never sober. Eh, it's an ill world.'

She drew her hands from the suds, wiped them on her wet apron, and, lifting a pint bottle from the chimneypiece, took a long draught.

'A body needs something to keep them up when they've to wash i' the nicht-time,' was her only apology; but almost immediately she became much more talkative, and began to regale Walter with sundry minute and highly-spiced anecdotes about the neighbours' failings, which altogether wearied and disgusted him.

'I'll away, then, mother, and see if Teen knows anything. Liz will maybe write her.'

'Maybe. She's fit enough,' replied Mrs. Hepburn stolidly; and Walter, more heavy-hearted than ever, bade her good-night and departed. Never had he felt more fearfully alone — alone even in his anxiety for Liz. He had, at least, expected his mother to show some concern, but she did not appear to think it of the slightest consequence. In about ten minutes he was rapping at the door of the attic where his sister's friend Teen supported existence.

'Oh, it's you! Come in,' she said, when she recognised him by holding the candle high above his head, and looking profoundly surprised to see him. 'What is't?'

'I thought you'd know. I came to ask if you could tell me what has become of Liz.'

'Liz!' she repeated so blankly that he immediately perceived she was in complete ignorance of the affair. 'What d'ye mean? Come in.'

Walter stepped across the threshold, and Teen closed the door. The small apartment into which he was ushered was very meagre and bare, but it was clean and tidy, and more comfortable in every way than the one he had just left. A dull fire smouldered at the very bottom of the grate, and the inevitable teapot sat upon the hob. The little seamstress was evidently very busy, piles of her coarse, unlovely work lying on the floor.

'Has onything happened to Liz?' she asked, in open-eyed wonder and interest.

'Yes; I suppose it has. She's run off, bag and baggage, on Tuesday, my mother says, and this is Thursday.'

'Oh my!'

Teen took a large and expressive mouthful of these two monosyllables. Walter looked at her keenly.

'Don't you know where she has gone? Did she tell you anything?'

'No' her. Liz was aye close aboot hersel', but maybe I can guess.'

'Tell me, then. Is anybody with her?'

'She's no' hersel', you bet,' Teen answered shrewdly. 'My, she's ta'en the better o's a'; but maybe I'm wrang. She's been sick o' Brigton for lang and lang, an' whiles she said she wad gang awa' to London an' seek her fortune.'

Walter sprang up, an immense load lifted from his mind. If that were all, he had needlessly tormented himself.

'Did she say that? Then it's all right. Of course that's where she's gone. Don't you think so?'

'Maybe. It's likely; only I think she micht hae telt me. We made up to gang thegither when we had saved the screw. She had a beau, but I raither think it's no' wi' him she's awa'; Liz could watch hersel'. But I'll fin' oot.'

'Did you know him? Who was he?' asked Walter.

'Oh, fine I kent him, but I'm no' at liberty to tell. It wadna dae ony guid till we see, onyhoo.'

'If you find out anything, will you let me know?'

'Yes, I'll dae that. Hoo are ye gettin' on yersel'? An' thon queer deil o' a lassie? I canna mak' onything o' her.'

'I'm getting on fine, thank you,' Walter answered rather shortly. 'Good-night to you, and thank you. Maybe Liz will write to you.'

'Very likely. I'll let ye ken, onyway. If she writes to onybody it'll be to me,' Teen answered, with a kind of quiet pride. 'She telt me a'thing she didna keep to hersel'. But I dinna think mysel' there's a beau in this business. The theatre wad be mair like it; she had aye a desire to be an actress.'

'Indeed!' said Walter, in surprise. He had never before heard such a thing hinted at, but no doubt it was true. He really knew very little about his sister, although they had always been the best of friends.

His heart was not quite so heavy as he retraced his steps to Colquhoun Street. If Liz, tired of the grey monotony and degradation of home, had only gone forth into the world to seek something better for herself, all might yet be well. He took comfort in dwelling upon her strength and decision of character, and came to the conclusion that he had judged her too hastily, and that she was a most unlikely person to throw away her reputation. What an immense relief that thought gave him was known only to himself and God.

Ten was pealing from the city bells when he reached home. When he entered the kitchen, a strange scene met his view. His master was propped up by pillows, and evidently suffering painfully from his breathing, and over his pinched features had crept that grey shadow which even the unpractised eye can discern and comprehend. The young doctor stood sympathetically by, conscious that he had given his last aid and must stand aside. Gladys knelt by the bed with folded hands, her golden head bowed in deep and bitter silence. She saw her last friend drifting towards the mystic sea, and felt as if the blackness of midnight surrounded her.

'Surely, doctor, this is a sudden and awful change?' Walter said to the doctor; but he put up his hand.

'Hush!' he said, pointing to the dying man, who essayed through his struggling breath to speak.

'Pray,' he said at last; and they looked from one to the other dumbly for a moment. Then the girl's sweet voice broke the dreary silence, and she prayed as one who has been long familiar with such words, and who, while praying, believes the answer will be given. The words of that prayer were never forgotten by the two young men who heard them; they seemed to bring heaven very near to that humble spot of earth.

'For Christ's sake.'

Abel Graham repeated these words after her in a painful whisper, and his struggling ceased.

'It is all over,' said the doctor reverently. And it was. Ay, all over, so far as this world was concerned, with Abel Graham.

CHAPTER XIV.

THOSE LEFT BEHIND.

That was a sad night for Gladys Graham and for Walter. Feeling that she required the help and presence of a woman, Walter ran up for the kind-hearted Mrs. Macintyre, whom Gladys had occasionally seen and spoken with since she took up her abode in Colquhoun Street. It is among the very poor we find the rarest instances of disinterested and sympathetic kindness — deeds of true neighbourliness, performed without thought or expectation of reward. Mrs. Macintyre required no second bidding. In five minutes she was with the stricken girl, ready, in her rough way, to do all that was necessary, and to take the burden off the young shoulders so early inured to care. When their work was done, and Abel Graham lay placidly upon the pure linen of his last bed, Mrs. Macintyre suggested that Gladys should go home with her for the night.

'It's no' for ye bidin' here yersel', my doo,' she said, with homely but sincere sympathy. 'My place is sma', but it's clean, an' ye're welcome to it.'

Gladys shook her head.

'I don't mind staying here, I assure you. I have seen death before. It is not dreadful to me,' she said, glancing at the calm, reposeful face of her uncle, and being most tenderly struck by the resemblance to her own father. Death is always kind, and will give us, when we least expect it, some sudden compensation for what he takes from us. That faint resemblance composed Gladys, and gave her yet more loving thoughts of the old man. He had been kind when, in his own rugged way, the first harshness of his bearing towards her had swiftly been mellowed by her own sweet, subtle influence. We must not too harshly blame Abel Graham; his environment had been of a kind to foster the least beautiful attributes of his nature.

The only being Gladys could think of to help her with the other arrangements was Mr. Fordyce. She seemed to turn naturally to him in her time of need. A message sent to St. Vincent Street in the morning brought him speedily, and he greeted her with a mixture of fatherly compassion and sympathy which broke her down.

'You see it has not been long,' she said, with a quiver of the lips. 'I do not know what to do, or how to act. I thought you would know everything.'

'I know what is necessary here, at least, my dear, and it shall be done,' he said kindly. 'The first thing I would suggest is that you should come home with me just now.'

Gladys looked at him wonderingly, and shook her head.

'You are very kind, but that is quite impossible,' she said quickly. 'I shall not leave here until all is over, and then I do not know what I shall do. God will show me.'

The lawyer was deeply moved.

'My dear young lady, has it never occurred to you that there might be something left for you, a substantial provision, which will place you at once above the need of considering what you are to do, so far as providing for yourself is concerned?'

'I have not thought about it. Is it so?' she asked quickly, yet not with the eager elation of the expectant heir.

'You are very well left indeed,' he answered. 'If you like, I can explain it to you now.'

But Gladys shrank a little as she glanced towards the bed.

'Not now. Let it be after it is all over. It does not matter now. I know it will be all right.'

'Just as you will; but I cannot bear to go and leave you here, Miss Graham. Will you not think better of it? My wife and daughters will be glad to see you, and they will be very kind and sympathetic, I can assure you of that. Let me take you away.'

But Gladys, though grateful, still shook her head.

'I promised your uncle to take care of you,' he urged. 'If I go and leave you in such sad circumstances here, so alone, I should feel that I am not redeeming my promise.'

'I thank you, and I shall come, perhaps, after, if you are so kind as to wish me to come, but not now. And I am not quite alone here. I have Walter.'

Mr. Fordyce did not know what to say. It was impossible for him to suggest that Walter's very presence in the house was one reason why she should quit it. She knew nothing of conventionalities or proprieties, and this was not the time to suggest them to her mind. He could only leave the whole matter at rest.

'Can I see this Walter?' he asked then. 'I have papers in my hand concerning him also. I may as well see him now.'

'He is up-stairs. Shall I call him down?'

'No. I shall go up,' answered the lawyer; and Gladys pointed him to the stairs leading up to the warehouse. Walter rose from his stool at the desk and stood at the door of the little office.

'Good-morning,' both said, and then they looked at each other quite steadily for a moment. Mr. Fordyce was astonished at the lad's youth, still more at his manly and independent bearing, and he told himself that this strange client had exhibited considerable shrewdness in the disposal of his worldly goods.

'This is a very sad affair,' said the lawyer, — 'sad and sudden. Mr. Graham was an old man, but he has always been so robust, he appeared to have the prospect of still longer life. It will make a great change here.'

'It will, sir.' Walter placed a chair for him, and a look of genuine relief was visible on his face. 'I am very glad you have come up. I was sitting here thinking over things. It is a very strange case.'

'You know something, I presume, of this business, whether it was a paying concern or not?' said the lawyer keenly.

'It is a large business done in a small way, sir, — a worrying, unsatisfactory kind of business, I know that much; but my master always kept his books himself, and I had no means of knowing whether it really paid or not. I know there were bad debts — a lot of them; but I am quite ignorant of the state of affairs. I have only one hope, sir, which I trust will not be disappointed' —

'Well?' inquired the lawyer steadily, when the young man stopped hesitatingly.

'That there will be something left for Miss Gladys. That has troubled me ever since the master took ill.'

'You may set your mind at rest, then. Miss Graham will be a rich woman.'

Walter looked incredulous at these words.

'A rich woman?' he repeated, — 'a rich woman? Oh, I am glad of it!'

His face flushed, his eye shone, with the intensity of his emotion. He was very young, but these signs betrayed an interest in the fate of Gladys Graham which stirred a vague pity in the lawyer's heart.

'Yes, a rich woman; and you are not forgotten. There is a will, which, however, Miss Graham desires shall not be read till after the funeral; but there is no harm in telling you a part of its contents which concerns you. Mr. Graham had the very highest opinion of your character and ability, and though he may not have seemed very appreciative in life, he has not forgotten to mark substantially his approval. You are left absolutely in control of this business, with the power to make of it what you will, and there is a legacy of five hundred pounds to enable you to carry it on.'

Walter became quite pale, and began to tremble, though he was not given to such exhibitions of nervousness.

'Oh, sir, there must be some mistake, surely,' he said quickly. 'It cannot be true.'

'It is quite true, and I congratulate you, and wish you every success. There are very few young men in similar circumstances who have such an opportunity given them. I hope you will be guided to use both means and opportunity for the best possible end. I shall be glad to be of any service to you at any time. Do not scruple to ask me. I mean what I say.'

'You are very kind.'

They were commonplace words, but spoken with an earnest sincerity which indicated a deeper feeling.

Mr. Fordyce looked round the large dingy warehouse with a slightly puzzled air.

'Who would think that there was so much money in this affair?' he said musingly. 'But I suppose it was carried on at very little expense. Well, the poor old man had little pleasure in life. It was a great mistake. He might have blessed himself and others with his means in his lifetime. It is strange that the young lady should appear to mourn so sincerely for him; it was an awful life for her here.'

'He was never unkind to her,' answered Walter; 'and latterly he could not do enough for her. She won him completely, and made a different man of him.'

'I quite believe it. One of the weak things of the world,' he said more to himself than to his listener. 'There's a different life opening up for her; it will be a great change to her. Well, good-morning. I wish you well, and you'll remember my desire to be a friend to you should you ever need me.'

'I won't forget,' replied Walter, with beaming eye. 'Miss Gladys said you would make all the arrangements for the funeral.'

'I will. They are easily made, because Mr. Graham left the most explicit directions. He desires to be buried by his own folk in the churchyard of Mauchline. I am going out this afternoon.'

Then the lawyer went away, but before proceeding to the station he wrote a note to his wife, and sent it by a messenger to his house at Kelvinside.

About four o'clock in the afternoon, as Gladys was putting a black ribbon in her hat, a cab rattled over the rough causeway, and a knock came to the house door; and when Gladys went to open it, what was her surprise to behold on the threshold a lady, richly dressed, but wearing on her sweet, motherly face a look so truly kind that the girl's heart warmed to her at once.

'I am Mrs. Fordyce,' the lady said. 'You, I think, are Miss Graham? May I come in?'

'Certainly, madam.'

Gladys held open the door wide, and Mrs. Fordyce entered the dark and gloomy passage.

'We have a very small, poor place,' said Gladys, as she led the way. 'I ought to tell you that I have no room to show you into, except where my poor uncle lies.'

'My dear, I quite know. Mr. Fordyce has told me. It is you I have come to see.'

When they entered the kitchen, she laid her two kind hands on the girl's shoulders, and turned her face to the light. Then, with a sudden impulse, she bent down and kissed her brow. Gladys burst into tears. It was the first kiss she had received since she came to Glasgow, and that simple caress, with its accompanying tenderness of look and manner, opened the floodgates of her pent heart, and taught her her own loneliness and need.

'I cannot leave you here, my dear child. My carriage is at the door. You must come home with me. I shall bring you back quite early tomorrow, but I must insist on taking you away tonight. It is not possible you can stay here.'

'I must, I will. You are truly kind, but I shall not leave my home till I must. I have my own little room, and I am not quite alone. Walter is up-stairs.'

Mrs. Fordyce saw that she was firm. She looked at her in wonder, noting with practised eyes the neat refinement of her poor dress, her sweet grace and delicate beauty. To find a creature so fair in such a place was like coming suddenly on a pure flower blooming in a stony street.

'Your position is very lonely, but you will not find yourself without friends. We must respect your wish to remain here, though the thought will make me unhappy tonight,' said the kind woman. 'You will promise to come to us immediately all is over?'

'If you still wish it; only there is poor Walter. It will be so dreadful for me to leave him quite alone.'

Mrs. Fordyce could not restrain a smile. The child-heart still dwelt in Gladys, though she was almost a woman grown.

'Ah, my dear, you know nothing of the world. It is like reading a fairy story to look at you and hear you speak. I hope — I hope the world will not spoil you.'

'Why should it spoil me? I can never know it except from you,' she said simply.

Mrs. Fordyce looked round the large, dimly-lighted place with eyes in which a wonder of pity lay.

'My child, is it possible that you have lived here almost two years, as my husband tells me, with no companion but an old man and a working lad?'

'I have been quite happy,' Gladys replied, with a slight touch of dignity not lost upon the lawyer's wife.

'Perhaps because you knew nothing else. We will show you what life can hold for such as you,' she answered kindly; and there came a day when Gladys reminded her of these words in the bitterness of a wounded heart.

When her visitor left, Gladys ran up-stairs to Walter. They had so long depended on each other for solace and sympathy, that it seemed the most natural thing in the world for her to share this new experience with him.

'You heard the lady speaking, did you not, Walter?' she asked breathlessly. 'It was Mr. Fordyce's wife; she is so beautiful and so kind. Just think, she would have taken me away with her in her carriage.'

'And why didn't you go?' asked Walter in a dull, even voice, and without appearing in the least interested.

'Oh because I could not leave just now,' she said slowly, quite conscious of a change in his voice and look.

'But you will go, I suppose, after?'

'I suppose so. They seem to wish it very much.'

'And you want to go, of course. They are very grand West End swells. I know their house — a big mansion looking over the Kelvin,' he said, not bitterly, but in the same even, indifferent voice.

'I don't know anything about them. If that is true, it is still kinder of them to think of such a poor girl as I.'

To the astonishment of Gladys, Walter broke into a laugh, not a particularly pleasant one.

'Six months after this you'll maybe take a different view,' he said shortly.

'Why, Walter, what has come to you? You have so many moods now I never know quite how to talk to you.'

'That's true,' he answered brusquely. 'I'm a fool, and nobody knows it better than I.'

CHAPTER XV.

HER INHERITANCE.

In the cheerful sunshine, the following afternoon, a small funeral party left the house in Colquhoun Street, and drove to the railway station. It consisted of Mr. Fordyce the lawyer, the minister of the parish, Walter Hepburn, and Gladys. It was her own desire that she should go, and they did not think it necessary to dissuade her. She was a sincere mourner for the old man, and he had not so many that they should seek to prevent that one true heart paying its last tribute to his memory. So for the first time for many years the burying-ground of the Bourhill Grahams was opened, somewhat to the astonishment of Mauchline folks. The name was almost forgotten in the place; only one or two of the older inhabitants remembered the widow and her two boys, and these found memory dim. Nevertheless, a few gathered in the old churchyard, viewing with interest the short proceedings, and with very special interest the unusual spectacle of a young fair girl standing by the grave. They did not dream how soon her name was to become a household word, beloved from one end of Mauchline to the other.

The two elderly gentlemen were very kind and tender to her, and the clergyman regarded her with a curious interest, having had a brief outline of her story from Mr. Fordyce. But it was noticeable that she preferred Walter's company, that she spoke oftenest to him; and when the lawyer and the minister went into the inn to have some refreshment while waiting for the train, the two young people walked up the road to Mossgiel. Walter was very gloomy and downcast, and she, quick to notice it, asked the cause.

'You know it quite well,' he said abruptly. 'I suppose you are going away to these grand folks tonight, and there's an end of me.'

'An end of you, Walter! What do you mean?' she asked, with a puzzled air.

'Just what I say. When you turn your back on Colquhoun Street, it's bound to be for ever. You'll be West, I East. There's no comings and goings between the two.'

'I think you are very unkind to speak like that, and silly as well,' she said quickly.

'Maybe, but it's true all the same,' he answered, with a slight touch of bitterness.

'And you deserve to be punished for it,' she continued, with her quaint dignity; 'only I cannot quite make up my mind how to punish you, or, indeed, to do it at all today. Look, Walter,' she stopped him on the brow of the hill, with a light touch on his arm which thrilled him as it had never yet done, and sent the blood to his face.

'See, away over there, almost as far as you can see, on yon little hill where the trees are so green and lovely, is Bourhill, where the Grahams used to live. I told you how Uncle Abel said papa had such a desire to buy it. If I were a rich woman I think I should buy Bourhill.'

'So you will. I wish I could give it to you,' cried Walter quickly.

'Do you? You are very good. You have always been so good and kind to me, Walter,' she said dreamily. 'Yes, that is Bourhill; and just think, you can see the sea from it — the real sea, which I have never seen in my life.'

'You'll get everything and see everything you want soon,' he said in a quiet, dull voice; 'and then you'll forget all that went before.'

'We shall see.'

She was hurt by the abrupt coldness of his manner, and, having her own pride of spirit, did not seek to hide it.

'See, that is Mossgiel there, and we have no time to go up. I think Mr. Fordyce said we must turn here,' she said, changing the subject, womanlike, when it did not please her. 'But when it is summer you and I will come to Mauchline for a day together, and gather some daisies from the field where Burns wrote his poem to the daisy — that is,' she added, with a smile, 'if you are not disagreeable, which I must say, Walter, you are today — most disagreeable indeed.'

She turned and looked at him then for a moment with an earnest, somewhat critical look, and she saw a tall, slender youth, whose figure had not attained to its full breadth and stature, but whose face — grave, earnest, noble, even — spoke of the experience of life. These two years had done much for Walter Hepburn, and she became aware of it suddenly, and with secret amazement.

'Why do you look at me like that?' he asked almost angrily. 'Is there anything the matter with my clothes?'

'No, nothing, you cross boy. I was only thinking that you had grown to be a man without any warning, and I am not sure that I did not like you better as a boy.'

'That is more than likely,' he answered, not in the least gently; but Gladys only smiled. Her faith in him was so boundless and so perfect that she never misunderstood him. In her deep heart she guessed that the shadow of the coming parting lay heavy on his soul. It lay on hers likewise, but was brightened in some subtle fashion by a lovely hope which she did not understand nor seek to analyse, but which seemed to link the troubled past and the unknown future by a band of gold. Wherever she might go, or whatever might become of her, she could never lose Walter out of her life. It was the love of the child merging into the mysterious hope of the woman, but she did not understand it yet. Had he known even in part how she felt, it had saved him many a bitter hour; but as yet that solace was denied him. That hot, rebellious young heart must needs go through the very furnace of pain to bring forth its fulness of sweetness and strength.

As the two came side by side up the middle of the village street, the lawyer and the minister stood upon the steps at the inn door.

'Is it a case of love's young dream?' asked the latter significantly.

Mr. Fordyce laughed as he shook his head.

'Scarcely. They've been companions — in misfortune, I had almost said — for a long time, and it is natural that they should feel kindly towards each other. Miss Bourhill Graham must needs aim a little higher. I like the young fellow, however. There's an honesty of purpose and a fearless individuality about him which refreshes one. Odd, isn't it, to find two such gems in such a place?'

'Rather; but I don't agree with all you say,' replied the minister, 'and I'll watch with interest the development of Miss Graham's history. If that determined-looking youth doesn't have a hand in it, I've made a huge mistake, that's all.'

Mr. Fordyce had made his plans for the day, and arranged with his wife to bring the carriage to Colquhoun Street at five o'clock. Gladys had been made acquainted with this arrangement, and acquiesced in it. It was about four o'clock when they returned to the empty house, which looked more cheerless than usual after the beauty and freshness of the country.

'Now, my dear,' said the lawyer, 'we must have a little talk before Mrs. Fordyce comes. I have a great deal to say to you. You remember you would not allow me to speak to you about business affairs until all was over?'

'Yes,' answered Gladys, and seated herself obediently, but without betraying the slightest interest or anticipation.

'I shall be as brief and simple as possible,' he continued. 'I told you that you need have no anxiety about your future, that it was assured by your uncle's will. You were not aware, I suppose, that he died a rich man?'

'No; I have heard people call him rich, but I never believed it. He spoke and acted always as if he were very poor.'

'That is the policy of many who have earned money hardly, and are loath to spend it. Well, it is you who will reap the benefit of his economy. About six months ago your uncle called upon me at my office for the first time in connection with the purchase of a small residential estate in Ayrshire. He wished to buy it, and did so — at a bargain, for there were few offers for it. That estate was Bourhill, and it was for you it was bought. You are absolutely its owner today.'

'I — owner of Bourhill?' she repeated slowly, and as if she did not comprehend. 'I owner of Bourhill?'

'Yes, my dear young lady; I congratulate you, not only as mistress of Bourhill, but also as mistress of what, to you, must seem a large fortune. Your uncle has left you Bourhill and the sum of ten thousand pounds.'

She received this announcement in silence, but all the colour left her face.

'Oh,' she cried at length, in a voice sharp with pain, 'how wrong! how hard! To live here in such poverty, to be so hard on others, to act a lie. It was that, Mr. Fordyce. Oh, my poor uncle!'

Her distress was keen. It showed itself in her heaving breast, her saddened eye, her drooping lips. She could not realise her own great fortune; she could only think of what it had cost. The lawyer was deeply moved, and yet not surprised. It was natural that a nature so fine, so conscientious, and so true, should see at once the terrible injustice of it all.

'My dear, I must warn you not to dwell on the morbid side. We must admit that it was a great pity, a very great pity, that your poor uncle did not realise the responsibility of wealth, did not even take some comfort for himself from it. But I may tell you it was a great, an inexpressible joy to him to leave it in your hands. I daresay he felt assured, as I do, that, though so young, you would know how to use it wisely.'

It was the right chord to touch. The colour leaped back to her cheek, the light to her eyes, her whole manner changed.

'Oh, I will, I will! God will help me. I will do the work, his work. If only he had told me how he wished it done.'

'I have a letter for you, written by his own hand the day he died; but it is not here. I will bring it when I come from my office at night; and meanwhile, my dear, I would suggest that you should get ready to go. My wife will be here very shortly.'

Immediately thought was diverted into another channel, and a great wistfulness stole over her.

'And what,' she asked in a low voice, — 'what will become of Walter?'

'Has he not told you what his future is likely to be?'

'No, he has told me nothing.'

'Your uncle has left him this business to make of it what he likes, and five hundred pounds to help him to carry it on. It is a very good lift for a friendless young fellow — a waif of the streets.'

'He's not a waif of the streets,' cried Gladys hotly. 'He has a home, not so happy as it might be, perhaps, but it is a home. It is this dreadful drink, which ruins everything it touches, which has destroyed Walter's home. I am so glad for him. He will get on so quickly now, only he will be so dreadfully lonely. I must come and see him very, very often.'

'My dear, I do not wish you to turn your back on your old friend, but it might be better for you both, but more especially for him, if you let things take their course. Your life must be very different henceforth.'

'I do not understand you,' said Gladys quite calmly, 'Please to explain.'

Not an easy task for Mr. Fordyce, with these large, sorrowful, half indignant eyes fixed so questioningly on his face. But he did his best.

'I mean, my dear, that for you, as Miss Graham of Bourhill, a new life is opening up — a life in which it will be quite wise to forget the past. Your life here, I should think,' he added, with a significant glance round the place, 'has not held much in it worth remembering. It will pass from you like a dream in the midst of the many new interests which will encompass you now.'

It was the wisdom of the world, not harshly nor urgently conveyed, but it sounded cruelly in the girl's ears. She rose to her feet, and somewhat wearily shook her head.

'You do not know, you cannot understand,' she said faintly. 'I can never forget this place. I pray I may never wish to forget it. If you will excuse me, I shall get ready now, so as not to keep Mrs. Fordyce waiting when she comes.'

CHAPTER XVI.

FAREWELL.

The carriage was at the door, and they stood face to face, the young man and the maiden, in the little office up-stairs, to say farewell.

'I am quite ready, Walter,' Gladys said in a still, quiet voice. 'I am going away.'

'Are you? Well, good-bye.'

He held out his hand. His face was pale, but his mouth was set like iron, and these apparently indifferent words seemed to force themselves from between his teeth. Sign of emotion or sorrow he exhibited none, but the maiden, who understood and who loved him, — yes, who loved him, — was not in the least deceived.

'Have you nothing else to say than that, Walter? It is very little when I am going away,' she said wistfully.

'No,' he replied in the same steady, even tone, 'nothing. You had better not keep them waiting, these grand people, any longer. They are not used to it, and they don't like it.'

'Let them wait, and if they don't like it they can go away,' she answered, with unwonted sharpness. 'I want to say, Walter, that if I could have stayed here, I would. I would rather be here than any-where. It once seemed very dreadful to me, but now I love it. But though I am going away, I will come to see you very often, very often indeed.'

'Don't come,' he answered sharply. 'Don't come at all.'

A vague terror gathered in her eyes, and her mouth trembled.

'Now you are unkind, Walter, unkind and unreasonable. But men are often unreasonable, so I will forgive you. If I may not come here, will you promise to come to Bellairs Crescent and see me?'

Then Walter flung up his head and laughed, that laugh which always stabbed Gladys.

'To have the door slammed in my face by a footman or a smart servant? No, thank you.'

'Very well. Good-bye. If you cast me off, Walter, I can't help it. Good-bye, and God bless you. I hope I shall see you sometimes, and if not, I shall try to bear it, only it is very hard.'

She was a woman in keenness of feeling, a very child in guile-lessness. She could not hide her pain.

Then Walter, feeling it all so keenly, and hating himself with a mortal hatred for his savage candour, condescended to make an explanation.

'In a week,' he began, 'you will view everything in a different light. You are going away to be a great lady, and you'll soon find that you want nothing so badly in this world as to forget that you ever knew this place, or me. It will be far better to understand and make up my mind to it at the very beginning. Perhaps some day it will be different, but in the meantime I know I am right, and you'll soon be convinced of it too, and perhaps thank me for it.'

'If that is what you think of me, Walter, it will indeed be better as you say. Good-bye.'

She scarcely touched his hand or looked at him as she turned away. She was wounded to the heart; and the poor lad, putting a fearful curb upon himself, suffered her to leave him. He did not even go down to the door to see the carriage leave, and in a few minutes the rattle of wheels across the stony street fell upon his ears like a last farewell. Then, there being none to witness his weakness, he laid his head down upon the battered old desk, and wept as he had not wept since his childhood. He had a proud spirit, and circumstances had made him morbidly sensitive. He was very young to indulge in a man's hopes and aspirations; but age is not always determined by years. Already he had dreamed his dreams, had his visions of a glorious future, in which he should build up a home for himself. Yet not for himself alone — it could be no home unless light was given to it by her who had been the day-star of his boyhood. The very loneliness and bitterness of his experience had caused his heart, capable of a strong and passionate affection, to centre with greater tenacity upon the gentle being who had shown to him the lovelier side of nature and life, and had awakened in him strivings after all that was highest and best. But this morbid sensitiveness, which is the curse of every proud spirit, and turns even the sweets of life to ashes in the mouth, had him in bitter bondage. He lashed himself with it, reminding himself constantly of his origin and his environment, and magnifying these into insuperable barriers which would for ever stand blankly in his way. Although common-sense told him that there was no other course open to Gladys than to accept the kindness offered her by the lawyer and his wife, and though in his inmost better heart he did not doubt her, it pleased his harder mood to regard himself as being despised and trampled on; there was a certain luxury in the indulgence which afforded him a melancholy pain. By and by, however, better thoughts came, as they always will if we give them the chance they seek. Out of his fearful dejection arose a manlier, nobler spirit, which betrayed itself in his look and manner. He rose from the stool, walked twice across the narrow office floor out to the warehouse, and finally down-stairs. In a word, he took an inventory of the whole place, and it suddenly came home to him, with a new accession of hope and strength, that it was his — that he was absolutely monarch of all he surveyed, and could make or mar it as he willed. It was not a stupendous heritage, but to one nameless and unknown it was much. Nay, it was his opportunity — the tide in his affairs which might lead him on to fortune. Wandering the length and breadth of his kingdom — only a drysalter's warehouse, but still his kingdom — hope took to herself white wings again, and, fluttering over him, built for him many a castle in the air — castles high enough to reach the skies. Then and there Walter Hepburn took courage and began to face his life — laid his plans, which had for its reward a maiden's smile and a maiden's heart. And for these men have conquered the world before, and will again. Love still rules, and will, thanks be to God, till the world is done.

Meanwhile Gladys, all unconscious alike of his deep dejection and his happier mood, sat quite silently in the corner of the luxurious carriage, her eyes dim with tears. Her kind friend, noticing that she was moved, left her in peace. Her sympathy was true, and could be quiet, and that is much.

'Suppose you sit up and look out, my dear?' she said at last. 'We are crossing Kelvin Bridge. Have you been as far West before?'

Gladys sat up obediently, and looked from the carriage window upon the river tumbling between its banks.

'Is this Glasgow?' she asked, wondering to see the trees waving greenly in the gentle April breeze.

'Yes, my dear, of course; and we are almost home. I am sure you will be glad, you look so tired,' said Mrs. Fordyce kindly. 'Never mind; you shall have a cup of tea immediately, and then you shall lie down and sleep as long as you like.'

'Oh, I never sleep in the day-time, thank you,' said Gladys; and as the carriage swept along a handsome terrace and into Bellairs Crescent, where the gardens were green with all the beauty of earliest summer, her face visibly brightened.

'It is quite like the country,' she said. 'I cannot believe it is Glasgow.'

'Sometimes we feel it dingy enough, my love. We are talking of the Coast already, but perhaps we shall fall in love with the Crescent a second time through you. Eh, my dear?' she said, with a nod. 'Well, here we are.'

The carriage drew up before the steps of a handsome house, the door was opened, and a dainty maid ran down to take the wraps. Gladys looked at her curiously, and thought of Walter. Well, it was a great change. Gladys had an eye for the beautiful, and the arrangement of the hall, with its soft rugs, carved furniture, and green plants, with gleams of statuary here and there, rested and delighted her.

'We'll just go to the drawing-room at once. My girls will be out of all patience for tea,' said Mrs. Fordyce. 'Nay, my dear, don't shrink. I assure you they are happy, kind-hearted girls, just like yourself.'

Gladys long remembered her first introduction to the brighter side of life. She followed Mrs. Fordyce somewhat timidly into a large and handsome room, and saw at the farther end, near the fireplace, a dainty tea-table spread, and a young girl in a blue serge gown cutting a cake into a silver basket. Another knelt at the fire. Gladys was struck by the exceeding grace of her attitude, though she could not see her face.

'My dears,' said Mrs. Fordyce quickly, 'here we are. I hope tea is ready? We are quite ready for it.'

'It has been up an age, mamma; Mina and I were thinking to ring for some fresh tea. Is this Miss Graham?'

It was the one who had been kneeling by the fire who spoke, and she came forward frankly and with a pleasant smile, though her eyes keenly noted every detail of the stranger's appearance and attire.

'This is Clara, my elder daughter, my dear; and this is Mina. Is Leonard not home?'

'Yes, but he won't come up. Leonard is our brother,' Clara explained to Gladys, — 'rather a spoiled boy, and he is mortally afraid of new girls, as he calls them. But you will see him at dinner.'

In spite of a natural stateliness of look and manner, Clara had a kind way with her. She took off their guest's cloak, and drew a comfortable chair forward to the tea-table, while her sister made out the tea.

'Where's papa? Did he not come with you?' she asked her mother, leaving Gladys a moment to herself.

'No; he went off at St. Vincent Street. He has been away from business all day, you know.'

'Oh yes. This has been a sad day for you,' said Clara sympathetically, turning to Gladys. 'Mamma has told us how lonely you are, but we shall try to cheer you. Won't we, Mina?'

'Suppose you begin by giving her some tea?' said Mrs. Fordyce. 'Then she must have a little rest. She has very long cared for others, she must have a taste of being cared for now.'

Gladys could not speak a word. She felt at home. A vague, delicious sense of rest stole over her as she listened to these kind words, and felt the subtle, beautiful influences of the place about her. It was only a pleasant family room, which taste and wealth had appointed and adorned, but it seemed like a king's palace to the girl who had long walked in the darker places of the earth. Seeing her thus moved, mother and daughters talked to each other, discussing the pleasant gossip of the day, which always seems to gather round the table at five-o'clock tea.

'Now, Clara, you will take Miss Graham up-stairs. I think you must allow us to call you Gladys, my dear,' said Mrs. Fordyce. 'I am going to leave you in charge of Clara. When you know us better, you will find out that it takes Mina all her time to take charge of herself.'

Mina shook her finger at her mother, and a slight blush rose to her happy face.

'Too bad, mamma, to prejudice Miss Graham against me. The difference between my sister and me,' she added, turning to Gladys, 'is that Clara is always proper and conventional, and I am the reverse. You can never catch her unawares or in an untidy gown, she is always just as immaculate as you see her now; while I am — well, just as the spirit moves me.' She swept a little mocking courtesy to her sister, who only smiled and shook her head, then taking Gladys by the arm, led her from the drawing-room.

'You must not mind Mina. She often speaks without thinking, but she never wishes to hurt any one,' she said. 'We have both been so sorry for you since papa told us about you, and we hope you will feel happy and at home with us here.'

'Oh, I am sure I shall, you are all so kind,' cried Gladys impulsively. It was natural that she should exaggerate any little courtesy or kindness shown to her, she had known so little of it in her life.

'It is such a romance! To think you are an heiress, and that beautiful Bourhill is all your own,' continued Clara.

'Do you know it?' interrupted Gladys, with more interest than she had yet betrayed.

'Yes; I have been there. We have a house at Troon, and of course when we are there we drive a good deal. Papa pointed it out to us one day, and said it was sad to see it going to decay. We had no idea then that we should ever know you. This is your room; it is quite close to Mina's and mine. See, the river is just before the windows. I always think the Kelvin looks so pretty from here, because one cannot see its impurity.'

'It is beautiful — a great change for me,' said Gladys dreamily, as her eyes roamed round the spacious and elegant guest-chamber. 'How pleasant it must be always to live among so many beautiful things! I have loved them all my life, but I have seen so few since I came from the fen country with my uncle.'

'It was very strange that he, so rich, should keep you in that wretched place,' said Clara. 'How much better had he shared it all with you while he lived.'

'Yes; but I think he was happier as it was, and it pleased him at the end, I know, to think that he had given me Bourhill.'

'I am sure it did. Well, I shall go now, dear, and leave you to unpack. You will find the wardrobe and all the drawers empty. Mamma will be coming to you immediately, likely.'

With a nod and a smile, Clara took herself off to the drawing-room again.

'What do you think of Miss Graham of Bourhill?' asked Mina, with her mouth full of cake. 'Quite to the manner born. Don't you think so?'

'Quite. And isn't she lovely? Wait till mamma has taken her to Redfern, and then you and I may retire, my dear; we shall be eclipsed.'

'If so, let us be resigned. One thing I know, you don't believe in presentiments, of course, you matter-of-fact young person, but I feel that she is to be mixed up with us in some mysterious way, and that some day, perhaps, we may wish we had never seen Miss Graham of Bourhill.'

CHAPTER XVII.

THE WEST END.

Now Gladys had her opportunity of seeing the beautiful side of life. Her taste being naturally refined and fastidious, found a peculiar satisfaction in the beauty of her surroundings. It was a very real pleasure to her to tread upon soft carpets, breathe a pure air, only sweetened by the breath of flowers, and to rest her eyes with delicate combinations of colour and the treasures of art to be found in the lawyer's sumptuous house. Never had she more strikingly betrayed her special gift, of which Abel Graham had spoken on his death-bed, 'ability to adapt herself to any surroundings;' she seemed, indeed, as Mina Fordyce had said, 'to the manner born.'

She endeared herself at once by her gentleness of manner to every inmate of the house, and very speedily conquered the boy Leonard's aversion to 'new girls.' In less than a week they were chums, and she was a frequent visitor to his den in the attics, where he contrived all sorts of wonderful things, devoting more time to them than to his legitimate lessons, which his soul abhorred. But though she was invariably cheerful, ever ready to share and sympathise with all the varied interests of the house, there was a stillness of manner, a 'dreamy far-offness,' as Mina expressed it, which indicated that sometimes her thoughts were elsewhere.

The three girls were sitting round the drawing-room fire one wet, boisterous afternoon, chatting cosily, and waiting for tea to come up. Between Clara and Gladys there seemed to be a peculiar understanding, although Mr. Fordyce's elder daughter was not the favourite of the family. Her manner was too stiff, and she had a knack at times of saying rather sharp, disagreeable things. But not to Gladys Graham. In these few days they had become united in the bonds of a love which was to stand all tests. Clara was sitting on a low chair, Gladys kneeling by her side, with her arm on her knee. So sitting, they presented a contrast, each a fine foil to the other. The stately, dark beauty of Clara set off the fairer loveliness of the younger girl; neither suffered by the contrast. These days of peace and restful, luxurious living had robbed Gladys of her wearied listlessness, had given to her delicate cheek a bloom long absent from it. Her simple morning gown, made by a fashionable *modiste* who had delighted to study her fair model, seemed part of herself. She was a striking and lovely girl, of a higher type than the two beside her.

'Oh, girls,' cried Mina, with a yawn, and tossing back her brown unruly locks with an impatient gesture, 'isn't it slow? Can't you wake up? You haven't spoken a word for half an hour.'

'Do you never want to be quiet, Mina?' asked Gladys, with the gleam of an amused smile.

'No, never. I'm not one of your pensive maidens. One silent member in a family is enough, or it would stagnate. Clara sustains the dignity, I the life, of the house, my dear. Oh, I wish somebody would come in. I guess half a score of idle young women in the other houses of this Crescent are consumed with the same desire. But nobody ever *does* come in, by any chance, when you want them. When you don't, then they come in in shoals. I say, Clara, isn't it ages since we saw any of them from Pollokshields?'

'Yes; but you know we ought to have gone to ask for Aunt Margaret long ago.'

'I suppose so. We don't love our aunt, Gladys. It's the misfortune of many not to love their relations. Can you explain that mystery?'

'Perhaps they are not very lovable,' suggested Gladys.

'That's it exactly. Aunt Margaret is — Well, you'll see her some day, and then you'll admit that if she possesses lovable qualities she doesn't wear them every day. They are so rich, so odiously rich, that you never can forget it. She doesn't allow you to. And Julia is about as insufferable.'

'Really, Mina, you should not speak so strongly. You know papa and mamma wouldn't like it,' protested Clara mildly; but Mina only laughed.

'It is such a relief on a day like this to "go for" some one, as Len would say, and why not for one's relations? It's their chief use. And you know Julia Fordyce has more airs than a duchess. George is rather better, and he is so divinely handsome that you can't remember that he has a single fault.'

Was it the firelight, or did the colour heighten rapidly in Clara's cheek?

'Such nonsense you talk, Mina,' she said hastily.

'It isn't nonsense at all. Have we never exhibited the photograph of our Adonis, Gladys?'

'I don't think so,' answered Gladys, with a smile. 'Suppose you let me see it now?'

'Of course. That was an unpardonable oversight, which his lordship would never forgive. He is frightfully conceited, as most handsome men unfortunately are. It isn't their fault, poor fellows; it's the girls who spoil them. Here he is.'

She brought a silver frame from a cabinet, and, with an absurd assumption of devotion, dropped a kiss on it before she gave it to Gladys. Gladys sat up, and, holding the photograph up between the light, looked at it earnestly. It was the portrait of a man in hunting dress, standing by his horse, and certainly no fault could be found with his appearance. His figure was a model of manly grace, and his face remarkably handsome, so far as fine features can render handsome a human face; yet there was a something, it might be only a too-conscious idea of his own attractions, which betrayed itself in his expression, and in the eyes of Gladys detracted from its charm.

'It is a pretty picture,' she said innocently. 'The horse is a lovely creature.'

Then Mina threw herself back in her chair, and laughed till the tears ran down her cheeks — a proceeding which utterly perplexed Gladys.

'Oh, Clara, isn't that lovely? If I don't tell George Fordyce that the first time I see him! It'll do him all the good in the world. Only, Gladys, he will never forgive you.'

'Why? I have not said anything against him.'

'No, you have simply ignored him, and that is an unpardonable offence against my lord. You must let me tell him, Gladys. It is really my duty to tell him, and we should always do our duty by our relations, should we not?'

'I am sure I don't mind in the least if you do tell him,' replied Gladys serenely. 'Do you think I said anything very dreadful, Clara?'

'Not I. Never mind Mina, dear. You should be learning not to mind anything she says.'

'There's the bell. That's mother, I hope. We never miss mother more than at tea-time,' said Mina, jumping up. Love for her mother was the passion of her soul. It shone in her face, and betrayed itself in a hundred little attentions which touched Gladys inexpressibly. Clara was always more reserved, but though her feelings found slower expression they were not less deep and keen; and though Gladys felt at home and happy with every member of that singularly united household, it was to Clara, who was so seldom the favourite outside, that her heart went out in love.

'It is not mother. It's callers, I do believe,' cried Mina, giving her hair a tug before the mirror, and shaking out her skirts, while her face brightened with expectation.

'Mr. and Miss Fordyce.'

Clara rose and went hastily forward to receive her cousins, while the irrepressible Mina strove to hide her laughter, though her eyes danced in the most suspicious manner. It was with rather more than ordinary interest that Gladys regarded the new-comers. They were certainly a handsome pair, and so closely resembling each other that their relationship was at once apparent.

'To what do we owe this unexpected felicity?' inquired Mina banteringly. 'On such a day, too.'

'Yes, indeed; we quite expected to see you in the house we have just left,' said Julia a little stiffly.

'Where, where?'

'Evelyn Stuart's. Have you forgotten this is her first reception day?'

'So it is, and we forgot all about it. Clara, whatever shall we do? Was there a crowd?'

'Yes, an awful crowd.'

While answering Mina, Miss Julia inclined her head in recognition of Gladys, to whom Clara introduced her. The slightest possible surprise betrayed itself in the uplifting of her straight brows, as her keen, flashing eyes took in every detail of the girl's appearance. Needless to say, the new inmate of the lawyer's household had been freely discussed by the Pollokshields Fordyces, and it was in reality curiosity to see her which had brought them to Bellairs Crescent that afternoon.

'I should just say it was a crowd,' added George, giving his immaculate moustache a pull. 'I was sorry for Stuart, poor beggar. Really, though a fellow marries, he should not be subjected to an ordeal like you. I don't see anything to hinder a fellow's wife from receiving folks herself. It's an awful bore on a fellow, you know.'

He spoke languidly, and all the time from under his drooping lids surveyed the slender figure and fair face of Gladys. She was so different from the brilliant and showy young ladies he met in the society they moved in, that he was filled with a secret admiration.

'So the unfortunate young woman who marries you, George, may know what to expect. Do you hear that, girls? Be warned in time,' cried Mina. 'Won't you take off your cloak, Julia, and stay a little? Mother and tea will be here directly.'

'I daresay we have half an hour — have we, George? You are not going back to the mill, are you?'

'Not I; my nose has been pretty much at the grindstone for the last month. And now, girls, what's the best of your news? We're waiting to be entertained. How do you like the West End of Glasgow, Miss Graham?'

'Very much, thank you,' answered Gladys, and somehow she could not help speaking distantly. There was something about the young man she did not like. Had she looked at Clara just then she would have seen her eyes filled with a lovely, wavering light, while a half trembling consciousness was infused into her whole appearance. These signs to the observant are not difficult to read. Clara loved her handsome cousin, and unfortunately he was not blind to the fact.

'We are going to Troon first week in May, Julia,' she said quickly. 'Has Aunt Margaret thought or spoken of your going yet?'

'She has spoken of it, but we haven't encouraged it,' replied Julia languidly, as she drew off one of her perfectly-fitting gloves, and displayed a long firm white hand, sparkling with diamonds. 'I know she has written to the housekeeper to have Seaview aired, but I suppose it depends on the weather.'

'If you are all going down, it wouldn't be half bad, Julia. We must see what the mater says. Does Miss Graham go with you?'

'Of course,' replied Clara, with a smiling glance at Gladys.

She replied by an answering smile, so swift and lovely that George Fordyce looked at her with a sudden access of admiration. Gladys shrank just a little under the continued persistence of his gaze; and when he saw it, it added a new zest to his interest in her. He was accustomed to find his admiration or attention always acceptable to the young ladies of his acquaintance, and the demeanour of Gladys was at once new and interesting to him. He determined to cultivate her acquaintance, and to awaken that fair, statuesque maiden into life.

Just then tea came up, and, rising lazily, he began to make himself useful to his cousin Clara, murmuring some nonsense to her over the tea-table, which deepened the lovely light in her eyes. He enjoyed seeing the delicate colour deepening in her face, and excused himself for bringing it there on the ground of cousinship. But when he carried her cup to Gladys, he remained by her side, while Julia entertained the other two with a description of the bride's drawing-room and reception gown.

'It's an awful romance, Miss Graham, upon my word it is,' began George, standing with his back to the others, and looking down most impressively into the girl's face, — 'your story, I mean, of course. Uncle Tom has told us how you, the heiress of Bourhill, have lived in the slums — positively the slums, wasn't it?'

Now, though his words were not particularly well chosen or in good taste, his manner was so impressively sympathetic that Gladys felt insensibly influenced by it. And he *was* very handsome, and it was quite pleasant to have him standing there, looking as if there was nobody in the world half so interesting to him as herself. For the very first time in her life Gladys felt the subtle charm of flattery steal into her soul.

'I suppose you would call it the slums,' she answered. 'My uncle lived in Colquhoun Street.'

'Don't know it, but I guess it was bad enough, and for you,

too, who look fit for a palace. And did you live there all alone with the old miser?'

'Don't call him that, please; he was very kind to me, and I cannot bear to hear him hardly spoken of, she said quickly. 'There were three of us, and we were very happy, though the place was so small and poor.'

'Who was the third?'

He managed to convey into his tone just sufficient aggressiveness as to suggest that he resented the idea of a third person sharing anything with her.

'Walter Hepburn, my uncle's assistant.'

Had she looked at him then, she must have been struck by the strange expression, coupled with a sudden flash, which passed over his face.

'Ah yes, just so. Well, I'm glad the fates have been kind, and brought you at last where there's a chance of being appreciated,' he said carelessly. 'Nice little girls my cousins — awfully good-hearted little souls, though Mina's tongue is a trifle too sharp. Yes, miss, I'm warning Miss Graham against you,' he said when Mina uttered his name in a warning note.

'Now, to punish you, I shall tell you my latest anecdote,' Mina said; and, heedless of the half laughing, half eager protest of Gladys, she related the incident of the portrait, with a little embellishment which made him appear in rather a ridiculous light.

In the midst of the laughter which the relation provoked, Mrs. Fordyce entered the room.

CHAPTER XVIII.

'THE DAYS THAT ARE NOT.'

The last days of April came, the family in Bellairs Crescent were making preparations for an immediate departure to the Ayrshire coast, and as yet Gladys had not seen or heard anything of Walter. She had a longing to revisit the old home, and yet a curious reluctance held her back. She felt hurt, and even a trifle irritated against Walter; and though she understood, and in a measure sympathised with his feelings, she thought him needlessly morbid and sensitive regarding their new relation towards each other.

'Gladys,' said Clara one day, when she had watched in silence the girl's sweet face, and noticed its half sad, half wistful expression, 'what is the matter with you? You are fretting about something. Tell me what it is. Do you not wish to go to Troon with us, or would you rather go to Bourhill? Do tell us what you would like best to do?'

They were quite alone in the little morning-room, which had been given up to the girls of the house to adorn as they liked. It was a pretty corner, dainty, homelike, cosy, with a long window opening out to the garden, which was as beautiful as it is possible for a city garden to be.

Gladys gave a little start, and coloured slightly under Clara's earnest gaze.

'I am quite happy at the idea of going to Troon; remember I have never seen the sea,' she answered quickly. 'What makes you think I am unhappy?'

'My dear, you look it. You can't hide it from me, and you are going to tell me this very moment what is vexing you.'

Clara knelt down on the rug, and, with her hands folded, looked up in her friend's face. Gladys passed her hand lightly over the smooth braids of Clara's beautiful hair, and did not for a moment speak.

'Did you ever have a great faith in any one who after a time disappointed you?' she asked suddenly.

'No, I don't think so. I am not naturally trusting, Gladys. I have to be very sure before I put absolute faith in any one.'

'I cannot believe that of you, Clara. How kind you have been to me, an utter stranger! You have treated me like a sister since the first happy day I entered the house.'

'Oh, that is different. You know very well, you little fraud, that your very eyes disarm suspicion, as somebody says. You are making conquests everywhere. But now we are away from the point. *What* is vexing you? Shall I make a guess?'

'Oh, if you like,' answered Gladys, with interest.

'Well, you are thinking of past days. You have not forgotten the companions of the old life, and it is grieving you, because it would appear that they have forgotten you.'

'He might have come, only once,' cried Gladys rebelliously, not for a moment seeking to deny or admit in words the truth of Clara's words. 'We were a great deal to each other. It is hard to be forgotten so soon.'

'Gladys dear, listen to me.'

Clara's voice became quite grave, and she folded her hands impressively above her companion's.

'You must not be angry at what I am going to say, because it is true. Has it not occurred to you that this young man, in thus keeping a distance from you, shows himself wiser than you?'

'How?' asked Gladys coldly. 'It can never be wise to wound the feelings of another.'

'My dear, though your simplicity is the loveliest thing about you, it is awfully difficult to deal with,' said Clara perplexedly. 'You must know, must admit, Gladys, that everything is changed, and that while you might be quite courteous, and even friendly after a fashion, with this Mr. Hepburn, anything more is quite out of the question. He must move in his own sphere, you in yours. People are happier in their own sphere. To try and lift them out of it is always a mistake, and ends in disaster and defeat. Would you have liked mamma to invite him here?'

'He would not come,' said Gladys proudly. 'He would never come. He said so again and again.'

'Then it seems to me that it is you who are lacking in proper pride,' said Clara calmly.

'What is proper pride?'

Gladys smiled with the faintest touch of scorn as she asked the question.

'You know what it is just as well as I can tell you, only it pleases you to be perverse this morning,' said Clara good-humouredly, 'and I am not going to say any more.'

'Yes you are. I want to understand this thing. Is it imperative that the mere fact that my uncle has left me money and a house should make me a different person altogether?'

'It affects your position, not necessarily you. Don't be silly and aggravating, Gladys, or I must shake you,' said Clara, with the frank candour of a privileged friend. 'And really I cannot understand why you should be anxious to keep in touch with that old life, which was so awfully mean and miserable.'

'It had compensations,' said Gladys quickly. 'And I do think, that if it is all as you say, there is more sincerity among poor people than among rich. There is no court paid, anyhow, to money and position.'

'My dear, you are not at all complimentary to us,' laughed Clara. 'Your ingenuousness is truly refreshing.'

'I am not speaking about you, and you know it quite well,' answered Gladys. 'But if the world is as fond of outward things as you say, I do not wish to know anything of it. I could not feel at home in it, I am sure.'

'My dear little girl, wait till your place is put in order, and you take up your abode in it, Miss Graham of Bourhill, the envied and the admired of a whole county, and you will change your mind about the world. Just wait till the next Hunt Ball at Ayr, and we'll see what changes it will bring.'

There was no refuting Clara's good-natured worldly wisdom, and Gladys had to be silent. But she pondered many things in her heart.

'When do we go to Troon? Isn't it next week?'

'Yes, on Tuesday.'

'Do you think,' she asked then, with a slight hesitation, 'that Mrs. Fordyce would allow me to pay a little visit to my old home before I go, for the last time?'

There was all the simplicity and wistfulness of a child in her manner, and it touched Clara to the quick.

'Gladys, are you a prisoner here, dear? Don't vex me by saying things like that. Do you not know that you can go out and in just as you like? Of course you shall go. I will take you myself, if mamma cannot, and wait for you outside.'

True to her promise, Clara ordered the brougham on Monday afternoon, and carried Gladys off to Colquhoun Street. Clara was, like most quiet people, singularly observant, and she noted with interest, not unmixed with pity, how nervous Gladys became as they neared their destination. Mingling with her pity was a great curiosity to see the young man whose image seemed to dwell in the constant heart of Gladys. It was a romance, redeemed from vulgarity by the beauty and the sweet individuality of the chief actor in it.

'I shall not knock. Don't let James get down,' cried Gladys, when the carriage stopped at the familiar door. 'I shall just run in. I have a fancy to enter unannounced.'

Clara nodded, and Gladys, springing out, opened and closed the familiar door. Her very limbs shook as she went lightly along the dark passage and pushed open the kitchen door. It was un- changed, yet somehow sadly changed. A desolateness chilled her to the soul as she looked round the wide, gaunt place, saw the feeble fire choking in the grate, and the remains of a poor meal on the uncovered table. The light struggling through the barred windows had never looked upon a more cheerless picture. All things, they say, are judged by contrast. Perhaps it was the contrast to what she had just left which made Gladys think she had never seen her old home look more wretched and forlorn.

So lightly had she entered, and so lightly did she steal up the warehouse stair, that the solitary being making out accounts at the desk was not aware of her presence until she spoke. And then, oh how timid her look and tone, just as if she feared greatly her reception.

'Excuse me coming in, Walter. I wanted so much to see you, I could not help coming. I will not hinder you long.'

He leaped up in the greatness of his surprise, in his agitation knocking over the stool on which he had been sitting. His face was dusky red, his firm mouth trembling, as he touched for a moment the outstretched, daintily-gloved hand.

'Oh, it is you? Won't you sit down? It is a battered old chair, but if you wait a moment I'll bring you another,' he said awkwardly.

'No, don't. I have often sat on this box. I can sit on it again,' she said unsteadily. 'I won't sit on ten chairs, Walter, though you should bring them to me this moment.'

She sat down, and her movement sent a faint whiff of perfume about her, dainty as herself. And then there was just a moment's painful silence. The awkwardness of the moment dwelt with them both; it would be hard to say which felt it more.

'I suppose,' said Walter stiffly, 'you are getting on all right?'

'Yes. I thought you would have come to see me before this, Walter,' said Gladys quietly.

'You need not have thought so. I said I wouldn't come, that nothing would induce me to come,' he answered shortly.

'We are going away into Ayrshire, so I thought I must come to say good-bye,' Gladys said then.

'To your estate?'

'No; to Troon, where the sea is.'

'Oh, and will you stay long?'

'Perhaps all the summer. How are you getting on here all alone, Walter? You must tell me that.'

'Oh, well enough.'

'Does Mrs. Macintyre come to work for you?'

'Yes, morning and night she looks in. I'm going to make this thing pay.'

He looked as if he meant it. His square jaw was firmly set, his whole look that of a man determined to succeed.

'I hope you will, Walter. I feel sure of it,' she said brightly.

'It'll be awful drudgery for a while,' he continued, almost in the confidential tones of yore. 'To have so much money, your uncle had the poorest way of doing business. He had the customers all under his thumb, and made them fetch and carry what they wanted themselves; in that way he saved a man's wages. I'm not giving anything on credit, and after they've once freed themselves, and can pay cash for what they get, they'll want it delivered to them, and quite right. Then I'll get a man and a horse and cart, and when I once get that, the thing will grow like a mushroom.'

'How clever you are to think of all that!' said Gladys admiringly. 'I am quite sure you will succeed.'

'I mean to,' he said soberly, but with a quiet determination which convinced Gladys how much in earnest he was.

'But don't let success make you hard, Walter,' she said gently. 'Remember how we used to plan what we should do for the poor if we were rich.'

'Your opportunity is here, then,' he said sharply; 'mine is only to come.'

The tone, more than the words, wounded her afresh. Oh, this was not the Walter of old! She rose from the old box a trifle wearily, and looked round her with slightly saddened air.

'Have you heard anything of your sister?' she asked him.

'No, nothing.'

'She has never written to any one?'

'No. I think she has gone to London to join a theatre. The girl who was her chum thinks so too.'

'Are your father and mother well?'

'As well as they deserve to be. They wanted to come here and live. Had they been decent and respectable, it wouldn't have been a bad arrangement. As they are, I simply wouldn't have it; I'd *never* get on. Of course they cast my pride in my teeth, but God knows I have little enough to be proud of.'

His mood cast its dark spell over the girl's sensitive heart, and she turned to go.

'It is all so different,' she said in a low voice, 'but the difference is not in me. Shall we never meet now, Walter?'

'It will be better not. If I ever succeed, and I have sworn to do it, we may then meet on more equal ground,' he said steadily, and not a sign of the unutterable longing in his heart betrayed itself in his set face. His pride was as cruel as the grave.

'Till then it is good-bye, then, I suppose?' she said quietly.

'Yes, till then; the day will come, or I shall know the reason why.'

'But it may be too late then, Walter, for us both.'

With these words, destined to ring their warning changes in his ears for many days, she left him, without touch of the hand or other farewell.

'Well, dear,' said Clara, with a slightly quizzical smile, 'has it made you happier to revive the ghosts of the past?'

'No; you were right, and I wrong,' said Gladys, as she sank into the cushioned seat. 'It was a great mistake.'

But even Clara did not know how dark was the shadow which had settled down on the girl's gentle soul.

CHAPTER XIX.

THE SWEETS OF LIFE.

From that day a change was observed in Gladys Graham. It was as if she had suddenly awakened from a dream, to find herself surrounded by the realities of life. Her listlessness vanished, her pensive moods became things of the past. None could be more interested in every plan and project, however small, in which the Fordyce household were concerned. She became lively, merry, energetic; it seemed impossible for her to be still.

'Now, what do you suppose is the matter with Gladys, Clara?' said Mina, the morning of the day they were to leave town. 'You who pretend to be a philosopher and a reader of character ought to be able to solve that mystery.'

'What do you see the matter with her?' inquired Clara, answering the question by another, as was her way when she did not want to commit herself to an expression of opinion.

'Why, she is a different girl. Don't tell me you haven't noticed it. She carries that Len to outrageous lengths, and if you don't call her behaviour at Aunt Margaret's last night the most prominent flirtation, I don't know what it is.'

'Just put it to Gladys, Mina. If she ever heard the word flirtation, I am positive she doesn't know what it means.'

'Oh, fiddle-de-dee! — every woman, unless she is a fool, knows intuitively what flirtation means, and can put it in practice. But it struck me last night that Aunt Margaret rather encouraged George to pay attention to Gladys. Of course it was quite marked.'

'Why should she encourage it?' asked Clara, with a slight inflection of huskiness in her voice.

'Clara, really you are too obtuse, or pretend to be. Of course it would be a fine thing for them. She belongs to an old Ayrshire family, and poor Aunt Margaret adores lineage. If she could with any effrontery assume it herself, she would; but, alas! everybody knows where the Fordyces came from. They'll angle for our dear little ward this summer, and bait the hook with gold.'

'Really, you are vulgar, Mina,' said Clara a trifle coldly, and, bending over an open trunk, busied herself with some of the trifles in the tray. 'We are sure to forget a thousand things. Do you think everything is here which ought to go?' she said, deliberately changing the subject.

'Oh, I don't know. We shall be glad of any excuse to come up in a week. If it is fearfully slow I'm coming back to keep Leonard company. Well, I suppose we must make haste. The cabs will be here directly.'

'Not till after breakfast, surely. There is the gong. Are you ready?'

'Yes; just put in this stud for me, like a dear. How elegant you look, just as if you had stepped from a bandbox. How do you manage to be so tidy, and yet always so graceful? When I am tidy I am stiff as a poker.'

Clara laughed, and, having fastened the refractory collar-button, bent her stately head, and gave her sister a kiss.

'Don't attempt to be too tidy, it will spoil your individuality.'

> "*"They were two sisters of one race,*
> *She was the fairest in the face,"*'

sang Mina, as she bounded down-stairs — not disdaining, in spite of her eighteen years, to slide down the last few feet of the banisters; only she took care to see that nobody but Clara was in sight.

It was a very happy breakfast-table, though Leonard, whose classes kept him in town, affected a melancholy mood.

'I have only one piece of advice to give you, Gladys, in addition to my parting blessing,' he said teasingly. 'How much will you give for it?'

'How much is it worth?' she flashed back in a moment, her eyes dancing with fun.

'Untold gold, as you will find if you take it.'

'I can't buy it at the price,' she answered demurely.

'Well, I'll give it for nothing, in gratitude for the peace I shall enjoy this evening. Mamma, mayn't I come down Wednesday nights as well as Fridays?'

'No, my dear, you mayn't,' replied Mrs. Fordyce, shaking her head. 'If you work hard all week, you will enjoy your Saturdays all the more.'

'All right. Papa and I will have high jinks; see if we don't,' said the lad, with a series of little nods towards the newspaper which hid his father's face.

Mr. Fordyce did not hear this remark, though he looked up in mild surprise at the laughter it provoked.

'You seem very merry, Len, my boy. It is time you were off.'

'Yes, I know. That's the way a fellow's treated in this house — not allowed five minutes to eat a decent breakfast. Well, I'm off. Good-bye, all.'

'The advice, Leonard?' asked Gladys, when he came round to her chair.

He bent down, whispered something in her ear, and ran off.

'What did he say, Gladys. Do tell us?' cried Mina, in curiosity.

'I must, because I don't understand it,' answered Gladys. 'He said, "*Don't* let them take you for a walk on the Ballast Bank." What did he mean?'

'Oh, the Ballast Bank is the only promenade Troon can boast of, and Len has a rooted aversion to it,' replied Mina. 'He is a most absurd boy.'

In spite, however, of Leonard's advice, many a delightful blow did Gladys enjoy on the Ballast Bank.

The spring winds had not yet lost their wintry touch on the Ayrshire coast. Sweeping in from the sea, they made sport with the golfers on the Links, and taxed their skill to the utmost. The long stretch of grey sand upon which the great green waves rolled in and broke with no gentle murmur, the wide expanse of the still wintry-looking sea, the enchanting pictures to be seen in the clear morning light, where the Arran hills stood out so bold and rugged against the sky, and at sunset, when the tossing waters were some-times stilled into an exquisite rest, all these were revelations to the girl who had the soul and the eye of an artist, and she drank them in with no ordinary draught of enjoyment. She lived out of doors. Wind and weather could not keep her in the house. When the rain-drops blew fierce and wild in the gale, she would start across the garden, out by the little gate to the beach, and, close by the edge of the angry sea, watch the great waves rolling in to her feet, and as she looked, her eyes grew large and luminous, and she would draw great breaths of delight; the wideness of the sea satis-fied her, its wildest moods only breathed into her soul an ineffable calm.

In the course of a week the Pollokshields Fordyces also ar-rived at their Coast residence, and there began to be a quite unprecedented amount of friendly coming and going between the two families. It became evident before long that George Fordyce appeared to find some great attraction at The Anchorage, though in former years he had only presented himself at rare intervals during the months his people were at the sea-side. And those who looked on saw quite well how matters were drifting, and each viewed it in a different light. The most unconscious, of course, was Gladys herself. She knew that everybody was kind to her — George Fordyce, perhaps, specially so. He could be a very gallant squire when he liked. He was master of all the little attentions women love, and in his manner towards Gladys managed to infuse a certain deference, not untouched by tenderness, which she found quite gratifying. She had so long lived a meagre, barren existence that she seemed almost greedy of the lovely and pleasant things of life. She enjoyed wearing her beautiful gowns, living in luxurious rooms, eating dainty food at a well-appointed table. In all that there was nothing unnatural, it was but the inevitable reaction after what she had gone through. She began to understand that life has two sides, one for the rich and one for the poor, and she was glad, with an honest, simple gladness, that she had been permitted to taste the best last. She retained her simple, genuine manner; but her soul had had its first taste of power, and found it surpassing sweet. Beauty and riches had proved themselves valuable in her eyes, and there were times when she looked back upon the old life with a shudder. In the intoxication, of that first summer of her new life, memory of Walter grew dim in her heart. She thought of him but seldom, never of her own free will. Unconsciously she was learning a lesson which wealth and power so arrogantly strive to teach — to put away from her all unpleasant thoughts. Let us not blame her. She was very young, and experience has to lead the human heart by many tortuous ways to full understanding. So Gladys lived her happy, careless, girlish summer by the sea, enjoying it to the full.

'Tom,' said Mrs. Fordyce to her husband one afternoon, as they sat at the drawing-room window watching the young folks in the garden, 'do you think there is anything serious between Gladys and George Fordyce?'

'Eh, what? No, I don't think so.'

'Well, I do. Just look at them at this moment.'

They were sauntering arm in arm on the path within the shadow of the garden wall, Gladys with a bunch of pink sea daisies in her hand, a pretty bit of colour against her white gown. There was a tint as delicate in the fair cheek under the big sun hat, brought there, perhaps, by some of her companion's words. His attitude and bearing were certainly loverlike, and his handsome head was bent rather nearer the big sun hat than Mrs. Fordyce altogether approved.

'Well, I must say, my dear, it looks rather like it, only I've heard the girls say that George is a great flirt.'

'He is, but I don't think it's flirting in this case,' said Mrs. Fordyce seriously. 'I am afraid we, or at least I, have been very indiscreet.'

'You wouldn't approve then, Isabel? George is a trifle vain and silly, but I never heard anything against his character.'

'I suppose not. We would be the last to hear any such rumours. But it isn't fair to the girl; she has not had a chance. Do you know what people will say of us, Tom? That we took her away down here and shut her up among ourselves for the very purpose of matchmaking. It is a blessing our Leonard is only a boy, but it is bad enough that it should be our nephew.'

'There's a good deal of truth in what you say, but the world must just wag its stupid tongue. If the thing is to be, we can't prevent it.'

'We can, we must. She is only a child, Tom. I feel quite convicted of my own sinful want of observation. I have been thinking of it all day, and my mind is made up, provided you, as her guardian, will give your consent. She must go abroad. Do you remember Henrietta Duncan, who married the French officer? She is living in Bruges now, taking a few English ladies into her house. Gladys must go there.'

Mr. Fordyce looked at his wife in profound astonishment. He had not often heard her speak in such a very determined manner.

'Why, of course I can't have any objections, if the child herself is willing to go,' he said. 'Not that I believe it will do an atom of good. If there is a love affair in the matter, opposition is the very life of them. Don't you remember our own case?' he asked, referring, with a smile, to the old romance which had kept them true through years of opposition and discouragement.

'I haven't forgotten it,' she said, with an answering smile, 'only it is impossible these two in so short a time can be seriously involved. I'll find out this very day.'

'You are not in favour of it, Isabel, and a wilful woman must have her way.'

'It's not altogether fear of the world's opinion, Tom; there's something about George I don't — nay, can't like. He is very handsome, and can be very agreeable, but I never feel that he is sincere, and he is profoundly selfish. Even his mother says that.'

'Ay, well, she would need kind dealing, Isabel; she is a highly-strung creature,' said the lawyer thoughtfully, and the subject dropped.

CHAPTER XX.

PLANS.

While these golden days were speeding by the sea, Bourhill was being put in order for its young mistress. Her interest in the alterations was very keen; there were very few days in which they did not drive to the old house, and Mrs. Fordyce was surprised alike at the common-sense and the artistic taste she displayed in that interest.

'Do you think, dear Mrs. Fordyce,' she asked one day, when they happened to be alone together at Bourhill, — 'do you think the house could be ready for me by the end of September, when you return to Glasgow?'

'It will be ready, of course; there is really very little to do now,' replied Mrs. Fordyce. 'But why do you ask?'

'Why, because if it is ready, then I need not go up with you. You have been very kind — I can never, never forget it; but, of course, when I have a home of my own it would not be right of me to trespass any longer on your kindness,' said Gladys thoughtfully.

Mrs. Fordyce could not forbear a smile.

'How old are you, my dear? I do not know that I have ever heard your age exactly.'

'I shall be eighteen next month.'

'Eighteen next month? — not a very responsible age. Is it possible, my dear, that you feel perfectly fit to take possession here, that you would have no tremors regarding your lonely position and your responsibility?'

'I have no such feeling, Mrs. Fordyce. I could live here quite well. Is there any reason why I should not?' she asked, observing the doubtful expression on the face of her kind friend.

'It is quite impossible, my dear, whatever your feelings may be, — altogether out of the question that you should live here alone.'

'But tell me why? I am not a child. I have always seemed to occupy a responsible position, where I have had to think and act for myself.'

'Yes, you have; but your position is entirely altered now. It would not be proper for you to live in this great house alone, with no company but that of servants. Mr. Fordyce would but poorly fulfil his promise to your poor uncle if he entertained such an idea for a moment. If you are to live at Bourhill at all, you must have a responsible person to live with you. But we had other plans for you.'

'Tell me what plans, please,' said Gladys, with that simple directness which made evasion of any question impossible to her, or to any conversing with her.

'Mr. Fordyce and I have thought that it would be to your advantage to winter abroad. I have an old school-friend, who married a French officer, and who is now left widowed in poor circumstances in Bruges. You would be most happy and comfortable with Madame Bonnemain. She is one of the sweetest and most charming of women, musical and cultured; her companionship would be invaluable to you.'

'I do not think I wish to go abroad, meanwhile. Would you and Mr. Fordyce think it ungrateful if I refused to go?'

'Well, no,' replied Mrs. Fordyce, though with a slight accent of surprise. 'But can you tell me what is your objection?'

'I want to come here and live just as soon as it is possible,' said Gladys, looking round the dismantled house with wistful, affectionate eyes. 'I want to have my very own house; I can never feel that it is mine until I live in it; and I have many plans.'

'Would you mind telling me some of them?' said Mrs. Fordyce rather anxiously. She was a very practical person — attentive to the laws of conventionality, and she did not feel at all sure of the views entertained by her husband's ward.

'I want to be a help to people, if I can,' said Gladys, 'especially to working girls in Glasgow — to those poor creatures who sew in the garrets and cellars. I know of them. I have seen them at their work, and it is dreadful to me to think of them. Sometimes this summer, when I have been so happy, I have thought of some I know, and reproached myself with my own selfish forgetfulness. You see, if I do not help where I *know* of the need, I am not a good steward of the money God has given me.'

'But tell me, my dear child, how would you propose to help?' asked Mrs. Fordyce, inwardly touched, but wishing to understand clearly what Gladys wished and intended to do. There seemed no indecision or wavering about her, she spoke with all the calm dignity of a woman who knew and owned her responsibilities.

'I can help them in various ways. I can have them here sometimes, especially when they are not strong; so many of them are not strong, Mrs. Fordyce. Oh, I have been so sorry for them, and some of them have never, never been out of these dreadful streets. Oh, I can help them in a thousand ways.'

Mrs. Fordyce was silent, not knowing very well how to answer. She saw many difficulties ahead, yet hesitated to chill the girl's young enthusiasm, which seemed a beautiful and a heavenly thing even to the woman of the world, who believed that it could never come to fruition.

'There is something else which might be done. What would you say to Madame Bonnemain coming here to live with you as housekeeper and chaperon?'

'If you, knowing us both, think it would be a happy arrangement, I shall be happy,' Gladys said; and the wisdom of the reply struck Mrs. Fordyce. Certainly, in many respects Gladys spoke and acted like a woman who had tasted the experience of life.

'My love, anybody could live with you, and unless sorrow and care have materially changed Henrietta Bonnemain, anybody could live with her,' she said cheerfully. 'Suppose we take a little trip to Belgium, and see what can be done to arrange it?'

'Oh yes, that would be delightful. I shall know just at once whether Madame Bonnemain and I can be happy together. Is she a Scotch lady?'

'To the backbone. She was born at Shandon, on the Gairloch, and we went to Brussels to school together. She never came back — married at eighteen, Gladys, and only a wife five years. She has had a hard life,' said Mrs. Fordyce, and her eyes grew dim over the memories of her youth.

'Can we go soon, then?' asked Gladys fervently; 'just when they are finishing the house? Then we could bring Madame back with us.'

'My dear, you will not let the grass grow under your feet, nor allow any one else to loiter by the way,' said Mrs. Fordyce, with a laugh. 'Well, we shall see what Mr. Fordyce has to say tonight to these grand plans.'

Some days after that conversation, Mrs. Macintyre was labouring over her washing-tub in her very limited domain in the back court off Colquhoun Street, when a quick, light knock came to her door.

'Come in,' she said, not thinking it worth while to look round, or to lift her hands from the suds.

'Good-morning, Mrs. Macintyre. How are you today?' she heard a sweet voice say, and in a moment she became interested and excited.

'Mercy me, miss, is't you? an' me in a perfick potch,' she said apologetically. 'No' a corner for ye to step dry on, nor a seat to sit doon on. Could ye no' jist tak' a walk the length o' the auld place or I redd up a wee?'

'No, no, Mrs. Macintyre,' replied Gladys, with a laugh. 'Never mind, I'll get a seat somewhere. I have come to see you very particularly, and I'm not going to take any walks till our business is settled. And are you quite well?'

''Deed, I'm jist middlin',' said the good woman, and then,

with one extraordinary sweep of her bare arm, she gathered all the soiled linen off the floor and pushed it under the bed, then vigorously rubbing up a chair, she spread a clean apron on it, and having persuaded Gladys to sit down, stood straight in front of her, looking at her with a species of adoring admiration.

'Ye micht hae let a body ken ye were comin'. Sic a potch,' she said ruefully. 'My, but ye are a picter, an nae mistak'.'

Gladys laughed, and the sound rang through the place like sweetest music.

'Have you not been quite well? I think you are thinner,' she said kindly.

'No, I've no' been up to muckle; fair helpless some days wi' rheumatics. The washin's no' extra guid for them, but a body maun dae something for meat. I've anither mooth to fill noo. My guid-brither, Bob Johnson, is deid since I saw ye, an' I've been obleeged to tak' Tammy — no' an ill loon. He's at the schule, or ye wad hae seen him.'

'I don't suppose you would be sorry to leave this place and give up the washing if you could get something easier?' said Gladys.

'No' me; a' places are the same to me. Hae ye been up by?' asked Mrs. Macintyre significantly.

Gladys shook her head.

'I came to see whether you would come and live in the lodge at my gate. It is a nice little house, and I would like to have you near me; you were such a kind friend in the old days.'

Mrs. Macintyre drew her rough hand across her eyes, and turned somewhat sharply back to her wash-tub, and for the moment she gave no answer, good or bad.

'What aboot Tammy?' she asked at length.

'Oh, he could come with you, of course. He could go to school in Mauchline just as well as in Glasgow. Just say you'll come. I've set my heart on it, and nobody refuses me anything just now.'

'I'll come fast enough,' said Mrs. Macintyre, rubbing away as for dear life at her wash-board, upon which the big salt tears were dropping surreptitiously. 'Me no' want to leave this place? I'm no' that fond o't. Sometimes it's a perfect wee hell in this stair; it's no' guid for Tammy or ony wean. 'Deed, it's no' guid for onybody livin' in sic a place; but if ye are puir, an' tryin' to live decent, ye jist have to pit up wi' what ye can pay for. Ay, I'll come fast enough, an' thank ye kindly. But ye micht get a mair genty body for yer gate. I'm a rough tyke, an' aye was.'

'It is you I want,' replied Gladys; then, in a few words, she explained the very liberal arrangement she had in view for her old friend. After that, a little silence fell upon them, and a great wistfulness gathered in the girl's gentle eyes.

'So ye hinna been up by?' said Mrs. Macintyre. 'Are ye gaun?'

'Not today. Is Walter well?'

'Ay, he is weel. He's a fine chap, an' he's in terrible earnest aboot something,' said Mrs. Macintyre thoughtfully, as she shook out the garment she had been rubbing. 'There's a something deep doon in thon heart no' mony can see. But the place is no' the place it was to him or to me. What way wull ye no' gang up? Eh, but he wad be fell glad to see ye, my lady' —

'I am not going today,' replied Gladys quietly, and even with a touch of coldness. 'You can tell him, if you like, that I was here, and that I hoped he was well.'

'Ay, I'll tell him. And are ye happy, my doo?'

It was a beautiful and touching thing to see the rare tenderness in the woman's plain face as she asked that question.

'Yes, I — I think so,' Gladys replied, but she got up suddenly from her seat, and her voice gave a suspicious tremor. 'Money can do a great deal, Mrs. Macintyre, but it cannot do everything — not everything.'

'Aweel, no. I dinna pray muckle, — there's no' muckle encouragement for sic releegious ordinances this airt, — but I whiles speir at the Lord no' to mak' siller a wecht for ye to cairry. Weel, are ye awa?'

'Yes; good-bye. When you come down to Bourhill, after I come back, we'll have long talks. I shall be so glad to have you there.'

'Aweel, wha wad hae thocht it? Ye'll no' rue'd, my doo, if I'm spared, that's a' the thanks I can gie. An' wull ye no' gang up by?'

There was distinct anxiety in her repetition of the question. But Gladys, with averted head, hastened towards the door.

'Not today. Good-bye,' she said quickly; and, with a warm hand-shake, which anew convinced the honest woman that the girl in prosperity remained unchanged, she went her way.

But instead of going back through the lane to Argyle Street, she continued up the familiar dull street till she reached the warehouse door. She stopped outside, and there being no one in sight, she laid her slender hand on the handle with a lingering — ay, a caressing touch, and then, as if ashamed, she turned about and quickly hurried out of sight.

And no one saw that tender, touching little act except a grimy sparrow on the leads, and he flew off with a loud chirp, and, joining a neighbour on the old stunted tree, made so much noise that it was just possible he was delivering his opinion of the whole matter.

CHAPTER XXI.

ACROSS THE CHANNEL.

For the first time in her life Gladys tasted the novelty of foreign travel. It was quite a lady's party, consisting of Mrs. Fordyce
and her daughters, though Mr. Fordyce had promised to join
them somewhere abroad, especially if they remained too long
away; also, there were vague promises on the part of the Pollokshields cousins to meet them in Paris, after the main object of their
visit to Belgium was accomplished.

They stayed a week in London — not the London Gladys
remembered as in a shadowy dream. The luxurious life of a first-
rate hotel had nothing in it to remind her of the poor, shabby
lodging on the Surrey side of the river, which was her early and
only recollection of the great city. At the end of a week they
crossed from Dover to Ostend, and in the warm, golden light of a
lovely autumn evening arrived in quaint, old-world, sleepy
Bruges. Madame Bonnemain herself met them at the station, a
bright-eyed, red-cheeked, happy-faced little woman, on whom
the care and the worry of life appeared to have sat but lightly
during all these hard years. She was visibly affected at meeting
with her old school-friend.

'Why, Henrietta, you are not one bit changed; you actually
look younger than ever,' exclaimed Mrs. Fordyce, when the first
agitation, of the meeting was over. 'Positively, you look as young as
you did in Brussels eight-and-twenty years ago. Just look at me.
Yes, these are my daughters; and this is Gladys Graham, whom I
am so anxious to see under your care.'

The bright, sharp eyes of Madame Bonnemain took in the
three girls at one comprehensive glance, then she shook her head
with a half arch, half regretful smile.

'A year ago such a prospect would have seemed to lift me to
paradise. Times have been hard with me, Isabel — never harder
than last year; but it is always the darkest hour before the dawn, as
we used to say in Brussels, when the days seemed interminably
awful just before vacation. Two carriages we must have for so
many women. Ah, I am so glad my house is quite, quite empty.'

Beckoning to the drivers of two rather rickety old carriages,
somewhat resembling in form the old English chaise, she put all
the girls in one, and seated herself beside Mrs. Fordyce in the
other.

'Now we can talk. The children will be happier without us.

How good, how very good, it is to see you again, Isabel, and how my heart warms to you even yet.'

'It was your own fault, Henrietta, that we did not meet oftener. You have always refused my invitations — sometimes without much ceremony,' said Mrs. Fordyce rather reproachfully.

'Pride, my dear — Scotch pride; that is what kept me vegetating in this awful place when my heart was in the Highlands. Tell me about Gairloch and Helensburgh, and dear old Glasgow. I have never forgotten it, though I was too proud to parade my poverty in its streets.'

'I will tell you nothing, Henrietta, till I hear what all this means. Have you really been worse off lately?'

'My dear, for twelve months I have not had a creature in my house,' said Madame Bonnemain, and her face grew graver and older in its outline, — 'positively not a creature. Bruges has gone down as a place for English residents, and I don't wonder at it.'

'It is very beautiful, Henrietta,' said Mrs. Fordyce quickly, — 'so quaint; everything about it a picture.'

'People can't live on quaintness, my love, and the narrowness and tyranny of it is intolerable. I hate it. When I go away from Bruges I never want to set eyes on it again as long as I live.'

Her eyes shone, her cheeks grew red, her little mouth set itself in quite a determined curve. Mrs. Fordyce perceived that she had some serious umbrage against the old Flemish town — a grudge which would never be wiped away. And yet it *was* very picturesque, with its grey old houses, its quaint spires, its flat fields spreading away from the canal, its rows of stately poplar trees.

'There is nothing really more terrible, Isabel, than the English life in a foreign town. It is so narrow, so petty — I had almost said so degraded. I should not have taken your pretty ward into my house here suppose you had prayed me to do it. Nothing could possibly be worse for a young girl; she could not escape its influence. No, I should never have taken her here.'

'Why have you stayed so long, then, Henrietta, among such undesirable surroundings?'

'Because it is cheap. There is no other reason in this world would keep anybody in Bruges,' replied Madame promptly.

'But you have not yet told me why you cannot take the position offered you.'

Then Madame turned her bright eyes, over-running with laughter, to her friend, and there was a blush, faint and rosy as a girl's, on her cheek.

'Because, my dear, I have accepted another situation — a permanent one. I am going to marry again.'

'Oh, Henrietta, impossible!'

'Quite true, my dear.'

'Another foreign gentleman, of course?'

'Why of course? No, I am going to rise in the world. I am going to marry an English colonel, Isabel, and return to my own land. I believe I told him that was my chief reason for accepting him at first.'

'But not at last?' hazarded Mrs. Fordyce, with a teasing smile.

'Well, no; romance is not dead yet, Isabel. But I shall tell you my story by and by. Here we are.'

The carriages rattled across the market-place, and drew up before one of the quaint, grey, green-shuttered houses. The *concierge* rose lazily from his chair within the shadow of the court, and showed himself at the door. The ladies alighted, and were ushered into the small plain abode where Madame Bonnemain had so long struggled for existence. All were charmed with it and with her. She made them feel at home at once. Often Gladys looked at her, and felt her heart drawn towards her. Yes, with that bright, sympathetic little woman, she could be happy at Bourhill. But somewhat late that night Mrs. Fordyce came into her room and sat down by her bed.

'My dear, are you asleep? We have come on a fruitless errand; Madame Bonnemain cannot come to you. She is going to be married almost immediately, so what are we to do now?'

'It is a great disappointment,' said Gladys. 'I like her so much. Yes, what are we to do now?'

'You must just come to us for another winter, Gladys; there is nothing else for it.'

Gladys lay still a moment, revolving something in her mind.

'Would it be proper for me to have an unmarried lady to live with me, Mrs. Fordyce?' she asked suddenly.

'Quite, if she were old enough.'

'How old?'

'Middle-aged, at least.'

'Then I know somebody who will do; it is a beautiful arrangement,' cried Gladys joyfully. 'In the little fen village where we lived, my father and I, there is a lady, Miss Peck — we lived in her house. She was very kind to us, and yet so poor; yes, I think she would come.'

'Is she a lady, Gladys?'

'If to be a lady is to have a heart of gold, which never thinks one unselfish thought, she is one, Mrs. Fordyce,' said Gladys warmly.

'These are the attributes of a lady, of course, Gladys, but there are other things, my dear, which *must* be considered. If this Miss Peck is to sit at your table, help you to guide your household, and be your constant companion, she must be a very superior person.'

'She was well brought up. I think her father was a surgeon in Boston,' said Gladys; and these words at once relieved the lawyer's wife.

'If that is so, she may be the very person for whom we are seeking. You are sure she is still there?'

'Yes,' replied Gladys reluctantly. 'I wrote to her in the summer. Mr. Fordyce allowed me to send her some money, — not in charity, it was the payment of a just debt, — and when she replied I knew by her letter that she was still very poor. I have always meant to have her come to me at Bourhill, but it will be delightful if she can come altogether.'

'You have a good heart, Gladys; you will not forget those who have befriended you.'

'I hope not, I pray not; only sometimes I am afraid it is harder for some reasons to be rich than poor.'

These words slightly surprised Mrs. Fordyce, though she did not ask an explanation of them.

'Try to sleep, my child, and don't worry your dear brain with plans,' she said, and, with a motherly kiss, returned to the little *salon* to enjoy the rare luxury of recalling old memories she had shared with the friend of her youth. They sat far on into the night, and before they parted Mrs. Fordyce was in full possession of the whole story of these weary and sordid years through which Henrietta Bonnemain had uncomplainingly borne her burden of poverty and care.

'Then the Colonel turned up,' she concluded, with a curious little tender smile; 'just when my affairs were at the lowest ebb he came here to visit an old regimental friend who lives over the way. So we met, and both being unattached, we drew to each other, and next month we are to be married.'

'Tell me about him, Henrietta, tell me all about him. I declare I am as silly and curious as a school-girl — far more curious about this new lover of yours than I ever was about the old.'

'There is no comparison between the two, Isabel — none at all. Captain Bonnemain was a good man, and he loved me dearly, but it is nearly always a mistake to marry a foreigner. It seems a cruel thing to say, but I never felt to poor Louis as I felt to the noble Englishman who has done me so great an honour.'

Her eyes were full of tears. Mrs. Fordyce saw that she was deeply moved.

'I do not know what he sees in me. He is so handsome, so noble, and so rich, he might marry whom he willed. He has no relatives to be angry over it; and he says, if it pleases me, we can buy a place in Scotland, on the very shores of the Gairloch. Think of that, Isabel; think of your exiled Henrietta returning to *that*. God is too good, and I am too happy.'

She bent her head and wept, and these tears betrayed what her exile had been to the Scotchwoman's heart. Mrs. Fordyce was scarcely less moved. It was a pathetic and beautiful romance.

The Scotch travellers spent a happy week in the old Flemish town; and Gladys, who had the artist's quick eye for beauty of colour and picturesqueness of detail, carried away with her many little 'bits,' to be finished and perfected at home.

Madame Bonnemain journeyed with them to Brussels many times, but declined their invitation to accompany them to Paris. They would all meet, she said, after a certain happy event was over, in the dear land over the sea.

George Fordyce alone joined them in Paris, and, somewhat to his aunt's distress, constituted himself at once as cavalier to Gladys. Often, very often, the good lady was on the point of speaking plainly to him, but, remembering her husband's warning, decided to let matters take their course. She watched Gladys narrowly, however, but could discover nothing in her demeanour but a frank kindliness, almost such as she might have displayed towards a brother. George Fordyce, who had really learned to care for the girl, felt that the close companionship of these days in Paris had not advanced his cause. He did not know that her mind was so engrossed by great plans and high ideals for the life of the coming winter that she had no time to bestow on nearer interests. He was a prudent youth, and decided to bide his time.

After a month's pleasant loitering abroad, they returned to London. George took his cousins home, and Mrs. Fordyce went with Gladys into Lincolnshire.

And they found the fen village as of yore, in no wise changed, except that a few new graves had been added to the little churchyard. The little spinster still abode in her dainty cottage, not much changed, except to look a trifle more aged and careworn. The fastidious eye of the lawyer's accomplished wife could detect no flaw in the demeanour of Miss Peck, and she added her entreaties to those of Gladys. In truth, the poor little careworn woman was not hard to persuade. She had no ties save those of memory to bind her to the fen country, so she gave her promise freely, accepting her new home as a gift from God.

'I shall come one more time here only,' Gladys said, 'to take papa away. Mr. Fordyce promised to arrange it for me. He must sleep with his own people; and when he is in the old churchyard I shall feel at home in Bourhill.'

All these things were done before the year was out; and Christmas saw Gladys Graham settled in her new home, ready and eager to take up the charge she believed God had entrusted to her — the stewardship of wealth, to be used for His glory.

CHAPTER XXII.

A HELPING HAND.

All this time nothing had been heard of Liz. She was no longer known in her old haunts — was almost forgotten, indeed, save by one or two. Among those who remained faithful to her memory was the melancholy Teen, and she thought of her hour by hour as she sat at her monotonous work — thought of her with a great wonder in her soul. Sometimes a little bitterness intermingled, and she felt herself aggrieved at having been so shabbily treated by her old chum. She had in her quiet way instituted a very thorough inquiry into all the circumstances of her flight, and had kept a watchful eye on every channel from which the faintest light was likely to shine upon the mystery, but at the end of six months it was still unsolved. Liz was as irrevocably lost, apparently, as if the earth had opened and swallowed her.

Teen had come to the conclusion that Liz had veritably emigrated to London, and was there assiduously, and probably successfully, wooing fame and fortune. Sometimes the weary burden of her toil was beguiled by dreams of a bright day on which Liz, grown a great lady, but still true to the old friendship, should come, perhaps, in a coach and pair, up the squalid street and remove the little seamstress to be a sharer in her glory. In one particular Teen was entirely and persistently loyal to her friend. She believed that she had kept herself pure, and when doubts had been thrown on that theory by others who believed in her less, she had closed their tattling mouths with language such as they were not accustomed to hear from her usually reticent lips. These gossip-mongers, who flourish in the quarters of the poor and rich alike, speedily learned that it was just as well not to mention the name of Liz Hepburn to Teen Balfour. One day a visitor, in the shape of a handsomely-dressed young lady, did come to the little seamstress's door. Teen gave a great start when she saw the tall figure, and her face flushed all over. In the semi-twilight which always prevails on the staircases of these great grim 'lands' of houses, she had imagined her dream to come true.

'Oh, it's you, miss?' she said, recognising Gladys Graham at last. 'I thought it was somebody else. Ye can come in, if ye like.'

The bidding was ungracious, the manner of it as repellent as of yore; but Gladys, not easily repulsed, followed the little seamstress across the threshold, and closed the door. The heavy, close smell of the place made a slight faintness come over her, and she was glad to sink into the nearest chair.

'Do you never open your window? It is very close in here.'

'No, I never open it. It takes me a' my time to keep warm as it is. There's a perfect gale blaws in, onyhoo, at the chinks. Jist pit yer hand at the windy, an' ye'll see.'

Gladys glanced pitifully round the place, and then fixed her lovely, compassionate eyes on the figure of the little seamstress, as she took up her position again on the stool by the fire and lifted her work.

'You look just as if you had been sitting there continuously since I saw you last,' Gladys said involuntarily.

'So I have, maistly,' replied Teen dully, 'an' will sit or they cairry me oot.'

'Oh, I hope not; indeed, you will not. Have you had a hard summer?'

'Middlin'; it's been waur. Five weeks in July I had nae wark; but I've been langer than that — in winter, too. In summer it's no' sae bad. When ye're cauld, ye feel the want o' meat waur.'

'Have you really sometimes not had food?' asked Gladys in a shocked voice.

'Whiles. Do *you* ken onything aboot Liz?' she asked, suddenly breaking off, and lifting her large sunken eyes to the sweet face opposite to her.

'No; that is one of the things I came about today. Have you not heard anything of her?'

'No' a cheep. Naebody kens. I gaed up to Colquhoun Street one day to ask Walter, but he didna gie me muckle cuttin'. I say, he's gettin' on thonder.' She flashed a peculiar, sly glance at Gladys, and under it the latter's sensitive colour rose.

'I always knew he would,' she replied quietly. 'And he has not heard anything, either? Do you ever see her father and mother?'

'No; but it's the same auld sang. They're no' carin' a button whaur Liz is,' said Teen calmly.

'Have you *no* idea?' asked Gladys.

'Not the least. I may think what I like, but I dinna ken a thing,' replied the girl candidly.

'What do you think, then? You knew her so intimately. If you would help me, we might do something together,' said Gladys eagerly.

Teen was prevented answering for a moment by a fit of coughing — a dry, hacking cough, which racked her weary frame, and brought a dark, slow colour into her cadaverous cheek.

'Well, I think she's in London,' she replied at length. 'But it's only a guess. She'll turn up some day, nae doot; we maun jist wait till she does.'

'I am very sorry for *you*. Will you let me help you? I am living in my own home now in Ayrshire. It is lovely there just now — almost as mild as summer. Won't you come down and pay me a little visit? It would do you a great deal of good.'

Teen laid down her heavy seam and stared at Gladys in genuine amazement, then gave a short, strange laugh.

'Ye're takin' a len' o' me, surely,' she said. 'What wad ye dae if I took ye at yer word?'

'I mean what I say. I want to speak to you, anyhow, about a great many things. How soon could you come? Have you any more work than this to do?'

'No; I tak' this hame the nicht,' replied Teen. 'I can come when I like.'

'If I stay in town all night, would you go down with me tomorrow?'

'Maybe; but, I say, what do ye mean?'

She leaned her elbows on her knees, and, with her thin face between her hands, peered scrutinisingly into her visitor's face. There was a great contrast between them, the rich girl and the poor, each the representative of a class so widely separated that the gulf seems well-nigh impassable.

'I don't mean anything, except that I want to help working girls. I so wished for Liz, she was so clever and shrewd; she could have told me just what to do. You can help me if you like; you must take her place. And at Bourhill you will have a rest — nothing to do but eat and sleep, and walk in the country. You will lose that dreadful paleness, which has always haunted me whenever I thought of you.'

A curious tremor was visible on the face of the little seamstress, a movement of every muscle, and her nerveless fingers could not grasp the needle.

'A' richt,' she replied rather huskily. 'I'll come. What time the morn?'

'What time can you be ready? It is quite the same to me when I go. I have nothing to do.'

'Well, I can be ready ony time efter twelve; but, I say, what if, when I come back, they've gi'en my wark to somebody else? That's certain; ye should see the crood waitin' for it — fechtin' for it almost like wild cats.'

Gladys shivered, and heavy tears gathered in her eyes as she rose from her chair.

'Never mind that. It will be my concern — that is, if you are willing to trust me?'

Teen rose also, and for a moment their eyes met in a steady look. 'Yes,' she said, 'I trust ye, though I dinna, for the life o' me, ken what ye mean.'

There was no demonstration of gratitude on the part of the little seamstress; Gladys even felt a trifle chilled and disheartened thinking of her after she had left the house. But the gratitude was there. That still, cold, self-constrained heart, being awakened to life, never slept again. Both lived to bless that bleak November day when the first compact had been made between them.

From the city Gladys went by car to Kelvinside, and walked up to Bellairs Crescent. Habit is very strong; not yet could the girl, so long used to the strictest and most meagre economies, bear to indulge herself in small luxuries. The need of the world was always with her. She thought always of the many to whom such small sums meant riches. She was not expected at Bellairs Crescent, and she found her friends entertaining at afternoon tea. Some one was singing when she reached the drawing-room door, and when the song was over, she slipped in, surprised, and a little taken aback, to see so many people in the room. A number of them were known to her; there had been many pleasant gatherings at Troon in the summer, and, as was natural, Miss Graham of Bourhill, with her interesting personality and her romantic history, had received a great deal of attention from the Fordyces' large circle of friends. The warmth of the greeting accorded to her made the lovely colour flush high in her cheek, and her eyes sparkle with added brilliance.

'Yes, I came up only at noon. I have been in the city since then,' she replied, in answer to many questions. 'Oh, how do you do, Mr. Fordyce? I did not expect to see you.'

'Nor I you,' said George Fordyce impressively. 'I was dragged here by Julia against my will, and this is the reward of fraternal virtue.'

It was a daring speech, and the manner conveyed still more than the words. The colour broke again over her face in a wavering flood, and her eyes down-dropped under his ardent gaze. These things were noted by several present, and conclusions rapidly drawn.

'You must not talk nonsense to me,' she said, recovering herself, and speaking with her quaint, delightful dignity. 'Remember your promise at Paris.'

'What promise? Did I make one?'

'You know you did,' she said reproachfully. 'We agreed to be friendly, and between friends there should never be any foolish compliments.'

'Well, I can't keep faith; it's impossible to see you and remember any such promise. Besides, it's sober truth,' he replied, growing bolder still. 'Let me get you some tea. Isn't it rather lively here? Doesn't it make you regret having buried yourself in the backwoods at the very beginning of the season?'

'No; I don't care anything about the season,' replied Gladys truthfully. 'Yes, you may bring me some tea, if you don't stay talking after you have brought it. How beautiful Clara is looking today.'

'Clara — yes; she's a handsome girl,' said George, regarding his cousin with but a languid approval. She looked very handsome and stately in her trained gown of brown velvet, with a touch of yellow at the throat, but her expression was less bright than usual. The two who spoke of her at the moment did not guess that they were responsible for the sudden change from gay to grave in her demeanour.

'Oh, Gladys, we were coming down on Saturday, Len and I,' whispered Mina at her elbow; 'but now you will stay, and that will do as well. How are you supporting life down there just now? and how is that sweet little oddity, Miss Caroline Peck?'

'If you call her an oddity, Mina, I cannot talk to you,' said Gladys, with a laugh and a shake of the head. 'I am going home tomorrow. Could Leonard and you not go down with me?'

'Going home tomorrow! Not if we know it. The people are just going away, and we shall have a delightful cosy chat. Here's that tiresome George; but *isn't* he looking handsome? Really, one is proud to have such a cousin.'

It was now half past five, and the company began to disperse. In about ten minutes there were no guests left but Gladys and the two cousins from Pollokshields.

'Now I can talk to you, my dear child,' said Mrs. Fordyce. 'Why didn't you let us know you were coming to town, and one of the girls, at least, would have come to meet you?'

'I had something to do in the city, dear Mrs. Fordyce,' replied Gladys. 'There is something troubling me a good deal just now.'

'What is it? Nothing must be allowed to trouble Miss Graham of Bourhill. Her star should always be in the ascendant,' said Mina banteringly.

'It is a mystery — a lost girl,' said Gladys rather gravely. 'Some one I knew in the old life, who has disappeared, and nobody knows where she has gone.'

'How exciting! Has she not gone "ower the border an' awa', wi' Jock o' Hazeldean"?' asked Mina. 'Do tell us about her. What is her name?'

'Lizzie Hepburn; she is the sister of Walter, who was with my uncle,' said Gladys gravely. 'It is the strangest thing.'

'George, my dear, look what you are doing. Oh, my beautiful gown!'

It was Mrs. Fordyce who thus turned the conversation. Her nephew, handing the cup of tea she had never found time to drink while her guests were present, had deliberately spilled it on the front of her tea-gown. The incident was laughed over in the end, and the only person present who thought of associating his awkwardness with the name Gladys had mentioned was Mina, the shrewdest of them all; but though she had many a strange and anxious thought on the subject, she held her peace.

CHAPTER XXIII.

REAL AND IDEAL.

The little seamstress had never been out of Glasgow in her life. Even the Fair holidays, signal for an almost universal exodus 'doon the water,' brought no emancipation for her. It may be imagined that such a sudden and unexpected invitation to the country filled her with the liveliest anticipation. By eight o'clock that night she had finished her pile of work, and immediately made haste with it to the warehouse which employed her. When she had received her meagre payment, and had another bundle rather contemptuously pushed towards her by the hard-visaged forewoman, she experienced quite a little thrill of pride in refusing it.

'No, thank you, Mrs. Galbraith; I dinna need ony mair the day,' she said, and her face flushed under the forewoman's strong, steady stare.

'Oh, what's up?'

'I'm gaun into the country to visit a lady,' said Teen proudly.

'Oh, all right; there's a hundred waiting on the job, but don't expect to be taken on the moment you like to show your face. We can afford to be as independent as you.'

'I don't expect to need it,' said Teen promptly, though in truth her heart sank a little as she heard these words of doom.

If Gladys failed her, she knew of no other place in that great and evil city where she could earn her bread. She even felt a trifle despondent as she retraced her steps to her garret, but, trying to throw it off, she set herself immediately on entering the house to inspect her wardrobe. This was a most interesting occupation, and, after much deliberation, she took her best black skirt to pieces, and proceeded to hang it as nearly as possible in the latest fashion. Then she had her hat to retrim, and a piece of clean lace to sew on her neckband. At four o'clock her last candle expired in its socket, and she had to go to bed. At the grey dawn she was astir again, and long before the brougham had left Bellairs Crescent with Gladys, Teen was waiting, tin box in hand, on the platform of St. Enoch's Station.

Mrs. Fordyce accompanied Gladys to the station, and when Teen saw them she felt a wild desire to run away. Gladys Graham sitting on a chair in the little attic, talking familiarly of the Hepburns, and Gladys Graham outside, were two very different beings. Gladys glanced sharply round, and, espying her, smiled reassuringly, and advanced with frank outstretched hand.

'Ah, there you are! I am glad to see you. Mrs. Fordyce, this is Teen — Christina Balfour. I must begin to call you Christina; I think it is much prettier. Isn't this a pleasant day? The country will be looking lovely.'

Mrs. Fordyce smiled and bowed graciously to the seamstress, but did not offer her hand. Her manner was kind, but distant; her very smile measured the gulf between them. Teen felt it just as plainly as if she had spoken it in words, and felt also intuitively that her presence there was not quite approved of by the lawyer's wife. That, indeed, was true. There had been a long and rather warm discussion over the little seamstress that morning in Bellairs Crescent, and Mrs. Fordyce had discovered that, with all her gentleness and simplicity, Gladys was not a person to abandon a project on which she had set her heart.

'My dear Gladys,' she took the opportunity of whispering when Teen was out of hearing, 'I am more than ever perplexed. She is not even interesting — nothing could be more hopelessly vulgar and commonplace.'

Gladys never spoke.

'Do tell me what you mean to do with her,' she pursued, with distinct anxiety in her manner.

'Don't let us speak about it, Mrs. Fordyce,' said Gladys rather coldly. 'It is impossible you can understand. I have been like her; I know what her life is. You must let me alone.'

'I am afraid you are going to be eccentric, my dear,' said Mrs. Fordyce. 'I cannot help regretting that Madame Bonnemain was prevented coming to Bourhill. She would have set her foot down on this.'

'Then she would have been mistress of Bourhill,' answered Gladys, with a faint smile, 'and we should certainly have disagreed.'

Mrs. Fordyce looked at her curiously.

'There is a great deal of character about you, Gladys. I am afraid you are rather an imposition. To look at you, one would think you as gentle as a lamb.'

'Dear Mrs. Fordyce, don't make me out such a terrible person,' said Gladys quickly. 'Is it so odd that I should wish to brighten life a little for those whom I know have had so very little brightness?'

'No; it is not your aim, only your method, I object to, my dear. It will never do to fill Bourhill with such people. But I will say no more. Experience will teach you expediency and discretion.'

'We shall see,' replied Gladys, with a laugh, and for the first time she experienced a sense of relief at parting with her kind friend.

Mrs. Fordyce was a kind-hearted woman, and did a great many good deeds, though on strictly conventional lines. She was the clever organiser of Church charities, the capable head of the Ladies' Provident and Dorcas Society, to which she grudged neither time nor money; but she did not believe in personal contact with the very poor, nor in the power or efficacy of individual sympathy and effort. She thought a great deal about Gladys that day, pondering and puzzling over her action — a trifle nettled, if it must be told, at the calm, quiet manner in which her disapproval had been ignored. Gladys was indeed proving herself a very capable and independent mistress of Bourhill.

Meanwhile the two girls, whom fortune had so differently favoured, journeyed together into Ayrshire. A strange shyness seemed to have taken possession of Teen; she sat bolt upright in the corner of the carriage, clutching her tin box, and looking half scared, half defiant; even the red feather in her hat seemed to wear an aggressive air. In her soul she fervently rued the step she had taken, and thought with longing of her own little room, and with affectionate regret of the bundle she had so proudly returned to Mrs. Galbraith.

'What are you thinking of, Teen? You don't look at all happy,' said Gladys, growing a trifle embarrassed by the continued silence.

'I'm no; I wish I hadna come,' was the flat reply, which made the sensitive colour rise in the fair cheek of Gladys.

'Oh no, you don't; you are only shy. Wait till you have seen Bourhill; you will think it the loveliest place in the world,' she said cheerfully.

'Maybe,' answered Teen doubtfully. 'I feel gey queer the noo, onyhoo.'

This was not encouraging. Gladys became silent also, and both felt relieved when the train stopped at Mauchline Station.

The girl, whose only idea of the country was her acquaintance with the straight, conventional arrangement of city parks and gardens, looked about her with genuine wonder.

'My,' she said, as they crossed over the little footbridge at the station, 'sic a room folk have here! Are there nae hooses ava?'

'Oh, lots,' replied Gladys quite gaily, relieved to see even a faint interest exhibited by her guest. 'We shall drive through Mauchline presently; it is such a pretty, quaint little town.'

A very dainty little phaeton, in charge of an exceedingly smart young groom, waited at the station gate for Miss Graham. Teen regarded it and her with open-mouthed amazement. Again it seemed impossible that this gracious, self-possessed lady, giving her orders so calmly, and according so well in every respect with her changed fortunes, could be the same girl who accompanied Liz and herself to the Ariel Music Hall not much more than a year ago.

'My,' she said again, when Gladys took the reins and the pony started off, 'it's grand, but queer.'

'It is all very nice, I think,' said Gladys whimsically. 'Did I tell you that Mrs. Macintyre, who used to live in the Wynd, is at the lodge at Bourhill? But perhaps you did not know Mrs. Macintyre?'

'I have heard o' her frae Liz,' Teen replied; 'but I didna ken that she was here.'

'She only came a month ago. She is a great treasure to me. I wonder if you have thought why I wished you to come here?'

'I've wondered. Ye can tell me, if ye like,' said Teen.

'Well, you see, I have always been sorry about you, somehow, ever since that day I saw you in the Hepburns' house; I really never forgot your pale face. I want you here for your own sake, first, to try and make you look brighter and healthier, and I want your advice and help about something I am more interested in than anything.'

'My advice an' help!' repeated Teen almost blankly, yet secretly flattered and pleased. The idea that her advice and help should be desired by any one was something so entirely new that she may be excused being almost overcome by it.

'Yes,' answered Gladys, with a nod. 'It's about the girls — the girls you and I know about in Glasgow, who have such a poor time, and are surrounded with so much temptation. Do you remember that night long ago when Lizzie Hepburn and you took me to the Ariel Music Hall?'

'Yes, I mind it fine. I was thinkin' o't no' a meenit syne.'

'Well, don't you think that the girls we saw there might have some place a little pleasanter and safer for them to be in than a music hall?'

'Yes,' answered Teen, with unwonted seriousness. 'It's no' a guid place. I've kent twa-three that gaed to the bad, an' they met their bad company there. But what can lassies dae? Tak' Liz, for instance, or me. Had we onything to keep us at hame? The streets, or the music hall, or the dancin', ony o' them was better than sittin' in the hoose.'

'Oh, I know. Have I not thought of it all?' cried Gladys, with a great mournfulness. 'But don't you think if they had some pleasant place of their own, where they could meet together of an evening, and read or work or amuse themselves, they would be happier?'

'There are some places. I ken some lassies that belang to

Christian Associations. Liz an' me gaed twice or thrice wi' some o' the members, but' —

'But what?' asked Gladys, bending forward with keen interest.

'We didna like it. There was ower muckle preachin', and some of the ladies looked at us as if we were dirt,' responded Teen candidly. 'Ye should hae heard Liz when we cam' oot. It was as guid as a play to hear her imitatin' them.'

Gladys looked thoughtful, and a trifle distressed. Curiously, at the moment she could not help thinking of the many societies and associations with which Mrs. Fordyce was connected, and of her demeanour that day at St. Enoch's Station — an exact exemplification of Teen's plain-spoken objection.

'Liz said she was as guid as them, an' she wadna be patronised; an' that's what prevents plenty mair frae gaun. A lot gang just to serve themselves, because they get a lot frae the ladies. My, ye can get onything oot o' them if ye ken hoo to work them.'

This was a very gross view of the case, which could not but jar upon Gladys, though she was conscious that there was a good deal of truth in it. Somehow, in the light of Teen Balfour's unvarnished estimate of philanthropic endeavour, her dreams seemed to become all at once impossible of fulfilment.

'I do not think they mean, the ladies, to patronise. Do you not think the girls imagine, or at least exaggerate?'

'Maybe; but Susan Greenlees — a lassie I ken, that works in a print-mill — telt me one o' them reproved her for haein' a long white ostrich feather in her hat, and Susan, she just says, "Naebody askit you to pay for it," an' left.'

Gladys relapsed into silence; and Teen, all unconscious of the cold water she had thrown so copiously on a bright enthusiasm, sat back leisurely, and looked about her interestedly.

'Here we are,' said Gladys, at length rousing herself up, though with an evident effort; 'and there is Mrs. Macintyre at the gate. You have never seen her, you say? Hasn't she a nice kind face?'

Gladys drew rein when they had passed through the gate, and introduced the two. Mrs. Macintyre, who looked like a different being in her warm grey tweed gown, neat cap, and black apron, gave the pale city girl a hearty hand-shake, and prophesied that Bourhill air would soon bring a rose into her cheek. Gladys nodded, and said she hoped so, then drove on to the house. And when they went up the long flight of steps and into the wide, warm, beautiful hall, Teen's shyness returned to her, and if it had been possible she would have turned and fled.

CHAPTER XXIV.

THE UNEXPECTED.

It did not occur to Gladys to give her guest quarters at the lodge beside Mrs. Macintyre, where, it might have been thought, she would be more at home. Having invited her to Bourhill, she treated her in all respects like any other guest. Teen, after the first fit of shyness wore off, accepted it all as a matter of course, and conducted herself in a calm and undisturbed manner, which secretly astonished Gladys. All the while, however, her new surroundings and experiences made a profound impression on the awakened mind of the city girl. Nothing escaped the keen vision of her great dark eyes. Every detail of the beautiful old house was photographed on her memory; she could have told how many chairs were in the drawing-room, and described every picture on the dining-room walls. Between her and little Miss Peck — the brisk, happy-hearted spinster, who appeared to have taken a new lease of life — there was speedily established a very good understanding, which was also a source of amazement to Gladys. She had anticipated exactly the reverse.

'My dear, she is most interesting,' said Miss Peck, when the first evening was over, and Teen had gone to bed, not to sleep, but to lie enjoying the luxury of a down-bed and dainty linen, and pondering on this wonderful thing that had happened to her, — 'most interesting. What depths in her eyes — what self-possession in her demeanour! My dear, you can make anything of that girl.'

Miss Peck was given to romancing and enthusiasm, but the contrast between her opinion and that expressed by Mrs. Fordyce made Gladys smile. She did not feel herself as yet very particularly drawn towards her guest, whose reserve of manner was sometimes as trying as her outspokenness on other occasions.

'I am glad you like her, Miss Peck. I confess that sometimes I do not know what to make of her. But, you see, she is the only one who can be of any use to me; she knows all about working girls and their ways. If only I could find poor Lizzie Hepburn! She always knew exactly what she meant, and she was clever enough for anything,' said Gladys, with a sigh.

'But tell me, my dear, what is it you wish to do? I don't know that I quite comprehend.'

'Indeed, I am not quite clear about it yet myself, though, of course, I have an idea I want to help them, especially the friendless ones. If it could be arranged, I should like to establish a kind of friendly Club for them in Glasgow, where they could all meet, and where those who have no friends could lodge; then I should like to have a little holiday house for them here, if possible.'

'My dear, that is a great undertaking for one so young.'

'Do you think so? I must try it, and you must help me, dear Miss Peck, for Mrs. Fordyce won't. She doesn't approve at all of my having invited Christina Balfour down here.'

'My dear, the world never does approve of anything done out of the conventional way,' said Miss Peck, with a quiet touch of bitterness. 'I think you have a very noble aim, and the heart of an angel; only there will be mountains of difficulty in the way.'

'We must overcome them,' answered Gladys quickly.

'And you will meet with much discouragement, and a great deal of ingratitude,' pursued the little spinster, hating herself for her discouraging words, but convinced that it was her duty to prepare her dear charge for the worst.

'Not more than I can bear,' Gladys answered. 'And I am quite sure that, with all these drawbacks, I shall also receive many bright, encouraging things to help me on.'

'Yes, my dear, you will. God will reward you in His own best way,' said Miss Peck, with tears in her eyes.

Gladys sat late by the fire that night, pondering her new scheme, and developing its details with great rapidity. She found the greatest comfort and pleasure in such planning; for, though she was the envied of many, there were times, though unconfessed, when she was weighed down by her own loneliness, when a sense of desolation, as keen as any she had ever experienced in Colquhoun Street, made all the lovelier things of life seem of no account.

Next morning Gladys drove her guest into Troon, and at sight of the great sea, its breast troubled with wintry storms, tossing and rolling in wildest unrest, Teen appeared for the first time really moved.

'It's fearsome,' she said in an awe-stricken whisper, — 'fearsome! Michty me, look at the waves! It's fearsome to look at.'

'How odd that it should strike you so!' exclaimed Gladys. 'It always rests and soothes me; the wilder it is, the deeper the quiet it infuses into my soul. See the tall shadow yonder through the mists, the mountains of Arran; and that is Ayr, across Prestwick Bay; and these rocks jutting out into the sea, the Heads of Ayr. Do you see that house with the flagstaff, at the top of the Links? It is Mr. Fordyce's house, The Anchorage, where I lived all summer. It is splendid here today. Stand still, Firefly, you impatient animal; we are not ready to go yet.'

'I wad be feared to live in that hoose,' said Teen. 'The waves micht come up in the nicht an' wash it away. Jist look at that yin the noo.'

A great green wave, with its angry crest of foam, came rolling in with apparently resistless force, and spent itself on the pebbly shore with a sullen roar.

'"Thus far shalt thou come, and no farther,"' said Gladys, with a faint smile, and a momentary uplifting of her eyes to the grey wintry sky. '"He holdeth the sea in the hollow of His hand."'

'Some day, when it is very fine, I shall take you to Ayr,' said Gladys, as she turned the pony's head. 'I have often thought how I should like to bring Liz here. I cannot tell you how I feel about her; I think about her almost continually.'

'So dae I, though I think, mind, she's been very shabby to me; but she was my chum,' said Teen, with an unusually soft look on her face. 'She didna care a button what she said to a body, but at the same she wad dae onything for ye.'

'And you still think she is in London?'

'Yes,' answered Teen, without a moment's hesitation 'Learnin' to be an actress, as sure as I sit here.'

'Somehow I don't think it. I have an odd feeling at times about her, as if she were not so far away from us as we imagine.'

'She's no' in Glesca, onyway. She couldna be in Glesca withoot me kennin',' replied Teen confidently. 'There's some that think she gaed aff wi' a beau, but they never said it twice to me. I kent Liz better than that. She could watch hersel'.'

'Did you know him, the man you call her beau?' inquired Gladys, with a slight blush.

'Ay, I kent him,' said Teen, looking away over the landscape as if she suddenly found it of new and absorbing interest.

'And have you seen him since?'

'Ay.'

'Did you speak to him, or ask him if he knew anything about her?'

'No' me; it's nane o' my business to meddle; but maybe I wad ask him if I had a chance,' said Teen, with a peculiar pressure of the lips.

'Who is he, Teen? Do you know his name?'

'Ay, fine that; but it wad dae nae guid to say,' replied Teen guardedly. 'I dinna think he had onything to dae wi' her gaun away, onyway.'

Gladys perceived that Teen was determined to be utterly loyal to her friend, and admired her for it.

That very afternoon, however, Teen saw occasion to change her mind on the subject. After lunch, while Gladys was busy with letter-writing, Teen went out to pay a visit to Mrs. Macintyre at the lodge. She was walking very leisurely down the avenue, admiring the brilliant glossy green of the laurels and hollies, when the tall figure of a man in a long ulster came swinging round the curve which hid the gates from view. Teen gave a great start, and the dusky colour leaped in her face when she recognised him. His cheek flushed too with distinct annoyance, and surprise was also visible on his face.

'What are you doing here?' he asked, without the shadow of other greeting.

Teen looked up at him with a kind of quiet insolence in her heavy dark eyes.

'That's my business,' she said calmly, and picked to pieces the leaf she had in her hand.

'Are you staying here?' he asked then, with undisguised uneasiness, which secretly delighted Teen. If there was a human being she mortally disliked and distrusted, it was Mr. George Fordyce.

'Yes, I'm stayin' at the big hoose.'

'With Miss Graham?'

Teen nodded, and a faint, melancholy smile, half of scorn, half of amusement, touched her thin lips.

'How the deuce did you manage that?' he inquired angrily. 'I can't understand it.'

'Nor I; ye can ask her, if ye like,' responded Teen calmly; then quite suddenly she dropped her mask of indifference, and, laying her thin, worn fingers on his arm, lifted her penetrating eyes swiftly to his uneasy face. 'I say, where's Liz?'

'How should I know? How dare you question me?' he asked passionately. 'I shall warn Miss Graham against you, that you are not a proper person to have in her house. You are not fit to breathe the same air with her.'

'Maybe no'; but as fit as you,' she answered scornfully. 'I see through it a'; but if ye have harmed Liz, my gentleman, ye'll no' get off wi' it. Ye'll answer for it to me.'

Mrs. Fordyce had called her vulgar and commonplace; she did not look so now; passion transformed her into a noble creature. The man of the world, accustomed to its homage and adulation, cowed before the little seamstress of the slums. While she walked away from him, as if scorning to bandy further words, he looked after her in consternation. She had not only surprised, she had made a coward of him for the moment. He seemed to see in the slight, insignificant form of the city girl the Nemesis who would sooner or later bring his evil deeds home, and thwart what was at the present moment the highest ambition of his life.

His step lagged as he continued his way towards the house,

within whose walls dwelt the woman whom love and ambition prompted him to make his wife. It was not, however, the reluctance of a dishonoured soul to seek communion with one so absolutely pure, it was merely the hesitation of a prudence wholly selfish. He rapidly reviewed the situation, considered every possibility and every likely issue, and took his resolve. He could not afford to wait. If Gladys was ever to be his, she must be won at once. If she cared sufficiently for him to pledge herself to him, he believed that she would stand by him and take his word, whatever slander might assail his name. He had not anticipated this crisis when, in a careless, idle mood, he had left the mill, and followed the impulse which sent him to Bourhill.

By the time he reached the steps before the door every trace of disturbance had vanished, and he was once more the urbane, handsome, debonair gentleman who played such havoc among women's hearts.

Miss Graham being at home, he was at once shown into the drawing-room, and left there while the maid took his name to her mistress. Meanwhile Teen, instead of going into the lodge, passed through the gates, and walked away up the road. She was utterly alone, the only sign of life being a flock of sheep in the distance, trotting on sedately before a tall shepherd and a collie dog. Teen never saw them. She was fearfully excited, believing that she had at last discovered the clue to her missing friend.

CHAPTER XXV.

THE FIRST WOOER.

Gladys was writing a long letter to her guardian, setting forth in eloquent terms what she wished to do for the working girls of the East End, and asking him for some sympathy and advice, when the housemaid knocked at the door.

'A gentleman for me, Ellen? Yes, I shall be there presently,' she said, without looking at the card on the salver. 'Is Miss Peck in the drawing-room?'

'No, ma'am; she is taking her rest. Shall I tell her?'

'Oh no. Who is it?'

She added another word to her letter, and then read the name on the card. The maid standing by could not help seeing the lovely access of colour in the fair cheek of her mistress, and, as was natural, drew her own conclusions.

Gladys rose at once, and proceeded up-stairs. She did not, as almost every other woman in the circumstances would have done, go to her own room to inspect her appearance or make any change in her toilet. And, in truth, none was needed. Her plain black serge gown, with its little ruffle at the neck, which would have made a dowdy of almost anybody but herself, was at once a fitting and becoming robe. Her lovely hair, which in the early days had hung in straight heavy plaits over her back, was now wound about her head, and kept in place by a band and knot of black velvet. She moved with the calm mien and serious grace of a woman at ease with herself and all the world. A faint hesitation, however, visited her when she stood without the closed door of the drawing-room. That curious prevision, which most of us experience at times, that something unusual was in store, robbed her for a moment of her usual self-possession; but, smiling and inwardly chiding herself for her own folly, she opened the door and entered the presence of her lover. She knew him to be such, it was impossible to mistake his demeanour and his attitude towards her. There was the most loverlike eagerness in his look and step as he came towards her, and under his gaze the girl's sweet eyes drooped and her colour deepened.

'This is quite a surprise,' she said gaily. 'Why did you not bring some of the girls with you?'

'I haven't seen them for ages, and Julia has a dance on tonight for which she is saving herself. Besides, perhaps, I wanted to come quite alone.'

'Yes?' she said in a voice faintly interrogatory. 'And you had to walk from the station, too? If you had only wired in the morning, I could have come or sent for you.'

'But, you see, I did not know in the morning I should be here today. It is often the unexpected that happens. I came off on the impulse of the moment. Are you glad to see me?'

It was a very direct question; but Gladys had now quite recovered herself, and met it with a calm smile.

'Why, of course; how could I be otherwise? But, I say, you said a moment ago you had not seen any of the girls for ages; it is only forty-eight hours since we met in your aunt's drawing-room.'

'So it is,' he said innocently. 'I had quite forgotten, which shows how time goes with me when you are out of town. Are you really going to bury yourself here all winter?'

'I am going to live here, of course. It is my home, and I don't want any other. A day in Glasgow once a week is quite enough for me.'

'Hard lines for Glasgow,' he said, tugging his moustache, and looking at her with a good deal of real sentiment in his handsome eyes. She was looking so sweet, he felt himself more in love than ever; and there was a certain 'stand-offishness' in her manner which attracted him as much as anything. He had not hitherto found such indifference a quality among the young ladies of his acquaintance.

'I have just been writing to your Uncle Tom, telling him I want to spend a great deal of money,' she began, rather to divert the conversation than from any pressing desire for his opinion, 'and I don't feel at all sure about what he will say. Your aunt does not approve, I know.'

'May I ask how you are going to spend it?' he inquired, with interest.

'Oh yes. I want to institute a Club for working girls in Glasgow, and a holiday house for them here.'

'But there are any amount of such things in Glasgow already, and I question if they do any good. I know my mother and Ju are always down on them, and there's truth in what they say, too, that we are making a god out of the working class. It is quite sickening what is done for them, and how ungrateful they are.'

Gladys winced a little, and he perceived that he had spoken rather strongly.

'I know there is a good deal done, but I think sometimes the methods are not quite wise,' she said quietly. 'I am going to run my Club, as the Americans say, on my own lines. You see, I am rather different, for I have been a poor working girl myself, and I know both what they need and what will do them most good.'

'You seem rather proud of the distinction,' he said involuntarily. 'Most women in your position would have made a point of ignoring the past. That is what half of Glasgow is trying to do all the time — forget where they sprang from. Why are you so different?'

'I do not know.' Her lips curled in a fine scorn. 'As if it mattered,' she said half contemptuously, — 'as if it mattered what anybody had sprung from. I was reading Burns this morning, and I felt as if I could worship him if for nothing more than writing these lines —

> *"The rank is but the guinea stamp,*
> *The man's the gowd for a' that."'*

'That's all very good in theory,' he said a trifle lazily; 'and besides, it is very easy for you to speak like that, with centuries of lineage behind you. I suppose the Grahams are as old as the Eglintons, or the Alexanders, or even the great Portland family itself, if you come to inquire into it. Yes, it is very easy for you to despise rank.'

'I don't despise it, and I am very proud in my own way that I do belong to such an old family; but, all the same, it doesn't really matter. There is nothing of any real value except honour and high character, and, of course, genius.'

'When you speak like that, Gladys, and look like that, upon my word, you make a fellow afraid to open his mouth before you,' he said quickly, and there was something very winning in the humility and deference with which he uttered these words.

Gladys was not unmoved by them, and had he followed up his slight advantage, he might have won her on the spot; but at the propitious moment Ellen brought in the tea-tray, and the conversation had to drift into a more general groove.

'To return to my project,' said Gladys, when the maid had gone again, 'I have one of my old acquaintances among the working girls here just now. I expect she will help me a good deal. She was the friend of poor Lizzie Hepburn, whom we have lost so completely. Is it not strange? What do you think *can* have become of her?'

'I'm sure I couldn't say,' he replied, with all the indifference at his command.

Gladys, busy with the tea-cups, noticed nothing strange in his manner, nor did his answer disappoint her much. She was quite aware that he did not take an absorbing interest in the questions which engrossed so much of her own thought.

'The saddest thing about it is that nobody seems to care anything about what has become of her,' she said, as she took the dainty Wedgewood teapot in her hand. 'Just think if the same thing had happened to your sister or either of your cousins, what a thing it would have been.'

'My dear Gladys, the cases are not parallel. Such things happen every day, and nobody pays the least attention. And besides, such people do not have the same feelings as us.'

Gladys looked at him indignantly.

'You only say so because you know nothing about them,' she said quickly. 'I do assure you the poor have quite as keen feelings as the rich, and some things they feel even more, I think. Why, only today I had an instance of it in the girl I have staying here. Her loyalty to Liz is quite beautiful. I wish you would not judge so harshly and hastily.'

'I will think anything to please you, Gladys,' said George fervently. 'You must forgive me if I am a trifle sceptical. You see, a fellow has his opinions moulded pretty much by his people, and mine don't take your view of the lower classes.'

Again he was unfortunate in his choice of words. Gladys particularly disliked the expression, 'lower classes,' and his apologetic tone did not appease her.

'They judge them harshly because they know nothing about them, and never will. One has to live among them, as I have done, to learn their good qualities. It is the only way,' she said rather sadly.

George set down his cup on the tray, and lingered at the table, looking down at her with a glance which might have disconcerted her.

'You are so awfully good, Gladys,' he said, quite humbly for him. 'I wonder you can be half as civil as you are to a reprobate like me.'

'Are you a reprobate?' she asked, with a faint, wondering smile.

'I'm not as good as I should be,' he added frankly. 'But, you see, I've never had anybody put things in the light you put them in. If I had, I believe it would have made all the difference. Won't you take me in hand?'

He threw as much significance as he dared into his last question; but Gladys apparently did not catch his meaning.

'I don't like to hear you speak so,' was the unexpected reply. 'It is like throwing the blame on other people. A man ought to be strong enough to be and to do good on his own account.'

'If you tell me what you would like me to do, I'll do it, upon my word,' he said earnestly.

'Oh, I have no right to do that, but since you ask, I will say that you have not very far to seek your opportunities. Your Uncle Tom told me the other day you employed nearly seven hundred men and women at your mills. If that is not a field for you to work in, I don't know what is.'

George Fordyce bit his lip ever so slightly, and half turned away. This was bringing it home indeed, and the vision of himself taking up a new *rôle* among his own workpeople rather disconcerted him.

'Now you are offended,' said Gladys quickly; 'and, please, it is not my fault. You asked me what you should do.'

'Offended with you! No such thing. You could never offend me. Can't you see, Gladys, that the very reason I would be better is *you*, and you alone. I want to please you, because I want to win you.'

There was no doubt at all about his meaning now. The passion with which he spoke brought a blush to the girl's cheek, and she rose hurriedly from her chair.

'Oh, you must not say such things to me, please.'

'Why not? Every man has the right to speak when he loves a woman as I love you. Could not you care for me, Gladys? I know I am not half good, but I'll try to be better for your sake.'

'I have liked you very well. I do like you,' she answered, with a trembling frankness, — 'only, I think, not quite in that way.'

'If you like me at all, I shall not despair. It will come in time. Give me the hope that you'll try to think of me in that way,' he pleaded passionately; and Gladys slightly shook her head.

'Try?' she repeated. 'I do not know much, but it seems to me that that should be without trying.'

'But you need not give me a final answer now. Let me wait and try to win you — to be more worthy of you. I know I am not that yet, but you know we've got on awfully well together — been such chums — I'm sure it would all come right.'

He looked very handsome and very winning, pleading his cause with an earnestness which left no doubt of his sincerity. Gladys allowed him to take her hand, and did not draw herself away.

'If you will let me alone a long time — a year, at least — and never speak of it, I will give you an answer then. It is a very serious thing, and one must be quite sure,' she said slowly; and that answer was more than George Fordyce had dared to hope for. There was more deliberation and calmness in her disposal of the question than would have satisfied most men, but he had fared better than he expected, and left the house content.

As for Gladys, she felt restless and unhappy, she did not know why; only she knew that never had her thoughts reverted with such lingering persistence to the past, never had its memories seemed more fraught with sweetness and with pain. She was an enigma, she could not understand herself.

CHAPTER XXVI.

UNDER DISCUSSION.

Teen took quite a long walk along the bleak country road, and on her way back dropped in at the lodge.

Mrs. Macintyre and the redoubtable 'Tammy' — a very round and chubby urchin, as unlike a denizen of the slums as could well be imagined — were sitting at tea by the cosy hearth, and there was a warm welcome and a cup for the visitor at once.

'Come awa', my wummin; I saw ye gang by,' said the good soul cheerily. 'My, but ye hae a fine colour; jist gang ben an' look at yersel' in the room gless. Ye're no' like the same lassie.'

Teen smiled rather incredulously, and did not go 'ben' to verify the compliment.

'It's a fine place this,' she said, as she dropped into a chair. 'A body's never tired. I wonder onybody bides in the toon when there's sae much room in the country.'

The wideness of the landscape, its solitary freedom, and its quiet, impressed the city girl in no ordinary way. After the crush and struggle of the overcrowded streets, which she had not until now left behind, it was natural she should be so impressed.

'I walkit as far as frae the Trongate to the Briggate, an' I saw naething but twa-three sheep an' a robin red-breist sittin' in the hedge,' she said musingly. 'It's breist was as red as it had been pented. I didna ken ye could see them leevin'?'

'Oh, there's thoosan's o' them,' quoth Tammy enthusiastically. 'In the spring that hedge up the road will be thick wi' nests, filled wi' eggs o' a' kinds.'

'Which ye'll leave alane, my man, or I'll warm ye,' said his aunt, with a warning glance. 'Ay, my wummin, this is a hantle better nor the Trongate or the Briggate o' Glesca. An' what's the young leddy aboot this efternune?'

'Writin' letters, I think. Has she said onything to you, Mrs. Macintyre, aboot makin' a Club for lassies in the toon?'

'Tammy,' said Mrs. Macintyre, 'tak' the wee jug an' rin up to the dairy, an' ask Mrs. Grieve if she'll gie ye a hap'nyworth o' mair cream.'

She did not urgently require the cream, but it was necessary at the moment to get rid of Tammy, who was a remarkably shrewd boy, with very long ears and a wonderful understanding.

Just as Tammy departed, rather unwillingly it must be told, the carriage from the house came bowling down the avenue, and Mrs.

Macintyre ran out to open the gate. From her seat by the fire Teen could see over the low white window-blind that George Fordyce sat in it alone.

'There's something up,' said Mrs. Macintyre. 'D'ye see that?'

She held up a shining half crown, which in his gracious mood the hopeful lover had bestowed upon the gatekeeper.

'I wonder if that's to be the Laird o' Bourhill?' she said meditatively. 'Ye wadna see him as he gaed by? — a very braw man, an' rich, they say — a Fordyce o' Gorbals Mill. Hae ye heard o' them?'

'Ay, often.' Teen's colour seemed to have deepened, but it might be only the fire which glowed upon it. 'Ye dinna mean to say that *that* micht happen?'

'What for no'?' queried Mrs. Macintyre easily, as she cut a slice from the loaf and held it on a fork before the fire. 'She's bonnie an' she's guid, besides being weel tochered. She'll no' want for wooers. I say, did ye ken Walter Hepburn, that carries on auld Skinny's business noo in Colquhoun Street?'

'Yes, well enough,' answered Teen slowly.

'There was a time when I wad hae said the twa — him an' Miss Gladys, I mean — were made for ane anither, but it's no' noo. He seems to hae forgotten her, an' maybe it's as weel. She maun mak' a braw mairriage, an' Fordyce is a braw fellow. I wish ye had noticed him.'

'Oh, I've seen him afore,' said Teen, with an evident effort, and somehow the conversation did not flow very freely, but was purely a one-sided affair, Teen simply sitting glowering into the fire, with an expression on her face which indicated that she was only partially interested in the gatekeeper's cheery talk. It was rather a relief when Tammy returned with the 'wee jug' full of cream, and his own mind full of the arrival of a new calf, a great event, which had happened at the dairy that very afternoon.

Mrs. Macintyre was, on the whole, disappointed with her guest, and saw her depart after tea without regret. She was altogether too reticent and silent for that garrulous person's liking. She would have been very much astonished had she obtained a glimpse into the girl's mind. Never, indeed, in all her life had Teen Balfour been so troubled and so anxious. Once or twice that evening Gladys caught her looking at her with a glance so penetrating and so anxious that it impressed her with a sort of uneasiness. She did not feel particularly happy herself. Now that her lover had gone, and that the subtle charm of his personality and presence was only a memory, she half regretted what had happened that afternoon. She felt almost as if she had committed herself, and she was surprised that she should secretly chafe over it.

'Teen,' she said quite suddenly, when they were sitting alone at the library fire after supper, when Miss Peck had gone to give her housekeeping orders for the morning, 'had you ever a lover?'

This extraordinary and unexpected question drove the blood into the colourless face of Teen, and she could not for the moment answer.

'Well, yes,' she said at length, with a faint, queer smile. 'Maybe I've had twa-three o' a kind.'

'Two or three?' echoed Gladys in a surprised and rather disapproving voice. 'That is very odd. But, tell me, have you ever seen anybody who wished to marry you, and whom you wished to marry?'

'There was a lad asked me yince,' answered Teen, 'but he was only seventeen — a prentice in Tennant's, wi' aicht shillin's a week. I've never had a richt offer.'

'Then what do you mean by saying you have had two or three lovers?' queried Gladys, in wonder.

'Oh, weel, I've keepit company wi' a lot. They've walkit me oot, an' ta'en me to the balls an' that — that's what I mean.'

Gladys was rather disappointed, perceiving that it was not likely she would get much help from the experience of Teen.

'I think that is rather strange, but perhaps it is quite right, and it is only I who am strange. But, tell me, do you think a girl always can know just at once whether she cares enough for a man to marry him?'

'I dinna ken; there's different kinds o' mairriages,' said Teen philosophically. 'I dinna think there's onything in real life like the love in "Lord Bellew's Bride," unless among the gentry.'

'Do you really think not?' asked Gladys, with a slight wistfulness. 'I have not read "Lord Bellew," of course, but I do believe there is that kind of love which would give up all, and dare and suffer anything. I should not like to marry without it.'

'Dinna, then,' replied Teen quite coolly. Nevertheless, as she looked at the sweet face rendered so grave and earnest by the intensity of her thought, her eye became more and more troubled.

'Among oor kind o' folk there's a' kind o' mairriages,' she began. 'Some lassies mairry thinkin' they'll hae an easier time an' a man to work for them, an' they sometimes fin' oot they've only ta'en somebody to keep; some mairry for spite, an' some because they'd raither dee than be auld maids. I dinna think, mysel', love — if there be sic a thing — has ony thing to do wi't.'

It was rather a cynical doctrine, but Teen implicitly believed what she was saying.

'Are *you* thinkin' on mairryin'?' she asked then; and, without waiting for an answer, continued in rather a hurried, troubled way, 'I wadna if I were you — at least, for a while. Wait or ye see what turns up. Ye'll never be better than ye are, an' men are jist men. I wadna gie a brass fardin' for the best o' them.'

Gladys did not resent this plain expression of opinion, because she perceived that a genuine kindliness prompted it.

'I am quite sure I shall not marry for a very long time,' Gladys replied; then they fell to talking over the other subject, which was so interesting to them both.

Underneath all her cynical philosophy there was real kindness as well as shrewd common-sense in the little seamstress. She was in some respects one of the best advisers Gladys could possibly have taken into her confidence.

These sweet, restful days were a benediction to the weary, half starved heart of the city girl, and under their benign influence she became a different creature. Little Miss Peck, who adored Gladys, sometimes observed, with a smile of approval, the grateful, pathetic look in Teen's large solemn eyes when they followed the sweet young creature who had shown her a glimpse of the sunny side of life. It was not a glimpse, however, which Gladys intended to be merely transient. She had in view a scheme which was to be of permanent value to the poor little seamstress.

In the course of that week Gladys had occasion to be overnight in Glasgow, for the purpose of attending a concert with the family in Bellairs Crescent. It was a very select and fashionable affair, at which the *élite* and beauty of Glasgow were present. Gladys enjoyed the gay and animated scene as much as the music, which was also to her a rare treat. When they left the hall it was nearly eleven o'clock, and they had to wait some time in the vestibule till their carriage should move towards the door. It was a fine mild night, and the girls, with their soft hoods drawn over their heads, and their fleecy wraps close about their throats, stood close by the great doors, chatting merrily while they waited. The usual small crowd of loafers were hanging about the pavements, and as usual Gladys was saddened by the sight of the dejected and oftentimes degraded-looking denizens of the lower quarters of the city. It might be that, in contrast with the gay and handsomely-dressed people from the West End, their poverty seemed even more pitiable.

'Now, Gladys, no such pained expression, if you please,' said the observant Mina. 'Don't look as if you carried all the sins and sorrows of Glasgow on your own shoulders. Good, here is the brougham; and pray observe the expression on the countenance of James. Is it not a picture?'

Gladys could not but laugh, and they tripped across the pavement to the carriage. When they were all in, and Mr. Fordyce had given the word to the coachman, a woman suddenly swerved from the pavement and peered in at the carriage window. At the moment the impatient horses moved swiftly away, and when Gladys begged them to stop it was too late; the woman was lost in the crowd.

Gladys, however, had seen her face, and recognised it, in spite of the change upon it, as the face of Walter's sister Liz.

CHAPTER XXVII.

GLADYS AND WALTER.

The fleeting vision of Liz Hepburn's familiar face appeared to fill Gladys with excitement and unrest. As Mina looked at her flushed cheeks and shining eyes, she felt a vague uneasiness visit her own heart. They did not speak of her as they drove home, but when the girls gathered, as was their wont, round the cheerful fire in the guest-chamber before retiring for the night, Gladys asked them a question.

'Did you see her? She looked very ill, and very distressed. Do you not think so? Oh, I fear she has been in trouble, and I must do all I can to find out about her. If you will allow me, I shall remain another day in town, and I can send a telegram to Miss Peck in the morning.'

Mina, on her knees beside her chair, her plump bare arm showing very white and fair against the black lace of Gladys's gown, looked up at her with a slightly troubled air.

'Gladys, I wish you wouldn't bother about that girl. You lay things far too much to heart. It can't possibly concern you now. Let her own people look after her.'

Gladys received this remark with rather an indignant look.

'Mina, that is not like you. You only assume such hard-heartedness. If you saw her face as I saw it, it must haunt you. Her eyes were quite wild and despairing, I cannot forget them.'

'Oh, I think you exaggerate,' said Mina lightly. 'I saw her very well. It was the usual calm, rather insolent stare these girls give. I do not think she looked either very ill or very desperate, and she seemed comfortably clothed. What do you think, Clara?'

'Oh, I didn't see her,' answered Clara, with a slight yawn. 'Yes, Gladys dear, I do think you worry too much over things. What can that girl possibly be to you? Of course we are very sorry for her; still, if she is in trouble, she has brought it on herself. It will never do for you to mix yourself up with all sorts and conditions. I say, wasn't Sims Reeves heavenly tonight, and "Come into the garden, Maud," more entrancing than ever? To think what immense power that man wields in his voice! He can do with his audience as he likes. He was in splendid form.'

Gladys remained silent. The concert had given her a rare pleasure, but it was obliterated at the moment by the incident of the face at the carriage window.

'We had better get to bed, girls, or mamma will be sending

Katherine to us presently,' said Mina, as she picked herself up from the rug. 'Good-night, dear, and don't worry. If you wrinkle up your brows like that over every trifle, you will be old before your time.'

Gladys faintly smiled, and bade them good-night. She 'worried' a good deal more than either of them imagined.

'I say, Clara, I do wish we could induce Gladys to leave that girl alone,' Mina said to her sister, as she threw off her evening gown and began to brush out her hair. 'I have the oddest feeling about it, just as if it would make mischief. Haven't you?'

'No; but you needn't try to dissuade Gladys from anything she has set her mind upon. I never saw anybody so "sot," as Artemus Ward would say; she's positive to the verge of obstinacy. But what makes you have any feeling in the matter I can't imagine; you never even saw the girl in your life.'

'No, but I feel interested in her, all the same. And, I say' —

She broke off there rather suddenly, and meditatively brushed her hair for a few seconds in silence.

'Did you notice that afternoon we had the tea, after all the people were gone, you remember that Cousin George spilled the contents of a cup on mamma's gown?'

'Yes, I remember that, of course, but what can it have to do with Gladys and this Hepburn girl?'

'Did nothing occur to you in connection with his unusual awkwardness? Don't you remember what we were talking of at the time?'

'No,' replied Clara, and she paused with her bodice half pulled over her lovely shoulders, and a slow wonder on her beautiful, placid face.

'Well, Gladys was telling us at the very moment about the disappearance of this Hepburn girl, as you call her, and I happened to be looking at Cousin George while she was speaking, and, Clara, I can't for the life of me help thinking he knows something about it.'

No sooner were the words out of her mouth than Mina saw that she had made a profound mistake. The red colour leaped into her sister's face, dyeing even the curves of her stately throat.

'I think you are a wicked, uncharitable girl, Mina,' she said, with icy coldness. 'I wonder you are not ashamed to have such a thought for a moment. I only beg of you not to let it go any further. It may do more harm than you think.'

So saying, Clara gathered up all her wraps and marched off to her own room, leaving her sister feeling rather hurt and humiliated, though not in the least convinced that she had simply given rein to an uncharitable imagination. Mina was indeed so much troubled that she went off her sleep — a most unusual experience for her; and the morning failed to banish, as it often benignly banishes, the misgivings of the night.

Once more Gladys made a pilgrimage to the old home where Walter dwelt alone, working early and late, the monotony of his toil only brightened by one constant hope. It was a strange existence for the lad on the threshold of his young manhood, and many who knew something of his way of life wondered at the steady and dogged persistence with which he pursued his avocation. He appeared to have reached, while yet not much past his boyhood, the grave, passionless calm which comes to most men only after they have outlived the passion of their youth. He was regarded as a sharp, hard-working young man, with a keen eye for business, and honourable and just, but conspicuously hard to deal with — one whose word was as his bond, and who, being so absolutely reliable himself, suffered no equivocation or crooked dealings in others. By slow but certain degrees he had extricated himself from the strange network which old Abel Graham had woven about the business, and established it upon the basis of sound, straightforward dealing. The old customers, in spite of certain advantages the new system offered, dropped away from him one by one, but others took their place. When Walter balanced his books at the end of the first year, he had reason to be not only content, but elated, and he was enabled to carry out at once certain extensions which he had quite expected would only be justifiable after the lapse of some years. But, while prospering beyond his highest anticipations, what of the growth of the true man, the development of the great human soul, which craves a higher destiny than mere grovelling among the sordid things of earth? While supremely unconscious of any change in himself, there was nevertheless a great change — a very great change indeed. It was inevitable. A life so narrow, so circumscribed, so barren of beauty, lived so solitarily, away from every softening influence, was bound to work a subtle and relentless change. The man of one idea is apt to starve his soul in his effort to make it subservient to the furtherance of his solitary aim. To be a successful man, to win by his own unaided effort a position which would entitle him to meet Gladys Graham on equal ground, such was his ambition, and it never did occur to him that this very striving might make him unfit in other ways to be her mate. His isolated life, absolutely unrelieved by any social intercourse with his fellows, made him silent by choice, still and self-contained in manner, abrupt of speech. In his unconsciousness it never occurred to him that it is the little courtesies and graces of speech and action which commend a man first to the notice of the woman he wants to win. He was, though he did not know it, a melancholy spectacle; but his awakening was at hand.

Gladys made her second call at the house in Colquhoun Street, as before, early in the day. It seemed very familiar, though it was many months since she had passed that way. It seemed a more hopeless and squalid street than she had yet thought it. She picked her steps daintily through the greasy mud, holding her skirts high enough to show a most bewitching pair of feet, cased in Parisian boots, only there was nobody visible to admire them but a grimy butcher's boy, with a basket on his head, and he stared with all his might.

The warehouse door, contrary to the old custom, stood wide open, as if inviting all comers. Gladys gave a glance along the passage which led to the living-rooms, but was not moved to revisit them. She went at once up the grimy staircase, giving a little light cough as she neared the landing, a herald of her coming. She heard quite distinctly the grating of the stool on the floor, and a step coming towards her — a step which even now sounded quite familiarly in her ears.

'It is I — Gladys,' she said, trying to speak quite naturally, but conscious of a shrinking embarrassment which made her cheeks nervously flush. 'The door was open, so I came right in. How are you, Walter?'

In his face shone something of the old bright friendliness, but as she looked at the shabby youth, with his unshaved face and threadbare clothes, her fastidious eye disapproved of him just as it had disapproved of him when they met, boy and girl, for the first time in the rooms below.

'I am quite well,' he answered in his quick, abrupt unsmiling manner. 'But why do you always come without any warning? If you let me know, I should be ready for you. I am always busy in the morning, and a fellow who has so much hard work to do can't always be in trim to receive ladies.'

It was rather an ungracious greeting, which Gladys was quick enough to resent. The gentle meekness of the girl had merged itself into the dignity of the woman, which insists upon due deference being paid.

'I am quite sorry if I intrude, Walter,' she said rather stiffly. 'I shall not keep you long. All the same, I am coming in to sit down for a little, as I have something very particular to speak to you about.'

'Come in. Of course you know I am glad to see you,' he said hurriedly; and Gladys could not help rather enjoying his evident confusion. If he felt nervous and awkward in her presence, it was no more than he deserved to feel, since *she* was so entirely unchanged.

'I am glad you have the grace to be civil, at least,' she said, with a bewildering smile, which vanished, however, when she seated herself on the battered old office-stool; all her anxiety and troubled concern made her face grave to sadness as she put the question —

'Do you know that your sister is in Glasgow?'

CHAPTER XXVIII.

A TROUBLED HEART.

Walter did not know. His expression of surprise, tinged with alarm and a touch of shame, answered her before he spoke.

'How do you know that?' he asked.

'I saw her last night in Berkeley Street, just outside the Crown Halls, where we were at a concert,' said Gladys. 'Is it possible you have never seen her?'

'No; and I don't believe it was her you saw. You must have made a mistake,' replied Walter quickly.

'It was no mistake, because she looked into our carriage, and I saw her quite plainly. Besides, do you think that any one who has seen Liz once would ever forget her face? I have never seen one like it.'

'I don't know anything about it, and I care less,' Walter said with unpromising hardness.

Gladys did not know that the simple announcement she had brought to him in all faith, believing even that he might be in a sense relieved and glad to hear it, tortured him to the very soul. He felt so bitter against Gladys at the moment that he could have ordered her away. Her dainty presence, her air of ladyhood, her beautiful ways, almost maddened him; but Gladys was quite unconscious of it.

'Have you not been at your father's house lately, then?' she asked. 'Of course she must be there. How glad they will be to have her safely at home again! Do you think she would be glad to see me if I went today?'

'No, she wouldn't, even if she were there, which I know is not the case. I was there myself yesterday, and they had never heard anything about her. I wish to heaven you would leave us alone, and let us sink into the mire we are made for! We don't want such fine ladies as you coming patronising us, and trying to make pious examples of us. We are quite happy — oh, quite happy — as we are.'

He spoke with an awful bitterness, with a passion which made him terrible to look upon, but Gladys only shrank a little, only a little, under this angry torrent. Her vision was clearer than a year ago. She read the old friend now with unerring skill, and looked at him steadily with gentle, sorrowful eyes.

'You are very angry, Walter, and you think it is with me, but I know better, and you cannot prevent me trying to find out what has become of poor Lizzie. I loved her, and love has certain rights, even you will admit that.'

Her gentle words relieved the tension of his passion, and he became calmer in a moment.

'If it is true that she is in Glasgow, it is easy knowing what has become of her,' he said, with an ironical smile. 'Take my advice, and let her alone. She never was company for you, anyhow, and now less than ever. Let her alone.'

'Oh, I can't do that, Walter. You have no idea how much I have thought about her. It has often kept me from sleeping, I assure you. I have so many blessings, I wish to share them. To make others happy is all the use money is for.'

Walter was secretly touched, secretly yearning over her with a passion of admiration — ay, and of sympathy, but his passive face betrayed nothing. He listened as he might have listened to a customer's complaint, yet with even a slighter exhibition of interest. Strange that he should thus be goaded against his better impulses to show so harsh a front to the being he passionately loved, unless it was part of the *rôle* he had mapped out for himself.

'I heard that you had invited Teen Balfour to your estate; is she there yet?' he asked; and Gladys did not know whether he asked in scorn or in jest.

'Yes, she is at Bourhill still, and will remain for some time. Have you got anybody in Mrs. Macintyre's place? It was rather selfish of me, perhaps, to take her away without consulting you.'

'It didn't affect me in the least, I assure you. Mrs. Macintyre was not indispensable to my comfort. So you like being a fine rich lady? Don't you remember how I prophesied you would, and how indignant you were? After all, there is a good deal of worldly wisdom in the slums.'

'You prophesied that I should in a week forget, or wish to forget, this place, and that has not come true, since I am here today,' she said, trying to smile, though her heart was sore. 'Won't you tell me now how you are getting on? Excuse me saying that I don't think you look very prosperous or very happy.'

'Nevertheless, the thing will pay; there isn't any doubt about the prosperity. As for the happiness,' he added, with a shrug of the shoulders, 'I don't think there is much real happiness in this world.'

'Oh yes, there is,' she cried eagerly, 'a great deal of it, if only one will take the trouble to look for it. It is in little things, Walter, that happiness is found, and you might be very happy indeed, if you would not delight in being so bitter and morose. It is so very bad for you. Some day, when you want to throw it off, you will not be able to do so, because it will have become a habit with you. I must tell you quite plainly what I think, because it makes me so unhappy to see you like this. You always remind me of Ishmael, whose hand was against every man. What has changed you so terribly?'

'Circumstances. Yes, I am the victim of circumstances.'

'There is no such thing,' said Gladys calmly. 'That is a phrase with which people console themselves in misfortunes they often bring upon themselves. If you would only think of the absurdity of what you are saying. You have admitted your prosperity; and the other troubles, home troubles, which I know are very trying, need not overwhelm you. You are much less manly, Walter, now you are a man, than I expected you to be. You have quite disappointed me, and without reason.'

He was surprised, and could not hide it. The gentle, simple, shrinking girl had changed into a self-reliant, keen-sighted woman, and from the serene height of her gracious womanhood calmly convicted him of his folly and his besetting weakness, and, manlike, his first impulse, thus convicted, was to resent her interference.

'Whatever I may do, it can't affect you now, you are so far removed from me,' he said, without looking at her; and Gladys, disappointed, and a little indignant, rose to go.

'Very well; good-bye. It is always the same kind of good-bye,' she said quietly. 'If ever, when you look back upon it, it should grieve you, remember it was always your doing, yours alone. But even yet, though you may not believe it, Walter, your old friend will remain quite unchanged.'

His face flushed, and he dashed his hand with a hasty gesture across his eyes.

'I am not changed,' he said huskily. 'You need not reproach me with that. You know nothing about the struggle it is for me here, nor what I have to fight against. It was you who taught me first to be discontented with my lot, to strive after something higher. I sometimes wish now that we had never met.'

'Whatever happens, Walter, I shall never wish that; and I hope one day you will be sorry for ever having said such a thing,' she said, with a proud ring in her clear, sweet voice. 'I hope — I hope one day everything will be made right; just now it all seems so very wrong and hard to bear.'

She left him hurriedly then, just as she had left him before, at the moment when he could have thrown himself at her feet, and revealed to her all the surging passion of his soul.

Gladys felt so saddened and disheartened that she could not bear to return to Bellairs Crescent, to the inevitable questioning which she knew awaited her there. If the Fordyces were kind, they were also a trifle fussy, and sometimes nettled Gladys by their too obvious and exacting interest in her concerns. She ran up to the office in St. Vincent Street, and told Mr. Fordyce she was going off to Mauchline by the one-o'clock train, and begged him to send a boy with an explanation to the Crescent. Mr. Fordyce was very good-natured, and not at all curious; it never occurred to him to try and dissuade her from such a hurried departure, or pester her with questions about it. He simply set her down to write her note at his own desk, then took her out to lunch, and finally put her in her train, all in his own easy, pleasant, fatherly way, and Gladys felt profoundly grateful to him.

Her arrival being unexpected, there was no one to meet her at Mauchline Station, but the two-and-a-half-mile walk did not in the least disconcert her. It seemed as if the clear, cool south wind — the wind the huntsman loves — blew all the city cobwebs from her brain, and again raised her somewhat jaded spirits. She could even think hopefully of Liz, and her mind was full of schemes for her redemption, when she espied, at a short distance from her own gates, the solitary figure of Teen, with her hand shading her eyes, looking anxiously down the road. She had found life at Bourhill insufferably dull without its mistress.

'Have ye walkit a' that distance?' she cried breathlessly, having run all her might to meet her. 'Ye'll be deid tired. What way did ye no' send word?'

'Because I came off all in a hurry this morning,' answered Gladys, with a smile; for the warm welcome glowing in the large eyes of the little seamstress did her good. 'And how have you been — you and Miss Peck, and all the people?'

'Fine; but, my, it's grand to see ye back,' said Teen, with a boundless satisfaction. 'It's no' like the same place when ye are away. An' hoo's Glesca lookin' — as dreich as ever?'

'Quite. And oh, Teen, I have found Liz at last. I saw her last night in Berkeley Street.'

'Saw Liz in Berkeley Street? Surely, never!' repeated Teen, aghast.

'It is quite true. I think she cannot have been away from Glasgow at all. We must try and find her, you and I, and get her down here.'

'I'll get her, if she's in Glesca!' cried Teen excitedly. 'Did ye speak to her? What did she look like?'

'Very ill, I thought, and strange,' answered Gladys slowly. 'She only peeped into our carriage window as we drove away from the concert hall.'

'It's queer,' said Teen musingly, — 'very queer. I feel as if I wad like to gang back to Glesca this very day, and see her.'

'You might go tomorrow, if you like,' said Gladys. 'I daresay you will find her much quicker than I should; she would not be so shy of you.'

Teen turned her head and gave Gladys a strange, intent look, which seemed to ask a question. The girl was indeed asking herself whether it might not be better to let the whole matter rest. She suspected that there might be in this case wheels within wheels which might seriously involve the happiness of her who deserved above all others the highest happiness the world can give. The little seamstress was perplexed, saddened, half afraid, torn between two loves and two desires. She wished she knew how much or how little George Fordyce was to Gladys Graham, yet dared not to ask the question.

But so great was the absorbing desire of Gladys to find means of communication with Liz that she would not let the matter rest. Next day the visit of the little seamstress to Bourhill was brought apparently to a very sudden end and she returned to town — not, however, to sue for work at the hands of the stony-visaged forewoman, but to carry out the behest of the young lady of Bourhill.

CHAPTER XXIX.

AN AWAKENING.

The interview with Gladys upset Walter for the day. When she was gone, he found it impossible to fix his attention on his books or any of the details of his business. He could not even sit still, but wandered restlessly up and down his domain, trying to unravel his own thoughts. The subtle fragrance of her presence, like some rare perfume, seemed to pervade the place, and her words continued to haunt him, till he felt angry and impatient with her, with himself, with all the world. He had now two persons in his employment — a man who delivered goods on a hand-barrow, and a lad who filled a position similar to that which had been Walter's own in Abel Graham's days.

When this lad returned after the dinner hour, Walter left him in charge, and took himself into the streets, pursued by that vague restlessness he could neither understand nor shake off. Looking in at the mirrored window of a great shop in St. Vincent Street, he saw the image of himself reflected, a tall, lean figure, shabbily clad — an image which filled him with a sudden loathing and contempt. He stood quite still, and calmly appraised himself, taking in every meagre detail of his appearance, noting the grimy hue of the collar he had worn three days, the glazed front of the frayed black tie, the soft, greasy rim of the old hat. Yes, he told himself, he was a most disreputable-looking object, with nothing in his appearance to suggest prosperity, or even decent comfort. A grim humour smote him suddenly, and thrusting his hand into his pocket, he brought it out full of money, and rapidly counted it. Then he opened the door of the fashionable tailor's, and walked in. He was regarded, as was to be expected, a trifle superciliously by the immaculately-attired young gentlemen therein.

'I want a suit of clothes,' he said in his straight, abrupt fashion, — 'a good suit; the best you have in your shop.'

The young gentlemen regarded him and each other with such significance in their glances that their shabby-looking customer turned on his heel.

'I can be served elsewhere, I guess, without so much hesitation,' he said, and in an instant he was intercepted with profuse apologies, and patterns of the best materials in the shop laid before him.

'I'll take this,' said Walter, after refusing several.

'It is very expensive, sir — beautiful material, but a suit made

to measure will be five guineas,' said the young gentleman suggestively.

'I'll take it,' said Walter calmly. 'And I want an overcoat, and a
hat, and some other things. Show me what you have.'

The fascination of choosing new garments for personal wear
was upon Walter Hepburn, and he spent a whole hour in the shop,
selecting an outfit which did credit to his taste and discernment.
Before that hour was over he had risen very considerably in the
opinion of those who served him — his choice invariably falling
on what was not only most expensive, but in the best taste.

'Now, how much is to pay? I'll pay ready money today, and
send for the things when they are ready, which I hope will be
soon.'

'Very well, sir; but there is no hurry, I assure you,' said the
young gentleman suavely. 'Payment on delivery is always quite satisfactory.'

'I'll pay today,' Walter replied, with his hand in his pocket; and
when the bill was presented he ran his eye over it without a change
of face.

'Twelve pounds eight shillings and twopence,' he said slowly,
and counted out the bank notes carelessly, as if the handling of
them was his daily work. Then, having made arrangements for fitting, he went his way, leaving a very odd impression on the minds
of the shop people. Had he heard their surmises and comments,
he would have felt at once amused and chagrined.

From St. Vincent Street he sauntered back to Argyle Street,
and took a Bridgeton car. Thoughts of Liz were crowding thick
and fast upon him, and he found himself scanning the faces of the
people in the crowded streets, and even looking up expectantly
each time the car stopped, assuring himself he would not be in the
least surprised were his sister to appear suddenly before him. He
was ill at ease concerning her. If it were true that she was in
Glasgow, then his first fears concerning her were likely to have
some foundation. It was curious that all resentment seemed to
have died out of his mind, and that he felt nothing but an indescribable longing to see her again. Strange and unnatural as it may
seem, he had not for a very long time felt any such kindly affection
towards his parents. He did his duty by them so far as the giving of
money was concerned, but they lay upon his heart like a heavy
weight, and he lived in dread of some calamity happening, for
they were seldom sober. He could not help asking himself sometimes whether he was justified in giving them so liberal an allow-
ance, since relief from all pecuniary anxiety seemed to have only
made them more dissipated and abandoned. It was very seldom
indeed that his father now wrought a day's work. These were

heavy burdens for the young man to bear, and he may be forgiven his morbid pride, his apparent hardness of heart. It is a common saying that living sorrows are worse than death — they eat like a canker into the soul. It was his anxiety about Liz which took Walter to the dreary house in Bridgeton at that unusual hour of the day. He thought it quite likely that if she were in Glasgow they would have seen or heard something of her. He made a point of visiting them once a week, and his step was never buoyant as he ascended that weary stair, nor when he descended it on his home-ward way, for he was either saddened and oppressed anew with their melancholy state, or wearied with reproaches, or disgusted with petty grumblings and unsavoury details of the neighbours' shortcomings and domestic affairs. It is a tragedy we see daily in our midst, this gradual estrangement of those bound by ties of blood, and who ought, but cannot possibly be bound by ties of love. Love must be cherished; it is only in the rarest instances it can survive the frost of indifference and neglect. The drink fiend has no respect of persons; the sanctity of home and God-given affections is ruthlessly destroyed, high and holy ambitions sacri-ficed, hearts remorselessly broken, graves dug above the heaven-liest hopes.

Walter Hepburn was always grave, oftentimes sorrowful, because with the years had come fuller knowledge, keener percep-tion, clearer visions that the sorrows of his youth were sorrows which could darken his young manhood and shadow all his future. It was a profound relief to him that day to find his mother tidier than usual, busy with preparations for the mid-day meal. He never knew how he should find them; too often a visit to that home made him sick at heart.

'Ye are an early visitor, my man,' his mother said, in surprise. 'What's brocht ye here at sic a time?'

'Is Liz here?' he inquired, with a quick glance round the kitchen.

'Liz! No.'

In her surprise at this unexpected question, Mrs. Hepburn paused, with the lid of the broth-pot in her hand, looking won-deringly into her son's face.

'What gars ye ask that?'

'I heard she was in Glasgow, that's why,' Walter answered cau-tiously. 'Where's the old man? Not working, surely?'

'Ay; he's turned over a new leaf for three days, workin' orra at Stevenson's; they're short o' men the noo. He'll be in to his denner the noo. Wull ye tak' a bite wi' us? It's lang since ye broke breid in this hoose.'

'I don't mind if I do,' replied Walter, laying off his hat and drawing the arm-chair up to the fire. 'So you have never seen Liz? The person that saw her must have made a mistake.'

'Wha was't?'

'A lady. You don't know her. Have you never heard anything about her at all, then?'

'No' a cheep. She's in London, they say — the folk that pretend to ken a'thing. I'm sure I'm no' carin'.'

'And my father's really working this week? Oh, mother, if only he would keep steady, it would make all the difference. You look better yourself, too. Are you not far better without drink?'

'Maybe. We've made a paction, onyway, for a week, till we see,' said Mrs. Hepburn, with a slow smile. 'The way o't was this. We fell oot wan day, an' he cuist up to me that I couldna keep frae't, an' I jist says, says I, "Ye canna keep frae't yersel'," an' it's for spite we're no' touchin't. I dinna think mysel' he'll staun' oot past Seterday.'

Walter could not forbear a melancholy smile.

'It's not a very high motive, but better spite than no motive at all,' he answered. 'D'ye think, mother, that Liz can be in Glasgow?'

'Hoo should I ken? There's yer faither's fit on the stair, an' the tatties no' ready, but they'll be saft in a jiffy. He canna wait a meenit for his meat. As I say, he thinks it should be walkin' doon the stair to meet him. Ay, my man, it's you I'm on.'

She made a great clatter with knives and spoons on the table, and then made a rush to pour the water off the potatoes.

'Hulloa, Wat, what's up?' inquired the old man, as genuinely surprised as his wife had been to see his son.

'I heard Liz was in Glasgow, and I came to see if she was here,' answered Walter. 'So you're working again? I must say work agrees with you, father; you look a different man.'

'Oh, I'm no' past wark. If I like, I can dae my darg wi' ony man,' he replied rather ironically. 'Pit oot the kale, Leezbeth, or we'll be burnt to daith. Are ye slack yersel' that ye can come ower here at wan o'clock in the day?'

'I'm slacker than I was,' said Walter, 'but I can't complain, either.'

'An' what was that ye said aboot Liz, that she was here in Glesca? Weel, if she is, she's never lookit near. It's gentry bairns we hae, Leezbeth; let's be thankfu' for them.'

This mild sarcasm did not greatly affect Walter, he was too familiar with it.

'I heard she had been seen, but perhaps it was a mistake. It must have been, or she would surely have come here. You are working at Stevenson's, mother says; will it be permanent?'

'I'll see. It depends on hoo I feel,' replied the old man complacently. 'I've been in waur places, an' the gaffer's very slack. He disna work a ten-hoors' day ony mair than the rest o's.'

'Though you are paid for it, I suppose?' said Walter.

'Ay, but naebody but a born fule will kill himsel' unless he's made dae't,' was the reply.

'I wouldn't keep a man who didn't do a fair day's work for a fair day's wage, nor would you,' said Walter. 'I believe that nobody would make more tyrannical masters than working men themselves, just as women who have been servants themselves make the most exacting mistresses.'

'This is Capital speakin' noo, Leezbeth,' said his father very sarcastically. 'It's kind o' amusin'. We're the twa sides, as it were — Capital and Labour. Ye've no' been lang o' forgettin' whaur ye sprang frae, my man.'

Walter's father had been a skilful workman in his day, with an intelligence above the average; had he kept from drink, there is no doubt he would have risen from the ranks. Even yet gleams of the old spirit which had often displayed itself at workmen's meetings and demonstrations would occasionally shine forth. Walter was thankful to see it, and after spending a comparatively pleasant hour with them, he went his way with a lighter and happier feeling about them than he had experienced for many a day.

CHAPTER XXX.

TOO LATE!

George Fordyce was listening to a maternal lecture the morning after a dance, at which he had been distributing his attentions very freely among the most attractive of the young ladies present. The breakfast was nearly an hour late, and mother and son partook of it alone, Mr. Fordyce being in London on business, and the fair Julia not yet out of bed.

'It's all your nonsense, mother,' said George imperturbably. 'I didn't pay special court to anybody except Clara. She was the best dancer in the room and very nearly the handsomest girl.'

'You should have pity on Clara, my dear,' his mother said indulgently. 'You know she is fond of you; she can't hide it, poor thing, and it is a shame to pay her too much attention in public, when it can't come to anything.'

'I can't help it if girls will be silly,' was the complacent reply. 'Clara is all very well as a cousin, but I'd like more spirit in a wife.'

'It strikes me you will get enough of it if you should be successful where we wish you to be successful,' said his mother, with a keen glance across the table. 'Gladys Graham is a very self-willed piece of humanity. Your Aunt Isabel told me only yesterday of her absurd fad to have common girls visiting her at Bourhill. It is quite time somebody took her firmly in hand, or she will become that insufferable kind of person, a woman with a mission to set the world right.'

George emptied his coffee-cup, and returned his mother's look with one equally steady and keen.

'There is no use going on at me, mother. I've done all I can do in the meantime. I asked her, and she' —

'Did not refuse you, I hope?' exclaimed Mrs. Fordyce, with a gasp.

'Well, not quite; she said I must leave her alone for a long time, and I mean to. It isn't pleasant for a fellow to be sat on by a girl — especially,' he added, with a significant shrug, 'when he isn't used to it.'

'I wish you would tell me when all this happened. You have been very close about it, George,' his mother said reproachfully.

'I wish I had remained close; but now that I've let the cat out, I may as well tell the whole tale. It was only a fortnight ago — that Saturday afternoon I was down at Bourhill. I had no intention of committing myself when I went, but somehow I got carried away, and asked her. I believe I should have had a more favourable answer, but a confounded maid came in with tea — as they always do when nobody wants them.'

'And what did she say?' queried Mrs. Fordyce, in breathless interest.

'Faith, I can't remember exactly,' George replied, and his mother was more than astonished to see his cheek flushing. 'I know she asked me to wait, and not to bother her. I believe she'll have me in the end. Anyhow, I mean to have her, and it's the same thing, isn't it?'

'I hope it may be; but if you take my advice, my dear, don't leave her alone too much, in case somebody else more enterprising and not so easily repulsed should step in before you. If I were a man I wouldn't walk off for a girl's first No.'

'You don't know a blessed thing about what you're talking of, mother,' replied George, with calm candour. 'If you were a man, and had a girl looking at you with a steady stare, and telling you to get out, well, I guess you'd get out pretty quick, that's all.'

Mrs. Fordyce laughed.

'Well, perhaps so; but it is very important that you should follow up your advantage, however slight it may be. It would be a most desirable alliance. Think of her family; it would be a splendid connection. You would be a county gentleman, to begin with.'

'And call myself Fordyce Graham? Eh, mother?' said George lazily. 'There are worse sounding names. But Gladys herself affects to have no pride in her long descent; that very day she was quoting to me that rot of Burns about rank being only the guinea stamp, and all that sort of thing. All very well for a fellow like Burns, who was only a ploughman. It has done Gladys a lot of harm living in the slums; it won't be easy eradicating her queer notions, I can tell you.'

'Oh, after she is married, if you take her well in hand, it will be easy enough,' said his mother confidently. 'She did not give you a positive refusal, then?'

'No; but I'm not going to make myself too cheap,' said George; 'it seldom pays in any circumstances — in dealings with women, never. They set all the more store by a fellow who thinks a good deal of himself.'

'Then you should be very successful,' said Mrs. Fordyce, with a smile. 'Well, remember that nothing will give your father and me greater pleasure than to hear that you are engaged to Gladys Graham.'

'Well, I'd better get out of this. Twenty minutes to eleven! By Jove, wonder what the governor would say if he were to pop in just now? Thunder's not in it.'

So the amiable and self-satisfied George took himself off to the mill, and all day long thought much of his mother's advice, and somehow he felt himself being impelled towards paying another visit to Bourhill. Out of that visit arose portentous issues, which were to have the strongest possible influence upon the future of Gladys Graham. He found her in a lonely and impressionable mood, and left the house, to his own profound astonishment, an accepted lover.

That very evening, after he was gone, Gladys sat by the fire in her spacious drawing-room, turning upon her third finger the diamond ring George Fordyce had transferred from his own hand to hers, whispering as he did so that she should soon have one worthier of her. Watching the flashing of the stone in the gleaming firelight, she wondered to see tears, matching the diamonds in brilliance, falling on her gown. She did not understand these tears; she did not think herself unhappy, though she felt none of that passionate, trembling joy which happy love, as she had heard and read of it, is entitled to feel. She realised that she had taken a great and important step in life, and that it seemed to weigh upon her, that was all. In her loneliness she longed passionately for some sympathetic soul to lean upon. Miss Peck had gone back to the fen country to see a dying friend, and for some days she had heard nothing of Teen, who was pursuing in Glasgow her search for the lost and mysterious Liz. In the midst of the strange reverie she heard footsteps on the stair, and presently a knock came to the door. As it was opened, the silver chimes of the old brass clock rang seven.

'Mr. Hepburn.'

Gladys sprang up, struck by the familiar name, yet not expecting to behold her old companion in the flesh, and there he was, standing modestly, yet with so much manliness and courage in his bearing, that she could not forbear a little cry of welcome as she ran to him with outstretched hands. It seemed as if her prayer for the sympathy of one who understood her was answered far beyond any hope or expectations she had cherished regarding it.

'Oh, Walter, I am so very glad to see you! It is so good of you to come. I have so often wished to see you here. Come away, come away!'

The accepted lover, at that moment being whirled back by express train to Glasgow, would not have approved of those warm words, nor of the light shining all over the girl's sweet face as she uttered them. But he would have been compelled to admit that in Gladys's old companion of the slums he had no mean rival. The St. Vincent Street tailor had done his duty by his eccentric customer, and not only given him value for his money, but converted him, so far as outward appearance goes, into a new man. Philosophers and cynics have from time to time had their fling at the tyranny of clothes, but it still remains an undisputed fact that a well-dressed man is always much more comfortable and self-respecting than an ill-dressed one. When Walter Hepburn beheld the new man the tailor had turned out, a strange change came over him, and he saw in himself possibilities hitherto undreamed of. He realised for the first time that he looked fitter than most men to win a woman's approval, and I am quite safe in saying that Gladys owed this totally unlooked-for visit entirely to the St. Vincent Street tailor.

'So very glad to see you,' she repeated, and she thought it no treachery to her absent lover to keep hold of the hand she had taken in greeting. 'And looking so nice and so handsome! Oh, Walter, now I am no longer unhappy about you, for I see you have awakened at last to a sense of what you ought to be.'

It was a tribute to clothes, but it sank with unalloyed sweetness into the young man's heart.

'You are very kind to me, Gladys, and I do not deserve any such welcome. I was afraid, indeed, that you might refuse to see me, as you would be perfectly justified in doing.'

'Oh, Walter,' she said reproachfully, 'how dare you say such a thing? Refuse to see you, indeed! Do sit down and tell me everything. Do you know, it is just my dinner hour, and you shall dine with me; and how delightful that will be. I thought of sending down to say I didn't wish any dinner, it is so lonely eating alone.'

'Where is the lady who lives with you? You had a lady, hadn't you?'

'Yes — Miss Peck. She has gone back to Lincoln to see her aunt who is dying, and I am quite alone, though tomorrow I expect one of Mr. Fordyce's daughters. And now, tell me, have you heard anything of Liz?'

The voice sank to a grave whisper, and her eyes grew luminous with anxiety and sympathetic concern.

'Nothing,' Walter answered, with a shake of his head, 'and I have been inquiring all round, too. My father and mother have never seen or heard anything of her. I think you must have made a mistake that night in Berkeley Street.'

'If it was not Liz, it was her ghost,' said Gladys quite gravely. 'I cannot understand it. But, come, let us go down-stairs. You ought to offer me your arm, Walter. I cannot help laughing when I think of Mrs. Fordyce, she would be so horrified were she to see me now. She tries so hard to make me quite conventional, and she isn't able to do it.'

'She may be right, though,' said Walter, and though he would have given worlds for the privilege, he dared not presume to take Gladys at her word and offer her his arm. But they went into the dining-room side by side; and at the table, Gladys, though watching keenly, detected very little of the old awkwardness, none at all of that blunt rudeness of speech and manner which had often vexed her sensitive soul. For the first time for many many months Walter permitted himself to be at ease and perfectly natural in his manner, and the result was entirely satisfactory; self-consciousness is fatal to comfort always. Gladys wore a black gown of some shimmering soft material, with a quaint frill of old lace falling over the low collar, a bunch of spring snowdrops at her belt, and her lovely hair bound with the black velvet band which none could wear just in the same way — a very simple, unostentatious home toilet, but she looked, Walter thought, like a queen. Possessed of a wonderful tact, Gladys managed, while the meal progressed, to confine the conversation to commonplace topics, so that the servant who attended should not be furnished with food for remark. Both were glad, however, to return to the drawing-room, where their talk could be quite unrestrained.

'And now you are going to tell me everything about this wonderful metamorphosis,' she said merrily, — 'every solitary thing. When did it dawn upon you that even a handsome man is utterly dependent on his tailor?'

There was at once rebuke and approval conveyed in this whimsical speech, which made Walter's face slightly flush.

'It dawned upon me one day, looking in at a shop window where I could see myself, that I was a most disreputable-looking object, quite eligible to be apprehended as an able-bodied vagrant.'

'How delightful! I hope the shock was very bad, because you deserved it. Now that you have come back clothed and in your right mind, I am not going to spare you, Walter, and I will say that after my last visit to Colquhoun Street I quite lost hope. It is always the darkest hour before the dawn, somebody has said.'

'If I'd thought you cared' — Walter began, but stopped suddenly; for Gladys turned from the table, where she was giving her attention to some drooping flowers, and her look was one of the keenest wonder and reproach.

'Now you are weak, Walter, trying to bring your delinquencies home to me,' she said, with the first touch of sharpness he had ever seen in her. 'It has been your own fault entirely all along, and I have never had a solitary bit of sympathy for you, and I don't know, either, what you meant by going on in any such manner.'

'I didn't understand it myself then; I seemed goaded on

always to be a perfect brute when you came. But I believe I understand it now, and perhaps it would be better if I did not.'

He spoke with considerable agitation, which Gladys affected not to notice, while her white fingers touched the drooping blossoms tenderly, as if sympathising with them that their little day was over.

'Suppose you enlighten me, then?' she said, gaily still; then suddenly seeing his face, her own became very white.

'I don't dare,' he said hoarsely, 'it is too much presumption; but it will perhaps make you understand and feel for me more than you seem to do. Don't you see, Gladys, that it is my misery to care for you as happier men care for the woman they ask to marry them?'

There was a moment's strained silence, then Gladys spoke in a low, sobbing voice, —

'It is, as I said, Walter, too late, too late! I have promised to marry another man.'

CHAPTER XXXI.

WHAT MIGHT HAVE BEEN.

All the eagerness died out of Walter's face, and he turned away immediately as if to leave the room. But Gladys prevented him; her face still red with the hot flush his passionate words had called up, she stood before him, and laid her hand upon his arm.

'You will not go away now, Walter, just when I hope we are beginning to understand each other. Do sit down for a little. There is a great deal left to us, — we can still be friends, — yes, a great deal.'

'It will be better for me to go away,' he said, not bitterly nor resentfully, but with a quiet manliness which made the heart of Gladys glow with pride in him, though it was sore with another feeling she did not quite understand.

'By and by, but not yet,' she said coaxingly. 'Besides, you cannot get a train just now, even if you were at the station this moment. You shall be driven into Mauchline in time for the nine-fifteen, and that is an hour hence. I cannot let you go now, Walter, for I do not know when I shall see you again.'

She spoke with all the frank, childlike simplicity of the old time, and he turned back meekly and took his seat again, though it seemed for the moment as if all brightness and energy had gone out of him. Her hands trembled very much as they resumed their delicate task among the flowers, and her sweet mouth quivered too, though she tried to speak bravely and brightly as before.

'Do tell me, Walter, what you are thinking of doing now that your business has become so prosperous. Don't you think you have lived quite long enough in that dingy Colquhoun Street?'

'Perhaps so. I had thoughts of leaving it, but it is a great thing for a man to be on the premises. Your uncle would not have approved of my leaving the place so soon. Colquhoun Street was good enough for him all his days,' said Walter, striving to speak naturally, and only partially succeeding.

'Ah, yes, poor man; but just think how much he denied himself to give me all this,' she said, with a glance round the beautiful room. 'How much happier he and I would have been with something a little lower than this, and a little higher than Colquhoun Street. It often makes me sad to think of the poverty of his life and the luxury of mine.'

'But you were made for luxurious living,' was Walter's quick reply. 'You never looked at home in the old place. This suits you down to the ground.'

'Do you think so?' Gladys gave a little melancholy smile. 'Yet so contradictory are we, that sometimes I am not at all happy nor contented here, Walter.'

'You ought to be very happy,' he replied a trifle sharply. 'You have everything a woman needs to make her happy.'

'Perhaps so, and yet' —

She paused, and hummed a little scrap of song which Walter did not catch.

'I am becoming quite an accomplished violinist, Walter,' she said presently. 'I have two lessons every week; once Herr Döller comes down, and once I go up. Would you like to hear me play, or shall we talk?'

'I don't know. It would really be better for me to go away. I can walk to the station; the walk will do me good.'

'I will not allow you to walk nor go away, Walter, even if you are as cross as two sticks; and I must say I feel rather cross myself.'

They were playing with edged tools, and Gladys was keenly conscious of it. Her pulses were throbbing, her heart beating as it had never beat in the presence of the man to whom she had plighted her troth that very day. A very little more, and she must have given way to hysterical sobbing, she felt so overwrought; and yet all the while she kept on her lips that gay little smile, and spoke as if it were the most natural thing in the world that they should be together. But when Walter remained silent, she came forward to the hearth quickly, and, forgetting that what was fitting in the old days was not permissible in the new, she slipped on one knee on the rug, and suddenly, laying her head down on his knee, began to cry.

'Gladys, get up! For God's sake, get up, or I can't hold my tongue. This is fearful!'

The word was none too strong. The solitary and absorbing passion of his life, a pure and honest love for that beautiful girl, surged in his soul, and his face betrayed the curb he was putting on himself. He had had but a poor upbringing, and his code of honour had been self-taught, but he was manly enough to be above making love to another man's promised wife.

'Don't make it any harder for me,' he said hoarsely. 'I know you are sorry for me. You have been always an angel to me, even when I least deserved it; but this is not the way to treat me tonight. Let me away.'

'Let me be selfish, Walter, just this one night,' she said, in a low, broken voice. 'I don't know why I am crying, for it is a great joy to me that you are here, and that I know now, for ever, that you feel as you used to do before this cruel money parted us; there are not in all the world any friends like the old. Forgive me if I have vexed you.'

She rose up and met his glance, which was one of infinite pity and indescribable pathos. The greatest sorrow, the keenest disappointment which had ever come to Walter, softened him as if with a magic touch, and revealed to her his heart, which was, at least, honest and true in every throb.

'You can never vex me, though I have often vexed you. I need scarcely say I hope you will be happy with the one you have chosen. You deserve the very best in the world, and even the best is not good enough for you.'

A faint smile shone through the tears on the girl's face.

'What has changed you so, Walter? It is as if a whirlwind had swept over you.'

'I have never changed in that particular,' he answered half gloomily. 'I have always thought the same of you since the day I saw you first.'

'Oh, Walter, do you remember our little school in the evenings, with Uncle Abel dozing in the chimney-corner, and your difficulties over the arithmetic? Very often you asked me questions I could not answer, though I am afraid I was not honest enough always to say I did not know. Sometimes I gave you equivocal answers, didn't I?'

'I don't know; all I know is, that I shall never forget these days, though they can never come again,' answered Walter. 'I am learning German this winter, and I like it very much.'

'How delightful! If you go on at this rate, in a very short time I shall be afraid to speak to you, you will have grown such a grand and clever gentleman.'

Walter gave his head a quick shake, which made the waved mass of his dark hair drop farther on his brow. A fine brow it was, square, solid, massive, from beneath which looked out a pair of clear eyes, which had never feared the face of man. He looked older than his years, though his face was bare, except on the upper lip, where the slight moustache appeared to soften somewhat the sterner line of the mouth. Yes, it was a good, true face, suggestive of power and possibility — the face of an honest man. Then his figure had attained its full height, and being clothed in well-made garments, looked very manly, and not ungraceful. Gladys admired him where he stood, and inwardly contrasted him with a certain other youth, who devoted half his attention to his personal appearance and adornment. Nor did Walter suffer by that comparison.

'Must you go away?' she asked wistfully, not conscious how cruel she was in seeking to keep him there when every moment was pointed with a sorrowful regret, a keen anguish of loss which he could scarcely endure. 'And when will you come again?'

'Oh, I don't know. I can't come often, Gladys; it will be better not, now.'

'It is always better not,' she cried, with a strange petulance. 'There is always something in the way. If you knew how often I want to talk to you about all my plans. I always think nobody quite understands us like those whom we have known in our early days, because then there can never be any pretence or concealment. All is open as the day. Is it impossible that we can still be as we were?'

'Quite impossible.' His answer was curt and cold, and he was on his feet again, moving towards the door.

'But why?' she persisted, with all the unreason of a wilful woman. 'May a woman not have a friend, though he should be a man?'

'It would not be possible, and *he* would not like it,' he said significantly; and Gladys flushed all over, and flung up her head with a gesture of defiance.

'He shall not dictate to me,' she said proudly. 'Well, if you will go, you will, I suppose, but you shall not walk; on that point I am determined.' She rang the bell, gave her order for the carriage, and looked at him whimsically, as if rejoicing in her own triumph. 'I am afraid I am becoming quite autocratic, Walter, so many people have to do exactly as I tell them. If you will not come, will you write to me occasionally, then? It would be delightful to get letters from you, I think.'

Never was man so subtlely flattered, so tempted. Again he bit his lip, and without answering, he took a handsome frame from the piano, and glanced indifferently at the photograph he held.

'Is this the man?' he asked at hazard, and when Gladys nodded, he looked at it again with keener interest. It was the same picture of George Fordyce in his hunting-dress which Gladys had first seen in the drawing-room at Bellairs Crescent.

'A grand gentleman,' he said, with a faint note of bitterness in his tone. 'Well, I hope you will be happy.'

This stiff, conventional remark appeared to anger Gladys somewhat, and for the first time in her life she cast a reproach at him.

'You needn't look so resigned, Walter. Just cast your memory back, and think of some of the kind things you have said to me when we have met since I have left Colquhoun Street. If you think I can forget, then you are mistaken. They will always rankle in my mind, and it is only natural that I should feel grateful, if nothing else, to those who are a little kinder and more attentive to me. A woman does not like to be ignored.'

At that moment a servant appeared to say the carriage waited, and Walter held out his hand to say good-bye. Hope was for ever quenched in his heart, and something in his eyes went to the heart of Gladys, and for the moment she could not speak. She turned silently, motioned him to follow her from the room, and then stood in the hall, still silently, till he put on his greatcoat. Woman-like, in the midst of her strange agitation she did not fail to notice that every detail of his attire was in keeping, and that pleased well her fastidious taste. When the servant at last opened the door, the cool wind swept in and ruffled the girl's hair upon her white brow.

'Good-bye, then. You will write?' she said quickly, and longing, she did not know why, to order the servant to withdraw.

'If there is anything to write about, perhaps I will,' he answered, gripped her hand like a vice, and dashed out. Then Miss Graham, quite regardless of the watchful eyes upon her, went out to the outer hall, and her sweet voice sounded through the darkness, 'Good-bye, dear Walter,' and, putting her white fingers to her lips, she threw a kiss after him, and ran into the house, all trembling, and when she reached the drawing-room she dropped upon her knees by a couch and fell to weeping, though she did not know why she wept.

CHAPTER XXXII.

THE WANDERER.

It was half past ten before Walter alighted from the train at St. Enoch's Station. It was a fine dry evening, with a sufficient touch of frost in the air to make walking pleasant. As he made his way out of the station, and went among the busy crowd, he could not help contrasting that hurrying tide of life with the silence and the solitude he had left. The experience of the last few hours seemed like a dream, only he was left with that aching at the heart — that strong sense of personal loss which even a brave man sometimes finds it hard to bear manfully. For till now he had not realised how near and dear a part of his life was the sweet girl now lost to him for ever. Although it had often pleased him, in the bitterness of his mood, to say that an inseparable barrier had arisen between them, he had in his heart of hearts not believed it, but cherished the secret and strong hope that their estrangement was but temporary, and that in the end the old days which in their passing had often been shadowed, but which now to memory looked wholly bright and beautiful, would receive their crown. And now his dream was over, and again he felt himself alone in the world — more terribly alone than he had yet been. He was not a vain man, though he believed in his own ability, or, looking back, he might have taken no small comfort from the demeanour of Gladys towards him. He had not been untouched by it, her womanly tenderness had sunk into his soul; but he saw in it only the natural outcome of a kind heart, which felt always keenly the sorrow of others. He believed so absolutely in her singleness of heart, her honesty of purpose, that he accepted her decision as final. Since she had plighted her troth to another, it was all over, so far as Walter himself was concerned. He knew so little of women that it never occurred to him that sometimes they give such a promise hastily, accepting what is offered from various motives — very often because what they most desire is withheld. It must not be thought that in having accepted George Fordyce, Gladys was intentionally and wilfully deceiving him. His impassioned pleading had touched her heart. At a time when she was crying out for something to satisfy her need, in an unguarded moment, she had mistaken an awakened, fleeting impression for love, and passed what was now in her eyes an irrevocable word. She was no coquette, who gives a promise the one day to be carelessly withdrawn the next. George Fordyce had been fortunate in gaining the promise of a woman whose word was as her bond. There are circumstances in which even such a bond may become null and void, but Gladys did not dream of the tragedy which was to release her from her vow.

Walter felt in no haste to go home; nay, the very thought of it was intolerable to him. He saw it all before him, in sharp contrast to another home, which had shown him how lovely wealth and taste can make human surroundings, and he loathed the humble shelter of the old place, which memory hallowed only to wound, and from which the angel of hope had now flown.

With his hand in one pocket, his hat drawn a little over his brow, he sauntered, with heavy and reluctant step, up Renfield Street, in the direction of Sauchiehall Street. He did not know what tempted him to choose the opposite direction from his home. We are often so led, apparently aimlessly, towards what may change the very current of our lives. The streets, though quieter as he walked farther West, were by no means deserted, and just on the stroke of eleven the people from the theatres and public-houses made the tide of life flow again, apparently in an endless stream. Quite suddenly, under the brilliant light thrown by the illumination of a fashionable tavern, Walter saw standing on the edge of the pavement, talking to another girl, his sister Liz. He could not believe his eyes at first, for he had never credited the assertion of Gladys that she had really seen her, but believed it had been a mistake. But there she was, well dressed, stylish, and beautiful exceedingly. Even in that first startled look he was struck by the exquisite outline, of her face, the absolute purity of her colour, except where it burned a brilliant red on her cheeks.

He stepped back into a doorway, and stood silently waiting till they should separate, or move away. To his relief, they, separated at last, the stranger moving towards him, Liz proceeding westward. He followed her, keeping a few steps behind her, watching her with a detective's eye. Once a man spoke to her, but she gave no answer, and somehow that to Walter was a relief. He felt himself growing quite excited, longing to overtake and speak to her, yet afraid. At the corner of Cambridge Street she stood still, apparently looking for a car; then Walter stepped before her, and laid his hand on her arm.

'Liz,' he said, and in spite of himself his voice shook, 'what are you doing here?'

Liz gave a great start, and her pallor vanished, the red mounting high to her brow.

'I — I don't know. It's you, Wat? Upon my word, I didna ken ye; ye are sic a swell.'

'I heard you were in Glasgow, but I didn't believe it. Where have you been all this time?'

'To Maryhill; I'm bidin' there the noo,' Liz answered defiantly, though she was inwardly trembling.

'Maryhill?' Walter repeated, and his eye, sharp with suspicion, dwelt searchingly on her face. 'What are you doing there?'

'That's my business,' she answered lightly. 'I needna ask for you; I see you are flourishin'. Hoo's the auld folk? I say, here's my car. Guid-nicht.'

She would have darted from him, but he gripped her by the arm.

'You won't go, Liz, till I know where and how you are living. I have the right to ask. Come home with me.'

Liz was surprised, arrested, and the car, with its noisy jingle, swept round the corner.

'Hame wi' you!' she repeated. 'Maybe, if ye kent, ye wadna ask me, wadna speak to me,' she said, with a melancholy bitterness, and then her cough, more hollow and more racking than of yore, prevented further speech.

Walter drew her hand within his arm, and she, feebly protesting, allowed him to lead her back the way she had come. And then, as they walked, a strange, constrained silence fell upon them, each finding it difficult, well-nigh impossible, to bridge the gulf of these sad months.

'Are you not going to tell me anything about yourself, Liz?' he asked at length, and the kindness of his tone, unexpected as it was, secretly amazed and touched her.

'Naething,' she answered, without a moment's hesitation. 'An' though I've come back to Glesca, I'm no' seeking onything frae ony o' ye; I can fend for mysel'.'

Walter remained silent for a little. The subject was one of extreme delicacy, and he did not know how to pursue it. He feared that all was not with his sister as it should be, but he feared the result of further questions.

'What's the guid o' me gaun hame wi' you the nicht? I canna bide there,' she said presently, in a sharp, discontented voice. 'An' here ye've gar'd me miss the last car.'

'Where are you staying in Maryhill?'

'I have a place, me an' anither lassie,' she said guardedly. 'If ye are flush, ye micht gie me twa shillin's for a cab. I'm no' able to walk.'

At that moment, and before he could reply, a slim, slight, girlish figure darted across the street, and, with a quick, sobbing breath, laid two hands on the arm of Liz. It was the little seamstress, who had haunted the streets late for many nights, scanning the faces of the wanderers, sustained by the might of the love which was the only passion of her soul. At sight of Teen, Liz Hepburn betrayed more emotion than in meeting with her brother.[Pg 271]

'Eh, I've fund ye at last! I said I was bound to find ye if ye were in Glesca,' Teen cried, and her plain face was glorified with the joy of the meeting. 'Oh, Liz, what it's been to me no' kennin' whaur ye were! But, I say, hoo do you twa happen to be thegither?'

'I've twa detectives efter me, it seems,' said Liz, with a touch of sullenness, and she stood still on the edge of the pavement, as if determined not to go another step. 'I say, do you twa hunt in couples?'

She gave a little mirthless laugh, and her eye roamed restlessly up the street, as if contemplating the possibility of escape.

'Come on hame wi' me, Liz,' said Teen coaxingly, and she slipped her hand through her old friend's arm and looked persuasively into her face, noting with the keenness of a loving interest the melancholy change upon it. 'Ye're no' weel, an' ye'll be as cosy an' quate as ye like wi' me.'

'Has *your* ship come in?' asked Liz, with faint sarcasm, but still hesitating, uncomfortable under the scrutiny of two pairs of questioning, if quite friendly, eyes.

'Ay, has it,' replied the little seamstress cheerfully. 'Shouldn't she come hame wi' me, Walter? She wad be a' richt there, an' you can come an' see us when ye like.'

Walter stood in silence another full minute. It was a strange situation, strained to the utmost, but his faith in the little seamstress was so great that he almost reverenced her. He felt that it would be better for Liz to be with a friend of her own sex, and he turned to her pleadingly.

'It's true what Teen says, you are not well. Let her take you home. I'll get a cab and go with you to the door, and I'll come and see you tomorrow. We are thankful to have found you again, my — my dear.'

The last words he uttered with difficulty, for such expressions were not common on his lips; but some impulse, born of a vast pity, in which no shadow of resentment mingled, made him long to be as tender with her as he knew how. The manner of her reception by these two, whom she had wronged by her long silence, affected Liz deeply, though she made no sign.

'I dinna see what better I can dae, if ye'll no' stump up for the cab to Maryhill,' she said ungraciously. 'A' the same, I wish I had never seen ye. Ye had nae business watchin' for me, ony o' ye. I'm my ain mistress, an' I'm no' needin' onything aff ye.'

The little seamstress nodded to Walter, and he hailed a passing cab. All the time, even after they were inside the vehicle, she never relaxed her hold of Liz, but they accomplished the distance to Teen's poor little home in complete silence. Liz felt and looked like a prisoner; Walter's face wore a sad and downcast expression; the little seamstress only appeared jubilant.

It was nearly midnight when they ascended the long stair to the little garret, and Liz had to pause many times in the ascent to recover her breath and to let her cough have vent. She grumbled all the way up; but when Teen broke up the fire and lit the gas she sank into an old basket-chair with a more contented expression on her face.

'Noo, ye'll hae a cup o' tea in a crack,' Teen said blithely. 'I've gotten a new teapot, Liz; the auld yin positively fell to bits. Wull ye no' bide an' drink a cup, Walter?'

'Not tonight; I think you would be better alone. But I'll come tomorrow and see you, Liz. Good-night; I am sure you will be comfortable here.'

'Oh ay, I dinna doot. I say, ye are a toff, an' nae mistake; ye micht pass for a lord,' she said, with a kind of scornful approbation. 'Ye're risin' in the scale while I'm gaun doon; but I've seen something o' life, onyhoo, an' that's aye something.'

She gave him her hand, which was quite white and unsoiled, languidly, and bade him a careless good-night. As Walter went out of the kitchen, she was surprised, but not more so than he was himself, that two tears rolled down his cheeks. He dashed them away quickly, however, and when the little seamstress accompanied him to the door, he was quite calm again.

'You'll take care of her and not let her away, and I'll be eternally obliged to you. I trust you entirely,' he said quickly.

Teen nodded sagaciously.

'If she gangs oot o' this hoose, she tak's me wi' her,' she said, with a determined curve on her thin lips.

'And whatever you need, come to me,' he said, with his hand in his pocket; but Teen stopped him with a quick gesture.

'I have ony amount o' money I got frae Miss Gladys.'

'Keep it for yourself. You must spend my money on Liz, and see that she wants for nothing. It strikes me a doctor is the first thing she needs, but I'll be back tomorrow. Good-night, and thank you, Teen. You are a good little soul.'

'Middlin',' replied Teen, with a jerk, and closed the door.

CHAPTER XXXIII.

A FAITHFUL FRIEND.

The little seamstress was in a quiver of happy excitement, which betrayed itself in her very step as she returned to the kitchen.

Liz lay back in the old basket-chair with her eyes closed, and the deadly paleness of her face was very striking.

'Ye arena weel, Liz,' she said brusquely. 'It's the stair; ye never could gang up a stair, I mind, withoot bein' oot o' breath. Never mind; the kettle's bilin', an' ye'll hae yer tea in a crack.'

She busied herself about the table with nervous hands, astonished at her own agitation, which did not appear to have communicated itself to Liz, her demeanour being perfectly lifeless and uninterested.

Teen's stock of household napery did not include a tablecloth, but, desirous of doing honour to her guest, she spread a clean towel on the little table, and set out the cups with a good deal of cheerful clatter.

'What'll ye tak'? I have eggs, Liz — real country eggs. I brocht them up frae the country mysel',' she said, thinking to rouse the lethargy of her companion. 'I very near said I saw them laid; onyway, I saw the hens that laid them. Ye'll hae an egg, eh?'

'Yes, if ye like. I havena tasted since eleeven this morning, an' then it was only a dram,' said Liz languidly.

Teen stood still on the little strip of rag-carpet before the fender, and regarded her friend with a mingling of horror and pity. Whatever had been the tragedy of the past few months, Liz had not thereby bettered herself. With a little choking sob, Teen made greater haste with her preparation, and put upon the table a very tempting little meal, chiefly composed of dainties from Bourhill, a very substantial basket having been sent up to the little seamstress by order of Miss Graham. Liz threw off her hat, and, drawing her chair up to the table, took a long draught from the teacup.

'Eh, that's guid,' she said, with a sigh of satisfaction. Ye're better aff than me, efter a', Teen, an' I wish I was in yer place.'

'Ye'll bide here noo ye have come, onyhoo,' said the little seamstress cheerily. 'My ship has come in; but we'll speak upon it efter. I say, isn't Walter lookin' fine? He wad pass for a lord, jist as you said.'

'His looks are a' richt — he maun be makin' money. I say,

where is the lassie that used to bide there? The auld man's deid, isn't he?'

'Ay,' answered Teen; 'deid lang syne. Oh, she's turned into a graund leddy, livin' on an estate in the country. He left a fortin. See, eat up that ither egg, an' there's plenty mair tea. Look at that cream, isn't it splendid?'

'Fine,' said Liz; and as she ate and enjoyed the generous food her colour came again, and she looked a little less ghastly and ill, a little more like the Liz of old. Pen cannot tell the joy it was to the loyal heart of the little seamstress thus to minister to her friend's great need, though in the midst of her deep satisfaction was a secret dread, a vague and vast pity, which made her afraid to ask her a single question. It needed no very keen perception to gather that all was not well with the unhappy girl.

'Weel, I've enjoyed that,' she said, pushing back from the table at last. 'I've eaten ye oot o' hoose and hame, but as yer ship's come in, it'll no' maitter. Tell me a' aboot it.'

'Oh, there's no' much to tell,' answered Teen, with a touch of her natural reserve. 'I've made a rich frien', that's a'.'

'A man?' asked Liz, with interest.

'No; a lady,' replied Teen rather proudly. 'But hae ye naething to tell me aboot yersel'?'

'Oh, I have thoosands to tell, if I like, but I'm no' gaun to tell ye a thing,' replied Liz flatly; but her candour did not even make Teen wince. She was used to it in the old days, and expected nothing else.

'Oh, jist as ye like,' she answered serenely. 'But, tell me, did ye ever gang to London?'

'No,' replied Liz, 'I never went to London. Did ye think I had?'

'Yes. We — that is, some o's thocht — Walter an' me, onyway — that ye had gane to the theatre in London to be an actress. It was gey shabby, I thocht, to gang the way ye did, withoot sayin' a cheep to me, efter a' the plans we had made,' said Teen, with equal candour.

'Maybe it was,' said Liz musingly, and, with her magnificent eyes fixed on the fire, relapsed into silence again, and Teen saw that her face was troubled. Her heart yearned over her unspeakably, and she longed for fuller confidence, which Liz, however, had not the remotest intention of giving.

'I dinna think, judgin' frae appearances, that ye have bettered yoursel',' said the little seamstress slowly.

'Ye think richt. I made wan mistake, Teen — the biggest mistake o' a',' she replied, and her mouth became very stern and bitter, and a dull gleam was visible in her eyes.

Teen waited breathlessly, in the hope that Liz would still confide in her, but having thus delivered herself, she again relapsed into silence.

'What way are ye bidin' at Maryhill?' she asked after a bit, and the same note of suspicion which had been in Walter's questions sounded through her voice. It made the colour rise in the sharply-outlined cheek of Liz, and she replied angrily, —

'It's news ye're wantin', an' ye're no' gaun to get it. Ye brocht me here again' my wull, but ye'll no' cross-question me. I can gang hame even yet. It's no' the first time I've gane hame in the mornin', onyway.'

Teen wisely accepted the inevitable.

'Ye're no' gaun wan fit oot o' this hoose the nicht,' she replied calmly, 'nor the morn either, unless I ken whaur ye are gaun. I dinna think, Liz, ye hae dune very weel for yersel' this while; ye'd better let me look efter ye. Twa heids are aye better than yin.'

'Ye're gaun to be the boss, I see,' said Liz, with a faint smile, and in her utter weariness she let her head fall back again and closed her eyes. 'If I wis to bide here the morn, an' Wat comes, he'd better no' ask me ower mony questions, because I'll no' stand it frae neither you nor him, mind that.'

'Naebody'll ask you questions, my dear,' said Teen, and, lifting back the table, she folded down the bed, and shook up the old wool pillows, wishing for her friend's sake that they were made of down. Then she knelt down on the old rag-carpet, and began to unlace Liz's boots, glancing ever and anon with sad eyes up into the white face, with its haggard mouth and dark closed eyes.

'Ye are a guid sort, Teen, upon my word,' was all the thanks she got. 'I believe I will gang to my bed, if ye'll let me; maybe, if ye kent a', ye wad turn me oot to the street.'

'No' me. If the a's waur than I imagine, it's gey bad,' replied the little seamstress. 'Oh, Liz, I'm that gled to see you, I canna dae enough.'

'I've been twice up your stair, Teen; once I knockit at the door an' then flew doon afore you could open't. Ye think ye've a hard time o't, but there's waur things than sewin' jackets at thirteenpence the dizen.'

Teen's hands were very gentle as she assisted her friend off with her gown, which was a very handsome affair, all velvet and silk, and gilt trimmings, which dazzled the eye.

Thus partially undressed, Liz threw herself without another word on the bed, and in two minutes was asleep. Then, softly laying another bit of coal on the fire, Teen lifted the table back to the hearth, got out pen, ink, and paper, and set herself to a most unusual task, the composition and writing of a letter. I should be afraid to say how long it took her to perform this great task, nor how very poor an accomplishment it was in the end, but it served its purpose, which was to acquaint Gladys with the rescue of Liz. Afraid to disturb the sleeping girl, Teen softly removed a pillow from the bed, and placing it on the floor before the fire, laid herself down, with an old plaid over her, though sleep was far from her eyes. A great disappointment had come to the little seamstress; for though she had long since given up all hope of welcoming back Liz in the guise of a great lady, who had risen to eminence by dint of her own honest striving, she only knew tonight, when the last vestige of her hope had been wrested from her, how absolute and unassailable had been her faith in her friend's honour. And now she knew intuitively the very worst. It needed no sad story from Liz to convince the little seamstress that she had tried the way of transgressors, and found it hard. Mingling with her intense sorrow over Liz was another and, if possible, a more painful fear — lest this deviation from the paths of rectitude might be fraught with painful consequences to the gentle girl whom Teen had learned to love with a love which had in it the elements of worship. These melancholy forebodings banished sleep from the eyes of the little seamstress, and early in the morning she rose, sore, stiff, and unrefreshed, from her hard couch, and began to move about the house again, setting it to rights for Liz's awakening. She, however, slept on, the heavy sleep of complete exhaustion; and finally, Teen, not thinking it wise to disturb her, laid herself down on the front of the bed to rest her tired bones. She too fell asleep, and it was the sunshine upon her face which awakened her, just as the church bells began to ring.

With an exclamation which awoke her companion, she leaped up, and ran to break up the fire, which was smouldering in the grate.

'Mercy me! it's eleeven o'clock; but it's Sunday mornin', so it doesna matter,' she said almost blithely, for in the morning everything seems brighter, and even hard places less hard. 'My certy, Liz, ye've sleepit weel. Hae ye ever wakened?'

'Never; I've no' haen a sleep like that for I canna tell ye hoo lang,' said Liz quite gratefully, for she felt wonderfully rested and refreshed.

In an incredibly short space of time the little seamstress had the kettle singing on the cheery hob, and toasted the bread, while Liz was washing her face and brushing her red locks at the little looking-glass hanging at the window.

They were sitting at their cosy breakfast, talking of commonplace things, when Walter's double knock came to the door. Teen ran to admit him, and, with a series of nods, indicated to him that his sister was all right within. There was a strained awkwardness in their meeting. Liz felt and resented the questioning scrutiny of his eyes, and had not Teen thrown herself into the breach, it would have been a strange interview. As it was, she showed herself to be a person of the finest and most delicate tact, and more than once Walter found himself looking at her with a kind of grateful admiration, and thinking what an odd mistake he had made in his estimate of her character.

When the breakfast was over, Teen, under pretence of going to inquire for a sick neighbour, took herself off, and left the brother and sister alone. It had to come sooner or later, she knew, and she hoped that Liz, in her softer mood, would at least meet Walter half way.

When the door was closed upon the two there was a moment's silence, which Walter broke quite abruptly; it was not his nature to beat about the bush.

'Are you going to tell me this morning where you have been all this time?'

'No,' she answered calmly, 'I'm not.'

This was unpromising, but Walter tried not to notice her defiant manner and tone.

'Very well; I won't ask you, since you don't want to tell. You haven't been prospering, anyhow. Now, any one can see that; but we'll let bygones be bygones. I'm in a good way of doing now, Liz, and if you like to come along to Colquhoun Street and try your hand at housekeeping, I'm ready.'

Liz was profoundly amazed, but not a change passed over her face.

'Ye're no' feared,' was her only comment, delivered at last in a perfectly passionless voice.

'Feared! What for?' he asked, trying to speak pleasantly. 'You're my sister, and I need a housekeeper. I'm thinking of leaving Colquhoun Street, and taking a wee house somewhere in the suburbs. We can talk it over when you come.'

Then Liz sat up and fixed her large, indescribable eyes full on her brother's face.

'An' will ye tak' me withoot askin' a single question, Wat?'

'I can't do anything else,' he answered good-humouredly.

'But I've lost my character,' she said then, in a perfectly matter-of-fact voice.

Although he was in a manner prepared for it, this calm announcement made him wince.

'You can redeem it again,' he said in a slightly unsteady voice. 'I don't want to be too hard on you, Liz. You never had a chance.'

Liz leaned back in her chair again and closed her eyes. She

was, to outward appearance, indifferent and calm, but her breast once or twice tumultuously heaved, and her brows were knit, as if she suffered either physical or mental pain.

'You'll come, won't you, Liz, either today or tomorrow? You know the place,' he said rather anxiously.

'No,' she answered quietly; 'I'm no' comin'.'

'Why? I'm sure I will never cast up anything. I'm in solemn earnest, Liz. I'll do the best I can for you, and nobody shall cast a stone at you when I am by. I've lived to myself too long. Come and help me to be less selfish.'

The girl's breast again tumultuously heaved, and one deep, bursting sob forced itself from her lips; but all her answer was, to shake her head wearily, and answer, —

'No.'

CHAPTER XXXIV.

WHAT WILL SHE DO?

Walter looked at her perplexedly, not knowing what to say.

'Why will you not come?' he asked at length quite gently.

'I've disgraced ye enough,' she answered, a trifle sharply. 'Ye dinna ken what ye are daein', my man, askin' me to come an' bide wi' you. I've mair respect for ye than ye hae for yersel'. I'm much obleeged, a' the same, but I'm no' comin'.'

He perceived that the highest motive prompted her, and it convinced him as nothing else could have done that, if she had erred, she had also repented sincerely.

'What will you do, then?' he asked. 'Will you,' he added hesitatingly — 'will you go to the old folk?'

She gave a short, hard laugh.

'No' me. There wad be plenty castin' up there, if ye like. No; I hae nae desire to see them again this side the grave.'

It was a harsh speech; but, knowing what the past had been, Walter could not blame her. As he stood looking through the little window, beyond the forest of roofs to where the sun lay warm and bright on far-off country slopes, he thought of the sore bitterness of life. He might well be at war with fate; it had not given him much of the good which makes life worth living. It was all very well for Gladys Graham, the spoiled child of a happy fortune, to reprove him for railing at the cruelty of circumstances; her suffering, even when the days were darkest with her, had been of a gentler and less hopeless kind.

'Liz,' he said, turning to his sister again, after what had seemed to her an interminable silence, 'if you won't come to me, promise me you'll stay here. I have not asked any questions about your way of doing, but I can guess at it. Promise me that you will give it all up and stay here.'

'Sponging off Teen, like?' she asked sarcastically.

'No, no; I have plenty of money. You shall want for nothing,' he said, with a touch of irritation. 'She's a good little soul, Teen, and I won't forget her. I'm sure you and she could be quite comfortable here; you have always been good friends.'

'Yes,' answered Liz indifferently, 'that's true.'

'Will you promise, then,' he asked anxiously, 'to stay here in the meantime?'

'No,' she answered, 'I'll promise naething, because, if it comes up my back, I'll rise an' gang oot this very day.'

Walter's face flushed a little with anger. She was very perverse, and would give him no satisfaction whatever. He was at a disadvantage, because he really knew very little of her nature, which was as deep and as keen of feeling as his own.

'Then am I to go away and live in torture about you, Liz? I've a good mind to shut you up where you can't get out.'

'They wad be queer bolts and bars that kept me in,' she said, with a slight smile. 'Ye are very guid to tak' sae muckle thocht aboot me, and if it'll relieve yer mind, ye can believe that whatever I'm aboot, it's honest wark, and that if I need anything, I'll come to you.'

'You mean that, Liz?'

'Yes, I mean it; an' if I div say a thing I dinna gang back frae it,' she said, and again his mind was relieved. It was but natural that he should feel an absorbing desire to know exactly what her experience had been during the time she had been away from them, but since she seemed determined to keep silence regarding it, he could only keep silence too.

Presently Teen returned, and there was a furtive look of anxiety in her eyes as she regarded them, inly wondering what had transpired in her absence.

'Liz will bide with you in the meantime,' said Walter, affecting a cheerfulness he did not feel. 'I have been asking her to come and be my housekeeper, but she won't promise in the meantime.'

'Oh, she'll be fine here the noo,' answered the little seamstress, with a significance which did not convey anything to them, though it meant something to her. She was thinking as she spoke of the probable result of the letter she had just carried to the post, and which would be delivered at Bourhill in the morning. She was not mistaken in her calculations regarding it; for next morning, between eleven and twelve, when the two were sitting by the fire keeping up a rather disjointed conversation, during which Liz had exhibited distinct signs of restlessness, a light, quick knock came to the door.

'That's her!' cried Teen, springing up, her sallow face all aglow. 'I kent she wad come; yes, it's jist her.'

Liz sat up, her whole demeanour defiant, her face wearing its most ungracious look.

She had not the remotest idea who was meant by 'her,' and it is certain that had there been any other means of exit than the door in the building, she would have taken herself off there and then. What was her astonishment to behold presently a lissom, graceful figure and a sweet face, which seemed familiar, though she could not for the moment believe that they really pertained to Gladys Graham. And the face wore such a lovely look of gladness and wonder and sorrow all mingled, that Liz was struck dumb.

'Oh, Lizzie, I am so glad to see you. How could you stay away so long, when you must have known we were all so anxious about you? But we will forgive you quite, now that you have come back.'

She took the unwilling hand of Walter's sister in her firm, warm clasp, and, bending forward, kissed her, as she had done once before, on the brow. Then the face of Liz became a dusky red, and she started back, saying hoarsely, —

'Don't! Never dae that again. Oh, my God, if ye kent, ye wadna let yer eyes licht on me, far less that.'

'I know that we are very glad to see you again, and that you look very ill, dear Lizzie,' said Gladys, her voice tremulous with her deep compassion; 'and I have come to take you away to Bourhill. Here is somebody quite ready, I think, to go.'

She turned with a smile to the little seamstress, whose face still wore that intense, glorified look.

'Bourhill?' repeated Liz. 'Where's that?'

'That's my home now,' said Gladys gleefully. 'See what you have missed, being away so long. Has Teen not told you of all its glories? I thought she was so enthusiastic over it, she could not hold her tongue. Never mind, you shall soon see it for yourself.'

'I'm very much obleeged to ye, but I'm no' comin',' said Liz, with the same firmness which had set aside Walter's scheme concerning her.

'Why not? Nobody ever refuses me anything,' Gladys said.

'It wad be a sin for me to gang,' replied Liz quietly. 'I'm no' fit to speak to the like o' you. At least, that's what them ye belang to wad say.'

'I've nobody belonging to me to dictate to me, Liz, and I'm not afraid to trust you. You may have sinned, I don't know, but you have had many temptations. I want to show you a happier life. Tell her, Teen, how lovely it is at dear Bourhill.'

'I couldna,' answered Teen in a choking voice. 'It's like heaven, Liz.'

'Then it'll be ower guid for me,' said Liz wearily, 'an' I'll better bide whaur I am. But, I say, ye are queerer than ever, an' I thocht ye gey queer last time I saw ye.'

'Never mind what you think of me. Say you will come with me today. I came for the very purpose of taking you away,' said Gladys cheerfully. 'Do you remember that absurd story about "Lord Bellew's Bride" you were reading the first time I saw you? My own fortune is very nearly as wonderful as that of "Lord Bellew's Bride."'

Liz faintly smiled.

'Eh, sic lees there is in papers! It shouldna be printed. Things like yon never happen in real life — never, never!' She spoke with passionate emphasis, which indicated that she keenly felt what she said.

'Ye'll be gaun to get mairret next?' she added, looking at Gladys, who smiled and nodded, with slightly heightened colour.

'Well, what is to be done? Are you going down with me today?' she asked, looking from one to another, and tapping her dainty foot a trifle impatiently on the floor.

'I canna come the day, for my claes are a' at Maryhill,' said Liz.

'But I'll gang for them, Liz,' put in the little seamstress quickly. 'They can be easy got frae Maryhill afore nicht. It's only twelve o'clock the noo.'

'There need not be any such hurry; I think I shall stay in town all night,' said Gladys, 'and you can arrange it together, either to go with me or alone. Teen can manage it; she knows all about the trains, having been there before. I shall be sure to be home not later than tomorrow night, and if anything should prevent me getting down then, there is Miss Peck, Teen, who, you know, will make you very welcome.'

'Yes, I ken,' nodded Teen. 'If ye only kent what like a place it is, Liz, ye wad be jumpin'.'

'I'm sure I dinna ken what way ye want me doon there,' said Liz, relapsing into her weary, indifferent manner. 'I canna understand it.'

'Can't you?' asked Gladys merrily. 'Well, I want you, that's all. I want to have the pleasure of seeing you grow strong and well again. Nobody shall meddle with you. You shall do just as you like, and you two will be companions to each other.'

Teen looked reproachfully at her friend, wondering to see her so undemonstrative, never even uttering a single word of thanks for the kindness so freely offered. She shook hands with Gladys in silence, and allowed her to depart without further remark.

'You'll make sure that she comes down, Teen?' said Gladys, when they were outside the door. 'Poor thing, she looks dreadfully ill and unhappy. Where *do* you think she has been?'

Teen mournfully shook her head, and her large eyes filled with tears.

'I'll no' let her away,' she answered firmly. 'If she'll no' come doon to Bourhill, I'll see that she disna gang onywhere else withoot me.'

'You are a faithful friend,' said Gladys quickly. 'Has she — has she seen her brother?'

Teen wondered somewhat at the hesitation with which the question was asked.

'Ay; he was here yesterday.'

'And what did he say, Teen? Oh, I hope he was very gentle with her.'

'I wasna in a' the time, but I'm sure that kinder he couldna hae been. He wanted her to gang to Colquhoun Street an' bide, but she wadna.'

'Well, I hope she will come to Bourhill, and I think she will. Good-bye.'

'Weel, hae ye gotten me weel discussed?' queried Liz sarcastically, when the little seamstress returned to the kitchen. 'I canna understand that lassie by onybody.'

'Nor I a'thegither, but I ken she's guid,' she answered simply. 'Ye will gang to Bourhill, Liz?'

'Maybe; I'll see. I say, do ye ken wha she's gaun to mairry?'

'I have an inklin',' replied Teen, and said no more, though her face became yet more gravely troubled.

'Liz,' she said suddenly, 'will ye tell me wan thing afore we gang doon to Bourhill, if we gang?'

'What is't?'

'Had Fordyce onything to dae wi' you gaun awa' when you did?'

'Mind yer ain business,' replied Liz, with the utmost calmness, not even changing colour. 'I'm no' gaun to tell ye a single thing. My concerns are my ain, an' if ye're no' pleased, weel, I can shift.'

The girl's matter-of-fact, unruffled demeanour somewhat allayed Teen's burning anxiety, and, afraid to try Liz too far, lest she should insist on leaving her, she held her peace.

CHAPTER XXXV.

A REVELATION.

'Your Aunt Isabel was here this afternoon, George,' said Mrs. Fordyce to her son, when he came home from the mill that evening. 'She came over to tell me Gladys is in town. I said I thought you did not expect her.'

'No, I did not,' George replied. 'What's she up for? — anything new?'

'Oh, one of her fads. Something about one of these girls from the slums. Your aunt seemed to be rather distressed. She thinks Gladys is going quite too far, and she really took the opportunity, when the girls had all gone to a studio tea, to come over to consult me. We both think you are quite entitled to interfere.'

George shook his head.

'It is all very easy for you to say that, but I tell you Gladys won't stand that sort of thing.'

'But, my dear, she must be made to stand it. I must say her conduct is most unwomanly. If she is to be your wife, she must be taught that you are to be considered in some ways. You must be very firm with her, George; it will save no end of trouble afterwards.'

Mrs. George Fordyce was a large stout person, of imposing presence, and she delivered herself of this admirable sentiment most impressively; but though her son quite agreed with her, and wished with all his heart that the girl of his choice were a little less erratic and self-willed, he was wise enough to know that any attempt at coercion would be the very last thing to make her amenable to reason.

'What girl is it now?' he asked, with affected carelessness, but furtive anxiety. 'The same one who has been staying at Bourhill?'

'No; something far worse — a dreadful low creature, who has been missing for some time. If Gladys were not as innocent as a baby she would know that she is a creature not fit to be spoken to. Really, George, that Miss Peck is utterly useless as a chaperon. I wish we knew what to do. It is one of the most exasperating and delicate affairs possible.'

'That girl!' repeated George, so blankly that his mother looked at him in sharp amazement. 'Heavens! then it's all up, mother.'

'All up? What on earth do you mean?'

'What I say. Is it a girl called Hepburn?' he asked half desperately, afraid to tell his mother, and yet feeling that she, and she alone, might help him.

'I believe so. Yes, Hepburn was certainly the name your aunt mentioned. Well, what then?'

'Simply that if Gladys has got in tow with this girl, and takes her down to Bourhill, I'm ruined.'

'How?'

There was eager inquiry, anguish even, in the question. Mrs. Fordyce was a vain and silly woman, but she had a mother's feelings, and suffered, as every mother must, over her son's dishonour.

'This girl was one of our hands, and — and — well, you understand, she had a pretty face, and I was foolish about her. I never meant anything serious; but, you see, if Gladys gets to know about it, she is so absurdly quixotic, she is quite fit enough not to speak to me again.'

'You were foolish about her?' repeated Mrs. Fordyce slowly, and her comely face became rather pale, as she keenly eyed her son's troubled face. 'Does that mean that you were responsible for her disappearance?'

'Well, I suppose I was in the first instance,' he said frankly. 'Of course I was a fool for myself, but a man isn't always responsible, but' —

'Oh, hold your tongue, George Fordyce!' said his mother, her voice sharp with her angry pain. 'Not responsible, indeed! I am quite ashamed of you. It is a most disgraceful thing, and I don't know what your father will say.'

'There is no reason why he should say anything; he needn't be told,' said George a trifle sullenly. 'Of course I regret it, as every man does who makes such a deuced fool of himself. And the girl can't complain; it was more her fault, anyhow.'

'Oh, George, don't be a coward as well as a scoundrel,' said his mother, with more sharpness in her tone than she had ever before used towards her idolised son. 'Don't tell me it is the woman's fault. That is the poor excuse all men make when they get themselves into scrapes. I am very sorry for her, poor thing, and I think I'll go and see her myself.'

George remained silent, standing gloomily at the window, looking on the approach, with its trimly-cut shrubs and spring flowers, blooming in conventional lines. His mother had not received his information quite as he expected, and he felt for the moment utterly 'down on his luck.'

'You have indeed ruined yourself with Gladys, and with any other girl who has any respect for herself,' she said presently, with increased coldness, 'and I must say you richly deserve it.'

So saying, she left the room, and as she went up-stairs, two tears rolled down her cheeks. She was not a woman of very deep feelings, perhaps, but she had received a blow from which it would take her some time to recover. She sat down in her own room, and tried to think out the matter in all its bearings. She felt glad that her husband and daughter were not to dine at home, for after the first shock was over, worldly wisdom began to assert itself, and she pondered upon the best means of avoiding the scandal which appeared inevitable. She was not very hopeful. Had Gladys been an ordinary girl, entertaining less exalted ideas of honour and integrity, everything might have been smoothed over. Women, as a rule, are too lenient towards the follies of men, especially when the offenders are young and handsome; but Gladys was an exception to almost every rule. The only chance lay in the knowledge being kept from her, yet how was that possible, Liz Hepburn being at that very moment an invited guest at Bourhill? She made some little alteration in her dress, and went down, perfectly calm, and outwardly at ease, to a *tête-à-tête* dinner with her son. When they were left alone at the table she suddenly changed the subject from the commonplace to the engrossing theme occupying both their minds, and, leaning towards him, said quietly, —

'There is only one thing you can do now. It is your only chance, and if it fails, you can only retire gracefully, and accept your *congé* as your deserts.'

'I don't know what you mean,' he retorted a trifle ungraciously, for in his intense selfishness he had been able to convince himself that his mother had been rather hard upon him.

'I would advise you to go over to the Crescent tonight and see Gladys, and tell her what you have heard. Let her understand — as gently and nicely as you can, but be quite firm over it — that you, as her future husband, have some right to express an opinion about the people she makes friends of. You can lay stress on her own youth and ignorance, and don't be dictatorial. Do you understand me?'

'Yes, but it won't be an easy task,' he said gloomily.

'No, but it's your only chance — a very forlorn hope, I confess, it appears to me; but you can't afford to neglect it if you want to win Gladys, and it would be a most desirable marriage.'

These words were the keynote to Mrs. Fordyce's plan of action. To secure Gladys as a daughter-in-law at any price was her aim, and she had already stifled her womanly indignation over her son's fall, and even comforted herself by the cheap reflection that George had never been half so fast as dozens of other young men who were received into the best society. She had worshipped at the shrine of wealth and social position so long that all her views of life were centred upon a solitary goal, and consequently ran in a narrow and distorted groove.

'If the girl can be prevented going down to Bourhill, all may be well. Do you think she is one likely to hold her tongue?'

'I don't know anything about her. She'll speak, just as other women speak, when it comes up her own back, I suppose. The chances are, if Gladys and she have met, she's told the whole story already.'

'Oh no, she hasn't, because Gladys knew your aunt was coming here this afternoon, and sent a message that you might come over after dinner. She wouldn't have done that if she'd known that pretty story. You'd better go away to the Crescent at once.'

'I'm not very fond of the job,' said George, fortifying himself with a glass of whisky and water. 'I've a good mind to throw the whole bally thing up, and go off to the Antipodes. Marrying is an awful bore, anyhow; women are such a confounded nuisance.'

His mother listened to these lofty sentiments in silence, though she inwardly felt that it would relieve her feelings considerably to administer a sound box in the ear.

'I'm trying to help you, George, against my better judgment, but you don't appear to be very grateful,' she said severely. 'I've a good mind to let you bear the brunt of your folly, as you deserve; and you know very well that if your father knew about it, his anger would be terrific. I'm afraid you'd have to take to the Antipodes then, because the door would be shut upon you here. I would advise you to do what you can to redeem yourself, and your utmost to keep Gladys. Tell me something about the girl. Do you think she would accept a sum of money to leave Glasgow and hold her tongue?'

'No,' he answered, 'I don't.'

'Why, she must be very different from other girls of her class.'

'I don't know what are the characteristics of her class, but I know jolly well that if you offer money to her, she'll astonish you.'

Mrs. Fordyce looked with yet keener disfavour into her son's face.

'If she's that kind of girl, you must have promised her marriage.'

'Well, I daresay I did, but she might have known it was only talk,' he said, trying to speak coolly, though his mother's gaze made him decidedly uncomfortable. 'But I'm sick of the subject. I'll away over to Kelvinside, and have it either off or on. If the thing's out, I'll brazen it out; it's the only way.'

'You don't seem to realise the seriousness of the position, I'm sure I don't know what has made you go so far astray — not the training or example in this house. You have grievously disappointed me.'

'Oh, mother, don't preach. I've confessed to you, and it isn't fair to be so awfully down upon me,' he retorted irritably. 'I don't think you or the governor have had much to complain of as far as my conduct is concerned, and I'm not going to stay here to be bullied and snubbed for making a little slip. I tell you, you don't know what other fellows are. I've a good mind to open your eyes for you.'

'I don't want them opened, thank you; and if that is the spirit in which you are going to the Crescent, you deserve to fail, as you are sure to do. I am not sure whether I shall not tell your father, after all,' she said icily.

'I don't care if you do,' he retorted, and banged out in ill-humour, which, however, gradually cooled down as he walked rapidly to the station.

Finding no train for the city due for ten minutes, he threw himself into a hansom, and drove all the way, reaching his aunt's house before eight o'clock. Although he ran up the steps at once, he did not immediately ring, but even went back into the street, and took a turn up to the end of the houses, surprised and irritated at his own nervous apprehension. Glancing up to the house when he again came opposite to it, he saw the three long windows of the drawing-room lighted, and pictured the scene within. It was a new and unwelcome sensation for him to feel any reluctance in entering a drawing-room where there were three charming girls, and at last, calling himself a fool, he ran up the steps a second time, and gave the bell a furious pull.

'Is Miss Graham here, Hardy?' he asked the maid, an old servant of his aunt's, who opened the door.

'Yes, sir.'

'Anybody in the library?'

'No, sir. Mr. Fordyce is sleeping on the dining-room sofa.'

'Oh, all right. Just take my card to Miss Graham, and ask her if she would be so kind as to come down to the library for a few minutes.'

CHAPTER XXXVI.

TÊTE-À-TÊTE.

'How extraordinary!' exclaimed Gladys. 'Your cousin is in the library, why does he not come up?'

There was something so matter-of-fact in the question, that Mrs. Fordyce and her daughters could not refrain from exchanging glances.

'Well, my dear, I suppose he does not come up because he wishes to have you a little while to himself,' said Mrs. Fordyce, with a smile, 'and I must say I quite sympathise with him. Run away down, and don't stay too long; tell him not to be selfish.'

'But I don't think I want to go down. It is so strange, I think, for him not to come up here as usual. Why should there be any difference made?' inquired Gladys, as she rose with seeming reluctance to her feet.

'It is you who are strange, I think,' said Mina whimsically. 'You would require a very cool lover, Gladys, you are so cool yourself.'

'It is a pity one must have a lover,' said Gladys quite soberly, as she walked out of the room.

'Girls,' said Mrs. Fordyce, 'Gladys is an enigma, and I give her up; she is so different from any one I have ever met. Do you really think she cares anything for your cousin?'

'If she doesn't, why has she promised to marry him?' inquired Clara rather quickly. 'I think it is rather absurd to ask the question.'

'Well, I must say I should not particularly like to be in his shoes,' said Mina; and added, with light sarcasm, 'But it will do dear George good. Gladys will not fall down and worship him, like the rest of her sex. How I should like to be invisible at this moment in the library.'

But though Mina had had her wish she would not have seen anything very exciting, the greeting which passed between Gladys and her lover being remarkably cool. George Fordyce was not quite himself. Had Gladys been more absorbingly interested in him she could not have failed to observe the furtive look of anxiety with which he advanced to meet her; his demeanour was as different from the ordinary eagerness of a newly-accepted lover as could well be imagined. Nor did she betray these signs of maidenly shyness and trembling joy which in the circumstances she might have been expected to feel.

'Good-evening,' she said gaily. 'Why did you not come up, instead of sending a message to me, as if you were a person asking a subscription? I thought it so odd.'

George's courage rose. The gay unconcern of her demeanour convinced him that as yet nothing had lowered him in her estimation; with a little careful diplomacy, the dangerous currents might yet be avoided, and all go well.

'Is it so odd that I should wish to have you for a little while to myself?' he asked, and, putting his arm round her shoulders, took the kiss she could not deny him, though she almost immediately drew herself away.

'Do come up to the drawing-room. Why should we stay down here? Don't you think it rather silly?'

'I don't care whether it is silly or not,' he answered daringly. 'I don't mean to go up, or allow you to leave this room, for a good half hour at least.'

Gladys laughed a little, and dropped on one knee on a stool before the quaint fireplace, where the logs burned and crackled in a cheerful blaze.

'And I have a crow to pick with you, madam,' said the lover, made bolder by the perfect freedom of the girl's demeanour. 'I don't like second-hand messages. You might at least have sent me a nice little note by the hand of Aunt Isabel this afternoon.'

'I didn't think of it, or I might,' answered Gladys quite soberly, and the ruddy firelight lay warm and bright on her sweet face, and gave a deeper tinge to the gold of her hair. As George Fordyce stood as near to her as he dared, being deterred by a certain high dignity in her bearing, he was struck, not only by the perfect beauty of her features, but by the singular firmness mingling with the archness of her look. Twelve months had done a great deal for Gladys, and there was nothing of the child left, though the new womanliness was a most gracious and lovely thing.

'I had such a busy morning down town; and oh, I have a great deal to tell you, only you must promise to be sympathetic, because I have had a great deal to bear today, and have almost quarrelled with your aunt and the girls.'

'Yes?' he said, with all the fine indifference he could command. 'And what was it all about?'

He knew it must come sooner or later, and braced himself up to carry matters through with as high a hand as possible.

'About that poor girl of whom I told you, Lizzie Hepburn. She has come back, looking so very ill and unhappy, and of course I asked her down to Bourhill, and your aunt and cousins are so vexed about it, I am quite puzzled. It is so unlike them to blame one for wishing to be kind. Please, can you explain it?'

She raised her eyes to his face with something of the old child-like wistfulness in their depths, and it showed George Fordyce to be a very clever man indeed that he was able to meet that clear gaze without flinching.

'Well, you see, dear, I think it is regard for you which made Aunt Isabel appear a little harsh. She knows the world, and you do not, and, you know, a young and lovely girl, living without natural protectors, as you are, cannot be too careful.'

'Oh, that is just how they talk,' she cried petulantly, 'but it does not convey any meaning to me. Why should I not be kind to this poor girl? She can't eat me, or hurt me in the smallest degree. You must make it a great deal plainer to me before I see the smallest particle of reason in it.'

Here was a dilemma! The very irony of fate could not have devised a more trying and awkward position for any man. To say he felt himself on the brink of a volcano conveys but a faint idea of his peculiar state of mind.

'My own darling, it is extremely difficult to make it any clearer without giving offence, but I think you ought to have some idea of what is fitting. Can you not believe that we, who love you so dearly, would advise you to do nothing but what is right and best for you?'

This admirable plea, so earnestly and persuasively uttered, somewhat touched Gladys, though her face still wore a perplexed and even troubled look.

'Well, but how can it do me any harm to have these girls at Bourhill? Is it because they are poor that I must not have them?'

'Well, not exactly; though, of course, it is not customary for young ladies like you to invite such people to be your guests just in the same way as you would invite Clara or Mina; and I question very much, dear, if it is any real kindness to them, it is so apt to make them discontented with their own sphere.'

This was another clever stroke, this view of the case not having been as yet presented to Gladys. Hitherto the talk had all been of the influence such companionship was likely to have on her, and the new phase of the situation made her more thoughtful still.

'I never thought of that,' she said slowly, 'and I don't think it had that effect on Christina Balfour — in fact, I am sure of it. She is like a different creature, so much brighter and happier; and I am sure a week or two at Bourhill will do wonders for poor Lizzie Hepburn. If you saw her you would be quite sorry for her. She is such an interesting girl, so beautiful, and she has a great deal of character, quite different from Christina. I have asked them down, and of course I can't retract my invitations; they may have gone down to Miss Peck already, for aught I know. Promise to come down to Bourhill and see poor Lizzie, then I am sure you will say I have done quite right.'

A cold sweat broke over George Fordyce, and he was fain to take several turns between the window and the door to recover himself. He could almost have laughed aloud at the awful absurdity of the whole situation, only it had its tragic side too. He felt that his chance was almost over. He could not expect Liz Hepburn's visit to Bourhill to be barren of consequences the most serious; but he would wear the mask as long as possible, and make one more endeavour to save himself. He came back to the hearth, and, laying his hand hurriedly on the heart of the girl he loved with all the tenderness that was in him, he said, in that pleading, winning way so few women could resist, —

'My darling, if I ask you, won't you take Aunt Isabel's advice? I know I haven't any right yet to dictate to you, even if I wished to do it, but won't you believe that we only advise what is the very best for you? Couldn't you, instead of having the girls at Bourhill, send them to some other country place? It would only cost a very little more.'

'But that wouldn't be the same thing at all,' said Gladys wilfully. 'And if I were to retract my invitation now, they would never have the same faith in me again. I would not on any account disappoint them.'

'Even to please me?' he queried, with a slightly injured air.

'Even to please you,' she repeated, in the same wilful tone.

'And will it always be the same?' he asked then. 'Will you never allow me to have any say in your affairs?'

'I hoped you would help me to do good to people,' she said slowly, giving utterance for the first time to the feeling of disappointment and misgiving which sometimes oppressed her when she thought of her relation towards George Fordyce.

'My dear, you will get all your thanks in one day,' he said dryly. 'I know the class you have to deal with. They'll take all you have to give them, and laugh in your face. They have no such quality as gratitude in them.'

Gladys curled her lips in scorn.

'How unhappy you must be to have so little faith in humankind. That has not been my experience; but we shall never agree on that point. Shall we go up-stairs now?'

Her perfect independence of and indifference to his opinion, betrayed in the careless ease of her manner as she rose from the hearth, exasperated him not a little.

'No, I am not coming up-stairs,' he answered, as rudely as he dared.

'What shall I say to Mrs. Fordyce, then? That you are out of temper?' she asked, with a sly gaiety which became her well, though it only further exasperated him.

'You can say anything you like, I am very sorry indeed that my opinion is of so little value in your eyes, Gladys, and I ask your pardon if I have presumed too much in offering you a crumb of advice.'

'Oh, don't be cross because we don't happen to agree on that particular point,' she said sunnily. 'Each individual is surely entitled to his opinion. I am not cross because you would not agree with me. Come away up-stairs.'

'No, I'm not coming up tonight. Make my apologies to them. Gladys, upon my word, you are perfectly bewitching. I wish you knew how passionately I love you. I don't believe you care a tithe as much for me as I do for you.'

He would have held her again, but she moved away from him, and her face did not brighten as it ought to have done at such a loverlike speech.

'Will you promise me one thing, Gladys, before I go?' he pleaded, and he had never been more in earnest in his life. 'Promise me that if anybody speaks ill of me to you, you will at least give me a chance to clear myself before you condemn me.'

'Oh, I can promise that fast enough, because nobody ever speaks ill of you to me. It is quite the reverse, I assure you. I have to listen to your praises all day long,' she said, with a teasing smile. 'You ought to show your gratitude for such disinterested kindness by coming up to the ladies.'

'I'm not going up tonight,' he reiterated. 'Give them my kind regards. Are you really off?'

'I must, if you won't come.'

He held open the door for her, and as she passed out, stole another kiss with all a lover's passion, telling himself it might be the last. But it did not make her pulses thrill nor her heart beat more quickly, and she saw him depart without a regret.

'You don't mean to say that is George away?' they cried, when the outer hall door closed, and almost immediately Gladys entered the drawing-room alone.

'Yes, he has gone,' Gladys answered calmly.

'What have you been doing to him to set him off like that?' asked Mina. 'Have you had a quarrel?'

'No,' replied Gladys innocently; 'but I think he is rather cross.'

Mrs. Fordyce shook her finger reprovingly at the girl, and said regretfully, —

'My dear, you are incorrigible. I could almost regret Henrietta Bonnemain's marriage, because she is the only woman in this world who could have managed you.'

CHAPTER XXXVII.

CHUMS.

Never did mother watch more tenderly over a wayward child than the little seamstress over Liz, and though Liz was quite conscious of the espionage she did not resent it. She seemed to have no desire to leave the little house, and when Teen, in the course of that afternoon, offered to go to the house in Maryhill for her clothes, she made no demur, nor did she offer to accompany her.

'If the lassie I'm lodgin' wi' is in, Teen, ye can tell her I'm no' comin' back. I'm very gled to get quit o' her, onyway,' she said, as Teen buttoned on her shabby black jacket.

'What's her name? Had ye better no' write a line, for fear she'll no' gie me the things?'

'Oh, she'll gie ye them withoot ony bother; they wadna bring her abune ten shillin's, onyhoo. An', I say, dinna tell her onything aboot me, mind. She'd think naething o' comin' onywhere efter me.'

'Oh, I'll no' tell. Clashin' was never my sin,' said Teen. 'But her name? — ye havena telt me that yet.'

'Oh, weel, she ca's hersel' Mrs. Gordon, but I dinna believe she's a wife at a'. She's in the ballet at the Olympic the noo.'

'An' what way is she bidin' at Maryhill?'

'Oh, her man's there. She says she's mairret to yin o' the officers, but I've never set een on him.'

'Is she a nice lassie?'

'Oh, weel enough. She's no' mean, onyhoo, but she's gey fast. She was tryin' to get me ta'en on at the Olympic. If she says onything, jist tell her I've changed my mind.'

'An' are ye no' awn onything for the lodgin's?' queried Teen, who had a singular conscientiousness regarding debt, even of a microscopic kind.

'No; I paid up when I had it. I dinna owe her onything.'

Teen was silent as she put her long hat-pin through the heavy masses of her hair and pulled her fringe a little lower on her brow; but she thought a great deal. Bit by bit the story was coming out, and she had no difficulty in filling up for herself the melancholy details.

'Noo I'm ready. Ye'll no' slope when I'm oot, Liz?' she said warningly; and Liz laughed a dreary, mirthless laugh.

'I ken when I'm weel aff. I wish to goodness I had come to you when I was sick o' Brigton, instead o' gaun where I gaed.'

Teen stood still in breathless silence, wondering if full revelation was about to be made. When Liz saw this, the old spirit of contrariness entered into her again, and she said crossly, —

'What are ye waitin' on noo?'

'Naething,' replied Teen meekly. 'Weel, I'm aff. I'll be back afore dark. Ye can hae the kettle bilin', an' I'll bring in a sausage or a red herrin' for oor tea.'

It was not without some faint, excited curiosity that Teen found herself at the door of the house of which Liz had given her the address. It was a one-roomed abode, three stairs up a tall tenement, in one of these dreary and uninteresting streets which are only distinguishable from one another by their names. In answer to her knock, a shrill female voice cried, 'Come in,' an invitation which the little seamstress somewhat hesitatingly obeyed. It was now after sundown, and the freshness of the daylight had faded, leaving a kind of semi-twilight in the room, which was of a fair size, and comfortably, though not luxuriously, furnished. On the end of the fender sat the solitary occupant, in a ragged and dirty old dressing-gown of pink flannel, her feet in dilapidated slippers, and her hair in curl-papers along her forehead. Although she saw that her visitor was quite a stranger to her, she did not offer to rise, but simply raising her pert, faded, but still rather pretty face, said inquiringly, —

'Well?'

'Are you Mrs. Gordon? I've come for Lizzie Hepburn's things. She's no' comin' back here.'

'Oh, all right. Shut the door, and come in. What's up with her? Gone off with a handsomer man, eh?' queried Mrs. Gordon, as she bit her thread through, and held up a newly-trimmed dress bodice for admiration.

'No; she's gaun into the country the morn,' answered Teen, while the ballet-dancer gave several very knowing nods.

'That's a pity, for her luck's turned. You can tell her she'll be taken on if she likes to turn up at the Olympic tomorrow morning at ten sharp. I arranged it for her on Saturday night.'

'She said I was to tell you she had changed her mind aboot the theatre,' said Teen. 'She's no' weel enough for it, onyhoo. She'll be better in the country.'

'Are you her sister?'

'Oh no, only her chum.'

'Well, I say, perhaps you can tell me something about her. She was as close as the grave, though we've been pals for a while; she'd not tell me a single thing. Why is she out on her own hook? Is there a man in the business?'

'I dinna ken ony mair than you,' said Teen, looking rather

uncomfortable over this cross-examination. 'An' if ye'll tell me where her box is, I maun be gaun. I promised no' to be long.'

'It's there, at the end of the bed,' said Mrs. Gordon serenely, jerking her thumb in that direction. 'I see you mean to be close too. Not that it matters a cent to me; I've no earthly interest in her affairs. You can tell her, if you like, that Captain Dent was inquiring affectionately for her this morning. I met him on my way back from rehearsal.'

Teen listened in silence, mentally deciding that she would not tell her any such thing.

'And you can tell her, if you like, that I'll be glad to see her any time before the twenty-third. The Eighty-Fifth are ordered to Ireland, and of course my husband will wish me to go with him.'

A slow smile, in which there was the faintest touch of sarcasm, was in Teen's face as she glanced at the tawdry figure sitting on the fender end.

'A' richt; I'll tell her. An' guid-nicht to ye; I'm very much obleeged,' she said, and, taking Liz's tin box in her hand, she left a trifle hastily, as if afraid she should be longer detained.

She found Liz sitting where she had left her, in the same listless attitude, and her eyes were red about the rims, as if she had had a crying fit. The fire was very low, and the kettle standing cold where Teen had left it on the hearthstone.

'I forgot a' aboot the kettle, Teen,' she said apologetically. 'I'm a lazy tyke; but dinna rage. Weel, ye've got the box. Did ye see Emily?'

'Yes, if that's her name. She's a queer yin,' said Teen, as she let the box drop, and grasped the poker to improve the condition of the fire. 'Ye dinna seem to hae telt her much, Liz, ony mair than me.'

'No; it's aye best to keep dark. I dinna mean onything ill, Teen, but naebody shall ever ken frae me whaur I've been or what I've suffered since I gaed awa'. Ay, what I've suffered!' — she repeated these words with a passionate intensity, which caused Teen to regard her with a kind of awe. 'But maybe my day'll come, an' if it does, I winna forget,' she said, more to herself than to her companion; then, catching sight of Teen's astonished face, she broke into a laugh, and said, in quite a different tone, —

'Weel, is't the morn we're gaun among the swells? An' hoo d'ye pit in the time in the country?'

'Ye'll see,' replied Teen, with quiet satisfaction. 'The days are ower short, that's the only fault they hae. Efter we get oor supper, what wad ye say to gang roond to Colquhoun Street and see Wat, to tell him we're gaun to Bourhill?'

'No, I'm no' gaun. He micht say we werena to gang. I say,

Teen, he's in love wi' her. Onybody can see it in his e'e when he speaks aboot her.'

'I ken that; but it's nae use,' said Teen, 'she's gaun to mairry somebody else.'

'Is she? D'ye ken wha?'

'Ay; your auld flame,' said Teen, apparently at random, but all the while keenly watching her companion's face. She saw Liz become as pale as death, though she smiled a sickly smile, and tried to speak as indifferently as possible.

'Ye dinna mean it? Weel, I'd hae thocht she wad hae waled better. Hoo sune are we gaun the morn?'

She asked the question with eagerness, and from that moment the little seamstress observed that her whole manner changed. She suddenly began to display a new and absorbing interest in the preparations for their departure, and plied Teen with questions regarding the place and her former experiences there. The little seamstress, being a person of a remarkably shrewd and observant turn, saw in this awakened interest only another link in the chain which now appeared to her almost complete. Her former elation over their trip to Bourhill gave place to a painful anxiety lest it should hasten events to a crisis in which the happiness of Gladys might be sadly involved; but it was now too late to help matters, and, with a bit of philosophical calmness, she said within herself, 'What is to be maun be,' and went on with her preparations for the morrow's journey.

They set out, accordingly, about noon next day, carrying their belongings in the inevitable tin box, and arrived at Mauchline Station quite early in the afternoon — a lovely afternoon, when all the spring airs were about, and a voice of gladness over the spring's promise in the note of every bird singing on the bending boughs. With what keenness of interest did the little seamstress watch the effect of country sights and sounds upon Liz, and how it pleased her to see the slow wonder gather in her eyes as they wandered across the wide landscape over the rich breadths of the ploughed fields, in which the sowers were busy, to the sheltering woods glistening greenly in the sun, and the blue hills in the hazy distance seeming to shut in the world. It was her pride and pleasure to point out to her companion, as they walked, each familiar and cherished landmark, and though Liz did not say much, it was evident that she was in a manner lifted out of herself. The pure, fragrant air blowing about her, the wide and wonderful beauty of green fields and sunny slopes, filled the soul of Liz with a vague, yearning wonder which was almost pain. It brought home to her sharply a sense of all she had lost in the great and evil city; it was like a revelation of some boundless good of which she had hitherto lived in ignorance, and it awakened in her a bitter regret, which was in very truth rebellious anger, that the beauty of the earth should have so long been hid from her.

'It's a shame,' she said, — 'a horrid shame, that we should never hae kent there was a place like this ootside o' Glesca. Wha is't made for? — the rich, I suppose, as the best things are.'

'Oh no,' said Teen quite gently. 'There are plenty puir folk in the country, an' bad folk tae. Mrs. Galbraith says there's as muckle drink drucken in Poosie Nancie's on Seterday nicht as in Johnnie Shields' in the Wynd, but some way it seems different. Look, see, thonder's the big gate o' Bourhill. Eh, I wonder if Miss Gladys is hame?'

'I say, Teen, ye are very fond o' her, surely?' said Liz curiously. 'Since when? Ye didna like her sae weel that nicht I left ye to tak' her hame frae the Ariel.'

'No, but I didna ken her then. Yes, I'm fond o' her, an' there's naething I wadna dae for her. I wad let her walk abune me if it wad dae her ony guid,' said the little seamstress, her plain face glorified once more by the great love which had grown up within her till it had become the passion of her life.

'Ye needna fash; that's the way I've heard lassies speak aboot men, an' ye get a' yer thanks in ae day,' said Liz bitterly. 'The best thing onybody can dae in this world is to look efter number one. It's the only thing worth livin' for. I wish I had never been born, an' I hope I'll no' live lang, that's mair.'

'Oh, Liz, wheesht!'

'What for should I wheesht? It's no' the first time I've been doon at the Broomielaw takin' a look roon for a likely place to jump in quietly frae. That'll be my end, Teen Ba'four, as sure as I'm here the day; then they'll hae a paragraph in the *News*, an' bury me in the Puirhoose grave. It's a lively prospect.'

Teen said nothing, only made a vow within herself that she would do what she could to avert from the girl she loved such a melancholy fate.

CHAPTER XXXVIII.

IN VAIN.

Miss Caroline Peck had received that very morning a letter from Mrs. Fordyce of Bellairs Crescent — a letter which had put her all in a flutter. It was a letter of warning, counsel, and reproof concerning Miss Peck's duty towards her young charge, and laying a strong injunction upon her to be exceedingly judicious in her treatment of the eccentric guests whom Gladys had again invited to Bourhill. It was not a wise epistle at all, though Mrs. Fordyce had regarded it with complacency as a triumph of diplomatic letter-writing. Instead of stating plainly the whole facts, and pointing out how desirable it was that Gladys should not be thrown too much into the company of the girls from the East End, it threw out certain dark hints, which only mystified and distressed poor little Miss Peck, and made her anticipate with apprehension the arrival of the pair. It was a letter which, moreover, could not possibly do the smallest good, seeing Miss Peck, was not only far too fond of her young charge to cross her in the slightest whim, but that she secretly approved of everything she did. Of Mrs. Fordyce, Miss Peck, was mortally afraid and that very kind-hearted person would have been amazed had she known how the little spinster, metaphorically speaking, shrank into herself in her presence. The solemn warning she had received did not, however, prevent her giving the two girls a warm welcome when they presented themselves at the house that afternoon.

'Miss Graham has not come home, Christina,' she said fussily, as she shook hands with them both, 'but I feel sure she will be here tonight. Meantime I must do what I can to make you comfortable. Come with me to your old room, Christina, and you shall have tea directly.'

Though she had directed all her remarks to Teen, she did not fail at the same time to make the keenest scrutiny of her companion, whose appearance filled the little spinster with wonder. She was certainly a very handsome girl, and there was nothing forward or offensive in her manner — nay, rather, she seemed to feel somewhat shy, and kept herself in the background as much as possible. Acting slightly on Mrs. Fordyce's advice, Miss Peck gave the girls their tea, with its delightful adjuncts of new-laid eggs and spring chicken, in her own sitting-room, and she quite prided herself on her strength of mind as she decided to advise Gladys to give them their meals by themselves, except on a rare occasion, when she might wish to give them a treat. After tea, during which Miss Peck and the little seamstress sustained the conversation entirely between them, Liz apparently being too shy or too reticent to utter a word, the two girls went out for a walk. In their absence, to the great delight of Miss Peck, Gladys arrived home in a dogcart, hired from the Mauchline Hotel.

'You have something to tell me, haven't you?' cried Gladys eagerly, as she kissed her old friend. 'The girls have arrived, I am sure. And what do you think of poor Lizzie? Is she not all I told you?'

'She is certainly a fine-looking girl, but she has said so little that I don't know anything else about her.'

'But you have been very kind to them, I hope? I want you to be specially kind to Lizzie. I am afraid she has had a very hard time of it lately, and she is not strong.'

'My dear,' — Miss Peck laid her little hand, covered with its old-fashioned rings, on the arm of her young charge, and her kind face was full of anxiety, — 'tell me why she has had a hard time. I hope she is a good girl, Gladys? You have the kindest heart, my darling, but you must look after your own interests. I hope she has given you quite a satisfactory account of herself?'

'Dear Miss Peck,' said Gladys, with a light laugh, 'she has not given me any account of herself at all, nor have I asked it. But, tell me, do you think she looks like a wicked girl?'

'Well, no, not exactly; but I — I — have had a letter from Mrs. Fordyce this morning,' said the little spinster, with the most unsophisticated candour, 'and really, from it one might think your new *protégée* quite an objectionable person.'

Gladys looked distinctly annoyed. She had a very sweet disposition, but was a trifle touchy regarding her own independence. Sundry rather sharp passages which had occurred between Mrs. Fordyce and herself on this very subject made her now readier to resent this new interference.

'I really wish Mrs. Fordyce would mind her own business,' she said, and that was such a very harsh sentence to fall from the lips of Gladys that Miss Peck looked rather startled. 'She has really no right to be writing letters to you dictating what I shall do in my own house. Do you belong to me, or to her, I wonder?'

The momentary resentment died away as she asked this question with the old whimsical smile.

'I think she means it for your good, dear,' said the little spinster meekly, 'and I think in some particulars she is right. I never dictate to you, and for that very reason you will listen to what I am going to say. I think you should not make too much of these girls when they are here. Be kind to them, of course, and give them every comfort, but let them eat alone and be companions to each other. I am sure, dear, that would make them much happier, and be better for us all.'

'Do you think so?' Gladys asked, with all the docility of a child. 'Very well, dear Guardy, I will do as you think. But where are they now? I must bid them welcome.'

'They have gone for a walk to the birch wood. And how have you been since you went up to town? Have you been very gay, and seen a great deal of a certain gentleman?'

'No, I saw him once only, and we did not agree,' replied Gladys calmly. 'Do you know, dear Miss Peck, I think it was the greatest mistake for us to get engaged? I don't know in the least what made me do it, and I wish I hadn't.'

Miss Peck stood aghast, but presently smiled in a relieved manner.

'Oh, nonsense, my love — only a lover's tiff. When it blows over, you will be happier than ever.'

'I don't like tiffs,' Gladys answered, as she ran up-stairs to take off her wraps.

The lover's tiff seemed to be rather a serious affair, for a week passed away and no letter came from George; nor did Gladys write any. She felt secretly wounded over it, and though she often recalled that hour spent in the library at Bellairs Crescent, she could not remember anything which seemed to justify such a complete estrangement. Never since she came to Bourhill had so long a time elapsed without communicating with one or other of the Fordyce family, but as the days went by and they made no sign, the girl's pride rose, and she told herself that if they pleased to take offence because she reserved to herself the right to ask whom she willed to her own house, they should receive no advances from her. But she was secretly unhappy. Her nature craved sunshine and peace, and the conduct of her lover she could not possibly understand. In all her imaginings how far was she always from the truth! She did not dream that he believed his death-knell had been rung, and that he attributed her silence to her righteous and inexorable indignation over the story she had heard from the lips of Liz Hepburn. He never for one moment doubted that she had told, and between conscience and disappointed love he had a very lively week of it. All this time none could have been more discreet and reticent than the girl who was the cause of all this heart-burning. Her behaviour was exemplary. She was docile, courteous, gentle in demeanour and speech, grateful for everything, but enthusiastic over nothing, differing in this respect from Teen, who appeared to walk on air, and carried her exaltation of spirit in her look and tone. But Liz was dull and silent, content to walk and drive, and breathe that heavenly air which ought to have been the very elixir of life to her, but otherwise appearing lifeless and uninterested. Gladys was very kind and even tender with her, but just a little disappointed. She watched her keenly, not knowing that all the while Liz was in turn watching her, and at last she breathed a hint of her disappointment into the ear of the little seamstress.

'Do you think Lizzie is enjoying Bourhill, Teen? She looks so spiritless; but perhaps it is her health, though I think her looking a little better than when she came.'

'It's no' her body, it's her mind,' said Teen slowly. 'She has something on her mind.'

'Has she never said anything yet to you about where she was, or what she was doing, all the time she was lost?' asked Gladys anxiously.

'Naething,' answered Teen, with a melancholy shake of her head. 'But I think it's on that she's thinkin', an' whiles I dinna like her look.'

'I'm going to speak to her myself about it, Teen. Perhaps it is something it would do her good to tell. Like you, I am often struck by her look, it is so dreadfully sad. Yes, I shall speak to her.'

The little seamstress looked hesitatingly at the bright, radiant face of Gladys, and it was upon her lips to say it might be better to let the matter rest. But, with her old philosophical reflections that anything she might say could not possibly avert the march of fate, she held her peace.

Just after lunch that afternoon, as Gladys was writing some letters in her favourite window, she saw Liz sitting by herself in the drowsy sunshine on the lawn, and her face wore such a dejected, melancholy look that it was evident some hidden sorrow was eating into her heart. Closing her desk, Gladys ran down-stairs, caught up a garden hat from the hall, and crossed the green lawn to Liz.

'Dear me, how doleful you look!' she cried gaily. 'How can you look so dreadfully doleful on such a bright day? Now tell me every simple, solitary thing you are thinking.'

A swift, rather startled glance crossed Liz's face, and she gave rather a forced laugh.

'That wadna be easy. I don't think I was thinking onything, except a meenit syne, when I lookit up an' wished I was that laverock in the lift.'

'But why? It is much nicer to be a girl, I think. Tell me, Lizzie, don't you feel stronger since you came here? I think you look it.'

'I'm weel enough,' responded Liz dully; 'an' it's a lovely place — a lovely place. I'll never forget it, never as long as I live.'

It was the first note of enthusiasm Gladys had heard regarding

Bourhill, and it pleased her well.

'I hope you won't, and that you'll come often to see it.'

'I dinna think I'll ever come again; it's no' likely. Hoo lang are we to bide?'

'As long as you like,' answered Gladys frankly, — 'till you are quite strong, anyhow. Teen is in no hurry to go back to Glasgow; are you?'

'Sometimes it's very quiet,' said Liz candidly.

'But what are you going to do when you return?'

Liz shook her head, but her lips gave forth no answer.

'I hope you will go to your brother, as he wished,' said Gladys, and she could not for the life of her help a curious restraint creeping into her voice. 'It would be so very nice for him to have you; it is dreadful for him to live quite alone, as he does. Why won't you go?'

'He kens what way,' replied Liz quietly.

Gladys was perplexed. There was nothing particularly encouraging in the girl's look or manner, but she thought the time had come to put the question which had so often trembled on her lips. It was a proof of Gladys Graham's fine and delicate nature that she had not ere this sought to probe into Liz Hepburn's secret, if she had one.

'Lizzie,' she said gently, 'I hope you won't be angry at what I say; but often, looking at you, I see that you are unhappy. I have never sought to pry into your concerns, but perhaps, if you were to tell me something about yourself, you would feel more at rest.'

'D'ye think sae?' she asked, with a faint, ironical smile, which Gladys did not like. 'If it eased me, it micht keep you frae sleepin'. I'm very much obleeged to you for no' haein' pestered me wi' questions. I dinna ken anither in the world but Teen that wad hae treated me as you have. But my life's my ain, an' if I suffer, I'm no' askin' pity. I can bear the brunt o' what I've brocht on mysel.'

It was a flat repulse, but it was gently spoken, and did not vex the sensitive soul of Gladys.

'Very well, Liz,' she said kindly, 'I'll never ask any more; but remember that if I can help you at any time, I am ready, always ready, for your sake and for Walter's.'

'He worships the very ground you walk on,' said Liz calmly. 'I wonder what way him an' me was born? Is't true ye are gaun to be married to Fordyce o' Gorbals Mill?' As she asked this direct question, she flashed her brilliant eyes full on the girl's sweet face.

'I suppose I am, sometime,' Gladys answered rather confusedly. 'At least, I have promised.'

'Ay,' said Liz, 'but there's mony a slip atween the cup an' the lip; and in time, they say, a'body gets their deserts, even here.'

With this enigmatical speech Liz got up and crossed the lawn, with averted face, Gladys looking after her with a puzzled wonder in her eyes, thinking she was certainly a very strange girl, and that it was hopeless to try to make anything out of her.

CHAPTER XXXIX.

GONE.

Towards the end of the second week Liz began to exhibit certain signs of restlessness, which ought to have warned those concerned in her welfare that the quiet and seclusion of Bourhill were beginning to pall upon her. As she improved in her bodily health her mind became more active, and she began to pine for something more exciting than country walks and drives. They were not altogether unobservant of the growing change in her, of course, but attributed it to a returning and healthful interest in the simpler pleasures of life. All this time George Fordyce had not come to Bourhill, nor had any letters passed between him and his promised wife. It would be too much to say that Gladys was quite indifferent to this; if her feelings were not very deeply involved, her pride was touched, and the first advances were not at all likely to emanate from her. Liz had lived in secret dread, mingled with a kind of happy anticipation, of meeting George Fordyce at Bourhill, and as the days went by, and there was no sign or talk of his coming, she began to wonder very much what it all meant. She was a remarkably shrewd person, and it did occur to her to connect her visit and the absence of Miss Graham's lover. One day, however, she put a question to Teen as they sauntered through the spring woods on the hill behind the house.

'I say, is't true that she is gaun to mairry Fordyce, Teen? It's no' like it. What way does he never look near?'

Teen looked keenly into her companion's face, to which that fortnight of complete rest and generous living had restored the bloom of health. Without planning very much, or artfully seeking to mislead the little seamstress, Liz had thrown her entirely off the scent. Such careless mention of her old lover's name, and her apparent indifference as to whether they should or should not meet at Bourhill, had entirely convinced Teen that he had no share in that part of Liz's life which she had elected to keep a sealed book.

'It's quite true that they are engaged,' she replied tranquilly; 'but maybe he's awa' frae hame. But nane o' them hae been here for a long time.'

'She disna seem to be much in earnest,' put in Liz flatly. 'I dinna believe mysel' that she cares a button for ony o' the lot; do you?'

'I dinna ken,' answered Teen truthfully. 'It disna maitter to us, onyway.'

'Maybe no'. Let's sit doon here a meenit, Teen; the sun's fine an' warm,' said Liz, and plumped down among the bracken, while Teen stood still under the jagged branches of an old fir tree, and looked 'her fill,' as she expressed it, of the lovely world at her feet. It was still a spring world, clothed in a most delicate and exquisite garb of green, waiting only for the touch of later summer to give it a deeper hue. There were many touches of white and pink bloom, showing in exquisite contrast where the hawthorn and the gean were in flower. Nor was the ground left with its more sombre hues unrelieved; the blue hyacinth, the delicate anemone, the cowslip, and the primrose grew thickly on every bare hillside and in all the little valleys, making the air heavy with their rich perfume.

And all the fields now made glad the hearts of those who had in faith dropped their seed into the brown soil, and the whole earth, down to the sun-kissed edge of the sea, rejoiced with a great joy. Nor was the sea less lovely, with the silvery sheen of early summertide on its placid bosom, and the white wings of many boats glistening in the sun.

'It's jist like heaven, Liz,' said the little seamstress, to whom these things were a great wonder, revealing to her a depth and a meaning in life of which she had not before dreamed. But to these hidden lovelinesses of Nature the eyes of Liz were closed; her vision being too much turned in upon herself, was dimmed to much that would have made her a happier and a better girl.

'It's bonnie enough, but oh, it gets stale, Teen, efter a wee. If I were as rich as her I wadna bide here — no' if they paid me to bide!'

'What for no'?'

'Oh, it's that flat. Naething ever happens. Gie me the toon, I say; there's some life there, onyway.'

'I wadna care if I never saw the toon again,' said Teen gravely, for her friend's words troubled her.

'Hoo lang d'ye mean to bide here, Teen?' queried Liz presently. 'It'll be a fortnicht the morn since we cam'.'

Teen did not at once reply. She had not dared to count the days, grudging their sweet passing, and it jarred upon her to hear Liz state the exact period, as if it had appeared to her very long.

'This is the nineteenth; it was the twenty-third, wasn't it, that Mrs. Gordon said she was leavin' Glesca?'

'I've forgotten. Yes, I believe it was the twenty-third,' answered Teen listlessly, not being interested in the time.

'My, she'll see a lot, gaun to Ireland wi' a regiment. It's a lively life. I wish I was her.'

Teen turned sharply round, and looked with reproachful eyes

into her companion's face.

'I thocht ye was gled to get away from her, Liz? I dinna ken what ye mean.'

'Oh, I was doon in the mooth, because I wasna weel,' said Liz lightly. 'Seriously, though, hoo lang are ye gaun to bide doon here, Teen?'

'I wad bide aye if I had the chance, but I suppose we canna bide very much langer. Maybe we'd better see what Miss Gladys says.'

'Ay, I suppose sae,' said Liz a trifle dryly. 'Whatever you may think, I dinna think it's fair that she should hae sae much an' you an' me sae little. We're livin' on her charity, Teen.'

'Yes, but she disna mak' ye feel it,' retorted Teen quickly. 'An' she disna think it charity, either. She says aye the money's no' hers, she has jist gotten a len' o't to gie to ither folk.'

'Wad she gie me a thoosand, d'ye think, if I were to speir?' asked Liz; and Teen looked vexed at these idle words. She did not like the sarcastic, flippant mood, and she regarded Liz with strong disapproval and vague uneasiness in her glance.

'I dinna like the way ye speak, Liz,' she said quietly. 'But, I say, if ye were in Glesca the noo, what wad ye dae?'

'Dae? It's what wad I no' dae,' cried Liz. 'I'm no' the kind to sterve.'

'Ye wasna very weel aff when we got ye,' Teen could not refrain from saying.

'Oh, ye needna cast up what ye did. I never asked you, onyway. Ye ken you and Wat hauled me awa' wi' you against my wull,' said Liz rather angrily, being in a mood to cavil at trifles. 'I kent hoo it wad be, but I'll tak' jolly guid care ye dinna get anither chance o' castin' up onything o' the sort to me.'

Teen remained silent, not that she was particularly hurt by that special remark, but that she was saddened and perplexed by the whole situation. She had sustained another fearful disappointment, and she saw that Bourhill had utterly failed to work the charm on Liz which Teen herself experienced more and more every day. If she were not altogether blind to its loveliness, at least it did not touch any deeper feeling than mere eye pleasure; but more serious and disappointing still was the tone in which she spoke of Gladys. In her weak and weary state of health, she had at first appeared touched and grateful for the unceasing kindness and consideration heaped upon her, but that mood had passed apparently for ever, and now she appeared rather to chafe under obligations which Teen felt also, though in a different way, love having made them sweet. For the first time in her life she felt herself shrinking inwardly from the friend she had always loved since the days when they had played together, ragged, unkempt little girls, in the city streets. She looked at the brilliant beauty of her face. She saw it marred by a certain hardness of expression, a selfish, discontented look, which can rob the beauty from the loveliest face, and her heart sank within her, because she seemed dimly to foresee the end. The little seamstress did not know the meaning of a lost ideal, the probability is that she had never heard the word, but she felt all of a sudden, standing there in the May sunshine, that something had gone out of her life for ever. That very night she spoke to Gladys, seizing a favourable opportunity, when Liz had gone to enjoy a gossip with that garrulous person, Mrs. Macintyre, at the lodge.

'I say, Miss Gladys, hae ye noticed onything aboot Liz this day or twa?' she queried anxiously.

'Nothing,' replied Gladys blithely, 'except that she looks more and more like a new creature. Have you noticed anything?'

'Naething very particular; but I am feared that she's wearyin' here, an' that she wants to get away back to Glesca,' said Teen, with a slight hesitation, it must be told, since such an insinuation appeared to savour of the deepest ingratitude.

'Oh, do you think so? I thought she was quite happy. She certainly looks much brighter and better, and feels so, I hope.'

'Oh yes, she's better; that's the reason, I suppose. She was aye active an' energetic, Liz,' said Teen, feeling impelled to make some kind of excuse for her old chum. 'We've been here twa weeks; maybe it's time we left?'

'Oh, nonsense! What is two weeks? Suppose you stayed here all summer, what would it be? Nothing at all. But what do you think Lizzie has in her mind? Has she anything in view in Glasgow?'

'They'd be clever that fathomed her mind; it's as deep as the sea,' said Teen, with an involuntary touch of bitterness, for she could not help feeling that her faithful love and service had met with but a poor return.

'She can't think we will allow her to go back to Glasgow without knowing what she is going to do; we had too much anxiety on her account before,' said Gladys, with decision. 'There is no doubt her brother's house is the place for her. I must talk to her myself.'

'Dinna dae't the nicht, Miss Gladys, or she'll think I've been tellin' on her,' suggested the little seamstress. 'Liz is very touchy aboot a lot o' things.'

'Well, perhaps a better plan would be to write to Walter to come down and see her,' said Gladys thoughtfully. 'Yes, I shall just do that. How pleased he will be to see her looking so well! Perhaps he will be able to persuade her to go to housekeeping with him now, and in that case, Teen, you will stay on here. Miss Peck says she can't do without you anyhow, you are such an invaluable help with sewing and all sorts of things; perhaps we could make a permanent arrangement, at least which will last till I get my scheme for the Girls' Club all arranged. I must say it does not progress very fast,' she added, with a sigh. 'We always do so much less than we expect and intend, and will, I suppose, fall short to the very end. If you like to stay here, Teen, as sewing maid or anything else to Miss Peck, it will make me very happy.'

She regarded the little seamstress with a lovely kindness in her look, and what could poor Teen do, but burst into happy tears, having no words wherein to express a tithe of what she felt.

No further allusion was made that night to the question of the girls leaving, and all retired to rest as usual in the house of Bourhill. In the night, however, just when the faint streaks of the summer dawn were visible in the summer sky, Liz Hepburn rose very softly from the side of the sleeping Teen, and, gathering her things together in an untidy bundle, stole out of the room and down-stairs.

The Scotch terrier, asleep on his mat at the foot of the stair, only looked up sleepily and wagged his tail as she stepped over him and stole softly through the hall. The well-oiled bolts slipped back noiselessly, and she ran out down the steps, leaving the door wide to the wall.

And so they found it at six o'clock in the morning, just when Liz was stepping into the first train at a wayside station many miles from Bourhill.

CHAPTER XL.

THE MATRONS ADVISE.

'I think we had better go down and see what Gladys is about,' said Mrs. Fordyce at the breakfast-table. 'Could you go down with me this afternoon, Tom?'

'I daresay I could,' replied the lawyer. 'Surely we haven't heard anything about her for a long time?'

'I should just think we hadn't,' said Mina, with energy. 'Perhaps by this time she has gone off with somebody. We've shamefully neglected her.'

'George hasn't been down either, Julia told me yesterday,' said Mrs. Fordyce thoughtfully. 'There must have been a quarrel, girls. Did Gladys say anything more before she went away that day?'

'Nothing; but they are both so proud, neither will give in first. I certainly don't think, mother, that Gladys's feelings are very seriously involved. She takes the whole thing very calmly.'

'George should not be too high and mighty at this early stage, my dear,' said Mrs. Fordyce. 'He will find that Gladys has a mind of her own, and will not be dictated to. All the same,' she added, with a faint sigh, 'I admit that he was right to find fault with her having those girls at Bourhill. Tom dear, I really think it is your duty, as guardian, to interfere.'

'We can go down, anyhow, and see what she is about,' replied the lawyer; and that afternoon, accordingly, they went out to Mauchline.

Not being expected, they had to hire from the hotel, and arrived just as Gladys and Miss Peck were enjoying their afternoon tea. She was unfeignedly glad to see them, and showed it in the very heartiness of her welcome. It was somewhat of a relief to Mrs. Fordyce to find Gladys alone with Miss Peck. She had quite expected to meet the objectionable girls in the drawing-room, but there were no evidences of their presence in the house at all, nor did Gladys allude to them in any way.

She had a thousand and one questions to ask about them all, and appeared so affectionately interested in everything pertaining to the family, that Mr. Fordyce could not forbear casting a rather triumphant glance at his wife.

'As the mountain would not come to Mahomet, Mahomet has come to the mountain,' he said in his good-natured way. 'You should have heard the doleful conversation about you at breakfast this morning. Were your ears not ringing?'

'No, I had something more serious to take up my attention,' said Gladys a trifle soberly. 'I hope you have come to stay a few days — until tomorrow, at least?'

'Are all your other guests away?' inquired Mrs. Fordyce, with the faintest trace of hardness in her voice.

'Christina Balfour is here still. Her companion left this morning rather suddenly,' said Gladys, and it was evident that she felt rather distressed. 'In fact, she ran away from Bourhill.'

'Indeed!' exclaimed Mrs. Fordyce, in astonishment. 'Why should she have run away? It would have been quite sufficient, surely, for her to have said she wished to return to Glasgow. You were not keeping her here against her will, I presume?'

'No,' replied Gladys a trifle unsteadily. 'I cannot say she has treated us well. It was a very silly as well as a wrong proceeding to get up in the middle of the night and leave the door wide open, as she did. She has disappointed me very much.'

Mrs. Fordyce looked at Gladys in a kind of wonder. Her candour and her justness were as conspicuous as her decision of character. It evidently cost her pride no effort to admit that she had made a mistake, though the admission was proof of the correct prophecy made by Mrs. Fordyce when the hot words had passed between them concerning Liz at Bellairs Crescent. Mrs. Fordyce, however, was generous enough to abstain from undue triumph.

'Well, well, my dear, we all make mistakes, though we don't all admit so readily as you have done that they are mistakes,' she said good-humouredly. 'I suppose the girl felt the restraint of this quiet life too much. What was her occupation before she came down? I don't know that I heard anything about her.'

'She was once a mill girl with Mr. Fordyce,' answered Gladys. 'She is the girl who disappeared, don't you remember? — Walter Hepburn's sister.'

'Oh!'

The lawyer drew a long breath.

'Perhaps it is just as well she has disappeared again. I did not know *that* was the girl all the talk was about. Well, are you not tired of this quiet life yet?'

'Oh no; I like it very much. But when will you allow the girls to come down, Mrs. Fordyce? I think it is too bad that they have never yet paid me a proper visit at Bourhill.'

'They are talking of London again — wheedling their poor dear papa, as they do every May. I think you must go with us again, my dear.'

'Yes, I should like that,' replied Gladys, with brightening face; and Mrs. Fordyce perceived that she had sustained a very severe disappointment, which had made her for the time being a trifle discontented with her own fair lot.

She took an early opportunity, when Gladys conducted her to the guest-chamber, to put another question to her.

'Gladys, how long is it since George was here?'

'I have never seen him since that night in your house, when he didn't come up to the drawing-room,' answered Gladys calmly.

'But he has written, I suppose?'

'No; nor have I.'

'My dear girl, this is very serious,' said Mrs. Fordyce gravely. 'What was the difference about? You will tell me, my dear? I have your best interests at heart, but I cannot help thinking it is rather soon to disagree.'

'I don't think we disagreed, only I said I should ask whom I like to Bourhill. Surely that was within my rights?' said Gladys proudly.

'Oh yes, to a certain degree, but not when you harbour questionable characters — yes, I repeat it, questionable characters, such as the girl who ran off this morning I hope you counted your spoons today, Gladys?'

Gladys could have laughed, only she was too miserable.

'Oh, what absurd mistakes you make!' was all she said.

'Not so very absurd, I think. Well, as I said, I think George only showed that he had a proper regard for you and your peculiar position here. We know the world, my love; you do not. I think now, surely, you will allow us to be the judges of what is best for you?'

'I think he has behaved shamefully to me, not having come, or even written, for so long, and I don't think I can forgive him. Think, if he were to treat me so after I was his wife, how dreadful it would be. It would certainly break my heart.'

'My dear, the cases are not parallel. When you are his wife your interests will be identical, and there never will be any dispute.'

Gladys shook her head. She did not feel at all sure of any such thing.

'I cannot help thinking, my dear child, that the sooner you are married the better it will be for you. You are too much isolated here, and that Miss Peck, good little woman though she is, is only an old sheep. I must for ever regret the circumstances which prevented Madame Bonnemain coming to Bourhill.'

Mrs. Fordyce felt the above conversation to be so unsatisfactory that she occupied herself before dinner in writing a letter to her nephew, in which she treated him to some very plain-speaking, and pointed out that unless he made haste to atone for past shortcomings, his chance of winning the heiress of Bourhill was not worth very much.

This letter reached the offender when he was seated at his father's breakfast-table with the other members of the family. He slipped it into his pocket, and his mother, keenly watching him, observed a curious look, half surprise, half relief, on his face. She was not therefore in the least surprised when he came to her immediately after breakfast for a moment's private conversation.

'I've had a letter from Aunt Isabel, written at Bourhill last night; you can read it if you like.'

She took it from him eagerly, and perused it with intense interest. Like her son, she had really abandoned hope, and had accepted the silence of Gladys as her lover's final dismissal.

'This is extraordinary, George,' she said excitedly. 'The girl has been, and gone, evidently, and never uttered a word. Can you believe it?'

'I must. Gladys would not be fretting, as Aunt Isabel says she is, if she knew all that. What shall I do?'

His mother thought a moment. She had been very unhappy during the last two weeks, daily dreading the revelation of the miserable story which would make her idolised boy the centre of an unpleasant scandal. Her relief was almost too great, and it was a few minutes before she could collect her thoughts and gather up the scattered threads of her former ambition.

'You may have a chance yet. It is a slender one; but still I advise you to make instant use of it. Go down and make it up with Gladys, at any cost. If she has heard nothing, and is at all pliable, press for an early marriage.'

She gave the advice in all good faith, and without a thought of the great moral wrong she was committing. The supreme selfishness of her motherly idolatry blinded her to the cruel injustice she was meting out to the innocent girl whose heritage she coveted for her son. Yet she counted herself a Christian woman, and would have had nothing but indignant scorn for the individual who might presume to question her right to such a title.

This is no solitary or exceptional case. Such things are done daily, and religion is made the cloak to cover a multitude of sins. Mrs. Fordyce had so long striven to serve both God and Mammon that she had lost the fine faculty which can discern the dividing line. In other words, her conscience was dead, and allowed her to give this deplorable advice without a dissenting word.

'It would be deuced awkward,' said the amiable George, 'if anything were to come out after.'

'After marriage, you mean? Oh, there would be a scene, a few hysterics perhaps, and there the matter would be at an end. A wife can't afford to be so punctilious as a maiden fancy free. She has herself too much to lose.'

George accepted the maternal advice, and went out to Mauchline after business hours that very day.

CHAPTER XLI.

A GREAT RELIEF.

Next afternoon Gladys herself drove the lawyer and his wife from Bourhill to the station.

'Now, my dear,' said Mrs. Fordyce, as they were about to part, 'I shall allow the girls to come down on Saturday, on condition that you return with them at the end of a week, prepared to accompany us to London.'

Gladys nodded, with a bright smile.

'Yes, I shall do everything you wish. I believe I am rather tired of having my own way, and I should not mind having a change, even from Bourhill.'

As they stood lingering a little over their good-byes, a train from Glasgow came puffing into the station, and, with a sudden gleam of expectation, Mrs. Fordyce glanced anxiously at the alighting passengers.

'My dear, why, there is George! actually George himself.'

Gladys cast a startled glance in the direction indicated and the colour mounted high to her brow, then faded quite, leaving her rather strikingly pale.

'Why does he come here?' she asked quickly, 'I have not asked him.'

'Unless you have broken off your engagement with him, Gladys, he has a right to come whether you ask him or not. Tom dear, here is our train now, and we must run over that bridge. We dare not miss it, I suppose?'

'I daren't, seeing I have to take the chair at a dinner in the Windsor Hotel tonight,' replied the lawyer; 'but if you like to remain a little longer, why not, Isabel?'

Mrs. Fordyce hesitated a moment. Her nephew was giving up his ticket to the collector at the little gate, and their train was impatiently snorting at the opposite platform.

'I had better go,' she decided quickly, as her husband began to run off. Turning to Gladys, she gave her a hasty kiss, and observed seriously, —

'Be kind to poor George, Gladys; he is very fond of you, and you can make anything of him you like. Write to me, like a dear, this evening, after he is away.'

She would have liked a word in her nephew's private ear also, but time forbade it. She waved her hand to him from the steps of the bridge, but he was so occupied looking at Gladys that he did not return her salutation.

Gladys stepped composedly into the phaeton, and, sitting up in rather a dignified way, accorded him a very calm, cool greeting. His demeanour was significant of a slight nervousness as he approached the carriage, not at all sure of his ground.

'I am in luck, Gladys,' he said, trying to speak with a natural gaiety. 'Have I your permission to take a seat beside you?'

'If you are going to Bourhill, of course you may,' she replied quite calmly; then, turning to the groom, she said, without any hesitation, 'You can walk home, William. Put my letters in at the post as you pass, and bring me five shillings' worth of stamps.'

The groom touched his hat, took the money and the letters, and walked off, indulging in a grin when his face was turned away from the occupants of the carriage.

'Shall I take the reins, Gladys?' inquired George, with a very bright look on his face. He perceived that, though there might be 'rows,' as he mentally expressed it, they would be of a mild nature, easily explained; the bolt had *not* fallen, if anything was to be gathered from her demeanour.

'No, thank you. I dislike sitting idle in a carriage. I always drive myself,' she said calmly, and, with a rather tighter hand than usual on the reins, she turned the ponies' heads, and even gave each a sharp flick with the whip, which sent them up the leafy road at a very smart pace.

'I have come to make my peace, Gladys, and it's awfully good of you to send the fellow away,' George began impressively. 'I'm in luck, I tell you. I pictured to myself a long dusty walk through the sunshine.'

'I sent him away because we had a long drive this morning, and I wanted Castor and Pollux to have an easier load to pull up the hill,' she replied. 'I suppose if I had allowed you to walk instead of William, it would have been rather rude.'

Her manner, though very calm and unruffled, was rather unpromising. George looked at her a trifle anxiously, as if hardly sure how to proceed.

'Are you awfully angry with me, Gladys? I always expected a letter from you. I thought you were so angry with me that I was afraid to write.'

'You were quite wrong, then. I was not angry at all. But why should I have written when you did not?'

This was rather unanswerable, and he hesitated a moment over his next words. He had to weigh them rather carefully for the ears of this singularly placid and self-possessed young lady, whose demeanour was so little index to her state of mind.

'Well, if I admit I was in the wrong all the time, though I really, upon my word, don't know very well what the row was about, will you forgive me?' he asked in his most irresistible manner, which was so far successful that the first approach to a smile he had seen since they met now appeared on her lips.

'You know very well what it was all about; you have not forgotten a word that passed, any more than I have,' she answered. 'But you ought to have written all the same. I am generous enough to admit, however, that you had more reason on your side than I was induced to admit that night. The experiment I tried has not been a success. Have you heard that Lizzie Hepburn has run away from us?'

He swallowed the choking sensation in his throat, and answered, with what indifference he could command, —

'Yes, I heard it.'

'And is that why you have come?' she asked, with a keen, curious glance at him, — 'to crow over my downfall That is not generous in the least.'

'My darling, how can you think me capable of such meanness? Would it not be more charitable to think I came to condole and sympathise with you?'

'It would, of course,' she admitted, with a sigh; 'but I am rather suspicious of everybody. I am afraid I am not at all in a wholesome frame of mind.'

She looked so lovely as she uttered these words, her sweet face wearing a somewhat pensive, troubled look, that her lover felt that nothing would ever induce him to give her up. They had now left the town behind, and were on the brow of the hill where four roads meet. To the right stood the cosy homestead of Mossgiel, and to the left the whole expanse of lovely country, hill and field and wood, which had so often filled the soul of Burns with the lonely rapture of the poet's soul. Gladys never passed up that way without thinking of him, and it seemed to her sometimes that she shared with him that deep, yearning depression of soul which found a voice in the words —

'Man was made to mourn.'

The road was quite deserted. Its grassy slopes were white with the gowan, and in the low ragged hedges there were clumps of sweet-smelling hawthorn. All the fields were green and lovely with the promise which summer crowns and autumn reaps; and it was all so lovely a world that there seemed in it no room for care or sadness or any dismal thing. Being thus alone, with no witness to their happiness but the birds and the bees, the pair of lovers ought to have found it a golden hour; but something appeared still to stand between them, like a gaunt shadow keeping them apart.

'I have been awfully miserable, Gladys. You see, I didn't know what to do; you are so different from any girl I have ever met. I never know exactly what will please you and what will aggravate you. Upon my word, you have no idea what an amount of power you have in those frail little hands.'

Gladys smiled and coloured a little. She was not quite insensible to flattery; she was young enough to feel that it was rather pleasant, on the whole, to have so much power over a big handsome fellow like George Fordyce.

'I wish you would not talk so much nonsense,' she said quickly; but her tone was more encouraging, and with a sudden inspiration George followed up his advantage. He put his arm round the slender waist, to the great amazement of Castor and Pollux, who, finding the firm hand relax on the reins, had no sort of hesitation about coming to an immediate stop.

'But, all the same, I'm going to keep hold of these little hands,' he said passionately, 'because they hold my happiness in their grasp, and I'm not going to allow them to torture me very much longer. How soon can you be ready to marry me, Gladys?'

'To marry you! Oh, not for ages. Let me go. Just look at the ponies! They are utterly scandalised,' she cried, her sweet face suffused with red. But he did not release her until he had stolen a kiss from her unwilling lips, a kiss which seemed to him to bridge entirely the slight estrangement which had been between them.

She sat very far away from him, and, gathering up the reins again, brought Castor and Pollux to their scattered senses; but her face was not quite so grim and unreadable as before. After all, it was something to be of so much importance to one man. The very idea of her power over him had something intoxicating in it, thus proving her to be a very woman.

'I am going to London very soon with your Aunt Isabel and the girls,' she said, trying to lead the conversation into more commonplace grooves.

'And couldn't you see about your trousseau when you are there? Isn't London the place to get such things?' he asked. But Gladys calmly ignored this speech.

'I have engaged Christina Balfour to remain at least all summer at Bourhill. She can be useful to Miss Peck in many ways, and she is devoted to the place. Poor Lizzie has fearfully disappointed me. What would you advise me to do about her?'

'Nothing. There is nothing you can possibly do now but leave her alone,' he answered at once. 'Do you think it is wise to keep the other one here?'

'Oh yes; why not? I am really going to perfect that scheme for the working girls soon. Meantime, I think I have got a little dis-heartened; I am afraid I am not very brave. I hoped that you would help me in that.'

She turned to him with a look which no man living could resist.

'My darling, I'll do anything you wish. I'm not half good enough for you,' he cried, uttering this solemn truth with all sin-cerity. 'Only give me the right to be interested in all that interests you, and you'll find you can make of me what you like.'

Gladys was silent a moment, on her face a strange look. She was thinking, not of the lover pleading so passionately at her side, but of one who, while loving her not less dearly, had sufficient manliness and strength of will to go his way alone — conquering, unassisted, difficulties which would appear unsurmountable to most men. George Fordyce, looking at her, wondered at the cloud upon her brow.

'Promise me, my darling, that you won't keep me waiting too long. Surely three months is long enough for the making of the best trousseau any woman can want? Won't you promise to come to me in autumn, and let us have a lovely holiday, coming back in winter to work together in real earnest?'

She turned her head to him slowly, and her eyes met his with a long, questioning, half pathetic look.

'In autumn? That is very soon,' she said. 'But, well, perhaps I will think about it, only you must let me be till I have made up my mind. Why, here we are already at home.'

CHAPTER XLII.

A DISCOVERY.

It was some days before Gladys could summon courage to write to Walter about his sister. Had she known the consequences of that delay she would have been profoundly unhappy; it gave Liz the chance, which she took advantage of, to get clear away from the city.

Through these bright days of the early summer Walter kept plodding on at his business, but life had lost its charm. He was, indeed, utterly sick at heart; all incentive to push on seemed to be taken from him, and the daily round was gone through mechanically, simply because it waited his attention on every hand. As is often the case when success becomes no longer an object of concern, it became an assured matter. Everything he touched seemed to pay him, and he saw himself, while yet in his young manhood, rapidly becoming rich. But this did not make him happy — ah, how utterly inadequate is wealth to the making of happiness how many have bitterly proved! — on the contrary, it made him yet more restless, moody, and discontented. Looking ahead, he saw nothing bright — a long stretch of grey years, which held nothing beautiful or satisfying or worthy of attainment — a melancholy condition of mind, truly, for a young, prosperous, and healthy man. In the midst of this deep depression came the letter from Gladys conveying the news of Liz's sudden and strange flight from Bourhill. He smiled grimly when he read it, and, putting it in his pocket, returned to his work as if it concerned him not at all. Nevertheless, in the course of the afternoon, he left his place of business and took the car to Maryhill. Gladys had given him the address of Mrs. Gordon, with whom Liz had formerly lodged, and he felt himself impelled to make some listless inquiries there regarding her. The result was quite unsatisfactory. The landlady regarded him with considerable suspicion, and did not appear disposed to give him any information. But after repeated questioning, Walter elicited from her the fact that Mrs. Gordon had gone to Dublin with the Eighty-Fifth Regiment, and she believed Miss Hepburn was with her. Walter thanked the woman and went his way, scarcely affected one way or the other, at least to outward seeming. Liz was lost. Well, it fitted in with the rest of his dreary destiny; her ultimate fate, which could not be far off, weaved only some darker threads into the grey web of life.

Next morning Gladys received an answer to her letter, and it made her feel very strange when she read it. It ran thus: —

> 'Colquhoun Street,
> *Thursday Night.*
>
> 'Dear Miss Graham, — I received your kind letter this morn-
> ing, and I thank you for acquainting me with my sister's de-
> parture from Bourhill. The news did not surprise me at all. I
> was only astonished that she stayed so long. This afternoon I
> called at the address you gave me, and the landlady informed
> me that Mrs. Gordon has gone to Dublin with the Eighty-
> Fifth Regiment, taking my sister with her. After this there is
> nothing we can do. Poor Liz is lost, and we need not blame
> her too hardly. You reproved me once for calling myself the
> victim of circumstances, but I ask you to think of her as such
> with what kindness you can. Of one thing we may be sure,
> her punishment will far exceed her sin. — Thanking you for
> all your past kindness, and wishing you in the future every
> good thing, I am, yours sincerely,
>
> 'Walter Hepburn.'

It was a sad letter, conveying a great deal more than was actually expressed. Gladys threw it from her, and, laying her head on
her hands, sobbed bitterly.

'My dear,' cried the little spinster, in sympathetic concern,
'don't break your heart. You have done a great deal — far more, I
assure you, than almost any one else would have done. You cannot
help the poor girl having chosen the way of transgressors.'

'It is not Liz I am crying for at present, Miss Peck,' said Gladys
mournfully; 'it is for Walter. It is a heartbreaking letter. I cannot,
dare not, comfort him. I must take it to Christina to read.'

She picked it up, and ran to the stillroom, where the happy
and placid Teen sat by the open window with some sewing in her
hand, love making the needle fly in and out with a wondrous
speed. Her resentment against Liz for her ingratitude had taken
the edge off her grief, and she was disposed to be as hard upon her
as the rest of the world.

'Oh, Teen, I have had a letter from Walter. I shall read it to you.
It is dreadful!' Gladys cried; and, with trembling voice, she read
the epistle to the little seamstress. '*Isn't* it dreadful? Away to
Dublin! What will she do there?'

Teen laid down her sewing and looked at Gladys with the sim-
plest wonder in her large eyes. She could scarcely believe that a
human being could be so entirely innocent and unsuspecting as
Gladys Graham, for it was quite evident she did not really know
what Walter meant by saying Liz was lost.

'He says her punishment will be greater than her sin, what-ever he means. Do you know what he means?'

'Ay, fine,' was Teen's reply, and her mouth trembled.

'Tell me, then. I want to understand it,' cried Gladys, with a touch of impatience. 'There have been things kept from me; and if I had known everything I could have done more for her, and per-haps she would not have run away.'

'There was naething kept frae ye; if ye hadna been a perfect bairn in a'thing, ye wad hae seen through a'thing. That was why a' the folks — yer grand freen's, I mean — were sae angry because ye had Liz here. But I believed in her mysel' up till she ran awa'. Although a lassie's led awa' she's no' aye lost; but I doot, I doot — an' noo Liz is waur than we thocht.'

Gladys stood as if turned to stone. Slowly a dim comprehen-sion seemed to dawn upon her; and it is no exaggeration to say that it was a shock of agony.

'Do you mean to say that the poor girl is really bad, that she has deliberately chosen a wicked life?' she asked in a still, strained voice.

Teen gravely nodded, and her lips trembled still more.

'And what will be the end of it? What will become of her, Teen?'

'The streets; an' she'll dee in a cellar, or an hospital, maybe, if she's fortunate enough to get into wan; an' it'll no' be lang either,' said Teen, in a quite matter-of-fact way, as if it were the merest commonplace detail. 'She has nae strength; wan winter will finish her.'

Here the composure of the little seamstress gave way, and, dropping her heavy head on the sunny window-sill, she too wept passionately over the ruin of the girl she had loved. But Gladys wept no more. Standing there in the long yellow shaft cast by the sunshine, memory took her back to a never-to-be-forgotten night, when an old man and a maiden child had toiled through the streets of Glasgow after midnight, and how the throng of the streets had bewildered the wondering child, and had made her ask questions which never till this time had been satisfactorily answered.

'I begin to understand, Teen,' she said slowly, with a shiver, as if a cold wind had passed over her. 'Life is even sadder than I thought. I wonder how God can bear to have it so. I cannot bear it even in thought.'

She went out into the sunny garden, and, casting herself on the soft green sward, wept her heart out over the new revelation which had come to her. Never had life seemed so bitter, so myste-rious, so unjust. What matter that she was surrounded by all that was lovely and of good report, when outside, in the great dark world, such things could be? For the first time Gladys questioned the goodness of God. Looking up into the cloudless blue of the summer sky, she wondered that it could smile so benignly upon a world so cursed by sin. Little Miss Peck, growing anxious about her, at last came out, and bade her get up and attend to the concerns of the day waiting for her.

'You know, my dear, we can't stand still though another perverse soul has chosen the broad road,' she said, trying to speak with a great deal of worldly wisdom. 'I see it is very hard upon you, because you have never been brought into contact with such things, but as you grow older, and gain more experience, you will learn to regard them philosophically. It is the only way.'

'Philosophically?' repeated Gladys slowly. 'What does that mean, Miss Peck? If it means that we are to think lightly of them, then I pray I may be spared acquiring such philosophy. Is there nothing we can do for Lizzie even yet, Miss Peck?'

She broke off suddenly, with a pathetic wistfulness which brought the tears to the little spinster's eyes.

'Is there no way we can save her? Teen says she will die in a cellar or an hospital. Can you bear to think of it, and not try to do something?'

Miss Peck hesitated a moment. It was an extremely delicate subject, and she feared to touch upon it; but there was no evading the clear, straight, questioning gaze of Gladys.

'I fear it is quite useless, my dear. It is almost impossible to reform such girls. I had a cousin who was matron of a home for them in Lancashire, and she gave me often rather a discouraging account of the work among them. You see, when a woman once loses her character she has no chance, the whole world is against her, and everybody regards her with suspicion. Sometimes, my love, I have felt quite wicked thinking of the inequality of the punishment meted out to men and women in this world. Women are the burden-bearers and the scapegoats always.'

Gladys rose up, weary and perplexed, her face looking worn and grey in the brilliant sunshine.

Her heart re-echoed the words of the little spinster; for the moment the loveliness of the earth seemed a mockery and a shame.

'Why is it so?' was the only question she asked.

Miss Peck shook her head. That great question, which has perplexed so many millions of God's creatures, was beyond her power of solution. But from that day it was seldom out of the mind of Gladys, robbing all the sweetness and the interest from her life.

CHAPTER XLIII.

A WOMAN'S HEART.

The second summer of Gladys Graham's changed life was less happy than the first. Her young enthusiasm had received many chills, and somehow the wealth with which she had anticipated so large a blessing to herself and others, seemed a less desirable possession than when it first came into her hands. Doing good was not simply a question of will, but was often surrounded by so many difficulties that it could not be accomplished, at least after the manner she had planned. Her experience with Liz Hepburn had disheartened her inexpressibly, and for the time being she felt inclined to let her scheme for the welfare of the working girls fall into abeyance. In May she left Bourhill in possession of Miss Peck and the regretful Teen, and departed to London, apparently with relief, in company with the Fordyces. Her state of mind was entirely favourable to the furtherance of the Fordyce alliance, and when, early in June, George joined the party in London, she allowed him to take for granted that she would marry him in the autumn, and even permitted Mrs. Fordyce to make sundry purchases in view of that great event. All the time, however, she felt secretly uneasy and dissatisfied. She was by no means an easy person to manage, and tried her lover's patience to the utmost. Her sweetness of disposition seemed to have deserted her for the time being; she was irritable, unreasonable, exacting, as different from the sunny-hearted Gladys of old as could well be imagined. The only person who was at all shrewd enough to guess at the cause of this grave alteration was the discriminating Mina, who pondered the thing often in her mind, and wondered how it was likely to end. She did not believe that the marriage would ever come off, and her guessing at all sides of the question came nearer the truth than she herself believed. Gladys appeared in no hurry to return to Scotland; nay, after six weeks in London, she pleaded for a longer exile, and induced Mrs. Fordyce to extend their trip to Switzerland; and so the whole beautiful summer was loitered away in foreign lands, and it was the end of August before Gladys returned to Bourhill. During her long absence she had been a faithful correspondent, writing weekly letters to Miss Peck and Teen; but when she returned that August evening to her own, she was touched inexpressibly by the wistful looks with which these two, the most faithful friends she possessed, regarded her. They thought her changed. She was thinner and older looking; her grace and dignity not less marked, her beauty not impaired, only the brightness, the inexpressible air of vivacity and spontaneous gladness seemed to have disappeared. She smiled at their tearful greeting, a quick, fleeting, almost melancholy smile.

'Why do you look at me so strangely?' she asked, with the slightest touch of impatience. 'Do you see anything odd about me?'

'No, oh no, my child,' answered Miss Peck quickly. 'We are so thankful to have you home again; we thought the day would never come. Have we not counted the very hours this week, Christina?'

'Ay, we hae; but I dinna think she's fell gled to be hame hersel',' said Teen, and her dark eye was shadowed, for she felt that a subtle change had overcast the bright spirit of Gladys, and she did not know what it might portend.

'Oh, such nonsense you two talk,' cried Gladys lightly. 'Dear Miss Peck, just ask them to hurry up dinner. I am famishing to taste a real home dinner. Well, Teen, how have you been all this summer? I must say you look like a new creature. I believe you are quite beautiful, and we shall have somebody falling in love with you directly. I don't suppose you have heard or seen anything of poor Lizzie?'

'No, naething. Walter was here, Miss Gladys, last week, seeking ye.'

The colour rose in the face of Gladys, and she averted her head to hide her softened, luminous eyes from the gaze of Teen.

'And did you tell him I was coming home this week?'

'I didna. We only spoke aboot Liz, an' some aboot his ain affairs. Miss Peck saw him maist o' the time. He's gaun to sell his business, and gang awa' to America or Australia.'

'Oh!' exclaimed Gladys sharply. 'Why should he do any such thing, when he is getting on so well?'

'I am sure I dinna ken,' replied Teen quietly, though she knew — ay, as well as Gladys — what it all meant. 'His faither's deid; he de'ed efter a week's illness, jist at the Fair time, an' he's gaun to tak' his mither wi' him. She's bidin' at Colquhoun Street the noo.'

'A great deal seems to have happened since I went away,' said Gladys, with something of an effort. 'Is he going to do this soon?'

'Yes, I think immediately; at least, he cam' doon here to say guid-bye to you. But Miss Peck can tell ye mair nor me; she spoke a long time till him.'

A question was on the lips of Gladys, but she held it back, and again changed the theme.

'And what does he think about poor Lizzie? I suppose he has never gone to Dublin to seek for her?'

'No, I dinna think it.'

'It is all very sad. Don't you think life very sad, Teen?' asked Gladys, with a great wistfulness, which made the eyes of the little seamstress become suddenly dim.

'Ay, it is. Oh, Miss Gladys, excuse me for sayin't, but if ye had seen his face when I telt him ye were maybe to be mairried in September or October, ye wadna dae't.'

'Why not? That could not possibly make any difference to me, Christina,' replied Gladys quite coldly, though a slight tremor shook her. 'Well, I must go and change my gown. Bourhill is looking lovely today, I think. I have seen many beautiful places since I went away, but none so satisfying as this; you will be glad to hear I still think Bourhill the sweetest spot on earth.'

And, with a smile and a nod, she left the little seamstress to her work; but it lay unheeded on her lap, and her eyes were heavy with a grey mist which came up from her heart's bitterness. Yes, life did indeed appear sad and hard to Teen, and all things moving in an entirely contrary way.

Miss Peck came bustling into her darling's dressing-room very shortly, and began to fuss about her in her tender, nervous fashion, as if it were not possible for her to show her gladness at having her back. Gladys did not say very much for a little; but at last, when she was brushing at her soft shining hair, she turned round suddenly, and looked into the old lady's face with rather an odd look on her own.

'Now, sit down, Miss Peck, and tell me every single, solitary thing about Walter.'

The little lady gave a nervous start. She had just been wondering how to introduce this subject.

'Christina has told you that he has been here. My dear, I was very sorry for him. He is a splendid young fellow, and I wish' —

She paused there, nor did Gladys ask her to finish her sentence.

'Teen tells me he is giving up his business. Do you think that is a wise step, Miss Peck?' Gladys asked, with a fine indifference which rather surprised the old lady.

'It may be wise for him, my dear. He seems to feel he cannot remain any longer in this country.'

'Did he ask any questions about me?'

'Yes, Gladys, a few.'

'Well, I hope you did not give him any unnecessary information?' said Gladys rather sharply.

'My dear, I told him everything I could think of. I did not think you would wish anything kept back from your old friend. His interest is very genuine.'

'I suppose so,' said Gladys coolly, as she began to coil her long tresses round her shapely head; 'we must take it for granted, anyhow. And what did he give you in exchange for all your interesting information? Did he condescend to tell you anything about himself?'

Miss Peck was wounded by the tone; such bitter and sarcastic words she had never heard fall from those gentle lips before.

'We had a long talk, Gladys, and I imagined — perhaps it was only imagination — that it relieved and made him happier to talk to me. His father is dead, and he has taken his mother home to his own house, and she will go with him abroad.'

'Where to? Is it quite decided? or has he already gone away?'

'Not yet, I think.'

'Did he ask where I was?'

'Yes.'

'For a particular address?'

'No.'

'Well, I think the least he might have done was to write and let me know all this.'

'My dear child, be reasonable,' said the little spinster, in gentle reproof. 'He came expecting to see you, and he left a kind message for you. I don't see that it would have done either you or him any good to write a letter; your ways must lie so far apart now. I told him we expected your marriage shortly.'

'I have never said it will take place,' said Gladys calmly. 'I wish people would leave me and my concerns alone.'

Miss Peck could see the girl's face in the long glass, the red spot burning on her cheeks, and the beautiful lips angrily quivering, and she became more and more perplexed. Of late Gladys had become a being difficult to understand.

'What is the use of talking in that manner, Gladys?' she said, with a faint show of sternness. 'I saw Mr. Fordyce in town the other day, and he told me it is quite likely the marriage will take place on the eighth of October. It is quite impossible that it could be definitely fixed without you.'

'I suppose so. And what did Walter say when you told him my marriage-day was fixed?' inquired Gladys, as she tied the ribbon on her hair.

'I shall not tell you what he said,' answered the little spinster, quite severely for her. 'You are in a mood which would make you laugh at an honest heart's suffering.'

'You think very highly of me, Guardy, I must say,' said Gladys a trifle unsteadily. 'But why do you speak of an honest man's suffering? Do you mean to say it made Walter suffer to hear I was going to be married?'

'My dear, he loves you as his own soul. I can never forget how he looked and spoke of you,' said the little spinster. 'He is a good and noble man, and God will bless him wherever he goes.'

There was a few minutes' silence, then Gladys walked over to the window, and drawing aside the lace hangings, allowed the red glory of the setting sun to flood the whole room. Standing there, with her white shapely arm against the delicate lace, she looked out in silence upon the lovely prospect which had so often filled her soul with delight. A shadow, dark as a storm-cloud, had fallen upon that sunny scene, and she saw no beauty in it.

'I have loved this place well, Guardy — loved and longed for it. It has been an idol to me, and my punishment is here. I wish I had never seen it. I wish I had never left the city, never been parted from the old friends. I am a miserable woman. I wish I had never been born.'

With a quick gesture she let the curtain drop, and throwing herself on the end of the couch, buried her face in the pillows.

Here again it was Miss Peck's privilege to administer some crumbs of comfort to the sad heart of the woman, even as she had once comforted the child. Stooping over her, she laid her hand tenderly on the bent golden head.

'My dear, it is not yet too late. If you do not love this man, it will be a great sin to marry him — a wrong done to yourself and to him. If there is a chord in your heart responsive to Walter's, don't stifle it. What is anything in this world in comparison with happiness and peace of mind?'

'Nothing, nothing,' Gladys answered, with mournful bitterness. 'But it is too late. It is Walter's fault, not mine; he left me in my desolation, when I needed him most. I did everything I could to show him that I could never forget him, and he repulsed me every time, until it was too late. If he is unhappy, it is no more than he deserves, and I am not going to be so dishonourable as to draw back now from my plighted word. George has always been kind to me, he has never hurt my feelings, and I will try and repay him by being to him a good and faithful wife.'

'A good and faithful wife!'

The little spinster repeated these words in a half mournful whisper, as she walked slowly to and fro the room.

Ah, not thus was it meet for a heart like Gladys Graham's to anticipate the most momentous crisis of a woman's life. She felt powerless to help, but Heaven was still the Hearer and Answerer of prayer, and with Heaven Miss Peck left the case.

She prayed that her darling's way might be opened up, and that she might be saved from committing so great a wrong, which would bring upon her the curse of a loveless marriage.

CHAPTER XLIV.

THE MAGDALENE.

Summer seemed no longer to smile upon Bourhill. That sunny evening was the last for many days. A wild, chill, wintry blast ushered in September, if the Lammas spates had tarried, when they came they brought destruction in their train. All over the country the harvest was endangered, in low-lying places carried away, by the floods. Whole fields lay under water, and there were many anxious hearts among those who earned their bread by tillage of the soil. These dull days were in keeping with the mood prevailing at Bourhill. Never had the atmosphere of that happy house been so depressed and melancholy; its young mistress appeared to have lost her interest in life. Many anxious talks had the little spinster and the faithful Teen upon the theme so absorbingly interesting to both — unsatisfactory talks at best, since none can minister to a mind diseased. One day a letter came which changed the current of life at Bourhill. How often is such an unpretending missive, borne by the postman's careless hand, fraught with stupendous issues? It came in a plain, square envelope, bearing the Glasgow post-mark, and the words 'Royal Infirmary' on the flap. Gladys opened it, as she did most things now, with but a languid interest, which, however, immediately changed to the liveliest concern.

'Why, Miss Peck, it is a letter, see, about poor Lizzie Hepburn. I must go to her at once, I and Teen. Where is she? If we make haste, we shall catch the eleven-o'clock train.'

She handed Miss Peck the letter, and sprang up from a half finished breakfast. The little spinster perused the brief communication with the deepest concern.

Ward XII., Royal Infirmary, Glasgow,
'*September* 6, 188 .

'Madam, — I write to you at the request of one of the patients under my care, a young woman called Lizzie Hepburn, who, I fear, is dying. She appears very anxious to see you, and asked me to write and ask you to come. I would suggest that, if at all possible, you should lose no time, as we fear she cannot last many days, perhaps not many hours. — Yours truly,
'Charlotte Rutherfurd.'

'This is from one of the nurses, I suppose,' said the little spinster pityingly. 'Poor girl, poor thing! the end has come only a little sooner than we anticipated.'

Gladys did not hear the last sentence. She was already in the hall giving her orders, and then off in search of Teen, whose duties were not very clearly defined, and who had no particular place of habitation in the house. It said a great deal for Teen's prudence and tact that her rather curious positions in the house — the trusted companion of the housekeeper and the friend of the young lady — had not brought her into bad odour with the servants. She was a favourite with them all, because she gave herself no airs, and was always ready to lend a hand to help at any time, disarming all jealousy by her unpretentious, willing, cheerful ways. Gladys found her in the drawing-room, dusting the treasures of the china cabinet.

'Oh, Teen, there is a letter about poor Lizzie at last!' she cried breathlessly. 'It is from the Infirmary; the nurse says she is very ill, perhaps dying, and she wishes to see me. You would like to go, I am sure, and if we make haste we can get the eleven train.'

Teen very nearly dropped the Sèvres vase she held in her hand in her sheer surprise over this news.

'There is no time to talk. Make haste, if you wish to go; we must be off in fifteen minutes,' cried Gladys, and ran off to her own room to make ready for her journey, Miss Peck fussing about her as usual, anxious to see that she forgot nothing which could protect her from the storm. It was indeed a wild morning, a heavy rain scudding like drift before the biting wind, and the sky thickly overcast with ink-black clouds; but they drove off in a closed carriage, and took no hurt from the angry elements. They did not speak much during the journey. In addition to her natural excitement and concern for the poor lost girl, Gladys was also possessed by a strange prevision that that day was to be a turning-point in her history.

'Surely Walter will have seen his sister; he cannot have left Glasgow so soon,' she said, as they drove from St. Enoch's Station, by way of the old High Street, to the Infirmary. These streets, with their constant stream of life, were all familiar to the eyes of Gladys. Many an hour in the old days she had spent wandering their melancholy pavements, scanning with a boundless and yearning pity the faces of the outcast and the destitute, feeling no scorn of them or their surroundings, but only a divine compassion, which had betrayed itself in her sweet face and shining, earnest eyes, and had arrested many a rude stare, and awakened a vague wonder in many a hardened breast. She was not less compasionate now, only a degree more hopeless. Since she had been so far removed from the sins and sorrows, the degradations and grinding poverty of the great city, she had, while not thinking less seriously or sympathetically of it all, felt oppressed by the impotence of those standing on the outside to lift it up to any level of hope.

'The loud, stunning tide of human care and crime,' as Keble has it, beat more remorselessly and hopelessly on her ears as she looked up to the smoke-obscured sky that wet and dismal day. She felt as if heaven had never been so far away. Almost her faith had lost its hold. These sad thoughts, which gave a somewhat worn and wearied look to her face, were arrested by their arrival at the Infirmary gates. It was not the visiting hour, but a word of explanation to the porter secured them admittance, and they found their way to the portion of the old house where Lizzie Hepburn lay. The visiting surgeons and physicians had just left, so there were no impediments put in their way, and one of the housemaids speedily brought Nurse Rutherfurd to them. She was a pleasant-faced, brisk little body, whose very presence was suggestive of skill and patience and kindly thought for others.

'Oh yes, you are Miss Graham, and have come to see poor Lizzie,' she said. 'Will you just come in here a moment? Her brother is with her. I will tell her you have come.'

She took them into a little room outside the ward door, and lingered only a moment to give them some particulars.

'She has been here three weeks,' she explained; 'she was over in the surgical wards first, and then came to us; it was too late for us to do any good. The doctor said this morning that she will probably slip away today.'

The little seamstress turned away to the grey window and wept silently; Gladys remained composed, but very pale.

'And her brother is with her? Is this the first time?' she asked.

'Yes; it was only when we told her there was no hope that she mentioned the names of anybody belonging to her. She spoke of you yesterday, and asked only this morning that her brother might be sent for. Shall I tell her you have come?'

'If you please. Tell her her old chum is with me; she will quite understand,' said Gladys quietly, and the nurse withdrew. Not a word passed between her and Teen while they were alone.

The nurse was not many moments absent, and the two followed her in to the long ward. It was a painful sight to Gladys, who had never before been within the walls of an hospital. Teen, however, looked about her with her usual calm self-possession, only her heart gave a great beat when the nurse stopped at a bed surrounded and shut off by draught-screens from sight of the other beds. She knew, though Gladys did not, why the screens had been placed there. The nurse drew one aside, and then slipped away. There was absolute silence there when these four met again.

Walter, who had been sitting with his face buried in his hands, rose from the chair and offered it to Gladys, but he did not look at her, nor did any sort of greeting pass between them. Gladys mechanically sat down, then Walter walked away slowly out of the ward. With a low cry, Teen flung herself on her knees, laying her face on the white, wasted hand of Liz as it lay outside the coverlet. The figure in the bed, raised up in a half sitting posture, had an unearthly beauty in the haggard face, a brilliance in the eye, which struck her chilly to the heart; it was like Liz, and yet strangely unlike. Gladys felt a strange thrill pass over her as she bent towards her, trying to smile, and to say a word of kindly greeting. It brought no answering smile to the dying girl's face, and the only sign of recognition she betrayed was to raise her feeble hand and touch the bowed head of the little seamstress with a tender touch, never bestowed in the days of health and strength.

'Weel,' she said, looking at Gladys, and speaking in the feeblest whisper, 'I'm gled ye've come. I couldna dee withoot seein' ye. Ye bear me nae grudge for takin' French leave? Ye can see I've suffered for it. I say, is't true that ye are to be mairried to George Fordyce? Tell me that plain. I must ken.'

These words were spoken with difficulty at intervals, and so feebly that Gladys had to bend forward to catch the sound. She felt that there was not only anxiety, but a certain solemnity in the question, and she did not evade it, even for a moment.

'They have fixed my marriage for the eighth of October,' she answered; and the manner of the reply struck even Liz, and her great hollow eyes dwelt yet more searchingly on the girl's sweet face.

'It'll no' be noo,' she said. 'I've lain here ever since the nurse telt me she heard it was to be, wonderin' whether I should tell. If ye hadna been what ye are I wad never hae telt; but, though I hae suffered, I wad spare you. It was him that brocht me to this.'

Gladys neither started nor trembled, but sat quite motionless, staring at the sad, beautiful face before her, as if not comprehending what was said to her.

'It was him that led me awa' first, an' when a lassie yince gets on that road, it's ill keepin' straicht. He said he wad mairry me, an' I believed it, as mony anither has afore me. Wheesht, Teen; dinna greet.'

The sobs of the little seamstress shook the narrow bed, and appeared to distress Liz inexpressibly. Presently she glanced again at the face of Gladys, and was struck by its altered look. It was no longer sympathetic nor sweet in its expression, but very pale and hard and set, as if the iron had entered into the soul within.

'Is this quite true?' she asked, and her very voice had a hard, cold ring.

'When ye're deein', ye dinna perjure yersel',' replied Liz, with a faint return of the old caustic speech. 'If ye dinna believe me, ask him. Is Wat away? Teen, ye micht gang an' bring him back.'

The little seamstress rose obediently, and when they were alone behind the screens, Liz lifted her feeble hand again and touched the arm of Gladys.

'Oh, dinna tak' him! He's a bad man — bad, selfish, cruel; dinna tak' him, or ye'll rue'd but yince. I dinna want to excuse mysel'. Maybe I wasna guid, but afore God I lo'ed him, an' I believed I wad be his wife. Eh, d'ye think that'll be onything against me in the ither world? Eh, wummin, I'm feared! If only I had anither chance!'

That pitiful speech, and the unspeakable pathos on the face of Liz, lifted Gladys above the supreme bitterness of that moment.

'Oh, do not be afraid,' she cried, folding her gentle hands, whose very touch seemed to carry hope and healing. 'Jesus is so very tender with us; He will never send the erring away. Let us ask Him to be with you now, to give you of His own comfort and strength and hope.'

She knelt down by the bed, unconscious of any listener save the dying girl, and there prayed the most earnest and heartfelt prayer which had ever passed her lips. While she was speaking, the other two had returned to the bed-side, and stood with bowed heads, listening with a deep and solemn awe to the words which seemed to bring heaven so very near to that little spot of earth. The dying girl's strength was evidently fast ebbing; the brilliance died out of her eyes, and the film of death took its place. She smiled faintly upon them all with a glance of sad recognition, but her last look, her last word, was for Gladys, and so she passed within the portals of the unseen without a struggle, nay, even with an expression of deep peace upon her worn face.

A wasted life? Yes; and a death which might have wrung tears of pity from a heart of stone.

But the Pharisee, who wraps the robe of his respectability around him, and, with head high in the air, thanks God he is not as other men are, what spark of divine compassion or human feeling has he in his soul?

Yet what saith the Scriptures? — 'He that is without sin among you, let him first cast a stone at her.'

CHAPTER XLV.

THE BOLT FALLS.

From that sad death-bed Gladys passed out into the open air alone.

'When you are ready, Teen,' she said, 'you can go home, and tell Miss Peck I shall come today, sometime. I have something to do first.'

She neither spoke to nor looked at Walter, but passed out into the open square before the Cathedral, and down the old High Street, with a steady, purposeful step. The rain had ceased, but a heavy mist hung low and drearily over the city, and the wind swept across the roofs with a moaning cadence in its voice. The bitter coldness of the weather made no difference to the streets. Those depraved and melancholy men and women, the bold-looking girls and the wretched children, were constantly before the vision of Gladys as she walked, but she saw them not. For once in her life her unselfish heart was entirely concentrated upon its own concerns, and she was in a fever of conflicting emotions — a fever so high and so uncontrollable that she had to walk to keep it down. It was close upon the hour of afternoon tea at Bellairs Crescent when Gladys rang the bell.

'Is Mrs. Fordyce at home, Hardy?' she asked the servant; 'and is she alone — no visitors, I mean?'

'Quite alone, with Miss Mina, in the drawing-room, Miss Graham,' announced the maid, with a smile, but thinking at the same time that the girl looked very white and tired. 'Miss Fordyce is spending the day at Pollokshields, and will dine and sleep there, we expect.'

Gladys nodded, gave her cloak and umbrella into the maid's hand, and went up-stairs, not with her usual springing step, but slowly, as if she were very tired.

Hardy, who had a genuine affection for the young mistress of Bourhill, looked after her with some concern on her honest face.

'She doesn't look a bit like a bride,' she said to herself. 'There's something gone wrong.'

With a little exclamation of joyful surprise, Mina jumped up from her stool before the fire.

'Oh, you delightful creature, to take pity on our loneliness on such a day. Mother, do wake up; here is Gladys.'

'Oh, my dear, how are you?' said Mrs. Fordyce, waking up with a start. 'When did you come up? Were you not afraid to venture on such a day?'

'I had to come,' Gladys made reply, and she kissed them both with a perfectly grave face. 'Will you do something for me, Mrs. Fordyce?'

'Why, certainly, my dear. But what is the matter with you? You look as melancholy as an owl.'

'Will you send a servant to Gorbals Mill, to ask your nephew to come here on his way home from business? I want to see him very particularly.'

It was a very natural and simple request, but somehow Mrs. Fordyce experienced a sense of uneasiness as she heard it.

'Why, certainly. But will a telegram not do as well? It will catch him more quickly. He is often away early just now; there is so much to see about at Dowanhill.'

At Dowanhill was situated the handsome town house George Fordyce had taken for his bride, but the allusion to it had no effect on Gladys except to make her give her lips a very peculiar compression.

'How stupid of me not to think of a telegram! Will you please send it out at once?'

'From myself?'

'Yes, please.'

She brought Mrs. Fordyce her writing materials, the telegram was written, and the maid who brought in the tea took it downstairs.

'Gladys, you look frightfully out of sorts,' said Mina quickly. 'What have you been about? Have you been long in town?'

'Since twelve. I have come from the Infirmary just now, walking all the way.'

'Walking all the way! — but from the Western, of course?'

'No, from the Royal; it seemed quite short. Oh, that tea is delicious!'

She drank the contents of the cup at one feverish draught, and held it out for more. Both mother and daughter regarded her with increased anxiety in their looks.

'My dear, it is quite time you had some one to exercise a gentle authority over you. To walk from the Royal Infirmary here! It is past speaking of. Child, what do you mean? You will be ill on our hands next, and that will be a pretty to-do. Surely you came off in post-haste this morning without your rings?' she added, with a significant glance at the girl's white hand, from which she had removed the glove.

Gladys took no notice of the remark; but Mina, observant as usual, saw a look she had never before seen creep into the girl's eyes.

'But you have never told us yet what you were doing at the Infirmary?' she said suggestively; but Gladys preserved silence for a few minutes more.

'Please not to ask any questions,' she said rather hurriedly. 'You will know everything very soon, only let me be quiet now. I know you will, for you have always been good to me.'

A great dread instantly seized upon those who heard these words, and Mrs. Fordyce became nervous and apprehensive; but she was obliged to respect such a request, and they changed the subject, trying dismally to turn the talk into a commonplace groove. But it was a strain and an effort on all three, and at last Gladys rose and began to walk up and down the room, giving an occasional glance out of the window, as if impatient for her lover's coming, but it was an impatience which made Mrs. Fordyce's heart sink, and she feared the worst.

George was no laggard lover; within the hour he rang the familiar bell. Then the nervous restlessness which had taken possession of Gladys seemed to be quietened down, and she stood quite still on the hearth-rug, and her face was calm, but deadly pale.

'Shall we go before George comes up?' asked Mrs. Fordyce, involuntarily rising; but Gladys made answer, with a shade of imperious command, —

'No, I wish you to remain. Mina can go, if she likes.'

Mina had not the opportunity. A quick, eager footstep came hurrying up-stairs, and the door was thrown open with a careless hand.

'You here, Gladys?' he exclaimed, with all the eagerness and delight he might have been expected to display, but next moment the light died out of his face, and he knew that the bolt had fallen. Even those who blamed him most must have commiserated the man upon whom fell that lightning glance of unutterable loathing and contempt.

'I have sent for you to come here, because it was here I saw you first,' she said, and her voice rang out clear and sweet as a bell. 'You know why I have sent for you? — to give you back these things, the sign of a bond which ought never to have been between us. How dared you — how dared you offer them to me, after your monstrous cruelty to that poor girl from whose death-bed I have just come?'

She threw the rings down upon the table; they rolled to the floor, sparkling as if in mockery as they went, but none offered to touch them.

Mina opened the door hurriedly, and left the room. Mrs. Fordyce turned away also, and a sob broke from her lips.

Gladys stood quite erect, the linen at her stately throat not whiter than her face, her clear eyes, brilliant with indignation, fixed mercilessly on her lover's changing face. He was, indeed, a creature to be pitied even more than despised.

'Gladys, for God's sake, don't be too hasty! Give me opportunity for explanation. I admit that I did wrong, but there are extenuating circumstances. Let me explain, I entreat you, before you thus blight my life, and your own.'

'What explanation is there to give? If it is true that you ruined that poor girl, — and do you think that a lie can be uttered on a death-bed, — what more is there to say? Gather up these baubles, and take them away.'

Her bearing was that of a queen. Well might he shrink under that matchless scorn, yet never had she appeared more beautiful, more desirable in his eyes. He made one more attempt.

'Take time, Gladys. I deny nothing; I only ask to be allowed to show you, at least, that I am a repentant man, and that I will atone for all the past by a lifetime of devotion.'

'To whom?'

'To you. I have been a wild, foolish, sinful fellow, if you like, but never wholly bad,' he said eagerly. 'And, Gladys, think of the fearful scandal this will be. We dare not break off the marriage, when it is so near.'

'I dare; I dare anything, George Fordyce. And I pray God to forgive you the awful wrong you did to that poor girl, and the insult you were base enough to offer me in asking me to be your wife — an insult, I fear, I can never forgive.'

'Aunt Isabel, will you not help me?' said he then, turning desperately to his aunt. 'Tell Gladys what you know to be true, that there are hundreds of men in this and other cities who have married girls as pure and good as Gladys, and whose life before marriage would not bear investigation, yet they make the best of husbands. Tell her that she is making a mountain out of little, and that it will be madness to break off the marriage at this late date.'

Mrs. Fordyce slowly turned towards them. The tears were streaming down her face, but she only sadly shook her head.

'I cannot, George. Gladys is right. You had better go.'

Then George Fordyce, with a malignant scowl on his face, put his heel on the bauble which had cost him a hundred guineas, crushed it into powder, and flung himself out of the room. Then Gladys, with a low, faint, shuddering cry, threw herself upon the couch, and gave way to the floodtide of her grief and humiliation and angry pain.

Mrs. Fordyce wisely allowed it to have full vent, but at last she seated herself by the couch, and laid her hand on the girl's flushed and heated head.

'Now, my dear, be calm. It is all over. You will be better soon, my poor, dear, darling child.'

Gladys sat up, and her wet eyes met those of her kind friend, who had allowed her upright and womanly heart to take the right, if the unworldly side.

'Just think how merciful it was of God to let me know in time. In a few weeks I should have been his wife, and then it would have been terrible.'

'It would,' said Mrs. Fordyce, with a sigh; 'but you would just have had to bury it, and live on, as many other women have to do, with such skeletons in the cupboard.'

'I don't suppose I should have died, but I should have lived the rest of my life apart from him. Is it true what he says, that so many are bad? I cannot believe it.'

'Nor do I. There are some, I know, who have had an unworthy past, but you must remember that all women do not look at moral questions from your exalted standpoint. There are even girls, like Julia, for instance, who admire men who are a little fast.'

'How dreadful! That must lower the morality of men. It shall never be said of me. If I cannot marry a man who entertains a high and reverent ideal of manhood and womanhood, I shall die as I am.'

'He will be difficult to find, my dear,' said Mrs. Fordyce sadly. 'This is a melancholy end to all our high hopes and ambitions. It will be a frightful blow to them at Pollokshields.'

'I am not sorry for them. They will think only of what the world will say, and will never give poor Lizzie one kindly thought. If it is a blow, they deserve it; I am not sorry for them at all.'

'And you are not in the least disconcerted at the nine days' wonder the breaking of your engagement will make?'

'Not in the least. What is it, after all? The buzzing of a few idle flies. I have no room for anything in my heart but a vast pity for the poor dead girl who was more sinned against than sinning, and a profound thankfulness to God for His unspeakable mercy to me.'

She spoke the truth; and in her own home that night, upon her knees, she poured forth her heart in fervent prayer, and mingling with her many strange feelings was a strange and unutterable sense of relief, because she was once more free.

CHAPTER XLVI.

THE WORLD WELL LOST.

Gladys returned to her own home that night, and when she again left it it was in altered and happy circumstances. Those who loved her so dearly watched over her the next days with a tender and solicitous concern, but they did not see much, in her outward demeanour at least, to give them cause for alarm. She was certainly graver, preoccupied, and rather sad; but, again, her natural gaiety would over-flow more spontaneously than it had done for long, thus showing that pride and womanly feeling had been wounded; the heart was perfectly whole.

She lived out of doors during the splendid September weather, taking an abounding interest in all the harvest-work, finding comfort and healing in simple things and homely pleasures, and feeling that never while she lived did she wish to set foot in Glasgow again. There was only one tie to bind her to it — one spot beneath its heavy sky dear to her; how much and how often her thoughts were concentrated upon that lowly place none knew save herself.

Since that melancholy morning in the ward of the Royal Infirmary she had not heard of or seen Walter, but she knew in her inmost heart that she should see him, and waited for it with a strange restfulness of heart, therefore it was no surprise to her when he came one sunny evening up the avenue to the house. She saw him coming, and ran out to meet him — something in the old childish fashion — with a look of eager welcome on her face. His dark face flushed at her coming, and he gave his head a swift turn away, and swallowed something in his throat. When they met he was grave, courteous, but a trifle distant; she was quick to note the change.

'I knew you would come to see me again, Walter,' she said, as they shook hands with the undemonstrative cordiality of tried friends. 'I am very glad to see you.'

'Are you? Yet it was a toss-up with me whether I should come or not,' he said, looking at the graceful figure, and noticing with some wonder that she was all in black, relieved only by the silver belt confining her silk blouse at the waist; 'but I thought I had better come and say good-bye.'

'Good-bye! Are you going away, then, somewhere?' she asked in a quiet, still voice, which betrayed nothing.

'Yes; I have taken my passage to Australia for the fourteenth of

October, sailing from London. I leave on Monday, however, for I have some things to see to in London.'

'On Monday? And does your mother accompany you?'

'No; she is too old for such an undertaking. I have arranged for her to board with a family in the country. She has been there some weeks now, ever since I sold off, and likes it very much. It is better for me to go alone.'

'I suppose so. Are you tired with your walk, Walter, or can you go on a little farther? It is a shame that you have never seen anything of Bourhill. Surely you will at least sleep here tonight? or must you run away again by the nine-fifteen?'

'I can stay, since you are good enough to wish it,' he said a trifle formally; 'and you know I shall be only too happy to walk anywhere you like with you.'

'How accommodating!' said Gladys, with a faint touch of ironical humour. 'Well, let us go up to the birch wood. We shall see the moon rising shortly, if you care about anything so commonplace as the rising of a moon. To Australia? And when will you come back, Walter?'

'I can't say — perhaps never.'

'And will it cost you no pang to turn your back on the land of brown heath and shaggy wood, which her children are supposed to adore?' she asked, still in her old bantering mood.

'She has not done much for me; I leave few but painful memories behind,' he answered, with a touch of kindness in his voice. 'But I will not say I go without a pang.'

They remained silent as Gladys led the way through the shrubbery walk, and up the steep and somewhat rugged way to the birch wood crowning the little hill which sheltered Bourhill from the northern blast. It was a still and beautiful evening, with a lovely softness in the air, suggestive of a universal resting after the stress of the harvest. From the summit of the little hill they looked across many a fair breadth of goodly land, where the reapers had been so busy that scarce one field of growing corn was to be seen. All the woods were growing mellow, and the fulness and plenty of the autumn were abroad in the land.

'It's dowie at the hint o' hairst, at the wa' gaun o' the swallow,' quoted Walter in a low voice, and his eye grew moist as it ranged across the beautiful landscape with something of that unutterable and painful longing with which, the exile takes his farewell of the land he loves.

'Walter,' said Gladys quite softly, as she leaned against the straight white trunk of a rowan tree, on which the berries hung rich and red, 'I have often thought of you since that sad day. Often I wished to write, but I knew that you would come when you felt like it. Did you understand?'

'I heard that your marriage was broken off, and I thanked God for that,' Walter answered; and Gladys heard the tremor in his voice, and saw his firm, hue mouth take a long, stern curve.

'It did not surprise you?' she asked in the same soft, far-off voice, which betrayed nothing but the gentlest sisterly confidence and regard.

'No, but I suffered agony enough till I heard it. When, one lives through such dark days as these were, Gladys, faith in humankind becomes very difficult. I feared lest your scruples might be overcome.'

'I am sorry you had such a fear for me, Walter, even for a moment, but perhaps it was natural. And when will you come back from this dreadful Australia, did you say?'

'Perhaps never.'

He did not allow himself to look at her face, because he did not dare; but he saw her pick the berries from a red bunch she had pulled, and drop them one by one to the ground. Never had he loved her as he did then in the anguish of farewell, and he called himself a fool for not having gone, as prudence prompted, leaving only a written message behind.

'And is that all you have to say to me, Walter, that you are going to Australia — on the fourteenth, is it? — and that you will never come back?'

'It is all I dare to say,' he answered, nor did he look at her yet, though there was a whimsical, tender little smile on the lovely mouth which might have won his gaze.

'And you are quite determined to go alone?'

'Well, you see,' he began, glad of anything to get on commonplace ground, 'I might get plenty of fellows, but it's an awful bore, unless they happen just to be the right sort.'

'Yes, that is quite true, there are so few nice fellows,' said Gladys innocently. 'Don't you think you might get a nice girl to go with you, if you asked her properly?'

Then Walter flashed a sad, proud look at her — a look which Gladys fearlessly met, and thought at that very moment that she had never seen him look so well, so handsome, so worthy of regard. Sorrow had wrought her perfect work in him, and he had emerged from the shadow of blighted hope and frustrated ambition a gentler, humbler, ay, and a holier man than he had yet been. Suddenly that look of sad, quiet wonder, which had a touch of reproach in it, quite broke Gladys down, and she made no effort to stem the tears which might make him sad or glad, she did not care.

'Gladys,' he began hurriedly, 'it is more than man is fit to bear, to see these tears. If they mean nothing more than a natural regret at parting from one whom circumstances have strangely thrown in your way, perhaps too often, tell me so, and I shall thank you, even for that kindly regret; but if they mean that I may come back some day — worthier, perhaps, than I am today' —

'That day will never come,' broke in Gladys quietly. 'But if you will take me to Australia with you, Walter, I am ready to go this very day.'

His face grew dusky red, his eyes shone, he looked at her as if he sought to read her soul.

'Do you know what you are saying, Gladys? If you go, it can only be in one way — as my wife.'

'Well?'

She took a long breath, but was allowed to say no more until a long time after, when she raised her face from her lover's breast, and demanded that he should take her home.

'It is an awful thing we have done, Gladys,' he said, touching her dear head for the twentieth time, and looking down into her eyes, which were luminous with the light of love, — 'an awful thing for me, at least. We shall have to flee the country, and they will say I have abducted the heiress of Bourhill.'

'Oh, do! Run off with me, as the Red Reiver and all these nice, interesting sort of people used to do long ago. Let us abscond, and not tell a single living soul, except the faithful Teen.'

But Walter shook his head.

'It is what I should like to do above everything, but I must resist the temptation. No, my darling; for your sake, everything must be most scrupulously conventional, if a little hurried. I shall pay your guardian a visit tomorrow morning, which will some-what astonish him.'

Gladys looked at him with a sudden access of admiration. To hear him speak in that calm, masterful tone pleased her as nothing else could have done.

'But you won't let them frighten you, and abscond without me? That would be too mean,' she said saucily.

Walter made no verbal reply, and so, hand in hand, they turned to leave the moonlit woods, and there was a look on the face of Walter such as you see on the faces of reverent worshippers who have found rest and peace to their souls.

'Poor Liz!' he said under his breath, as he uplifted his eyes to the clear sky, as if seeking to penetrate its mystery, and find whither that wayward soul had fled.

Gladys laid her soft cheek against his arm, and silence fell upon them again. But the heart of each was full to the uttermost, and they asked no more.

It was, indeed, the world well lost for love.

*   *   *

On the morning of the ninth of October, this announcement appeared in the marriage list of the *Glasgow Herald*, and was read and discussed at many breakfast-tables: —

'At Bourhill, Ayrshire, on the 8th instant, Walter Hepburn to Gladys Graham.'

It may be added that it was a source of profound wonder to many, and of awful chagrin to a few. In the house of the Pollokshields' Fordyces the announcement was discreetly tabooed, though George must have felt it keenly, seeing Gladys had suffered so little over the unhappy termination of their engagement that she could substitute another bridegroom though retaining the same marriage-day.

On the fourteenth the young couple set sail for the land of the Southern Cross, and were absent exactly twelve months, the reason for their return being that they wished their first-born child to see the light first in Bourhill. And they never left it again; for Walter made use of the Colonial connection he had made to build up a new business in Glasgow, which has prospered far above his expectation. So fortune has blessed him in the end, and he can admit now that the bitterness of the old days was not without its purpose.

The faithful Teen, no longer melancholy, reigns in a snug house of her own, not a hundred miles from Mauchline, but retains her old adoration for Bourhill and its bonnie, sweet mistress.

There are occasional comings and goings between the Bellairs Crescent Fordyces and Bourhill, and the family are united in approving the marriage of Gladys now, though they had their fling at it with the rest of the folk when it was a nine days' wonder. But that is the way of the world mostly, to go with the crowd, which jumps on a man when he is down, and gives him a kindly pat or a cringing salute, as may seem most advisable, when he is up.

But the wise man takes no account of such, pursuing his own path with integrity and perseverance, cherishing the tried friends, and keeping warm and close in his heart, like a dove in its nest, the love which, through sunshine and storm, remains unchanged.

THE END